Pure Series: Book 4

Ghost Girl

Catherine Mesick

This book is a work of fiction. Names, characters, places, and incidents either are products of the author's imagination or are used fictitiously. Any resemblance to actual events or locales or persons, living or dead, is coincidental.

Once again, for my mother and brother

Chapter One

On the morning of my birthday, I woke early without any need for an alarm. Dawn was just a little way off, and I'd slept with the window open. The early morning was pleasantly cool, and I breathed in the fresh air contentedly. It was early October, but we'd been experiencing warmer-than-average temperatures, and I knew the high today was going to be about seventy-five.

It was going to be a beautiful day, and I was having a party.

And things had been very, very quiet.

I knew my grandmother would still be asleep, so I went downstairs to have a little quiet time by myself in the kitchen.

I made myself some hot chocolate, the old-fashioned way with a saucepan and milk, and then sat down at the kitchen table.

As I sat drinking my chocolate, the ground began to shake, and I could hear the dishes in the cupboards rattling.

I looked around, startled, and the shaking stopped as abruptly as it had started. I sat for several moments, gripping the edge of the table and waiting to see if it was all over.

But the shaking didn't return, and I began to relax. Earthquakes were rare in our part of the world, and I couldn't remember ever having experienced one before. This one didn't seem to have been too bad. The entire house had been shaken, but my hot chocolate had remained safely in the confines of my mug, and the salt and pepper shakers on the table hadn't fallen over.

I took a quick look around the house, and nothing seemed to be out of place—not a single book had fallen off a shelf, and none of the knickknacks in the living room had fallen over.

I went back to the kitchen to put my mug in the dishwasher, and then I went upstairs to take a shower.

As I walked into my room, I heard my phone buzz, and I hurried over to pick it up.

There was a text waiting for me, and it was an exact duplicate of the one before it.

Are you okay?

It was from William, and his earlier text had come just a few minutes before.

I answered quickly.

I'm fine.

You're sure?

Yes. I couldn't help smiling.

Ok. I'll see you in a few hours.

There was a brief pause, and then William texted again.

Happy birthday, Katie.

I smiled again and went to take a shower.

By the time my grandmother got up, I'd already come back downstairs and had eaten breakfast. I was just putting my dishes away in the dishwasher when she walked into the kitchen wearing a white silk robe. Her long, silver hair was tied back in a braid that flowed halfway down her back.

"Good morning, my dear girl," GM said, pressing a kiss to my forehead. "Happy birthday."

"Thanks, GM," I said.

"You look more like your mother every day," she said, touching a lock of my long, blond hair. She held it up for just a moment, and then she tucked it behind my ear. "Have you had breakfast yet?"

"Yes. Sit down and I'll make you something."

GM waved a hand. "No, no—it is your birthday. I should make you something. But since I am too late to do that, I will simply have a cup of tea. Then I will get ready, and we can go. We have a lot to do today."

"You really don't have to," I said. "It's just my friends. We don't have to make a big fuss for them. We can just do something simple for dinner, and that will be a lot easier for you."

"Nonsense!" GM said as she put the kettle on to boil. "I only have one granddaughter, and this is the only time you'll ever turn seventeen. I shall make all the fuss I like."

I had to smile at this speech. "Yes, ma'am."

"It is no laughing matter," GM said.

"I'm not laughing," I replied. "It's just that I love you."

I kissed her on the cheek, and she shooed me away.

"Hurry up and finish getting ready," she said. "Be ready to leave in half an hour."

I still had to get dressed and run a comb through my hair, and by the time I came back downstairs, GM was waiting by the front door with her keys in her hand and her purse on her shoulder.

We went out to her red sports car, and GM took off as soon as I had my door shut and my seat belt buckled.

GM had a thing for speed, and she had a drawer full of speeding tickets to attest to that fact.

We spent the morning getting our hair and nails done, and then we picked up our dresses and went to the party store to pick out decorations. After that, we went to the grocery store to buy ingredients for dinner, and finally we went to the bakery to pick up my cake. I'd hoped to bake a cake myself, but I had to admit that the cake from the bakery was really beautiful—a light, airy spice cake with cream cheese frosting. I'd never have been able to create something that fancy myself.

Somehow we managed to fit everything into GM's tiny trunk, and as we turned toward home, I received another text from William.

This time, he was counting down the hours till dinner.

GM saw me smile, and she glanced down at my phone.

"Is that from the boy?"

"Yes," I said. "And you know his name is William."

GM made no reply. She simply pursed her lips and stepped on the accelerator a little harder.

GM was not fond of William, but she tolerated him, and as William himself had pointed out, it wasn't really her fault. Many people felt uneasy around William—it was a purely instinctive reaction.

We reached home and began to carry our purchases into the house. Once we'd put everything away, GM and I sat down to lunch. After that, GM waved me out of the kitchen, and she got to work cooking and decorating. I wanted to help, but she insisted on doing everything herself.

I went upstairs to do some homework, and I tried not to mess up my hair.

Before I knew it, GM was calling up the stairs to me that it was time for me to start getting ready, and I took my dress out of the hanging bag it had come in.

The dress was long and silver, and it was GM's present to me for my birthday. She'd actually bought it about a week ago, but she'd also had the shop alter the dress so it fit me exactly. I slipped it on carefully, trying not to disturb my hair, and then I turned to look at myself in the mirror.

The dress fit well, and I'd never owned anything so elegant before.

There was a soft knock on the door, and then GM entered wearing a light gold gown.

"You look lovely, solnyshko," GM said.

"Solnyshko" was GM's pet name for me, and it meant "little sun" in Russian. It was a common endearment in Russia, where we'd both been born, but it just so happened that the term had another, more particular meaning for me.

"Thanks," I said as GM came to stand beside me. "I have to admit, I still feel a little bad about all of this. You're doing a sit-down dinner and decorations, and then there's this dress. We didn't do anything like this last year."

"My dear girl," GM said. She ran a hand over my hair, and I could see that she was wearing the necklace I'd given her at Christmas last year along with her usual cross.

GM looked at me for a moment and then sighed—but it was not an unhappy sound.

"Things were different last year," she said. "I wanted to keep you safe. And then you've had so much trouble lately—so many strange things have happened to you. And there was nothing I could've done. I realize now that it's better to celebrate what we have rather than fearing what could happen."

GM took a step back.

"And in the spirit of celebration," she said, producing a little white box that she'd been hiding behind her back, "I have this for you."

"GM—" I began.

She waved away my protest. "Do not say it is too much. It is exactly what I wanted to do."

Inside the box was a silver chain with a little silver sunburst pendant.

"Besides, it wasn't expensive," GM said. "A woman at the farmers' market was selling them, and she only had the one. This piece is unique."

"It's beautiful," I said. I took the necklace out of the box and put it on.

"As soon as I saw it, I thought of you," GM said.

"You thought of me?" I said.

"Yes," GM replied. "You were always such a quiet child. And now you seem bolder, brighter. Sometimes I swear you seem to be giving off sparks. I thought the sunburst suited you now."

I looked down at the pendant and pressed my hand to it. "Thanks, I love it."

GM's tone became brisk. "And I'm glad you're not wearing that ugly necklace he gave you. A handsome boy, I will admit, but he has no eye for jewelry."

The necklace in question—a roughly hewn iron cross on a plain leather cord—had indeed been given to me by William. But the necklace was not for adornment—its purpose had been purely practical. Iron was useful in warding off evil, and there was one evil in particular that the iron charm guarded against—a creature known as a kost. But I hadn't been troubled by a kost in a long time, and I hadn't worn the necklace lately.

But since this was my birthday, and William was coming to my party, I had been planning on wearing it.

Now, seeing how happy GM looked, I decided to keep her necklace on and figure out another way to wear William's charm.

Pleased with herself, GM went on.

"Dinner is nearly ready if you would like to come downstairs and wait for your guests."

"Sure," I said. "I'll be right down. I just have to finish getting ready."

GM touched my hair one last time and moved toward the door.

"GM," I said.

She stopped and looked back at me.

"Thanks," I said. "For everything."

"There is no need to thank me," GM replied. "Tonight we celebrate what we have now."

After she was gone, I went to my jewelry box and got out William's necklace. The iron charm was cool to the touch, and somehow looking at it always made me feel calmer and more peaceful. I held up the leather cord for a moment, and then I began to wrap it around my wrist—I would wear the necklace as a bracelet. Once I was satisfied with the results, I went downstairs.

The aroma from the kitchen was wonderful, and I found GM turning off the oven and peeking inside.

"The trick," she said as I came into the room, "is in the timing. You want to get everything ready at the same time. It is no job for an amateur—it requires great skill. Luckily, I have that in abundance."

As GM straightened up, her eyes fell on the necklace I had tied around my wrist.

"That's not too bad, actually," she said. "It's even a little rock and roll, if I don't sound too antiquated saying that."

"Do you need any help?" I asked.

The doorbell rang, and GM waved me away.

"No, no. I don't need any help. Go and greet your guests."

I walked to the front door and opened it to reveal my friend Simon Krstic. He was blond, a little under average height, and of stocky build.

"Hey, Simon," I said.

He stepped inside and gave me a hug. "Hey yourself, birthday girl."

Then he stepped back and gave me a wrapped package with a little green bow on top.

"Oh, thank you, Simon," I said, accepting the gift. "You really didn't have to. I was serious when I sent out those emails saying nobody had to get me anything. Your presence here is gift enough."

"Of course I had to get you something," Simon said. "You're my favorite person in the whole world."

Simon moved as if he was going to hug me again but then seemed to think better of it.

Instead, he glanced around. "So is what's-his-name here?"

"No," I said.

Simon brightened. "Does that mean he's not coming?"

"No—William's coming. You just happened to be the first one to arrive."

"Oh," Simon said. "Since no one else is around, can I ask you a question?"

"Yes, of course," I said. But I had a feeling that Simon was warming up to a familiar topic.

"Are you happy with this guy? I mean really, honestly happy? Because it just seems to me that you've run into a lot of trouble since you met him. I have to wonder who his friends are."

"Simon—" I began.

"Yeah, you're right," he said. "You don't even have to say it. This really isn't the time or place for this discussion. But we really do need to have a conversation about this sometime soon."

"Oh, Simon," I said.

He glanced at me as if noticing me for the first time.

"You look wonderful, by the way."

"Thanks," I said. "You know, I really don't think any amount of discussion is going to help—"

GM walked out into the hall at that moment.

"Why, Simon!" she said. "So good to see you!"

"Good to see you, too, Mrs. Rost," he replied. "You look lovely as ever."

"You are too kind," GM said. "And you are looking quite well yourself."

Simon looked down at his dress clothes and smiled sheepishly.

"Thank you."

"Come on back with me," GM said to Simon. "I want you to help me with something."

"Of course, Mrs. Rost," Simon said readily. "I'd be happy to help."

I looked at GM in surprise as she waved Simon forward. As the two of them turned toward the kitchen, I turned to follow them.

"No, no," GM said. "You stay here. Attend to your guests as they arrive."

I watched GM and Simon disappear down the hall, and moments later, there was a knock on the door.

I opened the door and found my best friend, Charisse, and her boyfriend, Branden, waiting on the other side.

Charisse stepped in and gave me a hug, and a swirl of cinnamon came with her.

"Happy birthday, Katie," Charisse said. "I know you said we didn't have to bring any gifts, but I made you some cinnamon rolls."

"Thanks," I said, stepping back and accepting her tin-foil wrapped package. "You look gorgeous, by the way."

Charisse was wearing a soft peach-colored dress that perfectly complemented her brown skin, and her black curls were piled in artful array at the nape of her neck.

Branden, by contrast, was wearing jeans and a T-shirt. He was very pale, and his long, brown hair flopped over his eyes. He was tall too—so much so that when he stepped in for a hug, the top of my head didn't even reach his shoulder.

"Happy birthday, Katie," Branden said.

"Thanks," I said. As I stepped back, I felt the ground give a brief rumble.

"Whoa," Branden said. "Was that an earthquake, or are you just glad to see me?"

"I think it was an earthquake," I said.

I glanced down the hall to the kitchen, half-expecting GM to rush out and declare that it wasn't safe to have a party, but luckily, she didn't make an appearance.

"Is there some place we can put these?" Charisse asked. "I don't want you to have to carry them around."

I turned back to see her tapping on the cinnamon rolls.

"Yes," I said. "Let's go into the living room."

The two of them followed me in, and then Branden stopped to right a knickknack that had fallen on its side. Then we all sat down, and I placed the cinnamon rolls on the coffee table.

"Ordinarily, I'd take these to the kitchen. But GM is up to something and doesn't want me in there."

The doorbell rang then, and my other guests began to arrive in quick succession. My friend Bryony was first, shyly offering a wrapped gift as she tucked a lock of her light brown hair behind her ear. Next was Irina, beautiful and imperious, with olive skin and glossy, jet-black hair, and her boyfriend, Terrance—handsome, tall, and athletic, with a shorn head and brown skin that glowed with health.

Irina offered me a beautifully wrapped gift, and I thanked her, but I sighed internally as she made no reply and went to sit down in the living room with the others. Irina and I had been friends when we were children, but we barely got along now. She'd once had a crush on Simon, and his lifelong crush on me had turned her against me. Though she'd clearly moved on to someone else, she still harbored a grudge against me. Our relationship had seemed to thaw a little a few months ago before refreezing again, but GM noticed none of that. She still saw us as the good friends we had been in childhood and invited Irina to everything.

Terrance, for his part, greeted me warmly and followed Irina into the living room.

The doorbell rang once again, and this time I opened the door on William.

William was tall and lean, with dark hair and unnaturally bright blue eyes. His eyes were the only really obvious sign that he wasn't quite like other people, but there were smaller, subtler things. He said people got a "feeling" around him that made them wary. I hadn't noticed anything of the kind, of course. To me, he was the most beautiful person in the world.

"Happy birthday," William said, walking in and handing me yet another wrapped gift.

"Thank you," I said. "I love it."

William gave me the little, crooked half smile that I loved so much.

"You don't even know what it is yet," he said.

"Whatever it is, I love it," I replied. "Any gift from you is special."

There was a noise that sounded suspiciously like a snort, and I turned to see that GM and Simon had joined us.

Simon was staring at William with ill-disguised dislike.

"Well," I said quickly, "now that we're all here—"

"I beg your pardon," GM said. "Everyone is *not* here."

I glanced around. "But—"

"No, solnyshko. Everyone is not here," GM said. "I've invited one more person."

The doorbell rang once more, and I hurried to open the door.

On the other side was a boy about my age. He had gray eyes, light brown hair, and a powerful, heavily muscled physique that was in stark contrast to his mild, friendly expression.

The boy gave me an uncertain smile. "You are Ekaterina Wickliff?"

"Yes," I said.

"Happy birthday, Ekaterina," the boy said. His Russian accent was noticeable, but he spoke English very well. "My name is Vadim Stepanov. Your grandmother was kind enough to invite me to your party this evening."

GM came up to stand beside me. "Vadim! I am so glad you could make it."

"Of course," Vadim said. "I am happy to make new friends. Thank you very much for inviting me."

"Vadim, this is my granddaughter, Katie," GM said. "Her full name is Ekaterina, but we call her 'Katie' for short."

"Yes, I understand," Vadim said. "Just like we say 'Katya' for Ekaterina."

He gave me a disarming smile. "It is a very pretty name."

"Thank you, Vadim," I said. "Won't you come in?"

"Yes, yes, do come in," GM said, waving him forward.

The two of us stood back so that Vadim could enter.

Vadim had very kindly brought a gift, just as everyone else had, and after his present was safely settled on the table with the others, GM ushered us all into the dining room.

She had actually hung up a curtain, and as we drew it back and walked inside, I could see that the room had been transformed.

The dining room was filled with gold and silver balloons with delicate, hanging streamers, and it was lit only by candles, also in gold and silver. The dishes on the table were gold, and champagne flutes filled with a pale, bubbling liquid—probably sparkling apple juice—sat next to every plate. On the far wall was a hanging banner that read "Happy Birthday, Katie" in silver letters on a gold background.

"Wow," I said.

"Sparkles for my sparkling girl," GM said, putting an arm around me. "Come, come, everyone. There are place cards. Find your name."

GM steered me toward the head of the table. She herself was seated in that spot as the hostess, and I was seated to her right. To her left she had placed Simon. And William was placed at the opposite end—as far from me as GM could place him.

Dinner was already on the table, resting under covered dishes, and GM walked around to uncover them. She had made salmon, risotto, and sautéed kale.

"I hope you don't mind serving yourselves," GM said, sitting down. "I'd considered hiring servers, and then I thought that that would be a little extravagant."

Everyone murmured polite approval of the arrangements, and then the food was passed around the table.

Once everyone was served, GM raised her champagne flute in a toast. The windows in the dining room were wide open, and the curtains fluttered softly in a light breeze.

"To Katie," GM said. "Happy seventeenth birthday."

Everyone raised their glasses and repeated the toast. I smiled and raised my glass also.

Then I sipped at the bubbly, amber liquid. It was definitely sparkling apple juice.

"So, Katie," GM said with an approving glance toward Vadim, who was seated next to me, "Vadim just moved here with his family, and he'll be attending school with you soon."

"Welcome to Elspeth's Grove," I said to Vadim. "I hope you'll be very happy here."

"Thank you," Vadim said. "I like very much your charming town."

"Vadim's uncle is my dad's boss," Irina said suddenly. She was seated down at the end of the table to William's right, and her dark eyes rested on Vadim with something that looked like dislike.

Vadim did not seem to hear her and instead seemed to have noticed Bryony for the first time.

"Yes, Irina is correct," GM said. "Vadim's uncle moved here to take charge of the operation of the North American office."

"The North American office of what?" Branden said.

"Pyrotechnics International," Irina replied.

"Pyrotechnics?" Branden said. He grinned. "You mean like fireworks?"

Irina gave him a faint smile. "Fireworks are one type of application. But my dad's company really works in research. They look for new ways to do things like mining and construction."

"Cool," Branden said.

William looked up suddenly, and his eyes darted to the window.

I followed his gaze but didn't see anything outside except the lawn and the soft mist that floated just above it.

William stood up abruptly.

"I've got to go."

GM looked up at him in surprise. "I beg your pardon?"

"I'm sorry," William said. "I have to leave right away."

He hurried from the room.

GM looked over at me. "Katie, what was that?"

"He probably got an emergency text," I said quickly.

"But he didn't look at his phone."

"He has one of those watches," I said. "You know, the ones that do everything? He probably got a text on that."

"Hmmm," GM said, but she didn't look convinced.

I gave her a reassuring smile and took a nonchalant sip of water, but I was far from feeling reassured myself. William had senses that were much keener than those of ordinary people, and if he'd seen or heard something unusual, that was definitely cause for concern.

"I'm sure he'll be back very soon," I said.

"Hmmm," GM said again.

Dinner resumed, but I didn't hear much of the conversation. I kept casting furtive glances out the window to see if I could spot what had caught William's attention.

And then I saw it.

I caught a flash of white cloth and golden curls—someone was outside the house and was lingering near the window.

I stood up quickly.

"I'll be right back," I said.

GM looked up at me. "Where are you going?"

"I—just have to leave for a moment," I said. I began to hurry around the table, and then I headed toward the curtain GM had hung up.

GM looked after me in concern. "Are you ill, Katie?"

"No!" I said quickly. "Yes! I—I'm not sure. I just have to leave for a moment. Please don't follow."

"All right," GM said doubtfully.

I plunged through the curtain and ran for the front door. I wrenched the door open, and standing on the other side was a girl who looked to be no more than nineteen years old. She had long, blond ringlets and pale white skin, and she was wearing a white summer dress and silver sandals on her dainty feet. The entire effect was one of fragile, angelic beauty, but the girl in front of me was far from angelic—and she was much older than nineteen.

Her lips curled into a smile when she saw me. "Hello, kitten."

I stepped out of the house and closed the door behind me firmly.

"Hello, Veronika," I said.

I grabbed her by the arm and pulled her away from the house. Her bare skin was ice cold, and I very nearly let go reflexively. But I forced myself to hang on, and I guided Veronika down the driveway to the sidewalk—I needed to get her away from my friends and family.

"What are you doing here?" I said.

Veronika gave me a long look. "I came to see you, my dear."

I glanced around quickly. "Is William out here too? Is that why he hurried out so quickly?"

Veronika smiled. "Oh no. I got him out of the way. He thinks he's out tracking a vampire. That should give us just enough time."

I glanced down the street to my house. A heavy mist was settling over everything, but no one seemed to be following us.

"What do you want?" I asked.

Veronika stopped walking and gave me one of her unnerving stares.

"The time has come for you to pay your bill."

I froze. "What do you mean?"

Veronika smiled. "Surely you've not forgotten? I saved William's life, and in return you are to give me whatever I want whenever I want it."

"I remember," I said.

"Well, now is the time that I want it."

"And what is 'it,' exactly?" I asked.

"I want you to find the ghost girl," Veronika replied.

I blinked. "I don't understand."

"There is someone out there making vampires disappear," Veronika said patiently. "They are calling her the ghost girl. I want you to find her."

I stared at her in disbelief. "Veronika, that's all over—you must know that. The ghost girl was rumored to be me—but I never did anything. And some others thought that the ghost girl was my friend Sachiko, but she never did anything either. She was just observing the incidents, and people happened to see her nearby."

"I do know this," Veronika murmured.

"And the ghost girl was just a myth anyway," I said. "There was never a person going around doing away with vampires. It was the healing waters from the Tears of the Firebird. The water was getting into the environment and making vampires sick—it made them crumble into dust instantly. It was environmental—no one was doing it."

Veronika made no reply and simply continued to stare at me. I began to wonder if she was okay.

"Veronika," I said. "Can you hear me?"

"Yes," she replied.

"The ghost girl thing is over," I said again. "The Order of the Hawthorne stopped using their cures. The Tears of the Firebird aren't getting into the air anymore. The disappearances have stopped."

"Slowed but not stopped," Veronika said.

"Oh," I said. "I didn't realize it was still going on. I'm sorry."

Veronika made no reply.

"Unfortunately, those are probably residual effects," I said. "There's nothing any of us can do. We just have to wait until the environment is clean again."

"They aren't residual effects," Veronika said.

"Veronika—"

"They aren't," she said firmly. "And your theory about the Tears of the Firebird was wrong."

"Sachiko saw the effects herself," I said.

Veronika waved a dismissive hand. "It happened to a small degree. A few have been affected that way. But your friend has taken that simple explanation too far. Something much bigger is at work here."

"So you're saying the Tears of the Firebird and the Order of the Hawthorne did not cause all those vampire deaths?"

"No, they didn't," Veronika replied. "In fact, they aren't deaths at all. They're disappearances. Vampires are not crumbling—they're being taken. Vampires are being spirited away."

"Then why have the incidents slowed down since the Order stopped using the tears?" I asked. "That would seem to indicate that the two are related."

"A coincidence. Like I said, a few deaths did happen that way. But most are not dead—they've been kidnapped."

"But—"

Veronika suddenly grabbed my wrist, and her cold fingers felt like iron bands.

"I've explained this." Her eyes blazed into mine. "You're wrong. And vampires are disappearing. I want you to find the one responsible."

Veronika's icy fingers tightened even more. "You owe me. And if you don't do this, I'll take back what I gave to you."

Panic surged through me. "You'd take William's life?"

"I would."

"But we both know the 'ghost girl' isn't real."

"That's just a name," Veronika said. "It doesn't have to be a girl. I don't know if it's a man or a woman or a whole crowd that's causing the disappearances. I just want you to find the person responsible."

"Why?" I said.

Veronika released my wrist. "My Promised One is missing. He was taken in this latest round of disappearances."

"Your Promised One?" I hesitated. "Is that like your boyfriend?"

Veronika's lips curved into a mocking smile. "A Promised One is much more than a lover—much more than your human concept of a marriage partner. I suppose you could call it a soulmate—although it is really much more than that, and we are not supposed to have souls. We are connected on a level that you cannot comprehend."

"So you want me to rescue him?" I said. "What makes you think I can do that?"

"You can go places I cannot," Veronika replied. "Go to your friends. They surely know more than they are telling."

I glanced down the street toward my house. "My friends?"

"Not your school friends," Veronika said. "Your friends in the Order of the Hawthorne."

"The Order will just say the same things I've already said," I replied. "They've stopped using the tears—the disappearances should stop eventually too."

"The disappearances are going down," Veronika said, "because the ghost girl—whoever he or she is—is getting close to her goal. This is a fact. We will have no further discussion on this point."

"Veronika—"

Her eyes flashed fire. "Do this, or I will do what I said I'd do."

"But—"

"Do this or I take back his life!"

"Yes!" I said. "I'll do it."

Veronika seemed to relax, and she gave me a long look. "You will find the ghost girl?"

"Yes, I will."

"You'll do whatever it takes? Because I mean what I say. If you fail, I will take back William's life. I don't care how much you tried."

"What choice do I have?" I said.

Veronika smiled. "Exactly."

"So would you like to tell me where I should start?" I said. "Do you know anything about who the ghost girl actually is?"

"All I can tell you is that vampire magic is involved," Veronika said. "So that leads me to believe that the ghost girl is actually a vampire herself. And while the practitioners of that art have always been rare, they are even rarer in these modern times than they were. Vampires—like ordinary mortals—no longer believe in magic."

She tilted her head and gave me an appraising look. "By the way, are the rumors true? Have you lost your ability to use the clear fire?"

"Yes," I said.

"I suggest you get your powers back—you're going to need them."

"Why? The clear fire doesn't work on vampires. It only works on the kost."

"How do you know that's all it does?" Veronika asked. "How do you know it doesn't work on vampires? Or on other creatures? It may do more than you think."

"I—" I stopped. I couldn't remember how I knew that. I certainly had never tested it.

"Besides, even if it doesn't work on vampires," Veronika said, "it's still a part of who you are. You shouldn't hide from it. You shouldn't hide from what you can do."

"I'm not hiding," I said.

"Oh, but you are," Veronika said. "You're both hiding—you and that boy of yours."

She stopped, and her voice grew softer. "But maybe I judge you too harshly. Maybe you were too young."

"You don't know anything about it," I said.

"Perhaps not." Veronika turned her head suddenly and looked away over the houses. "I should be going now."

"Wait," I said. "How long do I have?"

"However long it takes," Veronika said. "Goodbye, Little Sun."

With that she vanished.

Chapter Two

Little Sun. Ghost girl. I'd been known by both of those names. One of them was accurate. The other wasn't.

Little Sun was a mantle I'd inherited. Unbeknownst to my grandmother, her husband—my grandfather—had been a member of the Sídh—an ancient race of great power. The child of their union was my mother, and she became the Little Sun—a child born with the ability to use the clear fire and protect the people of Krov, Russia, from an evil creature known as a kost. My mother died when I was very young, and at her death, I automatically became the new Little Sun. But after the death of both my parents, my grandmother whisked me out of Russia and away from our small town and what she called "superstition." I didn't know about my heritage until last year, and then I'd only worked with the clear fire for a brief time. My ability to use it had been blocked by the mysterious, distant Sídh, who disapproved of my relationship with William—he had once been one of them, and now he was an outcast.

As for the ghost girl, what I'd told Veronica was true—when vampires had started going missing earlier in the year, a rumor had begun to spread that I was responsible. A mysterious female figure had been glimpsed at some of the disappearances, and she'd been dubbed the "ghost girl." And then because of my "affinity" for the kost, who were hated by vampires, popular vampire opinion had decided that the Little Sun and the ghost girl were one and the same. But the female figure that had been glimpsed was actually my friend Sachiko—a vampire who was trying to solve the disappearances.

And as far as I knew, she *had* solved them—the disappearances were actually caused by an environmental factor—the water from a mystical spring known as the Tears of the Firebird. The tears were said to heal any creature—even vampires. But rather than healing them, it actually made them crumble into dust and disappear.

And now Veronika wanted me to find the "real" ghost girl and rescue her Promised One, or else she'd take back the cure she'd given me. Veronika was a vampire and a healer, and she'd brought William back from the brink of death.

And she was right—I had agreed to pay whatever she would ask for.

I stood now looking up and down the street as if somehow I could find an answer that way. I really didn't know where to start.

After a moment, I realized that I would have to go back to the party, and automatically, I began walking back in that direction.

As I walked, it occurred to me that Terrance was a member of the Order of the Hawthorne, and my steps quickened. Terrance and I hadn't spoken about anything related to the Order or my status as the Little Sun in months. And since the Order was actually an organization dedicated to vampire-hunting, I wasn't sure how Terrance would react to the news that I myself owed a debt to a vampire.

But it was at least a place to start, and it was the course of action that Veronika herself had suggested.

I hurried on toward the house.

Just as I reached the front door, I saw a figure coming toward me in the mist, and I realized with relief that it was William.

He hurried up to me, and his brow was creased with worry. "What are you doing out here?"

"I—"

I stopped. William knew that he had been dangerously ill several months ago. He also knew that I had purchased a cure from Veronika for him. But he didn't know just how near death he had been, and he didn't know what I had agreed to give her in return. He was aware in a general way of how steep the charges were for vampire healers, but he didn't know that I had promised to give her anything she asked for. And now his life was in danger again— because of me.

William didn't seem to notice my hesitation and went on quickly. "I came out here because I sensed a vampire. You didn't see anyone—suspicious—did you?"

"You sensed a vampire—and you found one," said a new voice.

Around the corner of the house came a tall, dark figure, shrouded by the mist.

After a moment, I could see a familiar face.

"Anton!" I cried.

I ran forward and gave him a hug.

Even though his arms were covered, I could feel how hard and cold his body was.

"You're okay!" I stepped back and looked at him. "You really are okay."

He looked down at me, and his dark eyes were unreadable.

"You were worried about me?" he said.

"Of course I was worried about you," I replied.

Anton and a group of others had made a stand against an ancient vampire known as the Hunter in order to protect me—and the Hunter was the most powerful vampire to have been revived in centuries. I didn't know what had happened to Anton after their fight, and I didn't know if I would ever see him again.

"How did you—" I began.

"Survive?" Anton said, a hint of amusement dancing in his dark eyes. "It wasn't easy, certainly, but then again, he wasn't really interested in us. He was interested in you. And you seem to have gotten rid of him pretty well on your own."

"It wasn't just me," I said. "It wasn't really me at all. It was all of us—including you and William."

Anton glanced over my head. "Speaking of William, somebody with that name has known for a long time that I was okay. It's too bad that person couldn't have mentioned that to you. But then I suppose our friendship has suffered of late."

"We were never friends," William said curtly.

"You wound me," Anton said with a mocking smile. "When you first came to us, I was the one who taught you everything, showed you how to be at home in our community."

"You? Helped me?" William's voice was bitter. "That's not the way I remember it."

"Well, your memory's never been too good, has it?" Anton replied.

William moved toward Anton, and I quickly intervened.

"Guys, please," I said. "There's a party going on inside, and I don't want to attract any unnecessary attention. My absence is going to be hard enough to explain as it is."

"A party?" Anton said. "What's the occasion?"

"It's my birthday," I replied.

Anton's eyebrows rose. "Really? How about that? Best wishes and many happy returns."

"So I'm sure you can understand," William said, "why you should be leaving now."

"Leaving?" Anton said. "But I just got here. And aren't you even a tiny bit curious about why I've come here to visit you two today?"

"I assume you're here to cause trouble," William said. "And if you're here with a message from Innokenti, you can tell him we're not interested."

I glanced around then. Innokenti was the first minister of the Russian court of vampires in Krov, and I had first met Anton in Innokenti's company. Anton usually—but not always—acted on his orders. If this was official business, it was a little strange that he wasn't present.

"You know," Anton said, "I really think you should let Katie should decide for herself whether she's interested or not. Besides, Innokenti doesn't know that I'm here. I'm on the run as it were."

"On the run?" William said.

"Well, not exactly," Anton replied. "No one's chasing after me—that I know of. I just thought I should get out while the getting's good."

"Why? What's happened?" I said.

"Happening," Anton amended. "It's ongoing."

"So—what's happening?" William said.

"There have been earthquakes," Anton said.

"Earthquakes?" I said sharply.

"Yes, earthquakes," Anton replied. "In tiny, little Krov. An area—which I'm sure you know—is not known for them."

I glanced up at William to see how he was taking the news, but his face remained impassive.

"Some of the earthquakes even seem to be localized in Zamochit Village," Anton said. He turned to me. "You remember Zamochit, don't you?"

"Of course I remember Zamochit," I said. "I'm not likely to forget it."

"And one of the earthquakes appeared to be localized right in Rusalka Castle," Anton said. "You remember—"

"Yes, of course I remember Rusalka," I said.

Anton flashed me a grin. "Well, one can never tell with humans—you're all so fragile and prone to little problems. Your senses are often not reliable."

His eyes flicked to William. "And then there's this one here, who never seems to remember anything—"

"Get to the point," William said. "You've had earthquakes. And then?"

"And then, well, not much of anything."

"That's a fascinating story," William said. "Thank you for stopping by. You had me going there for a moment—I thought you might actually have had something to tell us. And now, if you don't mind, Katie and I have a party to get back to. I suggest you move along."

"Now wait just a minute," Anton said. "I said 'not much.' I didn't say nothing happened. There have been small incidents—disappearances."

William frowned. "Disappearances?"

Anton nodded. "A wheelbarrow here, a ladder there. Somebody lost some shovels and a rope."

"Some shovels and a rope?" William said. "You're talking about a few petty thefts."

"Yes," Anton said.

"But no humans or vampires have gone missing?"

"No more so than usual."

"Come on, Katie," William said. "He's just wasting our time."

"I'm not, you know," Anton said. "I'm very serious about this."

"About the missing garden tools?" William replied. "What makes you think they are in any way connected to the earthquakes?"

"Just a feeling."

"And here I thought you didn't have any."

"Oh, ha-ha," Anton said. "That's very funny."

"Well, you're a funny guy," William said.

"I'm not funny when it comes to Katie's welfare," Anton said. "I did risk my life to protect her from the Hunter."

William hesitated. "You want to help Katie?"

"Yes."

"Then why are you acting this way?"

"That's just the way I am," Anton said. "I'm very genuinely here to tell you my concerns."

He tilted his head. "Why don't you believe me?"

"Because Innokenti isn't here."

"I already told you that Innokenti doesn't know I'm here," Anton replied.

"Then you're just here to cause trouble," William said.

"And why do you say that? What's so magical about Innokenti's presence?"

"Innokenti is a responsible—"

William paused, looking for a word.

"Grown-up?" Anton said. "Innokenti is a responsible grown-up, and I'm not?"

"You said it, not me," William said.

"Well, in that case, I might just keep on going."

"You know, I really think you should."

"Stop!" I said. "Enough arguing!"

I turned to Anton. "Anton, why are you here? And get to the point quickly."

Anton shot William a look of triumph, but he went on in a reasonable tone.

"I was trying to work up to it with the stuff about the earthquakes and the thefts, but I didn't quite make it. I'm actually here to warn you about Innokenti."

"Why?" I said.

"I think he may come here too," Anton said. "There's trouble at the castle—trouble in the court. And I think it could affect you."

"What kind of trouble?" I asked.

Anton shook his head, and his expression became unusually pensive. "Something's brewing, and I wish I knew exactly what. Things at Rusalka are—off. Nothing seems to be right, and a lot of things are happening that I can't explain. But I do know this— someone wants more power and is prepared to sacrifice a lot of people to get it."

"That's nice and vague," William said. "Very helpful."

"But you came here for a reason," I said. "And you mentioned Innokenti. Does that mean you suspect him?"

Anton was silent for a moment.

"Yes—I do," he said at last.

"Why?" William said. "What could he possibly want more power for? He's already first minister. There's no higher office."

"Except for king," Anton said.

William scoffed. "You really think Innokenti wants to be king?"

"Why not?" Anton said. "He's been at that first minister spot for a long time. Maybe he thinks it's time for a change. Maybe he thinks he'd be better at combating the Werdulac."

"But plotting against the current king?" William said. "That's not how it works."

Anton smirked. "Oh no? I'm curious—how do you think we get a new king?"

William opened his mouth to speak and then stopped.

"Exactly," Anton said. "This one killed the last one. And that's how this king will go too."

"So you think Innokenti might try to recruit us?" I asked.

"Maybe," Anton said. "I don't know what he's up to exactly, but if this does turn out to be about the Werdulac, you two would make pretty good allies."

He turned to William. "And someone did trick you into wandering into the Black Tomb where you very nearly got turned into a super-vampire. I don't suppose you remember who gave you the information that led you there?"

"No," William said.

"Sachiko did tell me she believed it was someone at the castle who did it," I said to William. "She said we couldn't trust anyone there."

"Is that all your evidence?" William said to Anton.

"Well, there was one little incident that got me thinking," Anton said.

"Don't keep us in suspense," William replied.

"I choose to ignore your tone," Anton said with dignity. "So I mentioned disappearances—most of which appeared to be pretty ordinary objects."

"Garden tools," William supplied.

"Just so," Anton replied. "Well, the small disappearances got me thinking—what if more important things have gone missing? And my thoughts turned naturally to the Vaults."

I glanced at Anton sharply. "You think something's gone missing at the Vaults?"

The Vaults were an underground network of secure chambers at Rusalka Castle where valuable—and dangerous—items were stored, including a great many weapons. If something had disappeared from the Vaults, that really was cause for concern.

"Well, that's what I wanted to find out," Anton said. "So I asked Innokenti if I could take a look. And he wouldn't let me go into the Vaults at all."

"I wouldn't let you in there either," William said shortly. "Besides, would you actually know if something was missing? Do you have the whole place memorized?"

"No," Anton said. "But I assume they keep an inventory. I would've been able to check that."

"But Innokenti wouldn't let you in," William said. "So you didn't find anything out."

"That's where you're wrong," Anton replied. "It turns out that an inventory for the Vaults is kept in the archives. And since that area is slightly less secure, I was able to look through that."

"And something is missing?" I said.

"Something is missing," Anton replied. "And do you know what it is?"

"Of course we don't," William said.

"It was a key," Anton replied.

"A key to what?" I said.

"I don't know," Anton said. "I got caught and thrown out before I could look that up. What the key was for was located in some other book or ledger or something."

"So what are you going to do?" William said. "Since you're suspicious?"

"I thought I'd hang out here for a little while," Anton said. "Fill you guys in on what's going on and keep myself far away from Krov and the trouble that's brewing."

"We've been having earthquakes too," I said.

"Yes, I noticed that," Anton replied. "Anything missing?"

"Not that I've noticed," I said. "But as far as I know, the first one only happened this morning."

"Well, unfortunately, I don't think this is a coincidence," Anton said. "Not with you and that weird cave here."

"Have you been over there to look?"

"No—I thought I'd come to see you first, seeing as friends are most important. But I'll go over there next."

"You're going to hang around here?" William said. "Here at Katie's house? Or here in Elspeth's Grove?"

Anton smirked. "Always the watchful little guard dog. I doubt very much that Katie's grandmother would put me up in the guest bedroom. I think I'll just wander around the town looking for a place to lay my weary bones."

"You don't have to stay, you know," William said. "I'm perfectly capable of keeping an eye on things here."

"I know," Anton said. "But I'd really like to have a look around myself. In fact, I think maybe I'll go have a look at that cave right now. It's in the Old Grove, right? That little forested area with the fruit trees and whatnot?"

Anton began to walk off.

"You know, I think I'll go with you," William said, following him.

Anton turned and grinned. "I had a feeling you'd say something like that."

He waved to me over William's head.

"Bye, Katie! And happy birthday!"

Anton turned and jogged off into the fog. William jogged after him.

Moments later, the front door opened, and GM came out.

"Who was that man?" GM asked.

Hoping she hadn't seen Anton, my answer was deliberately vague. "Who? You mean William?"

"No, not him," GM said. "The other one—the one with the dark hair."

"That was Anton," I said reluctantly.

"And who is he?" GM said.

"Someone William works with." The words felt strange, but they were actually the truth—William and Anton had worked together for years in Krov—though William now lived in Elspeth's Grove permanently and only consulted with the court occasionally.

"I see," GM said. "So now—he—William has gone running after his coworker?"

"Yes," I said.

"Instead of staying at your birthday party with you?"

"Yes."

GM watched the two of them run down the street.

"Your boyfriend is a very strange person."

Chapter Three

GM was right. William was strange—even by the standards of his own world.

William was one of the Sídh—just like my grandfather had been. But William had been attacked by a vampire—and had been partially turned. His transformation had been incomplete, and he had some attributes of a vampire but not all. He could drink blood, for example, but he didn't need to—in fact, he didn't need to eat at all. But vampire blood did run through his veins, and other vampires recognized him as one of their own. The Sídh considered his vampire-tainted blood to be an abomination, and William had been banished—cast out of their world entirely. They had taken his memories from him, and only his most basic, core memories were left—he knew his name, he knew that he had once been one of the Sídh—and he knew he had been attacked by a vampire. After being cast out, William had been left to wander our world alone. He had been found by the community of vampires in Krov, Russia, and they had taken him in and had hoped to make him one of their own.

For a time William had been one of them, and he had worked quite closely with Anton. But something remained between them—

some old argument, some old hurt—and neither of them would tell me what it was.

Anton, in fact, seemed to delight in tormenting William. I had no doubt that Anton had jogged off simply to make William look foolish. Both Anton and William were capable of great speed, and they could have gone off so fast that they would have appeared to vanish. Then again, maybe that would have been a bad idea. If GM had seen that—it would have looked very strange indeed.

GM and I went back to the party, and the mood seemed to be a little lighter now that William had departed—although some of that may have been due to GM's obvious delight that he was gone.

The party wrapped up shortly after that, as most of us had school in the morning, and I hugged my friends tightly as they said goodbye. I even managed to get a reluctant handshake from Irina and an enthusiastic one from Vadim.

Then I closed the door gratefully behind me—I was glad there was no more chance for any of them to get mixed up in something strange.

"Are you all right, Katie?" GM asked, coming up to me. "You look tired."

"I am a little tired," I said.

She placed a hand on my forehead. "You aren't getting sick, are you?"

"No," I said quickly. "I'm just a little—overwhelmed. It was a beautiful party, though. Really lovely. Thank you."

"You're welcome, solnyshko," GM said. "You know there's one more thing—"

She stopped.

"It can wait till morning," she said. "Go and relax now. Enjoy this last night of your weekend."

"GM," I protested, "there must be a ton of dishes."

"No, no, I'll see to it all." She waved me toward the stairs. "Go now and rest. I don't want you getting a cold. It's this unseasonably warm weather we're having. It makes everyone feel out of sorts."

I did as she asked and went up to my room. I changed out of my party dress and into some comfortable nightclothes. Then I lay down, intending only to rest my eyes a little, and before I knew it, I'd slipped into sleep.

In the morning, I woke well before the alarm, and for a moment, all I could think of was how well rested and comfortable I felt.

And then the events of the previous evening came flooding back to me.

Veronika had come to visit last night.

And she'd demanded that I do something impossible in order to save William's life.

I got out of bed and went to the window.

A fine white mist still lay over the ground and made everything look fresh and new and a little dreamy. I frowned a little as I opened the window to get in some morning air. The mist was lovely, but it was odd for fog to last this long. But the weather was warm and pleasant, and today was supposed to be another fine day.

Maybe the mist was a product of the unusually warm weather.

I got ready for the day and then went down to breakfast.

GM was waiting for me in the kitchen, and she greeted me with subdued excitement.

"Come with me, Katie," she said. "I have something to show you."

She led me to the front door and then paused with her hand on the knob.

"I was going to show you this last night, but you seemed a little tired. It's another birthday gift—sort of. I have purchased it, and now you will pay me back. But I don't think you will mind."

"That's very mysterious," I said.

"You will see in just a moment," GM said.

She opened the door and led me outside.

It was still early morning, and in the light mist I could see our street as it usually was, with cars parked in driveways and along the street—not many people had left for work yet.

"I don't really see anything," I said.

GM took my hand. "Come with me."

She led me down the driveway past her own cherry-red sports car, and she stopped next to a nondescript sedan in navy blue.

GM waved a hand over it. "This is yours."

I glanced at the car. "Wait. What?"

GM beamed. "I purchased the car, and you may drive it. In the summer, you can get a job and begin to pay me back. But not right now—your studies are too important."

I looked at the car again. "So you're going to help me buy a car—this car."

"Yes. Giving a car as a birthday gift is too extravagant. But I will assist you in buying one. My mechanic helped me to find this one. It is a very good car—very safe, very reliable. And I got an excellent price, even for a used car. It will not be too expensive for a teenager."

"Wow, GM," I said. "Thanks."

"Do you like it?" she asked.

"Yes," I said. "I love it."

"Good," GM said. "It is good to see you smile. Especially since you looked so out of sorts last night."

"Thanks," I said. "I really mean it. It's a complete surprise. I never expected to get my first car so soon."

"Now is the time," GM said. "I think it is not good for you to walk to school. I mean, it is good for you to walk—that is healthy. But you have a habit of meeting strange people. I think it is better if you do not walk alone anymore."

"Thanks, GM," I said again.

She continued. "Unfortunately, you cannot drive it to school today. First, you must go to your school's main office and register the car. Then you will need to get a parking permit. Once that is done, you can begin to drive it to school."

"Today's not a good morning for my first drive anyway," I said. "Not with all this fog."

GM gave me a curious look. "Yes, well, I suppose it is a little foggy." She took me by the arm. "But now you should go inside and have breakfast."

I went inside and had some cereal and juice, and then I came out again and began my walk to school.

The morning mist was really lovely—but I had no time to linger. I had to get to school and begin working on how to save William's life.

As I approached the schoolyard, I saw students heading into the school and hanging out at the picnic tables that dotted the front lawn.

Last year, Charisse and Branden had made a habit of hanging out at a particular picnic table in the schoolyard, but now that we were juniors, they'd stopped doing it—somehow the thrill of having the seniority to score a picnic table had worn off. I usually met them inside, and Simon was usually with them too. William, of course, didn't go to school, but he did sometimes come to visit me there. Despite how much I loved to see him, I hoped today wasn't one of those days. I wasn't really in the mood to talk to him or any of my friends, and I hoped that I didn't run into any of them.

The person I was really looking for was Terrance.

I went into the school and waded into the crowd.

I knew where Terrance's locker was, and I headed down that hallway. Terrance wasn't there, so I leaned against a nearby wall and tried to look casual. I got out my phone and scrolled through my messages for something to do, and I saw that I had a text from William. I quickly scrolled past it—I didn't want to read it just yet.

A moment later, a shadow fell across my screen. I looked up to see Vadim.

"Good morning, Katya," he said. "No—sorry, Katie."

I smiled. "Katya is close enough. How are you, Vadim?"

"I am very well," he said. "Thank you very much for inviting me to your party last night."

"You're welcome," I said. "Thank you for coming. I hope you had a good time."

"Yes, I had a very good time," Vadim said. "Katie, may I ask you something?"

"Of course."

Vadim hesitated and then smiled sheepishly.

"Could you introduce me to your friend Bryony? I think she is a very nice girl."

I had to smile back at him. "But you met Bryony already. In fact, I seem to recall that the two of you talked quite a bit."

Out of the corner of my eye, I saw Terrance approaching his locker with Irina walking by his side. Terrance smiled and waved when he saw me. Irina looked at me, then at Vadim, and then she glared at me.

Vadim looked up at the two of them and raised a hand in greeting. Then he turned back to me.

"Yes, we talked," Vadim said. "We had a good conversation. But I am not sure—I only saw her one time. Maybe she will not remember me."

"I'm sure she will remember you," I said. "But I'd be happy to introduce you again. What time do you have lunch?"

Vadim rummaged in his backpack and came up with a printed sheet of paper, which he held out to me.

"This is my schedule," he said. "The print is very small."

I ran my finger down the printed sheet and picked out his lunch period.

"There it is," I said, showing it to him. "You have lunch at the same time I do. Why don't you meet me in the cafeteria, and I'll ask Bryony if she would like to join us today. And some of my other friends from the party will be there also."

Vadim smiled again. "Thank you, Katie. I would like that very much."

"I'll see you at lunch, then," I said.

"See you at lunch," Vadim replied.

Then he waved and moved off into the crowd, and I made my way over to Terrance and Irina.

Irina eyed me warily as I approached, but Terrance looked up and smiled.

"Hey, guys," I said.

"Hey, Katie," Terrance said.

Irina simply looked at me.

"So, Terrance, could I talk to you for just a second?" I said.

"Sure. What's up?" he said.

"Well, it's kind of a private matter."

"We're busy this morning," Irina said sharply. "Terrance doesn't have time to talk to you right now."

Terrance smiled. "We're a little tied up at the moment. Maybe you could send me a text, and we'll work something out?"

"Sure, I'll do that," I said. "I wouldn't ask if it wasn't something important."

"I know," Terrance said. "I'll see you soon. I promise."

"Thanks, Terrance."

"No problem."

I waved at them and walked off. I hadn't gone very far when I heard Terrance's voice.

"What?" he said.

I glanced back.

Irina was glaring at him.

I made my way over to my own locker, and then I hurried to homeroom.

I made it to my seat and then got out my phone and read the text from William.

Can you meet me after school?

I didn't want to see William just yet—especially since I wasn't sure what I was going to do about the Veronika situation.

I decided not to answer right away. I needed time to think.

Instead, I sent Terrance a text asking him when he had some free time to meet up.

As I did so, Bryony walked into homeroom and slid into the seat next to me.

"Hey, Katie."

"Hey, Bryony." I put my phone away, glad of the distraction. "I ran into Vadim this morning."

"Oh really?" Bryony smiled shyly and brushed her hair behind her ear.

"He asked about you," I said. "And I was thinking—I know you usually have lunch with Irina and Annamaria. But Vadim is going to be having lunch with us today, and I was wondering if you wanted to join us too."

"I would like that," Bryony said.

"From what Vadim said, I think he would like that too," I replied.

The PA system crackled to life at that moment, and the morning announcements began, so further conversation was cut short.

Eventually, the bell rang to signal the start of the school day, and as I filed out into the hall, I noticed that I had a text from Terrance. He asked if I could meet him in the library after school, and I texted back quickly that I would meet him there.

I then texted William that I had to go to the library after school and wouldn't be able to meet him.

Then I shut off my phone, and I went to my first-period class.

By the time lunchtime rolled around, I was dreading meeting up with my friends. I didn't want to pretend that everything was normal and happy when it really wasn't. Yet, at the same time, I couldn't tell anyone what was wrong. No one would believe that I'd put William's life in danger, and the reason why would sound even crazier.

But I put on what I hoped was a carefree expression, and I turned my steps toward the cafeteria.

Simon and Charisse were already seated at a round table when I arrived, and as I sat down, Vadim approached hesitantly with a tray.

I waved him over. "Hi, Vadim. Please come and join us."

Vadim smiled and walked over to the table.

"Guys, you remember Vadim from last night?" I said.

"Of course," Charisse said. "It's good to see you again."

"Thank you," Vadim said as he sat down.

Simon didn't seem quite as enthusiastic as Charisse, but he nodded politely and did not object.

"I've also invited Bryony," I said. "I figured you guys wouldn't mind."

"Not at all," Charisse said. "I'm always happy to see Bryony."

Simon perked up. "He's here for Bryony? Oh, hey, in that case, welcome."

I had to sigh inwardly—Simon wasn't exactly subtle. Then again, I'd wondered myself about GM's seating arrangements last night. Putting me near Simon and far away from William hadn't surprised me, but I had puzzled over the fact that GM had placed Vadim near me too. Was GM hoping to set me up with Vadim? If so, it didn't seem to have worked.

Bryony walked out of the line next and stood for a moment, looking around. Then she spotted us and headed over to our table.

"Hey, guys," she said.

We all greeted her, and Vadim got up and pulled out a plastic chair for her.

As Bryony giggled and was seated, I happened to look up and saw that Irina was watching us. She stared at Bryony for a moment and then at me.

Then she walked off.

My view of Irina's retreating back was blocked by the arrival of Branden, who didn't throw his backpack on the table like he usually did. Instead, he dropped it on the floor and slid his tray quietly onto the table.

"Whoa, extra people," Branden said. "Hi, extra people. Bryony, always a pleasure. Vadim—good to see you again. Sorry I'm late, but I was collecting intel."

Simon snorted. "Intel? And what do you think you've found out?"

"Only that we're going to have an assembly tomorrow morning," Branden said. "So if you'd like to sleep in a little tomorrow and skip the assembly, I don't think anyone will notice."

"What's the assembly about?" Charisse said.

"Earthquake safety," Branden said, dropping into his seat and biting into a sandwich. "On account of all the seismic activity lately. They're going to tell us what to do in case an earthquake strikes while we're at school."

"That actually sounds pretty useful," Charisse said. "I don't think I want to skip that."

"And that's not really intel," Simon said. "I'm sure we were all going to find out soon. It's not like they would spring it on us first thing in the morning."

Branden shrugged. "Maybe not. But I found out about it first anyway." He continued chewing. "So I'm thinking these earthquakes must be what caused the cave-in at the cave in the Old Grove back in April."

I looked up at that. The cave-in hadn't been caused by an earthquake—it had actually been caused by Anton and me. But even though I had no intention of telling anyone that, the mention of the cave still made me nervous. Something was always going on over there, and I had just gotten used to the idea that maybe the trouble was over—that is, until Anton had brought the cave up again last night.

"That doesn't make any sense," Simon said. "The first earthquake was yesterday. The cave-in was months ago."

"It could have been an earthquake we couldn't feel," Branden said. "Something low level."

"I don't think so," Simon said.

"You're not a scientist," Branden said. "You don't know."

"You're not a scientist either," Simon replied.

"Simon is correct," Vadim interjected. "The cave-in was not caused by an earthquake."

Vadim—who had been talking quietly with Bryony—was now looking over at Branden and Simon.

"What?" Branden said. "How do you know?"

"That's why my uncle is here," Vadim replied. "Irina's father was working on clearing up the cave-in so the tunnels could be used again. But he was having trouble, so my uncle had to come in to oversee the operation himself. Part of that was uncovering the reason for the cave-in. It was caused by human actions."

"Wait," Branden said. "I thought you said your uncle made fireworks."

"He works in pyrotechnics," Vadim said patiently. "Fireworks are one application. My uncle actually works in mining. Pyrotechnics there involves controlled detonations and chemical processes to extract ores and minerals."

"Really?" Branden said. "That sounds cool. So what kind of human actions caused the cave-in?"

"It was deliberate sabotage," Vadim said. "Someone set a series of explosive devices and intentionally detonated them. It was very dangerous."

"Cool," Branden said again.

I shifted uncomfortably in my seat.

I was relieved when lunch was over, and I jumped up when the bell rang to signal the end of the period.

As I filed out of the cafeteria with the rest of the crowd, I found Charisse walking by my side.

She touched me on the arm. "Are you okay?"

"Yes—I'm great," I said.

"You keep jumping at everything everyone says," Charisse said. "You've been that way ever since you ran out at the party last night."

"I'm fine, really." I smiled, but I had a feeling the smile wasn't convincing.

"You weren't the same at all when you came back," Charisse said. "And William ran out first. Did something happen between the two of you?"

"No," I said. "This isn't William's fault at all."

"But something *is* wrong," Charisse persisted.

"No—maybe. I just have to get a few things worked out."

"Okay," Charisse said. "You know you can always talk to me if you need to."

"Thanks," I said. "That means a lot to me." I tried to look reassuring, but once again, I wasn't sure if it worked.

We walked along in silence until we came to a parting of the ways.

As I turned to walk down my hallway, and Charisse turned to walk down hers, I happened to glance back at her.

She was staring at me with a worried look on her face.

After classes had ended, I hurried to the library to meet Terrance. I'd thought, at first, that he'd meant the school library, which was open for an hour after the school day ended. But when I didn't see Terrance there, we quickly established through a series of texts that he was waiting for me over at the public library. Luckily, it wasn't far, and I hurried over there on foot.

As I walked, I realized that I'd forgotten to stop at the main office to find out about registering my car and getting a parking permit—I figured I would just do it in the morning.

Elspeth's Grove Public Library was a pretty brick building on a leafy, quiet street. The unseasonably warm weather made the walk a pleasant one, and I felt myself relaxing a little as I walked up the broad front steps to the library. At least I was finally doing something about the Veronika problem.

I didn't see Terrance at first, and I worried that I might have misunderstood his texts. And then I spotted him in one of the private study rooms with the big windows. He smiled when he saw me and waved me in.

"Hey, Katie," Terrance said as I closed the door behind me.

"Hey," I said.

"Sorry about the mix-up," Terrance said. "I chose this library because these study rooms are soundproof. I thought that would be useful in case you needed to discuss—business."

"Thanks," I said, sitting down at the table across from him. "That's exactly why I'm here."

"Business it is, then," Terrance said. "So what's up?"

I stared at Terrance for a long moment.

"It's okay," he said after a minute. "You can tell me anything. You're the Little Sun, and I'm a member of the Order of the Hawthorne. We've both seen some really weird stuff. You don't have to worry that I'm going to judge you."

"You might," I said.

"Would you like some water?" Terrance said. "How about a granola bar? I always carry like five or six of them. Eating something might make you feel better."

"Sure," I said. "Thanks."

Terrance reached into his backpack, pulled out two wrapped granola bars, and slid one over to me.

"Peanut butter and chocolate," he said. "I highly recommend them. I'll join you if you don't mind."

I took a sip of the water and then unwrapped the granola bar and took a bite.

"That's good," I said. "Thanks."

"You can't go wrong with that combo," Terrance said. "So seriously, what's wrong? It's pretty obvious that something's troubling you. And that's the whole point of the Order. We help people."

"It involves a vampire—or two," I said.

"Naturally," Terrance replied. "Please go on."

"I have a friend," I said. "A very, very good friend who is a vampire. And I don't want this person to get hurt."

"I understand," Terrance said. "I know you have at least one friend who is a vampire."

I looked up at Terrance. I knew he knew about Sachiko, who was a vampire, but I didn't know if he knew about William. I wanted very badly to ask, but I had a feeling it might not be safe.

Terrance continued. "And I respect your friendships. I know that we in the Order have a reputation for being vampire hunters. But what we really want to do is protect humans. We're not on a mission to eradicate vampires—and yes, we wouldn't mind curing them. But I've known a few good vampires in my time, and if you have a vampire friend that you trust, that's good enough for me."

"I'm glad to hear you say that," I said. "Because you're really the only person I can talk to about this."

"I'm listening," Terrance said.

"Okay," I said. "As I was saying, I have a good friend—a vampire who got sick—very sick. I was afraid my friend was going to die."

Terrance waited patiently, and I went on.

"I was so worried that I had to seek help. And I found it—I found a vampire healer who promised to help my friend. For a price."

"I see," Terrance said. "And the bill has come due?"

"Yes," I said. "To be fair, the vampire healer did exactly what she promised. She returned my friend to health. But now she wants payment, and I have no idea how to do what she asks."

"What does she want?"

"I agreed to give her whatever she asked for whenever she asked for it."

Terrance's eyebrows rose. "Wow. That's steep. And it sounds like she knew she had a very valuable client in you. She knew you could get her something big if she needed it. So what did she ask for?"

"She wants me to track down the ghost girl," I said. "Her Promised One has disappeared, and she thinks the ghost girl is behind it. I told her there is no ghost girl and that the Tears of the Firebird caused those disappearances."

"And the disappearances have stopped since we stopped using the tears," Terrance said. "So the disappearance of the Promised One is probably unrelated."

"I told her the disappearances have stopped," I said. "But she insisted that they were still going on. She said that there was a real ghost girl, and that she was actively going after vampires."

"What's the healer's name?" Terrance asked.

"Veronika," I said. "She lives in Zamochit Village."

Terrance nodded. "I know her—at least by reputation. She's supposed to be one of the best. I'm surprised that she's got a hold of the wrong end of things."

"She said I had friends who could go places she couldn't. She specifically mentioned the Order. And she said you guys knew more than you were saying."

"Not as far as I know," Terrance said. "I'll admit this is a real puzzle. But I'll do everything I can to help you. I'll bump this up the line, if that's okay with you—run everything by Maksim. He's got a lot of pull—and a lot of knowledge and skill."

"Thanks, Terrance," I said. "I really appreciate your help."

"How much time do we have?" he asked. "How soon does she want you to catch the ghost girl?"

"She didn't give me a time frame," I replied. "She just said to get it done."

"Curious," Terrance said. "Very curious. This is definitely a puzzle."

He lapsed into silence.

"You know, Katie," he said after a moment, "I think you should be really careful. There's something suspicious about the timing of all of this."

"What do you mean?" I said.

"A vampire shows up suddenly and wants you to go on a wild quest to look for someone who doesn't exist—a quest that could take you to some weird, out-of-the-way places. It just sounds like someone is setting you up to disappear."

"You think someone told Veronika to do this?"

"Or maybe even tricked her," Terrance said. "It's possible she believes everything she said to you. He *has* used vampires for his own ends before."

I felt a chill steal over me. I hoped I was wrong about what he was getting at. "Who?"

Terrance paused to take a deep breath. "I was thinking of the Werdulac."

"Oh," I said quietly. "Then you do know about the Werdulac?"

"Of course we do. He's the biggest vampire threat around. Something like his reconstitution would not escape our notice. And we know what you mean to him."

"Good to know you're on it," I said.

"I don't want to alarm you," Terrance said. "But it makes sense. The Werdulac has been in hiding for some time. His hybrids are in hiding too. No one knows where they are. But the Werdulac still needs you, and he hasn't made an attempt to kidnap you in quite some time. It seems to me that now is as good a time as any to try to get to you. And then he sends in someone you wouldn't expect— someone you owe a legitimate debt to."

"Oh," I said again.

Terrance looked at me for a moment.

"I'm sorry, Katie," he said. "I've upset you, and I didn't mean to do that. I'll come stake out your house tonight—keep an eye on things. You'll be okay. And like I said, I'll let Maksim and the Order know. I'm sure if any extra help is necessary, they'll send it."

"But you need your sleep," I protested. My head was swimming, and I was trying to focus on something normal to keep from giving into panic. "Isn't this football season? You play wide receiver, right?"

Terrance chuckled. "Don't worry about me. I'll be fine. It's all part of the job, and I'm used to it. Besides, I always have to hold back a little out on the field anyway. I can't let everybody see how fast I really am."

I had to chuckle myself at that, and Terrance smiled.

"It's good to see you haven't lost your sense of humor yet," he said. "Very genuinely, I think you're safe right now. If the Werdulac has chosen the subtle approach, I think he'll stick with it. I don't think you'll see any bold attacks. He's probably just hoping to lure you to some out-of-the-way place where none of us would be watching. So just be aware of your surroundings. And don't go walking anywhere alone—you don't want to disappear on your way home from school."

I took a deep breath. "Okay."

"We'll get through this, Katie," Terrance said. "*You'll* get through this. After all, you already took on the Werdulac's brother and won. How hard could it be to take the Werdulac out too?"

I laughed again, and Terrance smiled.

"Come on, Katie. How about I drive you home?"

Chapter Four

Werdulac.

Little Sun.

Both things my grandmother knew nothing about. GM did not know that her daughter had had Sídh blood and had been the Little Sun. But GM did know of the legend, and she didn't believe in it. She didn't believe in anything supernatural, and she certainly wouldn't have believed in an ancient vampire known as the Werdulac, even if she had heard of him.

Which was unfortunate because he was after me.

The Werdulac and his army had fought a war against the Sídh, many centuries ago, and the Sídh had emerged victorious. They had then burned the Werdulac and his followers to ash and buried the ashes in secret places—magical places—with powerful spells on them to keep them bound. But the power of the ancient vampires was great—and the Werdulac, wherever he was hidden, began to heal. His body began to reconstitute itself, and his powerful will drew followers to him. And those followers were working now to free him.

Those followers were also working to capture me because of my Sídh blood. The Sídh had long ago left the mortal world, themselves defeated by ordinary human beings, and they were said to live underground now—though I didn't know if that was actually true or simply poetic. They still existed though, and they were still powerful—but their ability to intervene in human affairs and interact with the human world was severely limited.

And that was what the Werdulac wanted to change. He wanted a rematch with the Sídh—another chance to defeat them—and in order to get that, he had to set them free. And in order to set them free, he needed me.

The ancient treaty that banished the Sídh from our world, also required them to protect it in certain circumstances. The Sídh had to send one of their number to the human world whenever it was necessary to create a new Little Sun, and if the Little Sun was killed by a vampire, the Sídh could be released from captivity to take their revenge on their ancient enemies. So the Werdulac planned to kidnap me, hold me until he was fully restored and freed himself, and then he would sacrifice me, so he could free the Sídh and get his war.

Toward this end, the Werdulac had instructed his followers to build an army made of creatures of his own invention—hybrids who were part vampire and part kost. The kost was actually an evil spirit in a reanimated corpse, and the hybrids were kosts that had been turned by vampires. William and I had already faced this hybrid army once, when it was in its nascent state, and we had fought them off. And though the army had surely grown since then, their numbers had been depleted again thanks to the same Tears of the Firebird that had killed off vampires—the hybrids were vulnerable to it because of their vampire blood.

The Werdulac had taken his hybrids into hiding after that, and they had lain dormant. It had been nearly a year since I had been troubled by the Werdulac or the hybrids, and I suppose I'd been hoping that they'd gone away for good. But if the Werdulac really was active again, then I was once more the target of a very powerful enemy.

And Terrance and the Order were really the only people who could help me at this point—especially since I no longer had my powers. And my powers, as far as I knew, had never been effective against vampires anyway.

A little voice in the back of my mind whispered that I should tell all this to William—he loved me, and he would want to know. But fear came in a rush right after and nearly overwhelmed me. I saw again how he had looked when he was near death—pale and still and covered with bruises that wouldn't heal. Even if Veronika was working with the Werdulac, she still held William's life in her hands, and I couldn't put him in any more danger.

My phone buzzed at that moment, and I reached over to pick it up. As I tapped the button, 10:00 p.m. flashed up in big, white numbers on my screen. I sighed. I had resolved to go to bed early, but so far I had been unable to stop worrying about William and the Werdulac. I had resisted the impulse all night to go to the window and see if Terrance was out there, standing guard. I'd be worried if I saw him and worried if I didn't.

I glanced at the phone again and saw that I had a new text from William.

Are you okay?

I wanted to answer him, but I didn't know what to say. I shut off my phone and turned off the light.

In the morning, I ate breakfast quickly and hurried to school. The weather was still warm for October, but I didn't feel much like lingering and enjoying the morning, which was finally clear—at long last the persistent mist had lifted. I had taken my new car for one brief drive yesterday after Terrance had dropped me off at home, and I was anxious now to get the paperwork done so I could start driving to school. At least while driving I couldn't be lured into any dark corners by agents of the Werdulac.

When I reached the school, I saw signs posted on all the doors about an emergency assembly on the topic of earthquake safety and preparedness, which was being held in the newly renovated auditorium. So it appeared that Branden had been right.

I had plenty of time before the assembly, so I went inside and headed for the main office to pick up my paperwork.

As I reached the office, I saw Charisse coming toward me from the other direction. Her head was down, and she was looking at her phone. For a brief moment, I considered ducking down a nearby hall so she wouldn't see me. And then I realized I was being ridiculous. I was really not in the mood to talk, but that was no reason to avoid my friends.

I continued walking toward the office door, and as I reached it, Charisse looked up and noticed me.

"Hey, Katie," she said, coming to stand beside me.

"Hey," I said.

"So what brings you to the main office this early in the morning?" Charisse asked.

"GM got me a car," I replied. "So I have to register it and get my parking permit and all the rest of it."

"Your grandmother got you a car?" Charisse said.

"Yes—it was a big surprise."

"That's wonderful," Charisse said. "Welcome to the club. It's good to know you'll be out on the road with the rest of us."

"Thanks," I said. "It's not exactly a gift—I'm going to pay my grandmother back for it. But she did all the researching and test-driving, and all of a sudden I've got a car."

"That's great, Katie," Charisse said. "Your first set of wheels. Did you get the car today?"

"No—actually I got it yesterday in the morning."

Charisse's face fell. "Why didn't you tell me?"

I glanced toward the main office door. "Did you have something you needed to do?" I said evasively. "I don't want to keep you."

"I just have some info to drop off about upcoming auditions for the fall play," Charisse said. "It can wait. Seriously, Katie, this was a big moment in your life. Why didn't you tell me?"

"I didn't think of it," I said.

"I'm your best friend. You didn't have two seconds just to send me a text?"

"I'm sorry, Charisse. I've just been a little preoccupied lately—it slipped my mind."

Charisse's expression softened. "Are you okay?"

"Yes," I said. "I'm good. I'm great. Everything's going really well."

"Are you sure?"

"Yes," I said. "Absolutely."

"Do you mind if we go sit down somewhere for a second?" Charisse asked.

"What about your play?" I said. "You've got to get that stuff in."

"There's no rush at the moment," Charisse said gently. "Let's go sit down."

Charisse steered me into a nearby classroom, and we sat down at two empty desks. There were other students in the room, and I glanced around—I knew some of the students vaguely.

"This is a freshman homeroom," I said. "We don't belong in here."

"It's just for a few minutes," Charisse said. "And it'll give us a measure of anonymity. Nobody in here knows us too well, and they won't be interested in what we're saying."

"But—"

"Katie, please stop acting so worried," Charisse said. "We're best friends. I care about you. This isn't an interrogation."

I took a deep breath and made an attempt to relax. "You're right."

"So what's going on?" Charisse said. "You look really freaked out. You have for a few days now."

"It's nothing," I said. "I'm just not feeling quite myself."

Charisse gave me a long look.

"You told me once," she said quietly, "that I never say anything. You don't either, you know. You never tell anyone how you feel anymore. You never tell anyone what you're thinking—not really. Katie, I'm really and truly your friend. You don't have to keep me out. You can tell me anything."

"Oh, Charisse," I said. "I wish I could."

"You can."

"You'd never believe me."

"I know you said there's nothing wrong between you and William," Charisse said slowly. "But the word this morning is that Irina and Terrance had a big fight last night, and it was about you. Irina said Terrance blew her off so he could meet up with you."

"That's crazy," I said.

"You didn't meet with him?" Charisse asked.

"No—I met with him, but he's helping me with something. It's absolutely not romantic. And I know for a fact that he really cares about Irina. He's told me before that their relationship means everything to him."

Charisse persisted. "What was he helping you with?"

I glanced around the room. It really was starting to fill up—there were people sitting all around us now.

"Can we go somewhere else?" I said. "It isn't very private around here."

"Fine," Charisse said, her voice rising. "I'll go. But only if you promise to answer my question."

"I will," I said. "Let's just go."

We stepped out into the hall, and I spotted a little recessed bench near the main office that was now unoccupied—people were starting to file into their respective homerooms ahead of the warning bell.

"Over here," I said.

I sat down on the bench, and Charisse followed me.

"So what is Terrance helping you with?" she said.

"It's William." I paused—I knew I had to choose my words carefully. I couldn't slip and say too much. "I'm worried about him, and I think Terrance can help me."

"I thought you said there was nothing wrong between you and William."

"There isn't," I said. "It's not something between us. It's something about him."

"Could you be any more cryptic?" Charisse said. "For once I'd like you to just say something straightforward."

"All right," I said. "I'll tell you. But you have to trust me—I need you to trust me. I need you to believe me and not think I'm crazy."

"Katie, of course I trust you," Charisse said. "Of course I'll believe you. I'd like to feel like you trust me too. I'm your friend—you have to know that. Just tell me."

"I'm afraid for William," I said. "His life is in danger, and it's my fault."

"What?" Charisse said. "You can't be serious."

"You said you'd trust me."

"William's life is in danger?" Charisse said. "You really believe that?"

"Yes."

"And you think Terrance can help with that?"

"Yes," I said.

Charisse looked at me for a long moment. "Okay. I believe you. If that's what's been bothering you, it's no wonder you look so freaked out."

She paused. "So why is he in danger? What has he done?"

"He hasn't done anything," I said. "It's something I've done. And I can't tell you what it is—just trust me on that."

"Is there anything I can do to help?" Charisse said.

"No," I said.

"What about the police? Can you go to them?"

"No."

"Is it something illegal?" Charisse said. "Is that why you can't go to the police?"

"No," I said. "It's nothing illegal. It's just very, very strange. They'd never believe me."

"Well, that ties up a little with something else I've heard."

"What's that?" I said.

"A strange man has been seen loitering around town. He's been hanging out at the cave in the Old Grove a lot—and William's been seen with him. The police are keeping an eye on him—the strange man, I mean."

"How do you know that?" I asked.

"Branden," Charisse replied.

I had to smile a little. "Branden knows everything."

"Is that guy part of the trouble William is in?" Charisse asked.

"No," I said. "That guy has nothing to do with it. I know who it is, and ultimately he's not bad—he's just a lot of mischief."

"So what are the two of them doing out by the cave?" Charisse asked.

"I don't know," I said. "Nothing with that cave is ever good news."

"What does that mean?" Charisse said.

The warning bell rang at that moment, and I got up quickly.

"Looks like we'd better get going," I said. "We've got that big assembly today."

Charisse stood up also.

"Okay," she said. "I guess those are enough questions for one day. But thanks for telling me about William."

I looked at her. "Do you believe me?"

"Yes," Charisse said. "I really do. And I hope he's going to be okay. I hope you are too."

"Thanks," I said.

"And I hope that someday you'll trust me enough to tell me the whole story."

"Oh, Charisse," I said.

"I mean that," she said. "I realize now that there may be good reasons why you're so guarded—and you are guarded, even if you don't think that you are. And maybe I haven't been the friend to you that I should have been all these years. But I am here if you need me. So do what you have to do—and just know that I'll support you."

"I—" I stopped, uncertain what to say.

"You don't have to brush it off, Katie," Charisse said kindly. "Just try to accept someone else's support for once. You don't have to do everything on your own."

She picked up her bag and took me by the arm. "Come on, let's go."

As we started to walk down the hall, a strange rumbling sound filled the air.

"Whoa, what was that?" Charisse said. "That must be the world's heaviest truck going by outside."

She stopped to peer out a nearby window, and as I looked out after her, the whole world began to shake.

"Earthquake!" someone cried. "Earthquake!"

Students began to pour out into the hallway, and a big crowd of people ran for the nearest set of double doors.

"Get out!" somebody shouted. "Everybody, get out! Before the building collapses!"

There were screams and more people pouring out into the hall. Soon everyone began jostling each other, and a knot of students made their way out through the nearest exit.

Through the window, I could see people running across the lawn and out toward the street, and as the violent shaking continued, I grabbed onto the wall and tried not to fall.

"Charisse!" I cried. "Charisse, where are you?"

"I'm here!" came a voice.

A hand slipped into mine, and I gripped it firmly.

A huge shudder ran through the building, and I was bounced away from the wall. My feet slipped out from under me, and I fell to the ground.

I could feel people rushing past me, and I couldn't see anything but a tangle of limbs and flickering lights.

"Just hang on!" Charisse shouted.

I felt her tugging on my hand, and I tried to stand, but I couldn't figure out which way was up.

The rumbling around me grew louder, and the screams intensified.

The lights went out completely in the hall, and I could hear shouts and scuffling nearby.

It sounded like people were fighting as they tried to get out the door.

The rumbling underneath me grew stronger, and I felt myself being bounced around on the floor.

Soon all I could hear was screaming, and Charisse's hand slipped out of mine.

"Stop!" shouted a voice. "Stop!"

The voice was strong and authoritative.

"Everyone, stop! Do *not* run outside! Stop right where you are!"

The screaming died down, and the scuffling stopped.

"Everyone, get away from the doorway, and get away from the windows!"

Though the rumbling continued, the crowd began to get quieter, and people stopped running.

The voice continued. "Get close to the walls! Drop down and cover your heads!"

Through the shaking, I could see students complying as one by one they dropped. The hallway was soon calmer and calmer, and I could see a boy walking through the crowd, bracing his hands against the wall as he went. He had close-cropped, light brown hair and a stern manner.

"Remain calm, and we'll get through this!" he shouted. "No one—I repeat—no one is to go outside!"

The shaking continued, but soon, everyone was on the floor along with me, and the crowd in the hall grew quieter until the only sound was that of the building shaking and the earth moving.

Eventually, the rumbling died away, and the floor underneath me was still once again.

"Is it over?" cried a voice.

"Everyone, stay right where you are!" the boy with the close-cropped hair cried. "Nobody move until I tell you to move!"

Silence reigned, and the earth remained still.

"All right, everyone," the boy said. "You may stand up now. But standing only! No one does any walking yet. And help anybody who seems to be hurt."

There was rustling, a low murmur of voices, and soon the whole crowd was on their feet. The lights were off, but there was light from the windows that lined the outside wall, and I could see a sea of tense, strained faces all around me. I spotted Charisse nearby, and I went to stand beside her.

"Okay!" the boy said. "I think we're good to go. When I say go, everyone form a line and file out slowly and calmly. We will have no panic. And be alert for aftershocks. If you feel the ground shake again, do *not* run. Drop to the ground again and cover your heads. Is that clear?"

There were murmurs of assent, and then the boy began to move through the crowd. He came to stand by the big double doors, and then he raised his hand.

"All right, everybody! Let's go. One at a time."

He opened the doors, and the crowd began to move slowly. Eventually, Charisse and I made our way out with the rest of the students, and we joined a group that was congregating around the flagpole.

An insistent buzzing sound came from Charisse's bag, and she got out her phone.

"I've got about a hundred texts," she said. "Branden, Mom, Dad."

I got out my phone too. I also had a long list—GM, Simon, and William.

I responded to my grandmother and Simon first. Then I sent a brief text to William.

I'm okay. Wasn't so bad.

I'd briefly considered adding a smiley face but had decided against it. As I looked at the text now, it seemed kind of dismissive. That wasn't what I'd intended at all, but I didn't know how to fix it. Anything I thought of to send next would only make things worse. I'd simply wanted to sound reassuring so that William wouldn't worry.

I also didn't want him to come looking for me.

"All right, everybody, listen up."

The boy with the close-cropped hair walked through our little group and came to stand next to the flagpole.

"I'm going to tell you exactly the same thing I've told everyone so far," he said. "The school is currently evacuating. All students and staff are to come out here to the front of the building. I want you all to go look for your homeroom teachers and then stand with your class. Your teacher will do a head count, and once everyone is accounted for—and I do mean everyone—you will be allowed to go home. There will be no classes today."

A subdued cheer went up, and the boy held his hand up for silence.

"I repeat," he said. "Everyone must be accounted for before anyone will be allowed to go home. Anyone leaving without checking in with their homeroom first will receive an automatic detention. Is that clear?"

"Wow," Charisse whispered to me. "That is one bossy kid. He seems to know what he's doing, though."

"As far as tomorrow goes," the boy continued, "the school will be checked thoroughly for structural damage. A determination as to whether or not the school will open tomorrow will be made tonight. Emails will be sent to the families that wished to receive communication by email, phone calls will be made to those that chose that option, and the decision will also be posted on the school website. So if school is open tomorrow, lack of knowledge of that fact will not be accepted as an excuse if you decide not to show up."

Some chatter arose about this, and the boy whistled for silence.

"Now that I have your attention again, I just want to say that I'm glad you all appear to be uninjured. Be sure to report any injuries immediately if you discover them later. Now go find your homerooms, and stay safe the rest of the day."

The boy then walked off to address the next group.

"That was a little odd," Charisse said. "Informative but odd. Do you know who that guy was?"

"No idea," I said.

Charisse looked over the crowd. "Okay, so it looks like your teacher is over there, and mine is over here. Would you like a ride home after we've all been checked in?"

"No thanks," I said.

"Are you sure?" Charisse asked. "It's really no trouble."

"No, that's all right," I said. "I'd really like to walk. I think I need to be alone for a little while."

"Okay," Charisse said. "Text me when you get home. I just want to make sure you made it."

"I will," I said.

Charisse then turned toward her homeroom class, and I turned to look for mine.

I spotted my teacher's familiar red hair, and I began to walk toward her.

As I did so, I noticed that a fine white mist was slowly creeping toward the school.

Chapter Five

I'd really intended to go straight home.

But after checking in with my homeroom and asking several other people about the mist, it occurred to me that I was the only one who could see it.

It hadn't escaped my notice that no one else had mentioned seeing any fog over the past few days. It also hadn't escaped my notice that my grandmother had given me a funny look when I'd mentioned it on Monday morning.

And it wasn't all that strange that I was the only one who could see it.

Something like that had happened to me before.

So I walked straight into the mist, hoping to follow it to its source. But fog by nature is hard to follow—it disappeared ahead of me and closed in behind me, and it seemed to press in on all sides. I plunged on, hoping to find an end to the mist. Maybe then I could get an idea of where it was coming from.

I had only been walking for a little while when a car pulled up beside me.

I glanced over. Even through the haze, I could tell it was William.

His passenger-side window was open, and he was leaning over with one hand on the steering wheel, looking out at me.

"Katie, are you okay?" he said.

"Yes," I said. "I'm great. How did you find me?"

"I stopped by the school first," William said. "I saw Charisse. She told me that you decided to walk. So I came to look for you."

I stopped walking. "Does it look hazy out here to you?"

William stopped the car. "No. Why do you say that?"

"It's nothing," I said. "Did you get my text?"

"I got it."

"I really am fine," I said. "I just need a little time to myself."

"Katie, I really need to tell you something," William said. "Can we go somewhere and talk?"

"I don't know—"

"Katie, please. It's important."

I glanced over at William. He was looking at me imploringly.

"Okay," I said. "But I don't have long."

"A little time is all I need."

"So where to?" I asked.

"You could start by getting in the car," William said.

"Yes, okay," I said.

I opened the door and got in.

As William drove off, I tried not to look at him.

Instead, I watched the car plowing through a haze of fog—it was a little hard for me to see where we were going.

"So it's a nice, sunny day, is it?" I said.

William gave me a strange look. "Yes, it is."

"Just checking," I said.

"Checking for what?"

"To make sure that we're both seeing the same thing."

William threw me a worried glance. "Are you sure you're okay?"

"Yes," I said.

"You didn't get hit by falling debris or anything like that?"

"No," I said. "The building shook, and we sat on the floor by the wall until it was over. Then we went outside."

"That doesn't sound too bad," William said.

"It wasn't." I looked out the window but couldn't see a thing. I wondered if the fog was getting thicker. "Where are we headed?"

"How about Hywel's Plaza?" William said. "I don't think we'll be overheard there."

"Overheard?" I said.

"Yes. Your grandmother's always at your house, and right now, Anton's over at mine. The tables at the plaza are all placed far apart from one another, and we should be able to see anyone coming long before they get near enough to hear what we're saying."

William smiled at me.

"Sometimes the most public places can be the most private."

Usually William's crooked little half smile tugged at my heart, but this time I felt myself frowning.

"Why is Anton staying at your house?" I asked.

"That's one of the things I want to talk to you about," William said. "But at the moment, he's sleeping."

That made sense to me. Sunlight would not make vampires burst into flame, as was popularly believed. But it did make them much weaker—in sunlight a vampire wasn't much stronger than an ordinary human being, and their extraordinary senses were also dulled. In addition, a vampire's body needed rest and healing just as a human body did, and they would suffer fatigue and illness without it. In other words, vampires had to sleep sometime too, and daytime was as good a time as any for a nocturnal creature to rest.

William, however, as a Sídh with vampire blood, never seemed to need sleep or tire at all, and sunlight had no effect on him. I had heard the vampire Innokenti say once that William could be stronger than vampire or Sídh if he chose to be, and I understood that to mean that William could increase his already superhuman strength and speed if he would drink blood. But the Sídh in him was horrified by the idea, and as far as I knew, he took in no sustenance at all. The only time he ever ate any food was when he ate with human beings—and then it was really just for show.

Somehow, William seemed to live off air alone.

Soon, William was pulling the car to a stop, and I saw through the haze that we had reached the plaza.

Hywel's Plaza was a large, open area that was used for farmers' markets and community events in the warm months and as an ice-skating rink in the cold months. When it wasn't in use for an event, it was basically a large park with picnic tables and sturdy, metal chairs. The unusually warm weather had delayed the opening of the skating rink, and I could see one picnic table with a chair winking at me out of the mist.

William and I got out of the car, and I headed toward the one table I could see.

Luckily, as I drew closer to it, I could see that there was another chair on the other side of the table—I didn't want William to notice that I was having any trouble seeing.

The two of us sat down, and William gave me a long look.

I had to look away. I couldn't believe how much danger I'd put him in.

"Katie," William said, "I don't know why you're mad at me, but I really need you to listen right now."

"I'm listening," I said. "And I'm not mad at you."

"You won't even look at me," William said.

I made an effort to look over at him.

"I'm not angry," I said. "I'm not angry at all. I just—need to figure something out alone."

William nodded and looked down.

"I understand why you're feeling this way," he said. "I've kept a lot of secrets from you—I've even kept quiet about ordinary, everyday things—blocked you out completely. So when you're going through something, like you are now, you don't feel as if you can talk to me. I have to accept responsibility for that."

I didn't say anything. There wasn't really anything I could say.

"This problem didn't start today," William said after a moment. "And it's not going to go away in a day either. But I'd like to start trying to fix it."

I glanced over at him.

"And I think the best way I can do that," William said, "is by being totally open with you. So from now on, I'm going to tell you everything that's going on as soon as I know it. I'm not going to sit on information anymore."

I was startled. "You really mean that?"

"I do," William said. "No more protecting you by keeping you in the dark. You deserve to know everything."

"Wow," I said. "Thank you."

"There's no need to thank me. It's what I should have done all along."

William paused again, and he seemed to be gathering himself.

"So I'd like to start with Anton," he said. "Anton is staying at my house, and that's because he's convinced me that he's genuinely concerned about what's happening in Russia. And you know Anton is seldom genuine about anything."

I frowned, trying to think back to what had happened on the night of my birthday party. I'd been badly rattled by Veronika's visit, but I remembered the conversation with Anton vaguely.

"Didn't he say something about a conspiracy involving Innokenti?" I said. "And something else about disappearing household objects?"

"Yes, he did," William said. "And I'm not saying that I believe he's right about any of it. But I believe he's sincere in his belief. Which makes me think he's noticed *something*—even if he doesn't know exactly what it is."

"You believe he believes what he's saying," I said.

"Basically, yes."

"He also mentioned earthquakes, didn't he?" I said. "Do you think he's right that they mean something? Do you think there's a connection to the earthquakes here?"

William shook his head. "I wish I knew. And if Anton is right that something is wrong at the Russian court, we can't really go to them and ask what they know."

He shifted in his seat a little.

"And since we're on the topic of Anton," he said. "He's always hinting that I don't tell you things. And in this case he's right—I haven't told you something."

"Is it something important?" I asked.

"Very important," William said.

He paused as if waiting for my reaction.

I sighed gently and tried to make my tone sound light so as not to hurt his feelings.

"Go ahead and tell me," I said.

"The hybrids are gone," he said.

"Gone?" I asked.

"Gone. As in deceased. As far as we can tell, it's every last one of them."

"What?" I said. I was genuinely stunned, and I wasn't sure I'd heard him correctly.

"It's true," William said. "The entire army of them. A few of them disappeared during the ghost girl crisis. But something else killed off the rest of them all at once."

"How do you know?" I said.

"Their bodies were found on the edge of the Wasteland, not far from Zamochit. There were about three hundred of them. We know the Werdulac had about one hundred when we met up with them last year, and we destroyed about forty. Then he took them into hiding and began to build their numbers up again. It's not easy to create kost-vampire hybrids, so their numbers don't grow quickly. But considering the challenges, he did a pretty good job in creating three hundred."

"And you really think that there were only three hundred total?" I asked.

"That's what our best information says," William replied.

"How long ago was this?" I asked.

"Several months ago," William said. "Shortly after we came back from Russia."

"What do you think caused it?" I asked.

"Our best information is that the Werdulac did it himself."

"Where did that information come from?"

"From the Russian court."

"And do you believe them?" I asked.

"Yes. The news came out several months ago when things were still very stable at the court—and I think when it comes to the Werdulac, you can trust them. That's the one thing they are always careful about."

"So the hybrids are really and truly gone," I said. "And they're no longer after me?"

"They're really and truly gone. All accounted for and given proper burials."

"Why didn't you tell me this?" I said. "We can all breathe easier now."

William shifted in his chair again.

"You don't think so?" I asked.

"I actually think it means just the opposite," William replied. "The Werdulac has gotten rid of the army that he was just starting to build, and he doesn't care that we know it. In fact, I think he wanted us to know it—that's why the hybrids were all left near the Wasteland. There's no way the community in Zamochit could fail to find them there."

"Do you think that's where the hybrids have been hiding all this time?" I asked. "Right under their noses near Zamochit?"

"No," William said. "I think the bodies were moved there purposefully. I don't believe the Werdulac would do anything to let us know where his hiding place is."

"So is leaving them somewhere they would be found a trick?" I asked. "Does he want us to believe he's given up?"

"Possibly," William said. "But I don't think so. Like I said, I think he wanted us to know, and I think he did that because he's putting us on notice—he's sending us a message."

"Oh," I said. A little frisson ran down my spine. "A message like a warning?"

William nodded grimly. "He has no more use for his hybrid army. That means he's planning something worse."

"Something worse than extra-undead vampire warriors?" I said.

"Yes."

"Any idea what it could be?"

"No."

"You're right," I said. "We can't really breathe easier now."

"That's why I didn't want to tell you at first," William said. "But that's no excuse. I realize now that you should know—that you deserve to know. And you need to be able to trust me, and that's not possible if I'm keeping secrets from you."

"I'm glad you told me," I said. "But what brought this on?"

"I had to," William replied. "It was only right."

He gave me a long look.

"I've been hiding," William said. "I've been hiding from you and from myself."

It was my turn to shift uneasily. Those words were very similar to the ones Veronika had used.

William continued. "I don't want to hide anymore. Not so long ago, I almost lost you. I almost lost my own life."

"Oh, William." I reached out to take his hand. Unlike other vampires, his skin was warm—a consequence of his Sídh blood.

William's fingers closed around mine.

"I was used to the idea that I was immortal. Now I realize I'm vulnerable. And I think I'm better off for that knowledge."

"Oh, William," I said again.

I wished we could stay just as we were—a happy couple on a lovely day holding hands.

"It hasn't escaped my notice," he said, "that you've been distant since the night of your birthday party—distant and worried. I know something's troubling you. Will you tell me what it is?"

William looked at me earnestly, and I looked back into his bright, beautiful eyes.

Then my gaze faltered. I couldn't tell him.

"I just need to think this through," I said.

"Okay," William said quietly. "I understand. Whatever you need. And I'm going to keep trying to earn your trust."

"It's not that," I said. "It's just—"

The words hung in the air.

I let my hand slip from William's grasp, and I stood up.

"I should probably get home. We did have an earthquake today, and my grandmother's inclined to worry."

William stood up also.

"I'll drive you home."

We were both silent on the short ride over.

As William pulled up in front of my house, he looked over at me.

"I'll let you know everything I find out," he said. "From now on, you'll know everything I know."

"Thanks," I said.

"And I want you to know that you can tell me anything," William said. "I'm only a phone call away."

"Thanks," I said.

I realized how inadequate that sounded.

"I'm sorry," I said. "I really mean that. And I really am grateful that you told me about the hybrids. I'm just a little—overwhelmed at the moment."

William nodded. "It's a lot for me to spring on you all at once. Just take your time. And I meant what I said—whatever's going on with the Werdulac, we'll face it together."

I very nearly said "thanks" again. Instead, I leaned over and kissed him and then got out of the car.

I went inside and assured a waiting GM that I was really and truly fine.

As I went upstairs to my room, I noticed that I had a text from Terrance.

I sat down on my bed and read it.

Maksim's on his way.

Wow, that was quick, I replied.

Turns out he was already coming here, Terrance wrote. *I didn't even have to ask him.*

Perfect timing, I said.

Have you seen Veronika again? Terrance asked.

No, I said.

I checked out your neighborhood last night. There was no vampire activity. But—

I waited for a moment, and then Terrance's next text appeared.

There's a vampire in the area. I don't know exactly where. I don't think you're in immediate danger, but be careful.

I wondered once again if Terrance knew about William, but I figured it was probably Anton he was referring to.

Okay, thanks, I said.

Will look for vampire and fill Maksim in, Terrance wrote. *He'll probably want to meet soon. Will let you know.*

Thanks, I said.

Stay safe, Terrance texted.

You too, I replied.

I waited for a moment, but there were no further messages from Terrance.

I quickly texted William.

Terrance knows there's a vampire in town. Please tell Anton to be careful.

After a moment, William replied.

I will.

Please look out for yourself too, I wrote.

I will, William said, and for some reason I felt as if I could sense a smile in his reply.

The rest of the day flew by—homework, dinner, more homework. And through it all, in the back of my mind, I kept working on the William problem—but I was no closer to figuring out what to do next.

I supposed that Terrance and Maksim would come up with something, but I had a feeling that that wouldn't be enough.

This was something I had to do myself.

I knew I should be suspicious of Veronika—especially if she was actually working for the Werdulac—but her suggestion that I should try to get my powers back was not a terrible idea.

They had given me clues once—visions and dreams that had helped me see what was ahead of me. I'd had the dreams as recently as April, but lately even that had deserted me. If I could get the visions or the dreams back, I might have some idea where to start.

As I lay in bed that night, I tried to remember how I had found the clear fire the first time—that seemed to be the key to the whole thing.

I knew my mother had sent the clear fire to the stone ring in the Pure Woods to keep it safe. And that's where I had been when I first summoned it.

But I also knew that the clear fire could be summoned from anywhere—I had called it to me when I was trapped in the tunnels under the Mstislav mansion, and it was theoretically possible for me to make it appear right here in my room.

I closed my eyes and began to search within myself as I had done back in Russia when I had first found the clear fire. As I did so, I began to hum the song my mother had taught me as a child. There were no words—just a melody. And the music was a vital part of unlocking the clear fire's hiding place.

I sang the melody, let the music flow through me, and searched for the spark within.

But there was nothing. There was no feeling inside that I could catch on to. The tiny spark that had once been there was gone.

This attempt to summon the clear fire was just as unsuccessful as my previous attempts had been.

I stopped singing and lay for a time just listening to the creaking of the house.

Eventually, I fell asleep.

Somewhere in the night, the ground began to shake, and I sat up suddenly.

Dreams were still clinging to me, and I looked around in the dark, unsure for a moment what was going on.

In the dim light, I saw a few bottles on my bureau wobble gently before settling back down, and I realized that we'd just had a small earthquake.

I lay back down, and as I closed my eyes, I had the strangest feeling that in the dream I'd just had, I'd seen a flash of dark eyes.

Chapter Six

The next morning, I walked to school through a light mist.

I was determined to put an end to my walking days, so I headed straight to the main office to pick up the paperwork for my car.

The school had been cleared as safe overnight, even with the second earthquake, and notice had gone out that we would all be receiving earthquake preparedness instruction during homeroom—after yesterday, the school didn't want to risk sending us all to the auditorium again.

There were flyers up on all the doors to remind us of the meetings, and there was a large notice on the door of the main office as I went in.

The office was buzzing with talk of the earthquakes yesterday, and I waited in a line to see the school secretary. I collected my forms and listened to the instructions, and then I headed for the exit.

As I opened the door and stepped out into the hall, I nearly collided with someone who was standing just on the other side. It was Irina.

"You've been avoiding me, haven't you?" she said.

"What?" I said, startled.

"I saw you go in there," Irina said. "You ducked in there to avoid me, didn't you?"

"No," I said. "Not that it's any of your business, but no. I had no idea you were out here."

"What are you doing texting my boyfriend?" Irina demanded.

"What?" I said.

"Don't act like you don't know. I saw your name in his phone—again. I know you met with him. And now you keep texting him."

The door opened behind me, and a student squeezed out.

"Could you guys move?" he asked. "You're kind of in the way."

I moved over to stand by the wall, and Irina glared at the boy for a moment before following me.

"Terrance is just helping me with something," I said.

"So you admit it?" Irina said.

"Admit what?"

"That you've been texting my boyfriend?"

"Of course I admit it," I said. "Terrance is just being a friend and helping me. There's nothing else in it."

"What are you texting him about?" Irina asked.

"You didn't read them?" I said carefully.

"No," Irina said. "I just saw your name."

"It's a private matter," I said. "I really can't tell you."

Irina exploded. "What I don't understand is why you have to take everything from me. Back when I liked Simon, you had to have him. Now you're secretly meeting up with my boyfriend and texting him. And as if that wasn't enough, you steal my best friend away, and you try to set her up with that—that horrible Vadim."

"What's wrong with Vadim?" I asked, suddenly angry myself.

"He's killing my father!" Irina cried.

"Vadim is killing your father?" I said.

"Not Vadim—his uncle," Irina said, exasperated. "He's the one who's been forcing my dad to work all these long hours these last few years. He never eats, he never sleeps—he's never at home."

Irina leaned closer, and I could see tears standing in her eyes.

"I know what you all think," she hissed. "I heard the rumors back when I was kidnapped—about how all my dad cares about is money, and that's why he didn't come back to look for me. About how all I care about is money, and that's why I chose to live with my dad after the divorce."

I was silent—I had heard those rumors too.

"Well, it's not true," Irina said tearfully. "It's not. My dad only works so hard because he's afraid to lose his job. And I love my parents both the same. I chose to live with my dad because he needs someone to look out for him. He doesn't have anyone at all."

"Irina—" I said.

"Just stay away from my boyfriend," she said.

She turned and marched off.

I made my way to my homeroom.

Basic earthquake preparedness consisted of "drop, cover, and hold on," which was essentially what the boy with the close-cropped hair had told us to do yesterday. There wasn't much anyone could really do in the event of an earthquake—all you could do was wait until the shaking ended and try to protect yourself from falling debris.

Everyone was a little on edge after the training was over—somehow it helped remind us all of just how much damage an earthquake could do.

By lunch, however, a new topic had taken over.

"Ghosts."

Branden's backpack hit the table with a heavy thud, making all the trays rattle. Bryony and Vadim had joined us for lunch again, and Branden seemingly felt comfortable enough with them to return to his old habits.

"What was that?" Charisse said, looking up.

Branden slid his tray onto the table and dropped heavily into his chair.

"Ghosts were sighted in town last night."

Simon snorted. "That's ridiculous."

"And yet, it is true," Branden said.

"Simon is correct," Vadim said. "No one could have seen any ghosts. Ghosts are not real."

"You don't always have to agree with him, you know," Branden said to Vadim.

"Go ahead and tell us your story," Charisse said kindly. "I'm interested at least."

"So am I," I said.

Branden seemed mollified. "It all started last night after the smaller earthquake—"

Simon interrupted. "I feel like we should be sitting around a campfire with a flashlight."

"I can guarantee that you've never heard this story at summer camp," Branden said with injured dignity.

"That's true," Simon replied. "I'm sure this one won't be nearly as good. But go on anyway."

Branden glared at him but continued. "So a group of kids from this very school were out late last night after the earthquake. Something drew them to the cave at the Old Grove, though they didn't know why, and after a moment, they all heard this shuffling and whispering. Then this guy dressed in old-timey clothes came stumbling out of the cave and said something to them in a strange language. The kids were about to run away when the guy just disappeared. And on the ground where he'd been standing, they found a ruby."

"I was right," Simon said. "That's not as good as a summer camp ghost story."

"Summer camp ghost stories are fake," Branden said. "This one actually happened."

"Really?" Simon said. "Who were the kids who saw this? Tell me their names."

Branden shrugged. "They were freshmen. Who cares?"

"That's what I figured," Simon said. "It's just a rumor. The story can't be traced back to its source."

"The source was a freshman, but I heard it from a senior," Branden said. "And I know his name."

"Well, no senior could get a hold of a phony story," Simon said. "So the whole thing must be true."

"I see what you're doing there with the sarcasm," Branden replied.

"What do you mean by 'old-timey clothes'?" I asked.

"Yeah," Simon said. "The guy could have been a magician. Maybe disappearing was just part of his act."

"He wasn't a magician," Branden said.

"Oh no?" Simon said. "Are you sure it was a ruby they found? Maybe it was just a piece of plastic."

"It wasn't plastic," Branden said.

"That wasn't what I meant," I interjected. "I wasn't implying that the guy wasn't real. I was just wondering if you'd heard any details about the clothes."

"See?" Branden said. "Katie believes me."

He turned to me. "I heard that the clothes were lacy and fancy—sort of like what actors wear at a Renaissance festival."

"Maybe he *was* from a Renaissance festival," Simon said. "Maybe it's just an act to drum up business."

"Did you hear anything else?" I asked Branden.

"Just that it was a scary experience," he replied. "But then again, ghosts are scary."

"Ghosts are not real," Vadim said firmly.

The boys kept arguing, but I had stopped listening.

I had seen a figure like the one Branden described at that very cave once.

And now I would have to go look for myself.

As lunch came to an end, and we filed out with the rest of the crowd, Charisse drew me aside.

"How are you doing?" she asked, and her dark eyes were filled with concern.

"I'm all right," I said.

"You don't look any better," Charisse said. "You still look like you're under a lot of stress. How's the 'situation' going?"

"I'm not making much progress," I admitted.

"Is there anything I can do to help?"

"Thanks, Charisse," I said. "I really mean that. I think I have to continue to do this on my own. But—"

I broke off.

"Do you mind if I ask you a weird, vague question?" I said.

"Sure, go ahead," Charisse replied.

"Have you ever been able to do something," I said, "but then you lost that ability? And then you needed to get that ability back, but you didn't know how? And also there might be someone trying to stop you?"

"So you're saying that this is something you want to do?" Charisse asked. "You had an ability. You lost it. And now you want to get it back? Is that it?"

"Yes," I said.

"Well, I can't say that I can relate," Charisse said. "But any time you're trying to learn something—or gain an ability—you just work on it a little every day. Get your brain used to the situation. Do it each day, and it'll add up."

"Okay," I said. "Just a little each day—sort of like practicing?"

"Yes," Charisse said. "You can practice just about anything. And it will add up, believe me."

"Okay," I said again.

"And as far as someone trying to stop you—don't let them."

"Don't let them?" I said.

"Don't let them," Charisse replied.

"It's as simple as that?"

"It's as simple as that."

"All right," I said. "I guess I've got some work to do."

"And whatever you think, Katie," Charisse said, "you're not alone. I'm always here for you. Even if you can't tell me what's going on—I'm here for you."

"Thanks, Charisse," I said.

She gave me a quick hug and then disappeared into the crowd.

I continued on to my next class.

At the end of the day, I walked home quickly. I wanted to get out to the cave as soon as possible, but I knew that I would have to act normal for GM. I didn't want her to know that I was up to anything, so we would have to go through our usual routine until I could find an excuse to get away.

I did my homework and then came downstairs for dinner. Afterward, GM and I began to clear away the dishes, and I was just about to broach the idea of my going out for the evening when an ominous rumble shook the house. The tremor only lasted for a few moments, but I could tell that GM was startled.

She was standing with her hand on her heart, and then her fingers quickly flew to the silver cross that she always wore.

"Thank goodness that is over!" she exclaimed.

GM's eyes quickly darted to me.

"Are you all right, Katie?"

"Yes, I'm fine," I said.

"Maybe you just think you are fine," GM said. "You should sit down. This surely has been a shock to your system."

I sat down at the kitchen table, amused, and GM swiftly sat down beside me. She pressed the back of her hand to my forehead and then to her own.

"You don't feel too warm," she said, "but there is no telling what this may have done to you."

"I'm fine. Really," I said.

"Well, all right," GM said doubtfully. "But if you start to feel bad later, you must tell me right away."

"I will."

"Now," GM said briskly, sitting back in her chair. "What is it you were going to say earlier?"

I stared at her, puzzled. "What's that?"

"Back before this terrible earthquake hit," GM said, "you were going to say something. You had not started to say it yet, but you were just about to—is that not so?"

"Yes," I said, surprised. "How did you know?"

"I can tell when you are working up to something."

"You can?" I said.

GM waved a hand. "It is a mother's—and a grandmother's—instinct. What did you want to tell me?"

"Well, I was thinking of going out tonight, just to—"

"No!" GM cried. "No, my darling Katie! You must not go out on such a dangerous night. It is already dark, and we could get another one of these terrible earthquakes."

"But—"

"No, Katie," GM said firmly. "You must not go out. It is far too dangerous."

I sighed. I was grateful now that GM could sleep through anything and had not been awake for the first earthquake that had shaken our house. Otherwise, I might not have been allowed to go out for a week.

"No, no," GM said. "You must not make sounds at me. Now is not a good time to go out. I am sure tomorrow night will be much better."

She stood up. "Now we must take a look around the house to make sure that nothing was damaged. I will take the upstairs, which I think could be more dangerous. You can search down here. Come, Katie. We must do this now."

I stood up also, and I watched as GM took a quick turn around the kitchen.

"Everything looks all right in here," she said, "but I would like you to look over it too, just to be sure. And make sure you check all the windows down here also. Broken glass could be very dangerous."

GM bustled out of the room, and I was left to inspect the kitchen in some amusement, mingled with disappointment.

Earthquakes were always a serious matter, but this one was so much milder than the one at the school that I wasn't really fazed by it— and now I would have to wait till later and sneak out of the house.

All the same, I looked over the downstairs carefully and paid particular attention to the windows.

Everything seemed to be in good order.

Once GM was convinced that the house was undamaged, we settled down to a quiet night, and I waited a little impatiently for GM to go to bed.

When I finally heard her come upstairs and go to her room, I waited for another twenty minutes, then tiptoed downstairs and slipped out of the house.

I was grateful once again that GM was a heavy sleeper, and I knew she wouldn't miss me as long as I came back before dawn.

Then I got in my car and began to drive.

A white, luminous mist hung over the town, and I was more convinced than ever that this was all related to something I had encountered before—the fact that the mist was actually glowing now made that very clear to me.

I continued on through the white-blanketed streets until I reached the Old Grove.

Then I got out of the car and walked through the woods to the cave that had so interested Anton—and where the "ghost" had been sighted. Sure enough, a heavy, shining white mist was pouring out of the cave.

I had found the source of the mysterious fog that only I could see.

I went closer, and wave after wave of the mist flowed out of the cave and rolled over me. The mist had no feel to it—it was neither wet nor cold, but here at the source it was much thicker, and as I held my hand out, it disappeared into the heavy, white cloud that surrounded me.

I held out my other hand and watched it disappear too.

As I did so, a dark figure came toward me out of the mist, and I heard a voice:

"Why is it that whenever we meet up here, I find you doing something strange?"

A moment later, Anton stepped forward out of the white haze that swirled around me.

"You're always waving your hands or talking to somebody imaginary," he said. "It's getting to be a habit with you."

"Anton," I said, "what are you doing here?"

"What am I doing here?" he replied. "I'm a vampire. I'm supposed to roam the night."

He walked toward me and stared pointedly at my outstretched hands.

I quickly lowered them.

"So the real question is," Anton said, "what are you doing out here? Shouldn't you be in bed, missy?"

"I was just testing something," I said. "And I asked why you were out here because I'm worried about you. I told William that a member of the Order of the Hawthorne is here, and he knows a vampire's in town. I don't want anything to happen to either of you."

Anton smiled and closed his eyes. He pressed a hand to his heart.

"It does me good to hear you say that," he said. "It really does."

"Don't make fun of me," I said. "I'm serious."

Anton opened his eyes. "So am I. I'm genuinely touched by your concern. I just always sound like I'm being sarcastic even when I'm not. I kind of can't help it."

"Oh," I said.

"Yeah," Anton replied. "I'm in the right as usual, but I'm misunderstood. So when you say Order of the Hawthorne, are you talking about that Terrance guy?"

"Yes."

Anton snorted. "He's a high school kid. I don't have anything to worry about."

"I don't know," I said. "I've seen Terrance in action, and he's good. In fact, he's more than good. He's amazing."

Anton snorted again. "When have you seen him 'in action' as you so colorfully put it?"

"Earlier this year," I said. "At Rusalka Castle. He went up against the castle guards."

"Oh, well, that explains it."

"What?" I said.

"The guards at Rusalka Castle—"

Anton let his voice trail off.

"Let's just say that I wouldn't let them guard my—well, my anything."

"So in your opinion, the guards at Rusalka aren't very good," I said.

"No, they aren't," Anton replied.

"Do you have any proof of that?"

"That's beside the point," Anton said, "which is that I am perfectly safe from your little high school friend. And that leads me back to my original question—what are you doing out here? To which I might add, why were you waving your hands around?"

"I heard a story about a ghost at school," I said. "The rumor is that he came out of this cave and then disappeared."

"And you thought you'd see for yourself," Anton said. "I can understand that. And the hand-waving?"

"I was waving my hands around in the mist," I said ruefully. "But I imagine you can't see it."

Anton glanced around. "Looks perfectly clear to me. Can you still see it?"

"There's a big cloud of it around you right now."

"Intriguing."

"You don't believe me?" I said.

"I believe you," Anton replied. "Tell me more about it."

"Well," I said, "I've been thinking about it, and I think that the mist and the earthquakes are related. The mist seems to appear every time we have an earthquake, and then it slowly begins to fade. Until we have another earthquake—and then it starts up again. I can see it during the day and at night, and right now it's pouring out of the cave in waves."

Anton looked back at the cave.

"Really?" he said. "Do you have any idea what's causing it?"

"At the moment, the cave seems to be the source of the mist," I said, "because it really is pouring out of there. And as far as what's causing it—"

"Yes?"

"I've been thinking—I'm wondering if it could be related to the smoke trails I used to see."

"Interesting," Anton said. "And disturbing. Those are the smoke trails that you used to track kosts and hybrids, right?"

"Right," I said.

"But you lost that power, didn't you?"

I frowned. "I'm not sure. I've definitely lost the ability to summon the clear fire. But I'm not sure about the smoke trails. I haven't seen one in a long time—but that could just be because I haven't been near a kost or a hybrid in a long time."

"That you know of," Anton said.

"That I know of," I said. "That's true. It would make sense for the two powers to be linked, so maybe I have lost that too. But there's something about this mist that makes me think I still have a little of that power remaining to me."

"And what's that?"

"Well, first of all," I said, "I'm the only one who can see it."

"I'd make a quip here about how that only shows that you're crazy," Anton said, "but I've already admitted that I believe you. So I'll have to concede that point."

"Thanks, I think," I said. "And the other reason is that the mist glows in the dark. The smoke I used to see used to do that too.

Actually, it was dark during the day and shining white at night, and this mist is white all the time—but it shines when it counts."

Anton nodded. "It shines when you have to follow a monster—or, in this case, a ghost—into a deep, dark cave."

"Exactly," I said. "The mist provides just enough light."

I glanced over at Anton. His figure was hazy and otherworldly in the luminous mist.

"There was another reason I wanted to come out here," I said.

"Oh? Do tell."

"I wanted to come out here because of the description of the ghost," I said. "It sounded like something I've seen before. The ghost was described as wearing 'old-timey' or medieval clothes."

"And you've seen a ghost like that?" Anton said.

"Yes," I replied. "It was actually on the day I ran into you in these woods."

Anton had the good grace to look embarrassed. "Oh, yeah. I was kind of a jerk that day."

"You were," I said. "But you've improved a little since then."

"If I could blush, I would," Anton said. "So you had a ghostly visitation that day?"

"I was actually having a visitation at that moment," I said. "When you came across me, I was having a vision of the Werdulac. He was dressed in medieval clothes, and he was walking toward me."

Anton blinked in surprise. "You could actually see the Werdulac?"

"Yes," I said. "I saw him as clearly as if he were standing in front me, which of course he wasn't. I didn't find out who he was till later."

"Wow," Anton said. "No wonder you were acting strange that day. Seeing the Werdulac would do that to anybody."

He stopped and looked around.

"You did say he wasn't actually here, right?"

"Right," I said. "It was just an image of him—some kind of psychic projection. He was trying to send me to someone who wanted to capture me."

"And it almost worked," Anton said. "Sorry about that. So I can understand now why you would want—nay, even need—to rush out here. If the Werdulac is appearing again—"

He let his voice trail off.

"Exactly," I said.

Anton glanced toward the cave. "So you want to head in?"

"Just like that?" I said.

"Why not? You've got the magical, white mist so you can see, and I've got extra-special vampire vision, so I can see too."

"Shouldn't we come up with a plan or something?" I said.

"Did you have a plan when you came over here?" Anton asked. "Or were you just going to barge in?"

"I didn't have a plan," I admitted.

Anton smirked. "So let's go."

He turned and walked into the cave.

I quickly followed him.

"Besides," Anton said as I caught up with him, "it's not like we haven't been in here before."

"That's true," I said. "But as I recall, last time we ended up setting off a chain of explosives and causing a cave-in that nearly crushed us."

"Which was entirely accidental," Anton said airily. "And anyway, we survived. I'm sure we'll be fine as long as we don't set anything on fire."

"I hope you're right," I said, dropping my voice to a whisper. "Shouldn't we keep our voices down?"

Anton shrugged. "I don't see why we should. Anything supernatural is likely to have very good hearing and will hear us coming anyway. But if it will make you happy, I'll go along with it."

Anton lowered his voice.

"This is my whispering voice," he said.

We walked deeper into the cave, and the white, shining mist was both a help and a hindrance. Without it, I wouldn't have been able to see, but the mist was thick, and it partially obscured what was up ahead of me.

As Anton and I navigated what looked to be a clear stretch of tunnel, I stumbled.

"Whoa, careful there," Anton said.

We walked a little farther, and I stumbled once again.

"Maybe you'd better take my arm," Anton said.

I started to protest, but Anton cut off my indignant whispers.

"As far as I can see," Anton said, "this floor is perfectly clear. But somehow, you seem to find every tiny little bump and imperfection. So I think you need some help. Unless you'd prefer to hold hands?"

I threw an irritated look at Anton, but he wiggled his eyebrows at me, and I couldn't help smiling.

He held out his arm, and I took it.

We proceeded, and things seemed to go a little more smoothly.

"So I gather you haven't told William about any of this?" Anton said.

I shifted uncomfortably and moved to take my hand out of the crook of Anton's arm.

He moved swiftly to cover my hand with his cold one. I froze, and he patted my hand gently.

"Okay, I can see that's a touchy subject."

"No, I haven't," I said.

Anton continued. "In fact, it seems like you guys haven't been talking much lately. It hasn't escaped my notice that young William is looking a little despondent these days."

"He's despondent?" I said.

"Yes, yes, dear Katie, he is, I'm sad to say. And your voice is rising a little. It doesn't bother me, but you were the one who wanted us to go along quietly."

I stifled a retort and tried not to let Anton distract me from what was important.

"You really think William is unhappy?" I said in a quieter tone.

"Miserable," Anton replied.

"And you think it's because of me?"

"He did say that he thought you needed help, but you wouldn't tell him anything."

I felt a sharp pang in my heart at Anton's words.

He glanced over at me through the mist.

"Is any of this related to your little problem?"

"My little problem?" I said.

"I couldn't help but overhear—" Anton said.

"Overhear what?"

"Your conversation the other day with your friend Charisse—the day of the big earthquake."

"You—"

"But that's mostly because I was eavesdropping," Anton said. "It's hard not to overhear people when you're purposefully listening in."

"You were at the school in the middle of the day?" I said, incredulous.

"Don't sound so shocked," Anton said. "You know vampires can go out during the day—we're just slower and weaker. Pretty much like humans. Did you know moonlight is actually just reflected sunlight? The moon doesn't actually shine. So if vampires couldn't go out in the sunlight, they shouldn't be able to go out in the moonlight either. People never think of that."

"Yes, I know you can do that," I said. "But you might have been seen. Terrance might have found you."

"I believe I already addressed the Terrance issue," Anton replied.

"What were you doing spying on me?"

"And Charisse. I was invading her privacy also."

"What were you doing spying on us?" I said.

"Well, you were acting weird, William was acting weird," Anton said. "I had to find out what was going on."

"You're—unbelievable," I said.

"I know," Anton said. "I really, really am."

"I didn't mean that in a positive way."

"Sure you did," Anton said.

"So did you find out anything?" I asked.

"Not much," Anton admitted. "You are very good at keeping things to yourself. But I believe I did catch something about William's life being in danger?"

I drew in my breath sharply.

"Ah, so I heard correctly," Anton said. "Want to tell me about it?"

"I can't tell you," I said.

"So you keep saying. I think you told Charisse that about ten times."

"If I can't tell William," I said, "then I can't tell you. It has to be my secret."

"But you can tell Terrance?" Anton said. "I gather that's what your meeting with him was about? As I recall, Charisse said that meeting caused quite a stir with Terrance's significant other."

"There's nothing going on," I said. "It's just that Terrance has special knowledge that might help me."

"I have special knowledge too," Anton said. "I bet I could be a lot of help."

"I just—can't."

Anton glanced over at me. "I guess I'll have to figure it out on my own, then. So the question is what could you possibly have done that would endanger William's life? Because it's pretty clear that you're blaming yourself."

I had no answer for that, so I looked around at the mist-filled cave.

"Have you noticed anything unusual yet?"

"Nothing apart from the obvious thing," Anton replied. "Otherwise, I wouldn't be doing so much talking."

"So why are you here?" I asked.

"I told you, I'm hiding out."

"No—I mean why did you come to the cave tonight? I assume you didn't come here looking for ghosts."

"No," Anton said.

"Well, then, what?" I asked.

Anton stopped walking. "Are you serious?"

"Yes."

"You don't see anything unusual?" Anton said. "You've been in this cave a few times. Just look around. Do you see anything familiar?"

I looked around in the mist. "No, not really."

"And why is that? And I don't mean your magical mist."

"Oh," I said, startled. "Because of the—"

"Cave-in," Anton said. "Exactly."

I looked around more carefully. "We shouldn't even be able to walk through here. This section of tunnel should be collapsed."

"Which means?" Anton prompted.

"That someone cleared this whole cave system out," I said.

"Bingo," Anton said. "I'm a little surprised that you didn't notice that before. In fact, I'm more than a little surprised. You must have something on your mind to miss something so obvious."

I ignored that. "So you're here to find out who opened all of this up again?"

"Yes," Anton said. "You really didn't notice? Because you're usually pretty sharp."

"The cave entrance never collapsed completely," I said. "You could still walk into the cave. The major tunnels didn't actually collapse until later. And, of course, the real damage was done in that section behind the hidden wall."

"Which we passed some time ago."

"Okay," I said. "I should have noticed."

"Thank you for admitting that." Anton seemed mollified. "So yes, I came here to find out who had cleared these tunnels out again. I heard that this guy was coming here—Sergey Stepanov. He was going to take over the mining operation in this little town. I mentioned it to Innokenti, and he didn't seem too interested. Probably because he's in on it."

"Sergey Stepanov," I said. "He must be Vadim's uncle."

"And who's Vadim?" Anton asked.

"He's new at my school," I said. "And he was at my birthday party. He said his uncle was using some kind of chemical process to clear out the cave."

"Chemical?" Anton said, looking around. "More like alchemy. It must have taken something pretty special to clear all this out again."

"And Vadim was really adamant that there were no ghosts here."

"Interesting," Anton said. "It might be worth checking him out—finding out what he knows. After all, we do know there's a vampire in charge of this operation—we just don't know who it is."

"You think the uncle could be a vampire?" I asked.

"Yes," Anton said. "Clever of you to know that I don't think it's the boy."

"William was at the birthday party," I said. "And if Vadim had been a vampire, he would have said something. And then you showed up at the house too, and you didn't say anything either."

"You're right," Anton said. "I would have sensed his 'vampireness' at the party. But even though Vadim isn't a vampire, he still may know more about this than you think."

"So you don't think the vampire in charge is Irina's dad?" I asked.

"Nope," Anton replied. "Never did think it was him."

"Why not?" I said.

"Because, as I just pointed out, we can sense each other."

"But Maksim suspects—"

"Maksim is just a crusty old knight," Anton said. "And not a vampire. If he thinks his son is a vampire, he's wrong. But Ivan Neverov could still be involved in this operation as a human and know exactly what's going on."

"Do you think they cleared out all the tunnels below?" I asked. "The ones with all the—"

I stopped and shuddered thinking of what was down there.

"With all the boxed-up vampires?" Anton said. "Probably."

"Why?" I said sharply. "What do they want?"

"I don't think anyone's trying to raise the dead," Anton said with a hint of amusement in his voice. "Those coffins were mostly full of dust anyway. And the coffins themselves had protective spells on them to keep anything inside that somehow got a little overly energetic."

"But why go to all this trouble?" I said.

"I don't know," Anton said. "That's what I'm here to find out. Maybe they wanted some of those fancy artifacts that were buried alongside the vampires. As I said when we first found the site, some of those things actually do have real value."

I hesitated. "Should we go check it out?"

"I thought you wanted to look for that ghost."

"I do," I said.

Anton grinned. "Then let's keep looking. One problem at a time."

There was an ominous rumble from somewhere deep in the cave, and Anton looked around wide-eyed.

"Or maybe this is a good time to stop looking," he said. "Maybe give ourselves a little break. A cave is no place to be in an earthquake."

The cave began to shake in earnest, and Anton grabbed my hand.

"Come on," he said.

We flew through the tunnels, and I was dimly aware of loose rocks falling all around us. But we were out of the cave before I knew it, and suddenly I was standing in the open air, staring back at the cave mouth.

The ground had stopped shaking, but I was feeling more than a little disoriented from our quick flight, and it took me a moment to realize it.

Anton glanced around. "I suppose we're safe out here for the moment. But that was quite a jolt, and I'd like to make sure that the earthquake has truly stopped before you attempt to go home."

He turned suddenly and stared fixedly at the cave, and I could see wave after wave of thick, white mist billowing out of it.

But I also knew that the mist was invisible to him.

"What are you looking at?" I asked.

"Nothing's collapsing," Anton said.

He stepped closer to the cave mouth and peered inside.

"What do you mean?" I said.

"The tunnels," he said. "They aren't collapsing."

"Well, they didn't collapse right away last time either," I said. "It took a little while. And I, for one, am very grateful that they didn't collapse and squash us."

Anton shook his head. "It's not that. It's almost as if the earthquake isn't—real."

"It certainly felt real to me," I said.

"I don't know," Anton said. "There's something unusual about it. Something not natural."

He stepped into the mouth of the cave, and his figure was swallowed up by the billowing mist.

"Anton?" I said. "Be careful."

"There's something moving in here," he called back to me.

Moments later, Anton came hurrying out of the cave.

"You'll want to see this," he said. "But you probably shouldn't. My advice is for you to stand back."

"What are you talking about?" I said.

And then I saw it.

Crawling along the floor of the cave was a man with his head bowed. As I watched him through the mist, he reached out for the cave wall, and using it to lean on, he began to pull himself to his feet.

I started forward, but Anton held out a hand to stop me.

"We should help him," I said. "He could be hurt."

"Just wait," Anton said. "Don't get too close."

The man staggered toward us, and as he stepped out of the cave, I could see him more clearly.

The man was dressed in rags that were trimmed with tattered lace, and a border of pearls lined his collar. Tangled dark hair hung down over his pallid face, and heavy, jeweled rings sat on his bony fingers.

He walked straight toward us but didn't appear to see us.

The man continued to stagger forward, and he blinked several times as if trying to focus his vision.

"I suggest now that you back slowly toward your car," Anton said. "I'll stay here and make sure that this guy doesn't follow you."

"But shouldn't we try to talk to him?" I said. "Find out what he's doing here?"

"No," Anton said. "Because this guy isn't really a ghost—he's a vampire. And by the looks of things, he's a very old one. He's probably been down in that cave for a very long time, and I doubt he's friendly."

"But—"

"Just go," Anton said. "We'll talk later."

Suddenly, the man's eyes oriented on Anton and then turned toward me.

He started straight toward me.

But just as Anton stepped in the man's way, there was another earthquake, and the ground rumbled underneath us. A fresh wave of mist rolled out of the cave and swirled around the man.

He raised his arms, and his eyes lit up in triumph.

"All praise to the Acolyte, the gift of the Moon!" he cried.

A moment later, he disappeared.

A shower of pearls fell to the ground, and beside them fell the heavy, jeweled rings the man had been wearing.

"Looks like you found your ghostly apparition," Anton said.

Chapter Seven

So what was that?" I said.

I was gripping the steering wheel tightly as I drove home, and I made an effort to relax.

"Well, it wasn't a ghost," Anton said. "It was a vampire."

"From one of the coffins that were buried in our explosion?"

"I think so."

"But I thought you said they couldn't get out," I said. "I thought you said they were only dust. And there were spells to keep them in."

"I was wrong," Anton said. "At least it wasn't the Werdulac. Or was it? I've never seen him in real life like you have. I've only seen paintings—and I'm not sure how accurate they are."

"I've never seen him in real life either," I said. "He sent out an image of himself—it was just an illusion. It walked toward me, but it wasn't real."

"So what did he look like?"

"Just like the paintings," I said.

"So definitely not him," Anton said. "Then he must have come up from the coffins."

We were both silent for a moment.

"If one got out, more could," I said.

"Yep," Anton said.

"How many are down there?" I asked.

"Hundreds—if not thousands," Anton said. "I didn't bother to count them. It's a royal tomb, so all those vampires are likely followers or, even more likely, soldiers for the Werdulac. That could be an entire army division down there."

"And that vampire," I said. "You're sure he was real? He walked toward us too, but maybe he was just an illusion."

"No such luck," Anton said. "I could definitely sense his presence."

He turned over the ring he held in his hand. "Besides, this jewel is real enough."

"I forgot about the jewels," I said ruefully.

"And the pearls," Anton said.

"Then why did he just disappear?" I said. "Solid bodies aren't supposed to disappear."

"I don't know," Anton said.

"And who is the Acolyte?" I said.

"I don't know that either," Anton replied. "You noticed that he said that in Russian?"

"Yes," I said.

Anton was silent for a moment.

"I'm going to have to tell William, you know."

"I know," I said.

I glanced over at Anton.

"So how are you here at all?" I asked. "How did you survive the Hunter?"

I still wondered how Anton had lived through the Hunter's attack back in April. The Hunter was not only an incredibly powerful vampire, he was also the brother of the Werdulac. I had feared that Anton and the other vampires who had banded together to protect me wouldn't survive—and Anton had said very little about the encounter.

"Way to change the subject," Anton said.

"I'm not changing the subject," I said. "I was worried about you. I was afraid I'd never see you again. And then you suddenly pop up here, and you're completely fine. What happened?"

"I'll admit it was a scary situation," Anton said. "I thought I was going to die."

"I thought you were going to die too," I said.

"Glad to hear you have so much confidence in me."

"It's not that," I said. "It's just that the Hunter is no ordinary vampire. We knew he could take out the whole group of you by himself."

"Which is exactly what he did," Anton replied. "Only he didn't do it quite the way I expected him to."

"I heard—screams," I said.

"Yes," Anton said. "At first, he just swatted us away. And let me tell you that a swat from him is no minor thing. And then—"

"And then?"

Anton shrugged. "There was no way to stop him. He just kept moving toward the house where you were holed up. We tried to block him—tried to form a wall in front of him—and he just plowed through us. But we kept coming too—we knew what was at stake. And that's when he began throwing us."

"Throwing you?" I said. "Like through the air?"

"Yep," Anton said. "I'm pretty sure that's when the screaming started. Being thrown by the Hunter isn't really like being thrown—it's more like being launched. I got thrown so hard I actually blacked out. I woke up in Azerbaijan."

"Azerbaijan?" I said. "How far is—"

"It's two thousand eight hundred miles from where we were," Anton said. "And Peter—you remember Peter? He got thrown up onto the wing of a passing plane. There's video on YouTube—a passenger saw him clinging to the wing and filmed it. People are saying it's fake, but he was really up there."

"So is he okay?" I asked.

"Yeah, he's fine. He climbed down off the wing when the plane landed."

"What happened to the others?" I said.

"All fine—all accounted for," Anton said. "The Hunter just cleared us out of the way and then kept going toward you. In some ways, he wasn't really a bad guy—aside from his wanting to steal your soul."

"There is that," I said. "But I'm glad you're okay. I'm glad you're all okay."

"Like I said," Anton replied. "Nice distraction."

"I wasn't trying to distract you," I said. "I agree that William should know about what happened here tonight. If I was trying to distract you, I would have said something else."

"Like what?"

"Like, Irina's father, Ivan, could still be a vampire."

"How do you figure that?" Anton said.

"Because of the Hunter," I said. "He had that emerald that masked his presence. If he wore it, other vampires couldn't sense him. Didn't you say that it was one of a set of five?"

"You're right," Anton said. "There are five of them, and they aren't all accounted for. It is actually possible that Ivan has one. I have to admit, that would have been a pretty good distraction."

"And here we are at my house," I said. "That's a pretty good distraction too."

I eased the car up to the curb and parked it.

"Yep," Anton said. "Time for me to go."

He glanced over at me. "Take care of yourself. And while you're busy keeping your big secret, just remember that things tend to get a little easier if you let a friend in to help you."

"Thanks, Anton," I said. "I really mean that."

"I really mean it too," he said.

Then he stepped out of the car and disappeared into the night.

I went inside and went up to my room.

In the morning, I hurried to school and dropped off the paperwork for my car at the main office. I was told I could pick up my parking pass at lunchtime, and I inwardly rejoiced that I would now be driving myself to and from school every day.

As I stepped out of the office, I received a text from Terrance.

Can you meet me today after school?

Sure, I replied.

I'll let you know where soon.

I was so busy thinking over what had happened last night that the day passed in a blur. Before I knew it, it was lunchtime, and I was heading to the main office to pick up my parking pass. And soon after that, the final bell was ringing, and I was streaming out of the school with the rest of the crowd.

All day long I had been working over two questions:

How had that vampire gotten out of his coffin?

And why had he disappeared?

I'd asked around to see if anyone knew anything else about the "ghost" that Branden had told me about, but no one, including Branden, had any new information.

So now I was on my way to meet Terrance at the town library again—he'd sent me a text later in the day with the location.

Since I hadn't driven that morning, I hurried to the library on foot.

I found Terrance once again ensconced in one of the soundproof reading rooms with the big windows, and I was surprised to see a tall, elegant figure waiting with him.

As soon as I saw him, I realized I shouldn't have been surprised—I'd known that Maksim Neverov was on his way to Elspeth's Grove, and I'd known that I was going to see him soon. Somehow I just hadn't expected to see him at the library.

Maksim turned as I entered and smiled. He was very handsome, with silver hair and a courtly manner. He was about the same age as my grandmother, and in fact, the two had known each other back in Russia when they were young—they had once been very much in love. Maksim was also a member of the Order of the Hawthorne, just as Terrance was, although these days Maksim was largely retired. Only the most serious matters drew Maksim's attention, and I knew that he had to be here for more than just my problem with Veronika. Considering what I'd seen coming out of the cave last night, I had a pretty good idea what it could be.

"Hello, Katie," Maksim said. "It's good to see you."

"It's good to see you too," I said.

"I apologize for this somewhat unorthodox meeting place," Maksim said, "but Terrance and I agreed that it was probably best to meet somewhere where we couldn't be overheard."

He smiled ruefully. "Although now that I think about it, I'm not sure if soundproofing is effective against vampires or not. But at the very least, it's more secure than my son's house. And I don't think anyone would think to look for me here."

He moved swiftly to a chair and pulled it out.

"But where are my manners? Please have a seat, Katie."

I sat down at the table, and Maksim and Terrance joined me.

Maksim fixed me with a friendly, fatherly stare.

"Terrance has filled me in on your vampire problem. I understand that a vampire named Veronika has ordered you to find the 'real' ghost girl as well as her Promised One. Otherwise, she will take back a cure that she gave to a friend of yours."

"Yes," I said.

Maksim continued. "And if this cure is rescinded, it will result in the death of your friend."

"Yes," I said.

"Terrance has also told me of a theory of his own," Maksim said. "Which is that Veronika is working for the Werdulac and is hoping to lure you into a situation in which you can be kidnapped."

He glanced over at Terrance, and Terrance nodded his assent.

"As I have already told Terrance," Maksim said, "I respectfully disagree with him. It is my belief that this Veronika is acting on her own."

"Why is that?" I said.

"I know only too well the selfishness of vampires," Maksim replied. "They are only concerned about their own wants and desires. When this vampire woman says that she wants to rescue her lover, I can well believe that that is her sole motivation. She doesn't care that she is putting your life in danger—like others of her kind, she only cares about what she wants."

"But that's not true—" I began.

Maksim held up a hand. "Yes, I understand that you have a friend who is one of their kind, and I trust your judgement. But I have studied vampires for years. Your friend is the exception, not the rule."

"But why would that mean she isn't working for the Werdulac?" Terrance said. "Maybe he knows Veronika's story and her connection to Katie, and maybe he's using her. Veronika could be doing this out of fear—I'm sure no vampire wants to make the Werdulac angry."

Maksim shook his head. "No—the setup is too vague. If Veronika was working for the Werdulac, she would have suggested a specific plan. She would have told Katie where to go exactly—the Werdulac would want results. I believe she genuinely doesn't know how to get what she wants—thus, the reason she approached Katie and told her to talk to her 'friends.' No vampire would voluntarily talk to the Order or seek their help—even by proxy."

Maksim turned to me. "You haven't seen Veronika again since she first approached you, have you?"

"No," I said.

"Then that settles it," Maksim said. "If Veronika was working for the Werdulac, she would keep after you—maybe even try to accompany you. I think we can take her at her word. She wants you to find the ghost girl and get her lover back."

"So then what do I do?" I said. "How do I find someone who doesn't exist? Unless you guys know something more about this?"

Terrance and Maksim exchanged a glance.

"Okay," I said. "What does that look mean?"

Terrance looked at me. "It means a whole lot of things are happening that we don't quite understand."

"Like what?" I said.

Maksim gave me a patient smile.

"Katie," he said, "I really think it's best if you just leave this to us."

"But—"

Maksim held up a hand again. "Please hear me out. I know you have handled situations like this quite successfully in the past. And I know that you are no stranger to supernatural threats. But in this case, Veronika has got you believing that you and you alone are responsible for the life of your friend. And that is simply not true. If Veronika were any kind of a healer—like she claims to be—she would not do this. It is no true healer who offers a cure and then takes it back. What Veronika is doing is wrong."

The words hit me strangely.

"I know," I said. "But I did promise to pay her whatever she asked for. And this is what she asked for."

"Oh, Katie," Maksim said, sighing. "Let me tell you what I think should happen here. I think you should stay quietly at home with your grandmother and not go looking for the ghost girl or anyone else. I will be here in town for some time, and I will make sure someone is watching over you at night and during the day while you're at school. Terrance will have to travel for us in the next few days, and while he's gone, Dylan will be his very capable replacement. One of the two of them will be watching you at all times."

"It's not me I'm worried about," I said.

"I appreciate your concern for your friend," Maksim replied. "I really do. And I promise you that we are going to do something on that front. Veronika's threat is a credible one—the whole purpose of the Order is to combat the threat posed by vampires to humans. And though her stated threat is against a vampire, I believe she also poses a threat to you, especially since I know enough of your character to know that you will go to great lengths to help a friend. And this particular quest could lead you to some dangerous places."

"Like what?" I said.

Maksim sighed again and then continued. "And so, the Order has decided that they will look into the matter and see if they can locate Veronika themselves."

I felt a flash of alarm. "What are you going to do?"

Maksim arched an elegant eyebrow. "Do I detect a note of concern for your oppressor? Fear not, Katie, we are just going to find Veronika and talk to her. Very often if a vampire feels a little bit of pressure, they will throw up their hands in defeat. This may be easier to end than you think."

He gave me another smile. "My advice to you is to just let us take care of this. I think of you like a granddaughter, Katie, and I can't bear to let anything happen to you. Especially not if I can prevent it."

It was my turn to sigh. I could see that I wasn't going to get anywhere with Maksim. But I couldn't leave without telling them what else what going on.

"There's something else you need to know," I said.

I told them quickly about my trip to the cave last night—and about the vampire that disappeared in a haze of mist that only I could see. I omitted the part about Anton's being present.

Terrance frowned. "And you're sure it was a vampire?"

"Yes," I said. "At least as sure as I can be. I saw something like it once, and that time it was definitely a vampire."

"I fear you may be right," Maksim said. "You've certainly seen enough of vampires to recognize the signs."

He drew in a deep breath. "Please tell me again what the vampire said—the exact words, if possible."

"He said, 'All praise to the Acolyte,'" I said, "'the gift of the Moon.'"

Maksim and Terrance exchanged another look.

"You're sure about this?" Maksim said.

"Positive," I said. "What does it mean?"

"Let's just say this is not good," Terrance replied.

"You should also know I'm not the only one who's seen something like this," I said. "There's been at least one other sighting of a vampire coming out of that cave. And he also disappeared. The story is all over school."

"That's the one I was telling you about," Terrance said to Maksim.

Maksim ran a hand over his face, and I was surprised to see how worried he looked—I had seldom seen him looking anything less than perfectly assured.

"Then the situation is worse than we thought," he said. "It was one thing when it was just a rumor. It's another thing entirely when we have a credible witness with experience—extensive experience, I might add—with the supernatural."

"Would either of you like to tell me what's going on?" I said.

"Katie," Maksim said, "I ask for your trust. I wish I had time to explain this, but we have to move now. Take care of yourself, and take care of your grandmother. This town is in danger, and we all have to look out for the ones we love."

"The town is in danger?" I said.

"It's nothing we can't handle," Maksim replied. "And by 'we,' I mean the Order. We can take care of you—all of you. But we'll need your cooperation. The best thing you can do is go to school, stay at home at night, and remain vigilant for you and your grandmother."

"And what exactly would I be looking out for?" I asked.

"I can't tell you any more right now," Maksim said. "Terrance and I have a lot to do tonight. You should go home and stay inside."

"But I can help," I said.

"I can't ask you to put yourself at risk," Maksim said quietly. "Please don't ask that of me."

"Come on, Katie," Terrance said. "I'll take you home."

Terrance rose and walked to the door of the study room.

I followed him out of the room and out of the library.

"So I suppose you're going to tell me you can't tell me anything either," I said.

"No, of course not," Terrance said, looking at me, surprised. "I'll drive you home, but we'll take the scenic route. We'll have plenty of time to talk."

Relief flooded through me. "I really appreciate that, Terrance."

He smiled at me. "I told you you could depend on me. And I meant that."

We got in the car, and he started to drive.

"So won't Maksim get upset if you tell me what's going on?" I said.

"Maksim's a smart guy," Terrance replied. "He has to know that I'll tell you something. Besides, I feel like you're one of us."

"One of the Order?" I said.

"Not exactly," Terrance replied. "I was thinking more of one of the 'supernatural' group. You've seen some really unusual things. You've done some really unusual things. And you've gone up against actual monsters. Not everybody's done that."

He glanced over at me. "Also, you're younger, like I am. Not too many people in this game are teenagers. I figure we need to stick together."

"So we're the younger, supernatural group?" I said.

"Yes," Terrance said. "That's exactly who we are. At any rate, Maksim is technically retired—he's just been called in to add a little expertise. I'm the active member of the Order. And we're all authorized to give information to non-members as we see fit."

"Then why wouldn't Maksim tell me anything?" I said.

"He's just worried about you," Terrance said. "He really means it when he says he thinks of you like his granddaughter. He feels like a bad parent if he brings you in on it."

"But I am in on it," I said. "No matter what anyone wants."

"I agree," Terrance said. "So what do you want to know?"

"Well, basically, what's going on?"

"That's a good place to start," Terrance said. "So Maksim. He's here for two things. First, he's here because of Sergey Stepanov. You know who he is, right?"

"Yes," I said. "He's the new guy who's in charge of the mining operation at the cave."

Terrance nodded. "And we also have reason to believe that he's the vampire who's running the covert operation too. And they're after something big—really big. I know you know about all the coffins down there, and I know you know that the Order tried to neutralize the situation there—just in case."

I nodded. Terrance was the one who had rigged all the explosives that Anton and I had accidentally set off earlier in the year.

"Well, these people have expended a lot of resources to dig all those coffins out again," Terrance said. "We don't know exactly why—but whatever it is, it can't be good. As far as we know, vampires that far gone can't be revived unless they're exceptionally powerful. But the appearance and disappearance of vampires at the cave points in an ominous direction."

I suppressed a shudder—I knew only too well what was hidden down in that cave.

Terrance continued.

"And the second reason Maksim is here," he said, "is because he needed to deliver a message to me. I'm actually being temporarily reassigned in a few days. Something's brewing that they need me to investigate."

"What is it?" I said.

Terrance glanced over at me. "There's a tomb we've had our eye on for a very long time, and there's been activity there lately. The tomb is known as the Temple of the Moon."

"The moon?" I said sharply.

"Yep," Terrance said. "I was very disturbed to hear that the vampire you saw mentioned that word, and I know Maksim was too. If her influence extends all the way over here—"

He broke off.

"'Her'?" I said.

"The lady interred there is known as the Queen of the Moon," Terrance said. "And she's one of the big ones. She was the personal sorceress to the Werdulac—she's the one who created the emerald medallions for him and his family—the ones they used to disguise their nature."

"So she's a vampire?" I said.

"Yes—and a very, very powerful one," Terrance replied. "She's one of the few vampire magic workers around. Or at least she was. She was defeated by the Sídh just like the Werdulac and was consigned to a special tomb that supposedly had supernatural protections on it."

"And now there's activity there?" I said. "Does that mean someone is trying to open it?"

"Yep—and they're working covertly. We can't get in ourselves—the tomb is still sealed. But it's a site we monitor all the time, and there are subtle changes to the structure itself and to the land around it. In one case, a statue at the tomb has actually shifted so that it's facing in a new direction."

"There are statues at the tomb?" I said.

"Yes," Terrance said. "It's really quite a beautiful place—or so I hear. Supposedly, it's like a Greek temple—only it's in Russia."

"In Russia?"

"Yes—it's a bit like the Hunter's tomb. It's one of the few ancient tombs that we know the exact location of. And I think the fanciful, temple-like appearance of the tomb may be part of the protective enchantments on it."

"And who is the Acolyte?" I asked.

"I don't know," Terrance replied. "But someone is working on opening that temple—and probably working on reviving the Queen of the Moon also. I imagine the Acolyte—whoever he or she is—is working on that."

"Reviving the Werdulac's vampire sorceress," I said. "That doesn't sound good."

"No, it doesn't."

"So you're going to go in and look around?" I said.

"That's the plan," Terrance said. "But the tomb is still sealed. Whoever is doing the work there has a secret way in we don't know about. I'm going to go there and try to find a way in. I'm good at getting into places that seem impossible. That's why they called me."

"And what about the disappearing vampire at the cave?" I asked.

Terrance was silent for a moment.

"We really don't know," he said at last. "There have been unsubstantiated reports of centuries-old vampires popping up and then vanishing—mostly in Russia. We wouldn't have put much store in them except that the rumors started around the same time that the activity began at the Temple of the Moon—there seemed to be a connection. As it stands, we've never actually seen one of these old vampires ourselves. And we were completely surprised by the stories of vampires appearing—and then disappearing—here."

"Is it the water from the Tears of the Firebird again?"

Terrance shook his head. "No. Like I said, we stopped using it completely back in May, after we realized it wasn't working the way we thought as a cure. And these vanishings are nothing like the ghost girl disappearances. Those were known vampires who disappeared. These new disappearances are vampires who aren't even supposed to exist. And there can't be that much left in the environment."

"But if it was strong enough to cause the disappearances in the first place?" I said.

"That's just it," Terrance said. "I've been thinking about it since you mentioned it, and I don't know that it was—or at least not to as large an extent as we thought. I know that the first big wave of disappearances coincided with our use of the tears, but I don't think it actually caused all of it. The vampire that I found down in the cave had been stabbed by one of our stakes and had been directly injected with the tears, but he didn't disappear. Unfortunately, he got sick, froze up, and then expired. But he got the biggest dose of all—it wasn't just environmental—and as I said, he didn't disappear. And the vampires I staked myself at Rusalka didn't disappear either. So I'm not sure that environmental contamination would be enough to cause all those disappearances."

"But didn't the disappearances stop after you guys stopped using the tears?" I asked.

"As far as we knew, they did," Terrance replied. "But maybe we were wrong. And then there are the rumors about the ancient vampires. The tears can't be causing that, and like I said, I don't think now that the tears caused all of the earlier disappearances."

"That's what Veronika said too," I said. "She didn't think the tears were really the cause either."

"It was a good theory," Terrance said. "It seemed to fit at the time. But recent events don't really bear it out."

"So does that mean the ghost girl could be real?" I asked.

Terrance glanced over at me. "It's a possibility. That's yet another thing I have to go to Russia to find out. As I mentioned, the rumors of vanishing ancient vampires started around the same time the activity began at the Temple of the Moon. And now there are vanishing ancient vampires here too."

"Do you think there could be a connection between the Queen of the Moon and those disappearing vampires?"

"That's what I have to find out."

"Terrance," I said, "I have to go with you."

"Can't do it," he said. "I can't take you on a mission. I can give you information, but a mission is my responsibility—and my responsibility alone. I can't take you along any more than a member of the regular military could take a civilian along."

"I understand," I said.

"I'm sorry, Katie," Terrance said. "I really am. I know a lot is at stake here for you. And if it were me, I know I'd feel exactly the way you do—I'd want to go too. But I can promise you that I will do everything I can to find out who's opening that tomb and to keep your friend safe."

"Thanks, Terrance," I said.

He turned the car in the direction of my neighborhood, and as I watched the familiar scenery flying by, I had some time to think.

I would have to find a way to get to the Temple of the Moon on my own.

Chapter Eight

Terrance dropped me off at my house, and I stood before my door in an agony of indecision.

I wanted to rush right over to William's house and tell him that I had a lead, and that I would fix everything.

But of course, William had no idea of the danger he was in, so I could hardly tell him what I was about to do.

At the same time, it couldn't hurt to let William know a little of what I had found out. Anton surely would have told him by now about what we had seen at the cave, and I could give him more information about what was down there and what we might be up against. Maybe the three of us could go look for ourselves.

In fact, I was more than a little surprised that I hadn't received a panicked text from William—or, even more likely, a visit.

Perhaps Anton had prevailed on him not to do that.

I resolved to go inside, act like everything was normal, and then drive over to William's house like I was a perfectly normal girl visiting her boyfriend.

Except I was anything but.

I shook off the weight of what I had to do and then went inside.

GM and I had dinner together, and then afterward I did as much homework as I could reasonably concentrate on.

When my mind became too full of plans and possibilities, I headed out with as casual an air as I could muster.

I got in my car and began to drive to William's house.

William's house was not far from the Old Grove, but it was actually a little hard to find unless you already knew where it was. It was an unassuming ranch house off of a small dirt road that was easy to miss. In all the years I had lived in Elspeth's Grove, I had never actually noticed the road until it was pointed out to me.

I drove up the road now and parked my car in the carport next to William's house. The house didn't actually have a garage, and the carport was little more than a roof with some sturdy supports—William's car was most definitely exposed to the elements. I had wondered more than once why he didn't just convert the space into an actual garage, but maybe he just liked the way it looked—somehow the carport made the house look more modest.

Modest and unassuming was probably a good thing if you wanted to remain anonymous—and I had a feeling that that was exactly what William was hoping for.

I went up to the door at the side of the house to knock, but as I raised my hand, the door flew open, and William pulled me inside.

Before I knew it, he had wrapped me in a tight embrace, and he hugged me as if he would never let me go.

"You're all right," he breathed into my ear. "Anton said you were okay, but I couldn't truly believe it until I saw you again."

It felt good to have William's arms around me, and I leaned against him.

He stepped back abruptly and took my face in his hands.

"Are you really okay?" William asked. "I mean really okay?"

"Yes," I said. "I'm really okay."

He continued to stare at me as if he didn't quite believe it.

"Oh, William," I said, "I've missed you so much."

"You don't have to miss me," William said. "I'll always be right here. I'll always be wherever you are."

I stared into William's bright blue eyes—eyes that were like no one else's—and for just a moment, I felt my resolve weakening. I wanted to tell him everything.

And then I remembered what I'd done. I remembered how I'd put his life at risk.

I couldn't bear the thought of losing him.

William had continued to watch my face, and he seemed to sense a change in me.

"Come on," he said. "I want to show you something."

He led me into the living room, and he had me sit down on the sofa. Then he sat down in the chair next to me and opened a drawer in a nearby table.

"This is what I wanted you to see," he said.

He handed me a rock.

Puzzled, I turned the rock over in my hands.

It was small and shaped a little bit like a pyramid. It was smooth and black and shot through with veins of white. The rock was strangely beautiful, and I felt an odd sensation when I held it—there seemed to be something stirring inside it—some kind of power or energy.

"What is it?" I said.

"I don't know," William replied. "I found it in my pocket after we left the house of Veronika the healer."

I felt a shock at the sound of her name, but I forced myself to be calm—I knew William didn't know anything about her visit, and mentioning her name wouldn't hurt anything.

William continued. "There seems to be some kind of power flowing through it. I've studied it—I've even put it through a few tests. I can't quite figure out what's going on with it."

I stared at it with more than a little trepidation. "Do you think Veronika gave it to you? Do you—think it was part of the cure?"

"No, I don't," William said. "I've never heard of a stone that can save a life. And, at any rate, she had to perform a whole ritual that took some time, didn't she?"

I thought back to the terrible hours I had spent waiting in Veronika's house while William's life hung in the balance.

"Yes," I said, a little unsteadily. "It did take a little time."

"Then I don't think this one stone has anything to do with her," William said. "Besides, I've been away from it quite often—and I've gone far. And I've suffered no ill effects. I don't think this rock is any part of the cure."

"So what do you think it is?" I asked.

William looked down at the rock in my hands. "I must have picked it up in Rusalka Castle or in the Black Tomb before I was attacked. I have a feeling it's something important."

He looked up at me. "I want you to have it."

I looked at him in surprise. "Me? Why?"

"This thing is a mystery," William said. "I have no idea what it is or what it can do. Once upon a time, I would have kept it to myself. But now I want you to keep it. Maybe you can figure out what it is—I sure wasn't able to do that in all the time that I've had it."

"What made you decide that?" I asked.

"When Anton came back last night," William said, "he told me about what you guys saw in the cave. And even though he assured me that you were all right, I wanted to rush right over to your house to see for myself. But you've been staying away from me lately, so I figured that that wasn't what you wanted. Then I waited, hoping you would call me, but you didn't."

William looked up at me. "I can tell you're not ready to trust me yet. But I want you to know that I trust you."

"It's not you I don't trust," I said. "It's me."

"Well, I do trust you," William said. "I trust you more than anyone else in the world."

If only it were that simple, I thought to myself.

"There's something you should know," I said aloud. "About the cave."

"Yeah, good," William said. "I'd like to hear about anything you've learned."

"I went to see Terrance," I said. "And Maksim—he's in town. He's on a special assignment for the Order."

I told him briefly about the Queen of the Moon, and about the fact that vampire disappearances had continued even though the Order had stopped using the tears.

"So Terrance is heading to Russia soon," I said. "He's going to see if he can find a way into the temple."

William nodded thoughtfully. "Then the ghost girl may actually be real—there may be a person, or even a group of people that are making vampires disappear."

"Yes," I said.

"Why?"

"I don't know," I said. "And the Order doesn't seem to know either."

"Anton told me that the two of you had been down in the cave before," William said. "That you saw hundreds, if not thousands, of coffins down there that were housing an ancient army of the Werdulac's. He also said that you both believe that the vampire you saw disappear was part of that army."

"Yes," I said.

"But surely that's impossible. Those vampires were turned to dust long ago."

"That's what Anton said," I replied. "He said the vampires were destroyed when the Werdulac was defeated, and their ashes were placed in those coffins. He said further protections were placed on the coffins to make sure that none of the vampires ever got out— just in case one of them did manage to wake up and revive himself."

"And yet that's exactly what did happen," William said. "One of them woke up and got out."

"At least two," I said. "There were rumors going around school about a man coming out of the cave and disappearing. That's why I went out to the cave in the first place."

"And this Temple of the Moon in Russia is somehow related?" William asked.

"It's a strong possibility," I said. "The Order started hearing rumors about ancient vampires appearing and then disappearing around the same time they noticed activity over at the temple."

"And the Queen of the Moon was a vampire sorceress for the Werdulac?" William said.

"Yes," I replied.

"That's a very disturbing coincidence," William said.

I glanced around. "Speaking of disturbing things, where's Anton?"

"He's been out all day," William said. "I think he's just looking around. He's been really worried about the vampire at the cave."

"I know how he feels," I said.

I glanced around once more.

"Well, I guess I should be going," I said. I stood up. "I just wanted to let you know about the things I learned from the Order. And I wanted to see you—I've missed you."

William stood also.

"I'm glad you came," he said. "And thank you for telling me. I'll do my best to figure out what's going on—and I'll let you know what I find out."

He glanced down at the rock in my hand.

"And I really do want you to keep that stone. Maybe it will bring you good luck."

"Thanks, William," I said.

He walked me out to my car, and after he went back inside, I sat for a moment just looking at the stone.

It really was beautiful, and I was struck again by the strange feeling that there was some kind of energy flowing through it. But the stone was cool to the touch, and there was no sound or vibration in it. The sensation of power was more of an indefinite feeling than anything that was actively happening.

I moved to put the stone in my bag but then thought better of it. I pushed it into the pocket of my jeans instead—somehow it felt safer to have the stone on me.

I started up the car, and though I thought first of heading home, I found myself turning toward the Old Grove instead. Since I was already in the neighborhood, I thought I would stop at the cave and just have another quick look around.

It wasn't possible to drive all the way up to the Old Grove or to the cave, but I got as close as I could and parked the car.

Though the weather was warm for October, the sun still set right on time, and the sky was already getting dark.

There was no glowing fog around tonight to light my way, and I figured that hanging around a cave that was potentially full of vampires after dark was probably not a great idea.

But there was no harm in a brief stop, so I got out of the car and began to walk.

My feet crunched audibly on the fallen leaves on the ground, and I made an effort to walk more quietly.

After a moment I gave up—my attempts at stealth weren't really working, and they only served to slow me down.

Besides, no one seemed to be around anyway.

I walked through the Old Grove to the cave, and I stood for just a moment at the cave mouth looking around.

It was very dark inside the cave, and nothing stirred. The silence should have been a relief, since it meant that no one was there, but somehow it just seemed oppressive.

I stepped inside and walked as far as I could without switching on the little flashlight on my key chain. Nothing about the silent, stone walls or the bare floor really stood out to me, and I realized that I didn't really know what I was hoping to find.

I started back toward the mouth of the cave.

I hadn't gone far when I heard a small sound that echoed in the cave behind me.

I turned, but I couldn't see anything in the darkness behind me, and the sound was quickly followed by footsteps.

I swiftly flattened myself against the wall and hoped that whoever it was wouldn't see me.

Of course, if it was a vampire, then I knew I had already been spotted.

I held my breath and tried to will my heart to slow its beating.

The footsteps came closer, and soon I could see the outline of a male figure in the dim light of the cave.

He came even closer and then passed by me without even glancing in my direction.

He moved quickly, and as he reached the relatively greater light of the entrance, I realized he looked familiar.

I moved as quickly and quietly as I could, and as I reached the cave mouth, I just caught a glimpse of the mysterious person's face as he rushed out.

It was Vadim.

He hurried toward the nearby trees, and I went after him, but I soon lost him.

Night was falling quickly, and I knew it would be easy for me to get lost in the woods in the dark. So I went back to the cave to get my bearings and then found my car and drove home.

I went upstairs to my room and sat on my bed.

I really needed to think—and I felt a sudden, strong need to meditate.

Meditating wasn't something I usually did, so I just closed my eyes and allowed my thoughts to wander.

I thought about the fact that I had just seen Vadim emerging from the cave in the Old Grove.

I thought about the fact that he hadn't been using a light.

I thought about the fact that William's life was in danger, and I still had no idea how to go about saving him.

And I thought about the fact that I was no longer able to use the clear fire, and that Veronika had said I might be able to use it in more ways than I thought.

But I had been blocked from using the clear fire because of my love for William, and I felt a flash of anger.

The clear fire is mine, I thought. *I inherited it from my mother. I should be allowed to summon it whenever I wish.*

I felt something—a spark—ignite within me, and I saw what I had seen before—the flash of a woman's dark eyes. As the woman's eyes shifted and seemed to look right at me, my own eyes opened.

The image faded away, and I was sitting on my bed in my room looking at all my normal, ordinary things.

No one else was there.

I tried to get the image to come back, but no matter how hard I concentrated or how hard I wished, the eyes did not reappear. The brief spark I had felt was also gone, and try as I might, I couldn't get that to come back either.

I decided to give up on it for the night, and I got ready for bed. I would do what Charisse had suggested—I would work on it a little each day.

Then I turned out the light and went to sleep.

Friday morning dawned cool and clear, and after saying goodbye to GM, I drove to school for the first time.

The feeling of freedom was wonderful.

I was early, so when I reached the student parking lot, most spaces were empty, and I could park anywhere I wished.

I pulled into a spot near the school and made sure that my parking sticker was clearly displayed.

Then I went inside, feeling no small amount of pride.

I went to my locker, and as I slammed the door shut, I found someone standing on the other side.

It was Anton.

"What are you doing here?" I said, looking around quickly. "Someone could see you."

"I'm pretty sure they all can see me," Anton replied. "I'm a vampire. I'm not invisible."

"You have to get out of here," I said. "Right now."

"Relax," Anton said. "I've been here a bunch of times. It's surprisingly easy to sneak into a high school. You just kind of walk right in."

"Get out," I said. "You look young, but you don't look quite young enough to be a student. And an adult male who doesn't belong here is going to cause a lot of suspicion."

"So I'll tell them I'm a substitute teacher—for Mr. Johnson. There's always a Mr. Johnson. Besides, if I get thrown in jail, I'll just go along quietly and then escape later that night when no one's looking—no harm done."

"Fine," I said. "What do you want?"

Anton glanced around. "Shouldn't we walk or something? I assume you have a classroom you have to get to."

"The fewer people I have to explain your presence to, the better," I said. "We should stay right here."

"Works for me," Anton said. "So I hear you went to see William last night."

"Yes."

"I also hear he gave you his special, magic rock."

"Yes, he did," I said.

My hand went involuntarily to the cross I was wearing. It was the same cross GM hadn't wanted me to wear at my birthday party—but I was wearing it today, as I had on my birthday, because William had given it to me. For the same reason, I had brought the stone William had given me to school today. I knew nothing about the rock—or if it was indeed special—but I kept it with me because it was from William.

"Do you have the rock with you now?" Anton asked.

I hesitated.

"Okay, so you do have it," Anton said. "May I see it?"

"William said he gave it to me because he trusted me."

"Yes, I know," Anton said. "William told me that too. He's becoming very talkative lately. I promise I'll give it right back to you. I only want to look at it."

I hesitated once more.

"I'm asking you to trust me now," Anton said. "Vampire's honor."

"Fine," I said. "I'll let you see it, but just for a moment. And please stop saying that word."

"I promise," Anton said. "I'll stop saying the V-word."

I took the stone from the pocket of my jeans, and I handed it to Anton.

He held the black stone carefully by the base. The rock was a little different there—grayer and rougher in texture.

"It's pretty," he said.

"Do you know what it is?" I asked.

"No," Anton replied. "Other than the fact that it is obviously a rock."

"Then why did you want to see it?"

"I just wanted to make sure it actually was special," Anton said. "And that it wasn't just William's imagination."

He looked down at the rock one last time and then handed it back to me.

"I have to admit there is something unusual about it," Anton said. "Feels buzzy—like there's some kind of energy in it."

"I agree," I said.

I slipped the stone back in my pocket.

"William told me about the Queen of the Moon thing," Anton said. "And I think you should know that he started talking about that sword again. You know, the one that can supposedly defeat the Werdulac? He thinks he needs to try and find it."

"But that sword's not real," I said. "And searching for it is how he got attacked in the first place."

"I pointed both of those things out to him," Anton said. "I'm not sure he heard me."

"He didn't tell me he was thinking about doing that," I said.

"Well, I don't think he'd thought it yet," Anton replied. "I saw him later in the night."

"I'm sure that's what it was," I said.

"And there's something else I need to tell you too," Anton said. "The uncle is definitely a vampire. I found out while I was snooping around yesterday."

"You mean Vadim's uncle?" I asked.

"Yeah, that's the one—Sergey. I tracked him to his house and found him peacefully sleeping the day away. And before you get worried about me, no, he did not wake up, and no, he didn't know I was there."

"Wow," I said. "So what about Vadim? Is he one?"

"No, I don't think so," Anton said. "He's here in school right now, isn't he? I don't sense any anywhere near here. And before you go bringing up those medallions again, there are only five of them, and everybody in the world can't have one. And since Stepanov is the guy running this whole thing, and he's not using one, I really don't think his nephew would have one either. So my official verdict is that Vadim is not a vampire—besides, he really doesn't have the look. But he still could be in on it."

"Okay, I believe you," I said. "Vadim is not a vampire."

"And just for the record, I still don't think Irina's dad is one, either. I checked on him over at his office yesterday, and I really don't think he has the look either. But he does look worried. Stepanov seems to have him working around the clock. And then Stepanov is off sleeping. The nerve of that guy."

"So did you find out anything else?" I asked. "While you were out snooping?"

"Unfortunately, no," Anton said. "I was really hoping to find some evidence of that secret entrance to the cave—do you remember how I said back in April that there has to be a secret entrance? I feel like if we could find that, we could really get a handle on the situation. But Stepanov and Ivan are both very careful.

They've kept meticulous notes on the operation, but everything is perfectly normal and aboveboard. If you looked at their records, you would think they really were just clearing out the cave."

"Well, maybe we don't need to find it," I said. "We found a 'ghost' on our own just going through the regular entrance."

"You're probably right," Anton said. "But I don't like leaving loose ends. By the way, you haven't seen any more fog lately, have you? Like you did that night we saw the ghost?"

"No, I haven't," I said. "But I've been seeing the fog since the evening of my birthday party. I actually watched you and William jog slowly away into it."

Anton smirked. "Yeah. That was pretty funny."

"You did that on purpose, didn't you? To make William look foolish?"

"Well, of course I did," Anton said. "Making William look foolish is one of the great joys of my life."

"Okay," I said. "You really need to stop that. And like I said, I think the fog is significant. First there's an earthquake, and then I see fog."

"And then there are ghosts?" Anton said.

"That seems to be the pattern," I said. "I'm pretty sure all three are related."

"I think you're probably right," Anton said. "By the way, you didn't happen to notice anything that looked like a conveyor belt in the cave, did you?"

"A conveyor belt?" I said. "No. And you probably would've seen something like that before I would have."

"Yeah, I was just hoping you might have seen a glimpse of some metal or something. Stepanov's records made mention of a large conveyor belt. I think they use it to remove the–spoils? Or whatever you call all the stuff they have to cart out. I was just thinking if we found it, we could probably follow it all the way to the secret entrance. Or exit in this case."

"No, I don't know anything about it," I said. "But I did stop at the cave again after I saw William, and I saw something else—I saw Vadim leaving the cave."

"What did I tell you?" Anton said. "He could be in on it."

The hall began to grow steadily more crowded, and Anton glanced around.

"All righty," he said. "Well, you have my cell phone number, right?"

"Yes, I do," I said. "Why?"

"If you see any more of the fog, just let me know. I think we really need to keep an eye on that."

"Okay," I said. "I'll do that."

Anton pushed away from the locker he'd been leaning on. "I'm out, then. I'll see you around."

"Wait," I said. "Where are you going?"

"To do more snooping," Anton said. "And I'm pretty sure you have to go to class or something."

He began to walk away.

"What about Vadim?" I called after him. "Are you going to do any snooping around him?"

Anton glanced over his shoulder at me and grinned.

"I thought I'd leave that part to you," he said.

Then he disappeared into the crowd.

Chapter Nine

After Anton was gone, my mind immediately went back to what he had said about William and the sword.

I had to make my way to homeroom—or I was going to be late—and I knew that I should probably be keeping an eye out for Vadim. But I was worried about William, and I couldn't really think about anything else.

There was an ancient sword—Ignis Sacer, or "holy fire"—that was supposedly able to defeat any vampire, including the Werdulac. And there was even a prophecy by a vampire seer named Orpheo that seemed to mention the sword: *Sacer ignis exitus mundi*—"the world will end in holy fire." Some interpreted that to mean that the Werdulac would return in his full strength and could be defeated by the sword. Others thought the prophecy actually meant the end of the world. Still others thought Orpheo was a charlatan and the prophecy was a fake.

The sword itself was largely believed to be a legend, and there was no record of its having been an actual, historical sword. No one had ever seen it, and there were no pictures, paintings, or descriptions of it. And the Vaults at Rusalka, which held many treasures and weapons, including famous swords, had never held the legendary blade.

But the story of the sword persisted, and there were always rumors about where Ignis Sacer could be hidden. And it was those rumors that had gotten William in trouble.

William believed passionately in the sword. He believed it was real, he believed he could find it, and he believed he could use it to defeat the Werdulac. And he wanted to do all of this so he could keep me safe.

A rumor had led him to the Black Tomb, where he believed the sword could be found. The tomb was actually a dangerous place— the lair of an ancient and powerful vampire—and William had been attacked and bitten.

Since William was already in an unusual half-state, balancing his Sídh and vampire nature, the new infusion of vampire blood after the attack threw William's body into a perilous state. It was possible after the attack that the extra vampire blood would have worked to complete the transformation that had only been semi-successful before, and William would have become a full-blooded vampire.

But something else happened instead—William's body rejected the new blood and then worked to reject the vampire changes that had already been incorporated into him. William was literally being torn apart from within. His basic Sídh physiognomy was incompatible with that of a vampire—and the end result was that he was going to die.

With the help of my friend Sachiko, I had taken William to a vampire healer—Veronika—and she had saved him. And now Veronika would take back what she had given if I couldn't get her what she wanted.

And to top it all off, William wanted to go back out once again and search for the sword—the same thing that had nearly gotten him killed in the first place.

Disturbingly, Sachiko also believed that the attack had been engineered—that someone up at Rusalka Castle—a member of the

Russian court—had spread the rumor about the Black Tomb on purpose. They had hoped to lure William in there and have the ancient vampire attack him—they wanted the transformation that had begun once to be completed. They had wanted to turn William into a full-blooded vampire. A vampire with the full strength of the Sídh would be a formidable creature indeed.

So not only was William in danger if he went after the sword again, he was also in danger from someone at the Russian court—someone who knew William had a mind of his own and wouldn't just follow their orders.

It was important to me to keep William out of all of this.

Yet, at the same time, I was feeling left out because William was talking about looking for the sword again, and he hadn't told me.

It did occur to me that it wasn't right for me to keep things from him and then be upset when he kept things from me.

It also occurred to me that it could be dangerous—if William ran off suddenly and got into trouble again, I might not be able to get him another cure.

I got out my cellphone and very nearly texted William that I needed to talk to him right away—but I hesitated.

I was the one who had gotten William into this, and I was the one who should get him out. It wasn't fair for me to spring all of this trouble on him. I would have to keep going with things the way they were.

I put my phone away and went to homeroom.

I watched the crowd carefully between classes, hoping I could catch a glimpse of Vadim. I was especially hoping to catch a glimpse of him at his locker—that way I would know where to find him at the end of the day.

Unfortunately, I didn't see Vadim until lunch, and then he and Bryony actually opted to sit at a small round table by themselves and didn't join the rest of us.

I watched them furtively as I ate, and when the period ended, I followed Vadim and Bryony out into the hall. I soon lost sight of them in the crowd, however, and I figured I should just give up on trying to spot Vadim at his locker. I knew where Bryony's was, and with any luck, that would be enough.

I waited anxiously until the end of the day, and when the final bell rang, I hurried to Bryony's locker. I tried to look nonchalant as I stood by a nearby wall, partially shielded by a bank of lockers.

Luckily, it was the end of the day, and everyone was too busy hurrying to get out to notice me standing resolutely in a corner.

Minutes ticked by, and neither Bryony nor Vadim appeared.

As the crowd in the halls thinned out, I began to wonder if I'd picked the wrong spot—maybe I should have just staked out the main entrance and tried to catch Vadim as he came out.

But Bryony and Vadim soon appeared, walking slowly and talking together quietly. They walked over to Bryony's locker, and they continued to talk in quiet voices as Bryony opened the small metal door and began putting books into it.

The hall was considerably less crowded than it had been, and I felt more conspicuous watching from my spot behind the lockers. So I turned a little to the side and got out my phone. I pretended I was reading something, but I was actually listening to Bryony and Vadim and waiting to hear when they moved on.

Eventually, I heard the door to Bryony's locker close, and I looked up. Bryony and Vadim were walking toward me, and I quickly scrunched back behind the lockers and looked down at my phone.

I waited until I heard the two of them pass by me, and then I looked up again. Vadim and Bryony were deep in conversation and didn't seem to have noticed that I was nearby.

I watched them walk down the hall and through a set of double doors.

Then I hurried quietly after them.

I continued to follow the two of them as they walked slowly through the school's increasingly deserted halls, and I was relieved when they finally made their way to the exit.

I followed them out into the October sunshine, and I tried to stay a reasonable distance behind them as they walked over to the student parking lot.

Eventually, Bryony and Vadim stopped at a car, and I tried to act nonchalant as I walked down a row of nearby cars and watched them out of the corner of my eye. Bryony got in the car, and Vadim stood for a moment, talking to her over the top of the door. Then Bryony waved at him, and he smiled and closed the car door.

Bryony drove off with another wave.

Vadim began to walk toward his car, and I tried once more to act casual as I walked to my car and surreptitiously watched him. He didn't seem to notice me, however, and he got in his car and drove away.

I quickly drove after him.

I didn't know much about following people in a car, but I figured it was a good idea to keep at least one car in between us as I drove after Vadim.

I imagined he had no idea he was being followed, but somehow I felt like the fact that I was following him was obvious.

Luckily, Vadim drove only a few miles and then turned into the Sherwood Estates community. After a few more minutes, he pulled up to a house and then drove into its garage. It was pretty clear he was just going home.

I drove down the street and parked the car by the side of the road in a spot where I could see Vadim's house. I realized then that I wasn't quite sure what to do. It was Friday night, and Vadim could certainly be heading out later in the evening. Then again, it was also possible that he wasn't.

I wished that I could place a tracking device on Vadim's car so that I would know when it began to move again. But no such option, technological or otherwise, was available to me, and GM was going to expect me home for dinner.

I decided to go home and then come back a little later tonight. It seemed likely to me that if Vadim were going to go anywhere near the cave that he would probably do so under cover of darkness.

I hoped that I would get back in time to catch him leaving—that is, if he did in fact leave at all.

I drove home and ate dinner with GM and tried not to look as though I was in a hurry. Dinner seemed to go by slowly, but afterward, GM announced that she was going out—and she didn't mind that I was going out either.

I waited for GM to head out in her bright red sports car, and then I pulled out in my own, more modest sedan once she had disappeared down the street.

I drove quickly back toward Sherwood Estates. Somehow, I felt it wasn't wise to park near Vadim's house again, so I parked near the entrance to the community instead. All traffic seemed to be funneled through the main gate, and while it wasn't impossible for there to be another gate, this one in the front opened on a widely traveled road that led pretty quickly to the center of town. It seemed like a convenient way to get in and out, considering where Vadim's house was situated.

Night was falling fast, so I parked by the curb as close to the entrance as I could.

I didn't want to miss Vadim's car in the dark.

I sat for a long time watching cars go in and out through the gate, but I didn't see Vadim's.

Then there was a long stretch when there were no cars going in or out at all.

I began to wonder if I had chosen the wrong spot. Or maybe Vadim wasn't going out at all.

My attention had begun to wander when I heard the familiar creaking, and the gate began to open again.

I sat up quickly and watched the gate.

Moments later, a sleek, silver car that looked like Vadim's slid through the gate and pulled smoothly out onto the road.

I wasn't entirely sure it was Vadim's car, but I didn't want to take a chance and miss it.

I started my car and drove after the silver one.

The light from my headlights picked out the numbers and letters on the license plate ahead of me, and I saw with relief that I was indeed following Vadim's car. Following someone at night, however, was harder than following someone during the daylight hours, and I worried that I was going to lose Vadim as another car squeezed in between us. At the same time, I felt like my following him was more obvious at night—if I wasn't careful, my headlights would constantly be in his rearview mirror, and I didn't want him to get suspicious. So it was really better for me to let some other cars in, but I had to watch carefully so as not to lose him.

We soon came to the point at which Vadim should have turned if he were going to the Old Grove and the cave, but instead he continued on straight ahead.

I glanced over at the turnoff with some alarm as I passed by it, but I continued to follow Vadim. The path his car was taking was one that would lead to Bryony's house, and I felt my hopes sinking.

But Vadim continued past Bryony's neighborhood and kept going.

I wondered where he was going, and I couldn't think of what was out this way. All of the town nightspots were behind us.

As Vadim drove on, I hung back so as not to appear too conspicuous.

Eventually, he pulled off the road and headed toward a building I had been to once before.

I was so surprised that I nearly followed him right into the parking lot.

He was driving right up to the old, abandoned high school.

I drove down the road until I was out of sight of the school. Then I parked the car and began to walk back toward the building.

The abandoned high school, or the "old school" as it was generally known, had been out of commission for as long as I could remember. I had been there once with Anton, who had been following the sound of music only he could hear, and inside, we had found a number of townsfolk—including my grandmother—who were trapped there under a spell. The spell was being broadcast by a vampire named Sebastian, and Sebastian was using an artifact from the cave in the Old Grove to cast the spell. Sebastian, of course, had entered the cave before its collapse, and he had pilfered more than a few treasures from it.

Anton and I had managed to free the prisoners from the spell, and Anton had chased Sebastian off. But aside from that one incident, the old school had not been used in years. The remoteness of the place was attested to by the fact that even though a large number of people had gone missing, no one had thought to look for them there.

I had to wonder what would bring Vadim to a derelict old building.

As I walked across the grass to the school, I saw that the building looked much as it had before. A lone security light shone out over the school and its parking lot, and large portions of the big, square building were swathed in shadow.

Vadim's car was already parked and empty, and he was apparently already in the school.

It seemed as if he knew exactly where he was going.

If things were the same at the school as the last time I was there, then there would only be one door open.

I hurried around to the back of the school, and sure enough, the door I had entered through months ago was once again open.

I stepped inside, and holding the door open, I saw the same long hallway that stretched into darkness on both sides. I switched on the tiny flashlight that I now carried on my key chain at all times and closed the door behind me.

I began to make my way toward the auditorium.

The only time I had been there, Anton had been guiding me, but the night had been a memorable one, and I had a vague recollection of where to go.

The auditorium had been the place where the prisoners had been kept before, so I figured it was as good a place as any to start looking for Vadim.

After several wrong turns, I finally found the long, downward-slanting hall that led to the auditorium. I stumbled a little in the dark, as my flashlight only threw out a small beam of light, and I reached out a hand to steady myself as I made my way down toward the auditorium doors.

This time, however, when I reached the doors, there was no light streaming out from under them, and when I opened a door tentatively and peered inside, all was darkness.

As far as I could tell, the auditorium was empty.

I decided it was best to be sure, and as I stepped over the threshold, I tripped on an old piece of carpet and fell to the ground.

The door to the auditorium slammed closed with a resounding bang, and I froze where I sat on the floor.

I listened as intently as I could, but I couldn't hear anything moving in the auditorium or out in the hall.

I got up slowly and made my way down the slanting floor to the stage. I picked out the stairs that led up to it with my flashlight and climbed up onto the stage.

As best I could, I looked out over the auditorium with my tiny light.

The room clearly hadn't been used in quite some time.

Just as I was heading back to the stairs, I heard one of the doors in the auditorium open and close quietly.

I froze right where I was and switched off my flashlight.

I heard a soft sound—it was little more than a whisper or a sigh. Then there was a small creak from the other side of the stage—it was so quiet it might only have been the building settling.

Then a light, bright and harsh, shone right in my eyes.

"What are you doing here?" demanded a voice.

"Would you mind lowering that?" I said. "I can't see a thing."

The light was lowered, and I saw Vadim standing before me.

"What are you doing here?" he repeated.

"What are you doing here?" I countered.

"I heard you stumbling around in the dark," Vadim said. "You make enough noise to wake the—"

He stopped. He seemed to collect himself.

Then he glared at me in the harsh light of the flashlight.

"I asked the question first," Vadim said. "What are you doing here?"

"I was following you," I replied.

Vadim's expression grew stormy. "Why?"

"I saw you at the cave last night," I said.

Even in the unforgiving light of the flashlight, I could see Vadim blanch.

"Vadim," I said. "Are you a—" I knew what Anton had said, but I needed to be sure. "Are you human?"

Vadim's expressive face registered outrage very clearly. "You ask me if I am human? Of course I am human!"

His face fell just as quickly as it had clouded up, and he sighed heavily.

"I understand why you ask," Vadim said. "These are difficult times—very difficult."

"Why do you say that?" I said.

Vadim's whole body seemed to droop. "My uncle—he is acting very strange. My father says nothing is wrong, but he can't see—or he will not see."

He paused, searching for words. "I—took an internship with my uncle's company to keep an eye on him. What I have found is not good."

"What did you find?" I asked.

Vadim paused again as if struggling with himself.

"I will show you," he said at last.

He turned and began to walk across the stage.

I turned on my flashlight and quickly followed him.

Vadim led me out of the auditorium and down a long, dark hall to a metal door. The door was unlocked, and we went down a metal staircase to another door.

Vadim paused before it. "I think this used to be a boiler room."

He opened the door on a big, black space, and we stepped inside. The door closed behind us.

At first, I could see nothing beyond our flashlights.

Then I could see little lights in the darkness.

They flickered on and off, and their appearance seemed to be random at first. A few lights appeared up where I figured the ceiling must be, and then there were a few down by the floor. Bare moments after they appeared, they vanished—only to be followed by lights that appeared along the side.

Soon lights appeared at the top, bottom, and sides and remained lit.

The lights began to extend deeper into the darkness, and I could see what looked like a tunnel forming. A moment later, I heard a low hum as of machinery.

"What is that?" I said.

Vadim shrugged. "The technology is not so amazing. It is pretty standard—it's designed to turn on when it senses motion. It's just that you don't expect to find it down in the basement of a school."

The tunnel continued to light up, and it ran off into the darkness until it disappeared.

As the tunnel lit up, a little bit of the room around us was illuminated, and I could see large carts that were filled with what appeared to be rocks looming out of the darkness.

At the same time, I could see the floor of the tunnel moving.

"Wait a moment," I said. "Is that a conveyor belt?"

Vadim frowned. "Yes. I believe 'conveyor belt' is the term."

I looked around at the carts full of rock and other debris. I could also see other objects now—machinery and equipment I couldn't put a name to, as well as helmets and protective clothing.

"This track brings out carts full of rock," I said. "And this place is where they store it."

"Yes," Vadim replied.

"So this school is the secret entrance to the cave," I said.

"I don't know what's so secret about it," Vadim said. "*I* have known about it for several days now."

"It all makes sense," I said to myself. "Sebastian had been raiding the cave, and then when he came out at the school, he realized he had the perfect setup for what he wanted to do."

Vadim shot me a suspicious look. "Who is Sebastian?"

"He's someone you probably wouldn't like very much," I said. "But I doubt he'll bother us tonight."

Vadim seemed mollified.

"So is this what you wanted me to see?" I asked.

"No," Vadim said shortly. "This is just mining. It's not really being done the best way, but it's not strange. To see what is wrong, we have to go on."

I glanced over at the conveyor belt. "On that?"

"Yes."

Vadim stepped onto the conveyor belt and was soon disappearing into the distance.

I hurried after him.

The ride on the conveyor belt was swift but surprisingly smooth, and I walked over to Vadim without any difficulty. Lights flew by all around us, and after a few moments, the conveyor belt suddenly slanted down, and we began to descend.

"What did you mean when you said that this is not being done in the best way?" I asked.

"This is not proper mining," Vadim said. "Not for what my uncle claims to be doing. He said he is mining for aggregate. But you don't do that in a closed area like this. All of this should be done in the open—and in an area that is not full of houses. Even if there is a good aggregate deposit here, it should not be done where people are. It doesn't make sense to do it this way. You'll never be able to get the volume you need out of this small space."

Vadim paused. "No, he is not mining for aggregate—not really. And if he is not mining for aggregate, he must be doing something else—something he doesn't want anyone to know about."

The conveyor belt angled down very steeply, and we flew along, but somehow I never felt as though I was going to fall.

"This contraption is pretty amazing," I said.

Vadim shrugged. "It is standard, like I said. Not so amazing."

The belt eventually leveled off and then came to an abrupt stop. The area ahead of us was all darkness.

"This is where we turn off the lights," Vadim said.

He switched off his flashlight.

"Are you sure that's a good idea?" I said. "We won't be able to see anything."

"These lights," Vadim said, gesturing to the tunnel, "are here for normal workers. There are other—things that do not need light. We are entering their area."

Vadim had been carrying a small bag, and he slipped it off his shoulder. He placed the flashlight into the bag and pulled out two small objects.

He handed one to me. "We'll use these to see—they attract less attention."

I looked at the small, yellow tube in my hand. "It's a glow stick."

"Yes," Vadim said. "It gives just enough light to see, but it doesn't cast a big beam that can be seen far away by others. You can also just slip it in your pocket to hide the light. You don't have a loud click like you do with a flashlight."

"I understand now," I said.

"What do you understand?" Vadim said.

"When I saw you yesterday," I said, "leaving the cave, you seemed to be walking through the dark without a light. I thought for a moment you were a—"

I stopped.

Vadim cracked his light stick. It was green, and it cast melancholy shadows over his face.

"Yes," Vadim said. "I can understand why you would think something was wrong. There are things down here that can see in the dark. Come, I will show you what I have found."

I shut off my tiny flashlight and slipped it back into the pocket of my jeans.

Then I cracked my yellow glow stick and watched the light spring to life.

"There is a glass vial inside that gets broken," Vadim said. "Then hydrogen peroxide mixes with phenyl oxalate ester. The reaction produces a photon."

"Wow," I said. "I didn't know that."

"I know many things," Vadim replied.

We stepped off the conveyor belt.

As we did so, the lights vanished, and I turned to look. It was now just as dark behind us as it was ahead of us.

"What happened to the lights?" I said.

"They always disappear," Vadim replied. "I think it is meant to disguise the conveyor belt. I can't usually find it again. Don't worry—we can go out another way."

We walked through the darkness, holding our glow sticks up.

Soon, Vadim held up his free hand and stopped.

"We are almost there," he whispered.

He knelt down to the ground and began to feel along the floor near the cave wall.

I stepped close and held my glow stick up to the same spot.

It was a little changed, but it looked like the hidden entrance to the chamber far below that Anton and I had found earlier in the year—the chamber that held the army of vampires.

"I have found it," Vadim said, straightening up. "I was looking for an air current, and it is here. Try not to be nervous now. I will show you something that seems very strange, but it is actually not so bad."

Vadim put out a hand, and it disappeared into the wall.

"I've seen this before," I said. "It's an illusion. The wall is not really there."

Vadim seemed relieved. "Yes, you have seen something like this before. That is good. You are not worried. I think there must be light beams that are embedded in the wall to create this effect."

I knew it was actually something different, but I decided not to say anything at the moment—Vadim seemed to have a little bit of trouble dealing with things he deemed "strange."

He gave me a serious look. "I must tell you now what is here. I must tell you what I saw the other night."

He paused, and his gaze faltered.

"Vadim," I said quietly. "What did you see?"

He looked up at me. "I saw a ghost."

His gaze was challenging, as if he expected me to laugh at him.

"I believe you," I said.

Vadim blinked. "What?"

"I believe in what you saw."

Vadim smiled then. "You are a special person. I am glad you came."

I smiled too. "Thanks."

Vadim sobered. "But all the same, this is strange, and I must tell you what is there. On the other side of this false wall, there is a ghost. But he is frozen. I went to check this area again, before I went to school this morning, and he was still there. I believe he is there now."

I frowned. "Frozen?"

"I do not understand it," Vadim said, shaking his head. "I didn't know you could freeze a ghost. But that is what happened. And there is one thing more you should know. The ghost is standing on the edge of a very, very deep hole. You must be careful not to fall."

"I'll be careful," I said.

Vadim nodded once and then stepped gingerly through the fake wall.

I waited until he disappeared, and then I followed him.

As I stepped through, I was suddenly face to face with a tall, white figure—a man with long, bedraggled hair and open, staring eyes.

I stepped back, startled.

Vadim reached out a hand to me and pulled me along the side.

"It is all right," he said. "He will not move."

"I can see why you were startled by that," I said.

I looked the man over. He was dressed in clothes that were clearly once fine but now were ragged and torn. Both of his hands were adorned with heavy, jeweled rings, and his skin was as white as new-fallen snow. But the really remarkable thing about him—apart from his preternatural stillness—was the swirl of shining white mist that wound around his body and enveloped him like a shroud.

"Do you see it?" I said to Vadim. "Can you see the white mist?"

Vadim frowned in the green light of his glow stick. "I do not see any mist. But I do see how white his skin is. Nothing alive has skin like that."

"I can see why you thought he was a ghost," I said. "But he is quite solid—not vapor at all."

I slipped my hand out of Vadim's grasp and inched closer to the silent, white figure.

I stretched out a finger through the light layer of mist and touched the man on the arm. He was solid and hard like marble.

"See?" I said. "He's got a real body. You can touch him."

"I know he is solid," Vadim said. "He is frozen, like I said."

"He may be frozen," I replied, "but he's not a ghost."

Vadim's face took on a stubborn cast. "Then what is he?"

"He's a vampire," I said.

Vadim's eyebrows shot up. "A what?"

"A vampire."

Vadim shook his head. "No. That cannot be true."

"You can check his teeth if you don't believe me," I said.

"Teeth mean nothing," Vadim said. "A person can have sharp teeth and not drink blood."

I glanced at him quizzically and then looked down into the deep hole we were standing next to.

"We've got to go down there," I said.

"Down where?" Vadim asked.

"Down into this deep pit," I said. "We have to see what's going on at the bottom."

Now that the initial shock of seeing the frozen vampire had worn off, I had a chance to look around. By the light of my glow stick and the shining mist surrounding the vampire, I could see that I was standing on a narrow ledge overlooking a deep, dark pit. The last time I had seen it, the pit had been full of rubble, piled up all the way to the top. But now it was empty, and a vast, dark space yawned before us. Last time, too, there had been a cable that had run down into the pit, and Anton and I had used that to climb down into the chamber below. But I couldn't see the cable now, and I wondered if maybe it was just too dark for me to see it. I also noticed that the ledge we were standing on seemed a bit wider than before. I wondered if it was a trick of the light or if it had actually been built out somehow.

I leaned as close to the edge as I dared.

"Do you see a cable?" I asked Vadim.

And then I spotted it.

There was a ladder attached to the side of the pit that trailed down into the darkness.

"Why do we have to go down this tunnel?" Vadim said.

"Because there may be more like him down there," I said.

"How do you know?"

"I came through here with a friend once," I said. "Before the cave-in. We saw what was down in this tunnel. There were rows and rows of coffins."

I didn't feel like it was necessary to tell Vadim that we had caused the cave-in.

He gestured to the frozen vampire. "You really think there may be more of them?"

"Yes," I said.

Vadim nodded as if steeling himself. "Then we have to go and look."

I edged a little closer to the ladder.

"This looks new," I said. "Do you think it's safe?"

Vadim gave the ladder a cursory glance. "I am sure it's safe. My uncle hires good people. But I think we should take the elevator instead."

"The elevator?" I said.

"Yes," Vadim replied. "It's right here. It's set into the wall."

I walked carefully with Vadim along the ledge, and sure enough, just a few feet away, there were metal double doors set into the wall. Next to the doors was a metal panel with a downward-facing arrow.

"Wow," I said. "That really is new."

"Yes, it is new," Vadim said. "I think my uncle has added many new things."

He reached out and pressed the button. The button lit up with a red light that was unnaturally bright in the dark cave chamber.

I heard the distant whir of machinery as the elevator began to ascend toward us.

After a few minutes, the elevator arrived, and the doors opened.

It was dark inside, and the elevator cab seemed to be vast.

"I will check it out," Vadim said, rushing inside quickly.

He swept from corner to corner, holding up his light stick to illuminate the darkness. Then he hurried back to the doorway.

"It is clear," Vadim said.

I followed him into the elevator cab, and we both looked over the control panel. There were two buttons: one marked "upper level" and one marked "lower level."

"Not many choices," Vadim said grimly.

He jabbed a thumb against the lower button, and it lit up red.

The doors closed on us, leaving us with only the glow sticks and the elevator button for light.

The elevator began to whir again, and we began our descent.

A few minutes passed, and then I felt the elevator slow down. A moment later, it settled on the ground.

The doors opened silently, and the first thing I saw was a soft, white glow.

"It is dark out there," Vadim said, starting forward.

I put a hand on his arm.

"Maybe you should let me go first this time," I said. "I'm pretty sure I can see better in this situation."

Vadim looked puzzled, but he stood aside so I could pass.

I walked out into the cave chamber, and all I could see at first was a huge cloud of mist.

As my eyes grew accustomed to the unexpected light, I saw figures in the mist.

Soon I could see that there were many, many figures standing before me—more than I could count.

They stood in rows and columns that stretched far back into the darkness, and I could see that each figure was like the man above. Each one stood frozen, eyes staring and skin infused with an unnatural, ghostly white pallor. And each one was surrounded by a thick, white swirl of mist.

The vampire army had been revived.

Chapter Ten

I walked out into the cave chamber and then in between two columns of frozen vampires.

They were mute and motionless, and each one was wrapped in a thick blanket of white mist.

They were all wearing clothes that had once been fine, and most were adorned in one way or another with jewels. Dimly, I could see the coffins that I had seen the last time I was in the chamber—they were attached to the cave walls in rows. The coffins still stretched all the way up into the darkness, but now they were broken and damaged with their lids off and their sides split. It was clear that their former prisoners had broken out of them.

"What is it?" Vadim called out to me. "What do you see?"

"Stay right there!" I called back to him. I walked just a little farther, trying to see if I could see the end of the columns of vampires, but I could not—they seemed to stretch on endlessly.

I hurried back toward Vadim, and as I did so, I tripped over something and sent it skittering along the cave floor. I ran after it and stooped down to see what it was. It was a large splinter of wood—clearly from one of the coffins.

I stepped over it and hurried on to Vadim.

"What's wrong?" Vadim said as I reached him. "Why are you out of breath?"

"Nothing's wrong," I said. "At least, not at the moment. I just wanted to make sure you didn't follow me without being warned."

"Why?" Vadim said.

"There are vampires out there. Hundreds and hundreds of vampires, if not thousands."

Vadim held his glow stick up. "I don't see anything."

"They're out there," I said. "Come with me, and I'll show you."

Vadim started forward, and I reached for his arm.

"Wait," I said. "You'd really better take this slowly."

I guided Vadim up to the closest vampire and held out my hand until I could just about touch the man's shoulder.

"He's right there," I said to Vadim. "You can probably see him if you lean in just a little."

Vadim took a step forward, squinting into what was for him darkness. Then he recoiled quickly.

"I saw a white face," he said.

"There are more of them," I said. "Many more of them."

I led him down between two columns, and Vadim gasped as he held up his glow stick and took in the sea of faces that loomed out of the darkness at him.

"But how can there be so many?" Vadim asked.

"I was told they were placed down here a very long time ago," I said.

Vadim glanced over at me. "How can you see so well in the dark?"

"I can't really," I said. "I can see a mist shining all around them, and it gives me plenty of light to see by. I think it's related to something I've seen once before, but I don't quite know what the connection is."

Vadim looked at me, puzzled. "I don't see any mist. But I believe you. Maybe it is just some kind of chemical reaction with the rock that you are seeing."

"Maybe," I said.

Vadim stopped and held his glow stick over his head. "You believe all these people are vampires?"

"Yes," I said.

"Why?"

"I've had more than a little experience with vampires," I said. "And I was told by someone who should know that this cave was full of them. At the time, he believed they were trapped, but now it looks as if someone set them free."

"Maybe they are just regular people who are frozen," Vadim said. "Maybe there was some kind of accident."

"Vadim," I said, "I know this isn't easy, but we have to accept that the people we've found down here aren't human."

"I suspected there were things down here," Vadim said. "But this is beyond anything I imagined."

He turned abruptly. "I think we should leave."

"I agree with you there," I said.

I led the way back to the elevator, and soon we were in its dark cab, riding back to the top.

"There are stories," Vadim said, "about my family. That sometimes they turn to darkness."

He had his glow stick in his hand down by his side, so I couldn't see his face—but I could well imagine the worry that was written there.

"When I was a very young child," Vadim said, "my uncle was a happy person. I loved to see him. I was happy when he came to visit. But while I was still young, my uncle changed. He became cold and distant—I did not like to see him anymore. As I grew older, I noticed that my uncle was not like other people—his habits are very, very strange. My father said my uncle just has many cares because of his business."

We reached the top, and the doors to the elevator opened silently.

Vadim and I walked carefully along the ledge and past the vampire who stood near the hidden entrance like a frozen sentry.

Then we stepped back through the wall illusion, and I glanced back in the direction of the conveyor belt that had deposited us here.

The area was still dark.

"You won't find it again," Vadim said. "You cannot go back on the conveyor belt. Once you step off it, it disappears completely. If you look for the belt, you will not find it, and if you look for the lights, you will not find them either. I think maybe they fold into the floor and walls. The only way to make them stay is to remain standing on them. I think that's what the workers must do."

We walked quickly through the cave to the regular entrance, and then out into the fresh air.

I stopped and looked back at the cave mouth, which yawned black and inscrutable behind us. I was relieved to be out of the cave, but uncertain as to what to do next.

There had been a lot of vampires down in that chamber.

Vadim came to stand beside me.

"I think this is bad," he said. "I think this is very bad."

"I'm inclined to agree with you," I said.

"Then what do we do?"

"I think we should go home," I said. "I don't think any of those vampires down in the cave are going to move tonight."

"How do you know?" Vadim said.

"I don't," I replied. "But I feel very strongly that we're safe tonight. For one thing, the cave was deserted—apart from the vampires. I think when this thing—whatever it is—really gets going, there will be a lot of activity—and people—at the cave."

Vadim nodded. "What you say makes sense. I will go home and keep an eye on my uncle. If he suddenly gets very busy or excited, I will let you know."

"Thanks," I said.

"What will you do now?"

"I'll go home, like I said, and maybe make a few calls."

"Who will you call?" Vadim said. "The police?"

"No," I said. "I have some friends who specialize in this kind of thing. They know how to work with the supernatural."

"That is good," Vadim said. "I don't want to call the police on my uncle."

He looked around. "We will need a cab. Our cars are over by the school."

I looked around too. "Are you sure we can't we go back through the cave?"

Vadim shook his head. "No. We will never be able to find the conveyor belt again. It only appears if you start at the school. It will not appear on this end. For some reason, it only works one way."

He got out his phone and winked. "I have my uncle's credit card. I will call a cab for us."

The cab soon arrived, and we rode over to the old school in silence.

The cab left us by Vadim's car, and he looked around at the otherwise empty parking lot.

"Where is your car?" he asked.

"I parked it a little way down the road," I said. "I didn't know what I was going to find when I got to the school."

"That was probably wise," Vadim replied. "If you will permit me, I will walk you to your car."

"Sure," I said. "Thanks."

We walked over to my car, and Vadim paused as I opened the door.

"Do you really believe they are vampires?" he said.

"Unfortunately, I do," I said.

"I don't want to believe that," Vadim said quietly. He turned to go.

As I started up the car, Vadim began to walk away, and I waited by the road until I saw that he had reached his car safely.

Then I drove home.

I parked the car and went inside and up to my room.

Then I texted Terrance—I figured the Order should know about what was down in the cave.

While I waited for Terrance's reply, I thought about texting William.

I decided to wait just to see what Terrance would say—I was worried William would rush right over to the cave, and I didn't want him doing it without a plan.

And then I thought of texting Sachiko.

She had contacted me shortly after the Hunter had been defeated to let me know that she and her friend David were both safe and had moved to a new hideout. I hadn't heard from her in a little while, but her number was still in my phone.

It occurred to me that Sachiko might have heard something— even a rumor—that could help us. She was good at finding things out, and Anton had said trouble was brewing in Russia.

And maybe she could help me with my Veronika problem.

I sent her a one-word text:

Sachiko?

I wasn't expecting a response right away, so I was surprised when she answered moments later.

I was just thinking of texting you, she wrote. *Is everything okay?*

We seem to have a bit of a vampire problem, I replied. *There's a whole cave full of them. Do you know anything about that?*

I don't know, Sachiko said. *I might. Is it okay if I come to see you?*

Here? I said. *In my town?*

Yes.

Of course, I said. *It would be good to see you.*

I'm leaving right now, Sachiko said.

Is something wrong? I asked.

I've got something to tell you, Sachiko said. *It's probably better if I tell you in person.*

A moment later another text came through.

I'll text you when I land.

I sat for a moment or two, looking down at my phone and trying to come up with a response, and I soon decided one wasn't necessary. I would see Sachiko in about twelve hours or so, and she would tell me everything then. And somehow she sounded as if she was in a hurry—I sensed she didn't really want to chat.

I lay back against the pillows on my bed and glanced at the clock. It was late.

I looked down at my phone and wondered when Terrance would answer.

I felt my eyelids growing heavy, and I figured I would close my eyes for just a moment.

When I opened them again, sunlight was streaming into my room, and I could tell the morning was well on its way.

I sat up quickly and looked at my phone. Terrance hadn't replied yet.

At the same time, I heard a voice at my door.

"Katie? Are you all right? It's not like you to sleep so late."

"Yes, I'm fine, GM," I said. "I'll be right out."

"You are sure you are all right?" GM asked.

"Yes," I said. "I'll be right down."

I heard her footsteps move away.

I hurried to take a shower, and as I got dressed, I looked for my jeans from last night and found the rock William had given me in the pocket. I slipped the rock into the pocket of my new jeans, and I put on the cross William had given me.

It felt important for me to have both of those things with me today.

I went downstairs and joined GM at the breakfast table.

"I can't believe how warm it is," she said as I sat down. "It feels like springtime out there."

"It has been warm lately," I said. "But we've had warm days in October before."

"Not for such a sustained amount of time," GM said as she sipped her tea. "We haven't had one genuinely cold day. This is not normal."

She glanced over the top of her teacup. "I don't think you are well, Katie."

I looked up at her. "Because of the weather?"

"No." GM gave me a long look. "You are not ill in the usual way. You look good. You always look good—very healthy. But you are worried. Yes, that is the word for it. You are worried."

"I'm really okay," I said.

"No, you aren't," GM said, sighing. "You have been worried ever since that boy ran out at your birthday party. I suppose this is about him, isn't it?"

I wanted to say no, but I knew that William was exactly what I was worrying about. William—and a cave full of vampires.

"It's not his fault," I said. And I knew that was true—William wasn't responsible for anything that was happening.

"Young love," GM said, sighing again. "I suppose you have to go through these things."

She gave me a sharp glance. "But you would tell me if something was really wrong, wouldn't you?"

I hesitated and then gave her a careful reply.

"If something was really wrong with our relationship, I would tell you," I said.

That was true too—it wasn't the relationship that was the problem.

"Well, I suppose that will have to do," GM said. Her tone became more conversational. "What are you planning to do today?"

I was a little startled by the question. "I really don't know. I suppose I'll see what develops."

GM arched an eyebrow. "What does that mean?"

I thought back to my texts of the night before.

"I'll have to see what everybody else is up to."

GM nodded approvingly. "Yes, yes. You should see all your friends. It would be good for you to see some other people this weekend."

I wished that was all I meant, but I definitely had more pressing concerns.

I ate breakfast at what I considered to be a sufficiently leisurely pace, and then I went up to my room.

There was still no text from Terrance, but there was a new one from Sachiko.

Stuck at Charles de Gaulle in Paris, she said. *Was supposed to be a brief stopover, but the plane has mechanical trouble. Don't know when we'll leave.*

Okay, I said.

Sachiko soon sent another text.

Is everything good there?

Yes, I said.

No trouble?

No more than usual, I said.

Okay. I'll get there as soon as I can, Sachiko said.

I wondered why she was in such a hurry, but I figured I had enough to worry about as it was. We could deal with Sachiko's news when she arrived.

I waited for a few minutes to see if she would text again, and then I called Terrance to see if I could catch him this morning. His phone went to voicemail, and I decided not to leave a message. I figured he would see that I had called.

My phone buzzed again suddenly, and I saw that I had a text from William.

Are you free today?

I stared down at the text in an agony of indecision.

I wanted to see William—a lot. I really missed him, and I just wanted to hear the sound of his voice.

But I really had to talk to Terrance—I had to tell him what was down in the cave, and then maybe the two of us, along with some input from the Order, could figure out how to contain a cave full of vampires.

A little voice inside my head whispered that William could help with that too, and I should really just talk to him. The same voice whispered that I was just avoiding him.

I realized I needed some time to think.

Can we meet for dinner? I texted back.

That would be great, William replied.

Morning soon turned into afternoon, and after lunch GM went out.

I waited and waited, but I didn't hear from Terrance or Sachiko.

Before I knew it, daylight was fading, and sunset was fast approaching.

I decided to fix myself a snack.

While I was eating, I received a text from William.

Where do you want to go for dinner?

Eating right now, I said. *I know you don't really need to eat, so I thought I would get it out of the way.*

Do you want to meet at my house, then? William said.

Sure, I replied.

I'm glad you're coming over, William said. *See you soon.*

I was glad I was going to see him too. And I decided I would tell him about the cave. He needed to know what was down there—and maybe if I was in the house, he wouldn't go rushing right out without me.

I finished my snack quickly and put my dishes in the dishwasher.

Then I went out to my car.

I drove in the direction of the Old Grove, and I turned off onto the dirt road that led to William's house.

I parked my car in the carport like I usually did and then walked up to the door at the side of the house.

William was waiting for me, and he held the screen door open as I walked in. The side door led directly into the kitchen, and William hovered uncertainly near the cupboards.

"Would you like some tea?" he said. "I know you don't usually drink coffee."

"No, thanks. I'm good," I said. I glanced around. "Where's Anton?"

"He's sleeping," William replied. "With any luck, he'll stay that way for a while."

William pulled out a chair at the kitchen table. "Would you like to have a seat?"

"Sure, of course," I said.

I sat down, and William sat in a chair next to me.

"I've been thinking," he said.

He stopped.

After a moment, he went on. "I've been thinking that I need to find that sword."

I was happy and relieved that he had told me, and I waited patiently for him to go on.

William continued. "With everything that's going on—with the Queen of the Moon, vampires vanishing like ghosts, and the Werdulac working his way toward freedom—I really think I have to try to find it again."

"You mean Ignis Sacer?" I said. "The holy fire sword?"

"Yes," William said. "It's the only thing that can stop the Werdulac. And if the Queen of the Moon is his sorceress, and her tomb is being opened, he must be behind it."

"I'm really glad you told me," I said.

"And I know how much trouble I got into last time," William said. "I know you had to rescue me. But I have to go looking for it again. I *need* to."

"Even though everyone says the sword is just a legend?"

"It's real," William said. "I know it is. And I know I can find it. I have to do this."

"Okay," I said. "I understand."

William shook his head. "You don't understand just yet. I'm not just starting off into the wild with no plan to find it. I need to go somewhere specific. I need to go back to the Black Tomb."

"But that's where you were attacked," I said.

"I know."

"And it was just a rumor," I said. "A rumor created to trick you into going there."

William frowned. "I don't know that."

"There's a dangerous vampire there," I said. "That vampire nearly killed you. Why would you want to go back?"

"I don't remember what happened," William said. "I don't even remember the vampire. But there's a feeling that remains. It's a strong feeling. There's something there that I have to see."

He paused.

"I have to do this. And I want you to go with me."

"Oh, William," I said. "I'm glad you've told me all this, but—"

"It's good that somebody is being forthright," said a voice. "Maybe someone else could do that too."

I turned to see Anton standing in the doorway to the kitchen.

"What is that supposed to mean?" William asked.

"It means that something is bothering Katie," Anton said. "And she won't tell either one of us what it is."

"Katie should confide in us in her own time," William said. "Or not at all. It's up to her."

"I thought you were sleeping," I said to Anton.

"I was," he replied. "But you guys were shouting so much it woke me up."

"We were hardly shouting," I said.

"Shouting, conversing in normal tones," Anton said, "it's all the same to me. My hearing is so keen that I hear even the leaves as they fall from the trees outside. It's no wonder all your chatter woke me up. I'm a sensitive fellow."

"What do you want, Anton?" I asked.

"I want you to realize we can help you."

"I actually came here to tell you guys something," I said. "Well, I came here to tell William something. But since you're awake now, I suppose you can't help but overhear."

"That doesn't sound overly enthusiastic," Anton said. "But I'm inclined to overlook it. And I'm graciously going to offer to help, whatever it is."

"What is it?" William said. "What's wrong?"

"Nothing's wrong exactly," I said slowly.

"Something's definitely wrong," Anton said. "I can tell by the expression on your face. You're making a very clear effort to appear calm and composed. That means something is wrong, and you don't want anyone to know."

"It's just that there's this cave full of vampires," I said.

Both William and Anton looked startled.

"You mean the cave near the Old Grove?" William said.

"The one where we saw the vampire disappear?" Anton said.

"That's the one," I said. "But it's okay. They're frozen right now."

"Frozen how?" William said.

I quickly told them about how I had followed Vadim and what we had found at the cave.

"So that's where the secret entrance is," Anton said. "That abandoned school. That totally makes sense."

I nodded. "Sebastian was down in the cave, and then he just stumbled on the perfect place to carry out his kidnapping plan."

"I really should have seen this before," Anton said. "There's really no other reason why he would even have known about an old, abandoned school in your town. It's not like he hung out here a lot. But I guess you don't really think about a cave opening up into a school. They must have dug a special tunnel."

"Okay, that's great," William said. "I'm glad the mystery is solved. But I think we need to focus on the army of revived vampires here." He turned to me. "And I'm also more than a little concerned about this white mist only you can see. How long has that been going on?"

"Ever since the earthquakes started," I said.

"Why didn't you tell me?" William said.

"I—don't know," I said. That was true—I really didn't know why I hadn't told him.

William hung his head for a moment. Then he looked up at me.

"Do you think the mist is related to the smoke trail you used to see with kosts and hybrids?"

I sighed. "I don't know. I *think* so. But I don't seem to have any of my other powers, so I'm not sure how it could be. Besides, they're vampires—not kosts. I don't know what it could mean."

"I think we have to assume it's related to your powers and that it indicates something dangerous," William said.

"I agree," Anton said. "I think we can assume that."

William looked over at him in exasperation.

"What?" Anton said. "I just wanted to participate. Besides, you're starting to sound like Katie's dad, and that's after you said Katie needed to do things in her own time."

"Yeah, okay," William said. "So back to the vampires."

"Back to the vampires," Anton said.

"You're really sure they aren't moving?" William said to me. "Because if they're released, an army that size could overwhelm this town pretty quickly."

"Like I said, they were completely frozen," I replied. "Each one had a blanket of the mist around him, so I could see them all pretty clearly. I think the situation's stable for right now—I don't think they're going anywhere at the moment."

"Do you know that?" Anton asked. "Or do you just think it?"

"I don't know it," I said. "But there's no activity over there. There's no one over there doing anything. I think when things are going to be set in motion, we'll see a lot more going on."

"And I think whatever's going on, it's already been set in motion," Anton said. "I think all the activity is done, and everybody got out of the way before it got set off. We're lucky we've had as much time as we've had."

"You really think those vampires will be released soon?" William asked.

"I do," Anton said. "And I wouldn't be surprised if it happened within the next five minutes."

William turned to me. "We'd better get over there right now. Which way do you think would be quicker? The Grove entrance or the school?"

"Definitely the Grove," I said. "We're so close already, and Anton knows the location of the hidden wall."

"And we can just shinny down the cable again," Anton said.

"There's actually an elevator now," I said.

"Wow," Anton said. "Fancy."

William stood up and moved to the door. "We'd better get moving."

Anton and I followed him, and we all stepped outside.

Then William took my hand, and we sped off into the trees.

The world blurred, and within moments, we had reached the cave. Anton appeared alongside us, and we all stood for a moment staring into the dark mouth of the cave.

"I don't see or hear anything," Anton said, glancing at William. "Do you?"

"No," William replied.

"As Katie said, I know where the illusion wall is," Anton said. "I'll lead the way, then, shall I?"

William nodded once and then gave my hand a reassuring squeeze.

Anton stepped into the cave, and William and I went after him.

We went slowly at first, but even so, I still found myself stumbling. Night had already fallen, and there was very little light filtering into the cave.

I quickly got out my tiny flashlight and switched it on.

Moments later, I still managed to stumble, however, and Anton turned to look at me.

"You seem to have a real problem with that," he said. "Why don't I go on ahead and make sure that the wall is where I think it is, and then we can speed this up a little."

Without waiting for an answer, Anton vanished into the cave.

William turned to me. "Are you feeling okay with this?"

"Yes," I said. "Dark caves don't really bother me. I've had a lot of experience with them by now."

"That's not what I meant," William said. "I mean, are you okay with my being here? With Anton's being here? Anton said time was short, so I just kind of sprang into action. But this was something you found. Maybe you'd like to deal with it in another way—without us."

"No," I said quickly. "I'm glad you're here. And there's an entire army of vampires in this cave. The more people who know about it, the better. And I'm not really sure what to do about all this."

William nodded. "I'm glad you want me here. But I can't help feeling there's still a constraint—a distance between us. I'm not asking you to tell me what it is. I truly meant what I said—I think you should do things in your own time. I just want you to know that I'm aware of how you feel, and I'm sorry I haven't earned your trust yet."

"Oh, William," I said, "that's not it at all—"

Anton suddenly reappeared. "Okay, you two, let's go."

He pointed to my flashlight. "You might want to put that out."

He turned to William. "And you might want to pick her up. Just in the interest of speed."

Soon, my flashlight was extinguished, and William had swept me up into his arms. We streaked along through the cave tunnels in the darkness, and within moments we came to a halt.

I couldn't see a thing, and I heard Anton's voice come out of the darkness.

"This is the illusion wall," he said. "I'll step through first, and I'll let you know if it's safe to come in after me."

There was a moment of silence, and then Anton's voice sounded again.

"Okay," he said. "You'd better come through first and leave Katie here for a moment."

I assumed Anton was talking to William, and moments later, he gave my hand a gentle squeeze.

"I'll be right back," William said.

He let go of my hand, and soon after, I heard a gasp followed by a chuckle.

"You did that on purpose," I heard William say.

"Yeah, I did," Anton said. "I didn't know it would work so well. You should have seen how startled you looked."

"Let's just go and get Katie," William said. "And I am not going to allow you to play this trick on her."

"Relax," Anton said. "I bet Katie won't have any problem with it. She's seen all this before, remember?"

Moments later, William was standing beside me again, and he took my hand.

"There's a vampire just on the other side of this wall," he said. "There's also a ledge. I want you to be really careful when you step through."

"It's okay." This time I gave William's hand a reassuring squeeze. "Anton's right. I've seen it before. I know about the vampire."

William moved slowly—very slowly—and I felt him pulling cautiously on my hand. Soon, I'd stepped through the illusion wall, and once again, I found myself face to face with the vampire sentinel who stood right by the entrance. His eyes were wide and staring, he was still an unnatural chalk-white color, and he was still surrounded by a swirl of glowing white mist that wrapped around him from head to toe like a blanket.

The vampire was definitely a startling sight, and it was no wonder that William had been surprised. But the mist at least gave me light to see by, and I looked up at William, who was looking at me anxiously.

"It's all right," I said to him. "The vampire doesn't bother me. And at least I can see now."

William looked at me, puzzled. "How?"

"There's a mist around the vampire."

William glanced over at the silent figure. "I don't see anything."

"It's there, trust me," I said. "And there's even more down below."

"So how do you want to do this?" Anton said. "Do you want to take the ladder or the elevator? There doesn't appear to be a cable like there was last time."

William glanced down at the ladder. "Let's not take that if we don't have to. I don't want to take a chance that Katie might fall."

"Elevator it is," Anton said.

He pressed the button, and the red light lit up.

The elevator doors opened right away, and the three of us stepped into the cab.

The doors closed behind us, and I was enveloped in darkness again until Anton pressed the down button and lit up its tiny light.

The elevator began to descend smoothly, and the three of us rode down in silence.

The doors opened, and I stepped out, guided by the shining white mist that surrounded the vampire army.

William and Anton stepped out after me, and I could see the startled looks on their faces.

"But there's so many of them," William said, incredulous.

He walked up to the nearest vampire and stood for a moment, staring at him.

"It's incredible," William said. "He's not moving. He's completely frozen. They all are."

He turned back to look at me. "Do you see mist down here too?"

"I can see a great big cloud of it," I said. "It swirls around each one of the vampires. This chamber is so bright that it's practically like daytime."

Anton had gone walking out among the columns, and now he hurried back.

"Guys," he said, "that's a lot of vampires."

He paused. "We're in a lot of trouble."

"Do you think they're going to attack the town?" William said.

"I don't see why else they'd be here," Anton replied.

"So any ideas about what we should do?" I said.

"Well," Anton said, "my first thought was that we should try to blow the place up again, like we did last time. However, I didn't bring any explosives with me, and I'm pretty sure you guys didn't either."

There was a deep rumble, and then the ground beneath us began to shake.

After a moment, the shaking stopped.

"All right, okay," Anton said. "I won't blow anything up."

"This cave is very sensitive," he said in a whisper. "I think we should get out of here."

William took my hand, and we began to speed toward the elevator.

Before we had gone very far, the ground began to shake again, this time more violently. William and I were thrown to the hard rock floor, and my hand was pulled from his grasp. The violent shaking continued, and I was bounced along the floor until I found myself in amongst the columns of vampires. The vampires, for their part, seemed rooted to the floor, and none of them toppled over or even moved. I temporarily regained my feet before being bounced into one vampire's hard, statue-like body, and then I was thrown to the ground once again. The entire cave floor seemed to tip then, and I found myself sliding across the cold stone and further into the crowd of frozen vampires.

And then suddenly, the shaking stopped.

I sat up and looked around.

All the vampires were still motionless, and they stood all around me, pale and silent like a forest of ghostly white trees.

"Are you guys okay?" called a voice I recognized as Anton's.

"Katie?" William cried. "Katie, where are you?"

I stood up. "I'm here."

Both William and Anton rushed over to me.

"Are you all right?" William said.

"Yes, I'm fine," I replied.

"We need to get out of here now," William said, taking my hand. "Before this whole place collapses."

We began to walk through the crowd.

"Well, that was weird," Anton said. "All that shaking and not one of these guys moved."

He put a hand out and gave one of the frozen vampires an experimental push.

The vampire didn't move at all.

"Don't you think that's weird?" Anton said, looking around. "Nothing in this cave moved. We didn't even get any rocks falling on us. It's like something's holding everything in place."

William kept moving, but I tugged on his hand.

"Wait," I said. "William, slow down. The floor's moving, and I'm getting dizzy. I'm going to fall."

William stopped. "The ground's not moving. Are you all right?"

"No, no, it is," I said. I looked around. "No, wait. It's the mist. It's moving along the floor."

"Are you sure?" William said. "I don't see anything."

"It's definitely there," I said.

As I watched, the mist grew thicker, and soon it was rolling over the floor like rippling waves from the ocean.

The mist began to fill the entire chamber, and it rolled up and over the frozen vampires.

As the mist swirled around the vampires, I saw one of them move.

"Wait," I said, "that vampire just moved his hand."

A second later, I saw one of them blink. Then another one turned his head.

"William," I said, "they're waking up."

"I see it too," William replied. "Anton, we've got to get out of here."

He gripped my hand, and we began to fly through the ranks of vampires.

"Forget the elevator," William shouted over his shoulder to Anton. "It's too slow. Head straight for the ladder."

As we flew through the crowd, the vampires became more mobile, turning their heads and moving their limbs. A few turned toward us and reached their hands out as if to grab us. Soon a few of them began to walk, and within moments, a group of them began to chase us, with some of them crashing into their slower brethren.

Luckily, William and I soon reached the ladder.

"Climb on my back," William said. "And hold on tight."

I wrapped my arms around his neck, and he began to climb the ladder swiftly.

I glanced down in time to see Anton reach the ladder and begin to climb after us.

Behind him, I could see the great, white crowd of vampires. Many of them were still moving slowly, but I could see a thin stream of white working its way through the crowd and heading toward the ladder.

Within moments, the white line had reached the ladder. It began to climb after us.

William continued to climb quickly, and soon we had reached the top of the ladder.

William reached the ledge and hurried along it and through the illusion wall.

I could no longer see anything, but I could feel that we were speeding along the cave tunnel toward the entrance, and I heard something behind us that I hoped was Anton.

I glanced back, but all I could see was darkness.

Moments later, the cave seemed to grow lighter, and I glanced over my shoulder again.

At first, I just saw a distant, white glow. Then I could see a dark blur just behind me, which I assumed was Anton. Soon after that, the white glow seemed to round a corner, and I could see a crowd of the ghostly pale vampires chasing after us, the white mist swirling all around them.

As we ran, the crowd kept coming, and though they didn't seem to be gaining on us, they also didn't seem to be losing any ground.

"Behind us!" Anton shouted.

"I know!" William shouted back.

Soon we reached the cave entrance and sped out into the open air. William reached the trees and kept running. I glanced back, and I could see a sea of white vampires streaming out of the cave, chasing after us.

As I watched, the stream of white divided in two and began to chase us on either side. To my horror, I realized that the vampires were gaining ground.

William ran all the way to Hywel's Plaza, and as we reached the big, open area, the two arms of the white stream surged ahead of us, cutting off our escape. William came to an abrupt stop, and Anton skidded to a halt beside him. The vampires had closed in a circle around us.

Hywel's Plaza was surrounded by shops and restaurants, and the whole area, including the plaza, was teeming with people. There were shouts and cries and screams, and as I looked at the circle of white that surrounded us, I could see that there were people trapped in the center along with us.

The vampires began to advance on us, reaching out with their ghostly white hands, and the screams around us intensified.

William, Anton, and I huddled together with the frightened people in the center as the circle of vampires closed in on us. I could tell that William and Anton were sizing the vampires up and trying to figure out how many of them they could take out. But there were far too many of them, and more vampires were arriving every minute.

Just as a vampire was reaching out to grab my hair, there was a short, sharp earthquake, and then a heavy wave of white mist rolled over the vampires like a tsunami.

A moment later, the vampires disappeared.

Chapter Eleven

Brightly colored jewels hit the concrete with a clatter, and a fine white mist still hung in the air, but the vampires were nowhere to be seen.

I straightened up slowly, and I could feel the crowd around me relaxing.

Soon everybody started talking at once.

"So what was that?" Anton said.

William turned to look at me. "Are you all right?"

"Yes, I'm fine," I said. "Just a little stunned."

"What about the mist?" William said. "Can you still see it?"

I looked around. "It's still there, but it's fading quickly. I think it'll all be gone soon."

"Where do you think they went?" Anton said. "Back to the cave?"

"Somehow, I don't think so," I said. "But it couldn't hurt to look."

"Your car is back that way anyway," William said. "Let's get away from this crowd, and we'll see what's going on over there."

The sounds of approaching police sirens filled the air, and we began to walk away slowly from the still-bewildered crowd. Once we were out of sight of the plaza, William took my hand, and we began to run through the trees, with Anton just behind us.

We returned to the cave and the underground chamber down below, but now it was empty. Even the mist had vanished.

William, Anton, and I left the cave and hurried back to William's house.

"So what do we do now?" Anton said. "An entire army doesn't just vanish."

"I really don't know," William replied.

"I tried to contact Terrance earlier," I said. "I'll see if he answered me yet."

I got out my phone, but there was no message from Terrance. And there was no message from Sachiko either—I double-checked both of their last texts just to be sure. I glanced up to see William watching me.

"Nothing from Terrance," I said.

"We don't need his help anyway," Anton said. "We don't need any help from the Order."

"Well, at any rate, we should be safe at the moment," William said.

"How do you figure that?" Anton said. "They don't mind coming out into the open. Tons of people saw these vampires disappear. Whoever did this is not at all worried about secrecy."

"I'm just saying there's no need for us to rush into anything," William said. "We should sleep on this and then talk it over in the morning."

"I've been sleeping all day," Anton said. "I'm wide-awake. And I think we should do something now."

William turned to me. "Katie, you look tired. I really think you should go home and get some rest."

"I agree with Anton," I said. "I think we should do something now."

"Like what?" William said. "Look around? Go back down into the cave and look for clues? There wasn't anything there."

He paused. "From what you've told me, you've been spending a lot of late nights looking into this. You should go home and get some sleep. We won't do anything without you."

"Speak for yourself," Anton said.

"Fine," William said. "I can't make any promises on Anton's behalf. But I won't do anything without you."

"I—" I realized I was getting tired. And the vampires were gone. And I wasn't really sure what to do next.

"Okay," I said. "I'll go home right now, and we can talk about it tomorrow."

"What?" Anton said. "I can't believe what I'm hearing."

"I need time to think," I said.

"Exactly," William said. "We all do."

"You're not going to pursue this tonight?" Anton said.

"I don't even know where to start," I said. "Where are you going to go?"

"I don't know," Anton said. "I've already checked out both Sergey and Ivan, and there's nothing more I can find out there— they didn't leave any plans lying around about their secret vampire army. But I'm going to do something."

I stood up. "I'm going to do something too. I'm going to get some sleep."

"Well, call me when you change your mind," Anton said. "Because I know you're going to change your mind."

William stood up too. "Are you okay to drive home?"

"Yes, I'm fine," I said. I began to move toward the door.

"Like I said, call me," Anton called after me.

William walked me out to the car, and as I got in, he leaned on the door for a moment.

"We'll figure this out, Katie," he said.

I nodded, and he closed the door. Then I watched as he went back into the house.

I sat behind the wheel for a few moments and then glanced down at my phone again. There were still no messages from Terrance or Sachiko—but I hadn't really expected there to be.

Then I started the car and drove home.

I wasn't sure what type of reception I would get from GM. It wasn't terribly late—especially not for a Saturday night—but I didn't know how fast news about the plaza had traveled, and I didn't know if anyone had called GM about the incident yet.

If she had heard about it, I didn't really know how I was going to explain it to her.

Luckily, GM seemed to be perfectly calm, and I found her in the kitchen drinking a cup of tea and reading a book.

She looked up as I came in. "Good evening, Katie."

"Hey," I said.

"Are you hungry?" GM asked.

"No," I said. "Thanks. I think I'll just head up to my room."

I turned to go.

"Oh, Katie," GM said. "A friend stopped by to see you."

I turned back, surprised. "A friend?"

GM frowned in thought. "Yes. She said her name was—Sachiko. I don't think I've seen her before."

"Oh!" I said. "Sachiko. I knew she was coming, but I didn't know she was here already. She's from Russia," I added by way of explanation, "but I actually met her here. She'll be visiting in town for a few days."

"Well, she said she'd stop by again," GM said.

"Great. Thanks," I said.

I turned to go again, and this time there was a knock on the door.

I hurried down the hall.

I opened the door, expecting to see Sachiko, but instead I found a boy about my age with light brown hair and a stern, military bearing—he was the same one who had led me and the others out of the school during the earthquake.

171

"Good evening, ma'am," he said.

"Good evening," I replied.

"My name is Dylan Bell," the boy said. "I have been assigned to watch over you and your house."

"Oh, you're Dylan," I said. "You're from the Order."

"Yes, ma'am."

"Terrance mentioned that you would be taking over for him," I said. "Does this mean he's left town?"

Dylan did not reply.

"Where is he?" I said. "Is he okay? I sent him a text last night, but I haven't heard from him."

"Terrance's whereabouts are classified, ma'am," Dylan said.

"Okay, I understand that," I said. "But is he okay? I just want to be sure."

"I am unable to comment on that at this time, ma'am."

"Fine," I said. "And you can stop calling me 'ma'am.' My name's Katie."

"Yes, ma'am."

"All right," I said. "Can I help you with something?"

"There was an incident this evening involving potentially hostile persons," Dylan said. "The incident took place at Hywel's Plaza, which is in close proximity to both your home and the school you attend. I am here to request that you remain in your house this weekend, and on Monday I will escort you to and from school."

"What?" I said.

"It's for your own safety, ma'am."

"And what if I don't agree?" I said.

"Then I will accompany you anyway, ma'am," Dylan said. "And I am authorized to intervene if necessary."

"Okay, thanks," I said. "I'll take that under advisement."

I closed the door.

"Who was that?" GM asked, walking up to me.

"It was a boy from my school," I said. "He said there was an incident at Hywel's Plaza. He said it was best if I stayed inside for now."

I figured this was the best way to introduce the topic. Maybe GM would hear the stories later and just assume they were wild rumors.

GM blinked in surprise. "What kind of incident? Did he say?"

I was grateful GM had given me an easy out. "No."

"Was he with the police?" she asked.

"No—like I said, he's from my school."

GM walked past me and opened the door.

She stood looking out into the night.

"How extraordinary," GM said, closing the door and turning back to me. "There's nothing out there now. I suppose the boy's just a little overzealous. Is he a neighbor of ours?"

"Actually, I don't know," I said.

"Well, I suppose if there's anything in it, we'll hear about it later," GM said.

She returned to the kitchen, and I went upstairs to my room.

I opened the door to see a girl standing over by my bedroom window. She was small and slim, with long, black hair. It was Sachiko.

"Hey," she said. "I hope it's okay that I sneaked in."

I closed the door and rushed over to give her a hug.

"Of course it's okay," I said. "How are you?"

"I'm good," Sachiko said.

"What happened at the airport?" I said.

"Nothing out of the ordinary," Sachiko said. "It was just simple mechanical trouble. And then we had to deplane. And then board a new one—eventually. But I'm here now."

"So what did you need to tell me?" I said.

Sachiko hesitated. "It can wait a moment. It might be better if I hear what's going on with you first."

"But your texts—"

"Yes, sorry about that," Sachiko said. "I was just anxious to get here. Something's going on, and I'm not sure quite what yet. Maybe what's happening here will help me put the pieces into place."

I told her quickly about the disappearing vampires, about what I'd learned from Terrance and Maksim about the Queen of the Moon, and about Veronika.

Sachiko nodded when I was done.

"You guys are right about all of this," she said. "I mean about the disappearances. They're still going on—and not just the dramatic ones like at the cave. The smaller, individual ones are still happening. I've seen it myself. When the Order stopped using the tears, the disappearances seemed to stop—and then they began again. I still think it's good they stopped using it, though. It really isn't a cure."

"No, it isn't," I said.

Sachiko continued. "But, like I said, the disappearances *are* still happening. And the disturbances I felt before are still occurring. And I've followed them. But I can't find the source—they're too diffuse. They're all over the place."

"Terrance said they started hearing about new—and different— disappearances right around the same time they found activity at the Temple of the Moon," I said. "He said ancient vampires are appearing and disappearing, and I think the temple is the key. Do you think you could help me find it?"

"Yes, absolutely," Sachiko said. "If the temple is in Russia, I'm sure I could find it. And if the disappearances and the Temple of the Moon are related, we may just be able to solve your Veronika problem for you."

"You think we may be able to find out who's behind the disappearances?" I said.

"It's possible," Sachiko said. "I can't guarantee that we can find the ghost girl. But at least we have a place to start."

She paused and shook her head.

"I knew Veronika was going to ask you for something difficult," she said. "But I never expected her to ask you for something this big. It's outrageous—find the ghost girl. You're only one person. She should never have asked you to do something so big on your own."

"So is that what you came here to tell me?" I asked. "That you knew that the disappearances were still going on?"

"No," Sachiko replied. "I wasn't thinking of that in connection with you—it was just a mystery I was hoping to solve."

"So what was your news?"

"I saw your cousin," Sachiko said.

I was startled. "You saw Odette?"

Sachiko nodded. "Two days ago. That's why I was going to contact you."

"You're sure it was her?" I said.

"Positive. I know who she is—we all do. And what's more, I think she wanted me to see her."

"Why?"

"Our community is small," Sachiko said. "And word gets around fast. It's well known now that you and I are friends, and I think Odette wanted me to see her because she knew I would tell you. I think she wants to get in contact with you again."

I was stunned. "Where did you see her?"

"At your old house," Sachiko said. "Which I guess is actually her house. Someone's been fixing it up again since the Hunter set it on fire. I heard a rumor that it was being rebuilt, so I went over to see. And I saw Odette there flitting around the house and doing her best impression of a ghost. I don't think it was any accident that I saw her there."

I sat down on my bed. "Wow," I said.

My cousin Odette had been missing since last year. She had once led me into a trap, then helped me, then disappeared. She was much loved by GM, although they weren't blood relatives—I was related to Odette on my father's side. She was also a vampire, and she was currently rumored to be working as a spy.

Sachiko came and sat down beside me. "I think Odette wants to see you. And I'm not sure it's a good idea."

"Do you think she could be leading me into a trap?"

"It's possible. In fact, it's very possible. But I just don't know. She could have good intentions too. That's why I wanted to see you so quickly. I didn't know if she would try to contact you more directly. I didn't know if she would try to lure you into a meeting."

"So Odette has resurfaced," I said. "And I should probably avoid her right now."

I felt a little twinge at that. I still missed my cousin—even after all she had done—and I knew that GM missed her too. I would've liked to have been able to tell her that Odette was okay.

"I think that's probably best," Sachiko said. "Let's work on the temple first. We'll worry about Odette later."

"So the temple," I said. "Do you really think you can get me there?"

"We'll find it," Sachiko said. "Do you have a passport? If you don't, I can get you one, but it'll be easier if you have one already."

"I have one," I said. "But I don't have a visa. I think you need a visa to get into Russia."

"You do," Sachiko said. "But those are easier to fake. I know a guy—we'll get you one."

"I don't really have any money," I said. "I'm not sure I can buy a fake visa—or a plane ticket, for that matter."

"One thing that vampires have a lot of is time," Sachiko said. "And when you have time, you can make a lot of money. Don't worry about any of it. I'll take care of it."

She paused.

"When did you want to leave?"

"Now would really be ideal," I said.

"Are you sure?" Sachiko asked. "Don't you need to tell someone, or pack, or something?"

I wanted to tell my grandmother I was leaving, but I knew I couldn't—she would never believe me or let me go. I thought too of William. He'd been trying to reach out to me, but the thought of freeing him from Veronika forever was too precious to pass up. I could do this right now, and William would never need to worry about her again.

"I'll leave a note," I said. "And I'll pack quickly."

I unearthed a bag and began to push clothes into it. Then I found my passport in my desk and then went to the bathroom to get a few toiletries.

When I returned, Sachiko was standing by the window, looking out.

"We've got another problem," she said. "It's just a minor problem, but we'll still have to get past it."

"What is it?" I said, as I put the rest of my things in my bag.

Sachiko dropped the curtain. "There's a guy on patrol around your house. He just finished a circuit through your backyard, and now I bet he's returning to his post at the front. I think it's someone from the Order of the Hawthorne."

I moved toward the window. "That's probably Dylan—he stopped by to talk to me right before you showed up."

Sachiko frowned. "I don't think I know Dylan."

"I believe he's filling in for Terrance, who often watches over me," I said. I continued to look out the window, but I couldn't see anyone. "He already advised me to stay in the house for the rest of the weekend."

I turned back to Sachiko. "Do you think he'll try to stop us from leaving?"

"It's possible," Sachiko said. "At the very least, he probably has orders to keep an eye on you. It's probably best if we lose him. Like I said, it isn't a big problem. I'm sure you can spot him if you go out front. Look toward the bushes by the house directly across the street."

I went downstairs quietly and walked toward the door. I could see GM still sitting in the kitchen with her tea and her book.

I opened the door and stepped outside.

It was getting very late, and many of the houses on our block had gone dark for the night. There was no one out on the street, and the streetlights threw long shadows over the sidewalks.

I walked down the driveway and peered into the shadows.

The house across the way had a thick row of bushes that ran along the side of the house. Though the weather was warm, it was still October, and the bushes were largely bare of leaves. I tried to act nonchalant as I walked across the street to get a better look.

I couldn't see anyone over by the bushes.

And then I saw a tiny flash of light on metal. The metal piece was just a small circle, and on either side of it were two larger, black circles—I was looking at a pair of binoculars.

As I watched, the binoculars were lowered, and I saw a face. It was the same boy with light brown hair and a strangely stern countenance who had come to the door.

I hurried inside and went back up to my room.

"It's definitely Dylan," I said to Sachiko. "It took me a moment to spot him."

"The members of the Order are good at blending in," Sachiko said. "I'll give them that. But we'll get around him—don't worry."

"I don't know," I said. "He seemed pretty capable at the school."

"Seriously, don't worry," Sachiko said. "We'll make it work."

She glanced over at my bag.

"So when you said you wanted to go now," she said, "did you mean *now* now?"

"I should probably wait until my grandmother goes to sleep," I said. "But that shouldn't be much longer. It's getting late even for her."

I looked over my bag one more time just to make sure I had everything, and then I turned off the overhead light and switched on the lamp on my desk.

While I was waiting, I would write my note for GM.

After a few starts and stops, I wrote a brief note telling her I had to leave and that everything was fine—I hadn't been kidnapped. I also told her that I was perfectly safe, and I would be back soon.

I certainly hoped that last part was true.

When I was finished with the note, I turned out the light. As I did so, I heard GM come up the stairs and go to her room.

I waited a few more minutes to make sure that she had settled in. Then I picked up my note and my bag.

"My grandmother sleeps very heavily," I whispered to Sachiko. "She won't hear us going down the stairs."

Sachiko, I knew, could see in the dark, and I knew my bedroom so well that I could walk across it even without the sliver of light that shone in through a part in the curtains.

We went to the door, which I eased open, and then the two of us walked noiselessly down the stairs.

I went to the kitchen without turning on any lights, and I left my note on the table.

Then I joined Sachiko by the front door.

"So what are we going to do about Dylan?" I whispered.

"Just wait here," Sachiko said. "I'll come back and get you soon."

Sachiko stepped out the door and closed it behind her.

I went to the living room and peeked out the window from behind the curtain.

At first I didn't see anything. Then I saw a dark streak come down the street and zip past my house.

Moments later, I saw Dylan extricate himself from the bushes across the way and go running down the street after the streak. Soon they had both disappeared.

I stood looking out the window for several minutes, but the street remained quiet. After a little while, I let the curtain drop and went to sit on the stairs near the front door.

I lost track of time as I sat, but eventually, I heard a soft tap on the door.

I opened it to find Sachiko standing on the step.

"I've stranded him on a rooftop in an awkward position," she said, "but he'll figure it out eventually. We'd better go."

I grabbed my bag and hurried out after Sachiko, locking the door behind me.

Sachiko took my hand, and soon we were flying down the street in the opposite direction from the one in which she'd led Dylan.

Within moments, we came to a stop by a sleek, purple sports car that was set low to the ground.

"Wow. That's fancy," I said. "Did you—borrow it?"

"I rented it," Sachiko said. "You can rent fancy cars too. I picked it primarily for speed. I didn't know what I'd find when I got here. I thought we might have to get away quickly."

We both got in, and Sachiko began to drive.

"So—" I said.

"We're going to get you that visa," Sachiko supplied. "Then we'll go to the airport."

"Is Saturday night a good time to get a fake visa?" I said. "Isn't it too late?"

"Saturday night is the best time to get a fake visa," Sachiko replied. "That's when you'll find the right people out and about. Like I said, I know a guy. Or, to be more accurate, I know a guy who probably knows a guy who can help us. At the very least, he can point us in the right direction."

Sachiko drove very fast through the darkened streets, and as I watched the blurred scenery flying by, it seemed to me that we were already headed in the right direction to get to the airport.

We reached the nearest city, but instead of continuing along the highway, we pulled off at an exit that led to a dark, run-down section of town.

Sachiko pulled the car to a stop behind a dark, abandoned warehouse.

I peered out the window at the ramshackle building. "Are you sure this is the right place?"

"It's the right place," Sachiko said. "It's an underground club. Can I have your passport? Just in case I can get what we need in there."

I pulled my passport out of my bag and handed it to her.

"Thanks," Sachiko said. "Whatever you do, don't get out of the car. I'll be right back."

She stepped out of the car and slammed the door shut behind her.

I heard the car doors lock as she walked away.

I must have fallen asleep because the next thing I knew, the door was opening again, and Sachiko was getting back into the car.

"Okay," she said. "What we need isn't here, but I know where we can get it now. It's just one more place."

I glanced at the clock on the dashboard—about twenty minutes had passed.

"I can't believe I fell asleep," I said.

"Go ahead," Sachiko said. "You probably need it."

"I don't think I should," I said. "At least not until we're done with this. It's safer for me to stay alert right now."

"This car's pretty sturdy despite the way it looks," Sachiko said. "So you're probably safe enough in here with the doors locked. But you're right—it's best to stay alert just in case. And cops are attracted by people sleeping in cars—that's a complication we don't need at the moment."

We ended up going to two more places rather than just one, but eventually, Sachiko obtained a visa for me, and we turned onto the highway and began to drive toward the airport.

I looked at the broad, rectangular stamp in my passport with its shiny, holographic sticker.

"Are you sure this will work?" I asked.

"It should be a good counterfeit," Sachiko said. "And if it's not quite good enough, I can always use a little charm and smooth things over. I don't like to do that, but I can. And I got us tickets to Russia. We can print out boarding passes at the airport."

We drove on through the night, and I resisted the impulse to sleep. We arrived at the airport just as the first rays of dawn were creeping up over the horizon, and we had no trouble checking in or printing out our boarding passes. Even our relative lack of luggage didn't cause any comment.

Our flight was scheduled to leave in the early morning, so Sachiko and I sat and watched the sunrise.

I got out my phone several times and considered calling William. He'd been trying so hard to be open and honest with me, and here I was, preparing to run off and not tell him anything.

But I kept picturing him as he was when Sachiko and I had found him at Rusalka Castle several months ago—pale, bruised, and unresponsive. Sachiko had said that a vampire healer was his only hope—otherwise he was going to die. And Veronika had done her job and saved him.

I couldn't risk getting him involved and sending him back to that.

I shut off my phone and put it away.

Sachiko was watching me.

"Are you thinking about your grandmother?" she said. "It's been a long time since I lived with a family, but I feel like any parent—or grandparent—in the world would be upset if their child took off and just left a note."

Sachiko had misread the reason for my pensiveness, but her point was well made.

"I can't tell her what's going on," I said. "She'd never believe me. And she'd try to stop me. But I have to do this."

"I know," Sachiko said. "But you could at least leave her a voicemail. That way she could hear your voice and know that you're okay—that the note wasn't a fake. And as for the rest of it—no matter what you tell your grandmother, I'm sure she'll forgive you."

"Maybe I'll call her when we land," I said.

"Just keep it in mind," Sachiko said. She looked over at me again. "You should probably eat something—even if you don't feel particularly hungry. It'll help you to sleep once you get on the plane."

I did as she suggested and got myself a little breakfast.

Then, a little while later, our plane boarded, and we walked through the tunnel and found our seats.

As soon as I sat down, a heavy wave of fatigue washed over me, and I closed the shade on the window next to me.

Shortly after we took off, I fell asleep.

Chapter Twelve

When I awoke, the cabin was dim, and all I could hear was the steady hum of the airplane's engines.

I sat up and looked around.

I was sitting in a seat that was kind of like a little booth. There was a wall on each side, and one wall had a console and a little table. Sachiko was sitting in a similar booth to my right. Other than that, the cabin appeared to be empty.

"Is this first class?" I said.

"Yes," Sachiko said. "Your seat actually reclines into a bed, but you seemed so tired that I didn't want to wake you up to tell you."

"Where is everybody?" I said.

"I bought up all twenty seats," Sachiko replied. "I figured we could use some privacy."

"Why is that?"

"I feel like you're running from something," Sachiko said.

"How can I be running from something?" I asked. "I'm actually running toward danger right now."

Sachiko shook her head. "That's not what I mean. You've always been brave. You've never run from physical danger. But I feel like you're avoiding something—something that's important."

"What do you mean?" I said.

184

"It's just that you run off in the middle of the night and don't say goodbye to your grandmother," Sachiko said. "And I'm assuming you didn't contact William either."

"You're right," I said. "I didn't tell him I was leaving."

"Why not?"

"I can't," I said. "William's life is in danger because of me."

"But William wouldn't have a life to be in danger if you hadn't saved him," Sachiko said. "You can't help what Veronika is demanding now. Don't you think he deserves to know?"

"I don't want him to be scared," I said.

The words sounded strange to me even as they left my lips.

"You don't want him to be scared?" Sachiko said. "I haven't known William very long, but I don't think that's something you have to worry about."

"That's not really the right way to put it," I said. "I meant I don't want him to have the threat of death hanging over his head."

"But he does have that," Sachiko said. "And it's not your fault."

She paused. "You can't blame yourself for not fixing everything and not making sure it was fixed for good. Life isn't like that."

I nodded.

"No one can do that," Sachiko said. "No one. There will always be new problems. And old ones you've had will sometimes come back. That doesn't mean you did anything wrong. It just means that you can't control everything."

I nodded again.

Sachiko sighed. "So what's all this about the clear fire? Veronika really said you should try to get it back?"

"Yes," I said.

"Did she say anything else about it that you might not have mentioned yet?"

I frowned as I thought back on it.

"She said it might do more than I think," I said. "She also hinted that I might be able to use it against vampires."

"Hmmm," Sachiko said. "That's interesting. But as far as you know, it doesn't work against vampires?"

"No," I said. "It wasn't necessary. The Sídh defeated the vampires in battle, and then the humans defeated the Sídh. The humans banished the Sídh and made them promise to send one of their number to create the Little Sun and fight the kost. They weren't worried about vampires—they were already defeated."

"So the clear fire wasn't designed to fight vampires or any of the other dark creatures," Sachiko said. "Just the kost."

"Yes," I said.

"But it is a source of light and power," Sachiko said musingly. "And it obviously has mystical properties. Maybe Veronika's right—maybe it can be used on vampires—and other things."

She looked at me. "But first we have to get it back for you. Have you tried it lately?"

"Yes," I said.

"And?"

"I feel *something*," I said. "I feel like something's there, but I can't make anything appear. I got my best result when I got angry."

Sachiko nodded. "That makes sense. This kind of power is about feeling."

"Feelings can't be strong enough to get past the Sídh," I said.

"Yes, they can be," Sachiko said. "This ability of yours is genetic, right? It's something you were born with?"

"Yes," I said.

"Then I don't see how they can stop you," Sachiko said. "The power is yours. They can put up barriers. But you can get over them."

"I don't know," I said. "It feels like an awfully big obstacle."

"Let's try an experiment," Sachiko said. "Close your eyes."

Sachiko had been a healer in her old, human life, so I knew she had helped people. But even though I trusted her skill, I doubted very much that she could help me.

But I closed my eyes anyway.

186

"What do I do now?" I said.

"You don't have to do anything," Sachiko replied. "Just think. Think back to the first time you summoned the clear fire."

"I was in the Pure Woods," I said. "And I sang the song my mother taught me."

"You don't need to tell me," Sachiko said. "Just picture it in your own mind."

"But I've already sung the song," I said. "And it didn't produce anything."

"You don't need to sing," Sachiko said. "Just put yourself back in that moment in time."

I opened my eyes and looked at Sachiko—sort of to reset myself.

Then I settled back in my seat and closed my eyes again.

I allowed my mind to wander.

I thought of my mother, the petrified forest known as the Pure Woods, and the ring of tiny stones I had stood in to find the clear fire.

I thought of the clear fire itself—the way it was bright but easy to look at. There was something warm and comforting about it—it was like a piece of sunshine that you could hold in your hand.

I thought too of William—how he had stood by my side looking at the clear fire, his eyes alight with wonder.

I kept thinking of him, and before long, I had fallen asleep again.

When I woke up, Sachiko called for a flight attendant, and I ordered a light snack.

After I was done eating, I felt a lot better—the rest and food had really helped me. Then Sachiko asked that the lights be turned down again.

I let my mind wander once more.

I saw myself walking through bare, white trees. I saw myself holding up my hands.

I heard myself singing.

As my mind continued to wander, I thought I felt a spark.

I tried to move toward it, but I felt it float away.

I settled my mind again, and then I let it wander once more.

This time when I felt the spark, I made myself remain calm. I didn't think about the spark or even focus on it. Instead, I ignored it and turned back to my own thoughts.

I saw myself in the woods…I heard singing…

Then I felt a tiny flame ignite within me.

I opened my eyes.

Floating in the air of the dark cabin were countless tiny lights, like small pieces of fire.

I reached out my hand toward one, and it floated toward me.

It hovered over my outstretched palm for just a moment and then disappeared.

Moments later, all the other tiny lights disappeared too.

I looked over to see Sachiko staring at me in shock.

"What just happened?" she said.

"I'm not sure," I said. "What did you see?"

"You were sitting there looking very relaxed," Sachiko said. "And then you started to sing just a little. And then the next thing I knew, the air was full of sparks."

"I didn't realize I was singing," I said.

"You did that a couple of times," Sachiko said. "But the sparks only appeared at the end."

I frowned. "I guess I must have summoned the clear fire—at least in part. I've never seen it in fragments before, though."

"Well, whatever it was," Sachiko said, "I don't think you should do it again. At least not at thirty thousand feet. Let's wait till we land to work on that again."

The rest of the flight was uneventful, and we landed in Moscow and disembarked without difficulty.

The line at customs was long—and Sachiko and I were actually in different lines since she had a Russian passport—but we made it through eventually. Sachiko and I then went to rent a car.

She picked out a car that was less ostentatious than the last one—but had the most powerful engine of any on the lot.

"So where to now?" I said as we settled into the car.

"I think we should head to Krov," Sachiko said, starting the car and driving off. "I've got a new house there, and I also think it's the best place to find out information about the Queen of the Moon and her temple."

"Why would there be information about her in Krov?" I said.

"We'll head to the Vaults at Rusalka Castle," Sachiko replied. "They don't just have treasures and weapons there. They also have archives. We can search their records to see what they know about the Queen."

"Doesn't the Order of the Hawthorne have a location in Russia?" I said. "We could go to them instead. After all, they do know where her temple is."

"The Order won't help us," Sachiko said. "They would capture me on sight, and they would ship you back to your grandmother. The only one who might help us is your friend Terrance, and you don't know where he is, right?"

"Right," I said.

"Then the Vaults are our best bet," Sachiko said.

"Will they let us in?" I asked.

"No," Sachiko said. "But we'll sneak in. I'm fast—very fast. We'll be in and out before they know it. And if they do catch us at the Vaults, all they'll do is throw us out. They won't try to detain us like the Order would."

"Why not?" I said. "I seem to recall that the current queen thinks I tried to stake her husband. I'm pretty sure she'd love to have me as a prisoner."

"The king recovered," Sachiko said. "So she probably hates you a little less. Besides, things are pretty chaotic up at the castle. We've had earthquakes in Krov, too, and a rash of petty thefts. But the disappearances are what really have everyone rattled. They seemed to stop, and then they started up again. There's a sense of unease—a feeling that someone at the castle has sold us all out."

"Innokenti?" I said. "That's who Anton thinks it is."

"I don't know," Sachiko said. "I hesitate to speculate at this point. Let's just say that no one is in any hurry to contact any member of the court right now—not even their own guards. If we get caught in the Vaults, I think they'll let us slide."

"What about the disappearances?" I said. "You said you feel disturbances again, didn't you?"

Sachiko frowned. "I do feel disturbances again—but they're different. They're fainter, and they seem to be coming from all around me."

"Are you sure you can't track them?" I said.

Sachiko shook her head. "No—I can't. I could follow them last time, but this time they're too diffuse for me to get a clear read on them. Maybe in an absolute emergency I could try doing that—but I'd rather not depend on it."

"So Krov it is," I said.

"Krov it is," Sachiko said. "This is a pretty long drive, so I won't be offended if you just want to take a nap."

We drove on for several hours and stopped once so I could get some food.

Then we drove on again.

The sun was setting as we reached the outskirts of Krov, and Sachiko stopped at a small café so I could get some dinner.

It was much cooler in Krov than it had been in Elspeth's Grove, and luckily, I had thought to throw some warmer clothes into my bag. I was grateful for my heavier jacket as we got out of the car and walked into the café.

I went up to the counter and ordered some tea and a sandwich in Russian and then sat down with Sachiko at a table.

"So do you want to drive by your old house?" Sachiko said. "Just for a moment—while we're here?"

"No," I said. "It'll be too much of a distraction."

"Are you sure?" Sachiko said. "Like I said, it's all fixed up now."

"Let's finish what we're here to do first," I said. "That matters more than anything."

"Speaking of distractions," Sachiko said, "it's possible that Odette will try to contact you now that you're in Russia."

I shook my head. "I can't see her right now."

"I was hoping you'd say that," Sachiko said. "I'll keep an eye out for her. If I see her, I'll lead her away. So if I suddenly disappear, you'll know that's why."

"Thanks," I said.

I finished eating quickly, and soon we were back in the car.

Sachiko turned down an unfamiliar road, and before long, we were driving through a neighborhood I had never been to. The houses and streets were clearly new, and everything had an air of cheerful, modern convenience to it.

Sachiko drove up to a big, comfortable house, and we parked in the garage.

I looked around the immaculate room as I got out of the car.

"This is the nicest garage I've ever seen," I said.

"I don't really use it much," Sachiko said. "So it's never really had a chance to get dirty."

We went into the house, and Sachiko led me to a bright, cheerful living room with new furniture.

There were lacy curtains covering a window over the sofa, and I pulled them back and looked out on the prosperous, well-lit street outside the house.

"This is undercover?" I said.

"It is if you're a vampire," Sachiko replied. "The neighborhood is new, there are humans all around me, and there are bright lights everywhere. No one would think to look for me here."

"What about your old house?" I said.

"I just left it as it was," Sachiko said. "I didn't really have too many things to move—just a few odds and ends. As far as I know, the house is empty now, unless someone moved in. But I thought it was best for me to leave, just in case someone knew I'd been crashing there."

"What about David?" I said. "Where's he?"

David was Sachiko's friend who had helped us with the Hunter back in April. He'd allowed himself to be captured by the guards at Rusalka to enable us to escape, and even though Sachiko had told me he was safe now, I'd still hoped to see for myself that he was okay.

"As strange as it may sound," Sachiko said, "David's actually visiting family. He's younger than a lot of us. I made him up to look older than he is, and then he went off. Come on. I'll show you to your room."

Sachiko led me upstairs to a small bedroom at the end of the hall.

"The house is actually a little smaller than it appears from the outside," she said. "Or at least the bedrooms seem to be a little smaller than you might think."

"No—this is great," I said. "It's perfect."

"And I've got some extra clothes for you in the closet," Sachiko said. "Just in case. I know it's colder here than it was in Elspeth's Grove."

"That's really thoughtful," I said. "Thanks."

I set my bag down on the bed.

As I did so, I heard my phone buzz.

I got it out quickly. There was a message from GM. It was just two words.

I understand.

"What is it?" Sachiko said.

"It's a text from my grandmother."

"What did she say?"

"She says she understands."

"What does that mean?" Sachiko asked.

"I don't know."

I texted her back.

Thank you, I said. *I'll come home as soon as I can.*

At the very least, GM would know I was safe—explanations would need to wait for now.

"So where to now?" I said. "Do we head straight over to the Vaults?"

"If you don't mind," Sachiko said, "I'd like to try to work on the clear fire just once before we go. Even if you can only produce the sparks again, that may be something we can use in case we get in trouble. It might convince whoever catches us to let us go—the bright light could spook them."

"I thought you said they'd just throw us out if they caught us," I said.

"Well, that's really a best-case scenario," Sachiko said. "I can't say there's *no* risk. Realistically I can't be one hundred percent sure of what they would do. But I don't think anyone will be too interested in us. And I still think it's a better idea than going to the Order. Anyway, we're always best leaving a place under our own power. And I think the clear fire could help."

"Okay," I said. "I'd like to try it again."

We went back down to the living room, and Sachiko had me sit down on the new, white sofa. She sat down on a chair nearby.

"Let's do it just like you did before," Sachiko said. "Just close your eyes, and let your thoughts flow. You don't need to make any special effort to find it—and you don't need to sing. Just go back to the first time you found the clear fire—let that be your starting point."

I closed my eyes and tried to let go of all worries.

Then I just let my thoughts wander.

I saw myself back in the Pure Woods again.

I walked toward the tiny stone ring again, where I had first summoned the clear fire. But as I walked toward it, I saw a flash of dark eyes. A moment later, the eyes turned to gold.

My own eyes flew open.

"Is anything wrong?" Sachiko said.

"I saw a pair of eyes," I said. "I've seen them a couple of times since I started trying to get the clear fire back."

"Do you know who it is?" Sachiko said.

"No," I replied. "But they look like women's eyes to me."

"It could be significant," Sachiko said. "Keep going. See where they lead you."

I closed my eyes again and tried to settle my mind once more.

Then I returned to the forest.

I began walking toward the stone ring again, but this time I didn't see any eyes. Instead, as I drew close to the ring, I saw a soft, white light. The light was growing steadily, and there was a long edge of shadow that was moving across it—it was like a door was opening and letting in the light.

I walked closer.

The light was not nearly as bright as the clear fire, but there was a special quality to it—there seemed to be power in it.

The door opened even wider, and soon I was bathed in the soft, white glow. I could see a long, dark figure standing beside me—very broad and very tall. I turned toward it, and my eyes flew open again.

"What happened this time?" Sachiko said.

"I saw a bright light," I said. "But it wasn't the clear fire. I don't know what it was."

"You're getting a lot of extraneous visions," Sachiko said. "Maybe you could try to block them out for now—focus just a little more on the clear fire."

I tried to do as she asked, and at one point I felt a brief burst of flame inside, but I couldn't make the sparks reappear, let alone the clear fire.

"Maybe I'm pushing you too hard," Sachiko said. "Are you getting tired?"

"Not physically," I said. "But I'm starting to feel a mental strain."

"Then I'm definitely pushing you too hard," Sachiko said. "This type of work is actually pretty delicate. I'm sorry."

"No harm done," I said. "Every time I do this, I feel a little more like I used to. I guess you could say I feel like my old self."

"That's good," Sachiko said. "That's a good sign."

"So, the castle," I said. "Let's go."

Sachiko got me a coat that was heavily perfumed to help me disguise my human scent, and she gave me a little metal box of highly spiced candies to help me disguise my breath. The breath of humans was lighter and sweeter than the breath of vampires—and the candies were very strong. I knew that from experience.

We went out to the shiny, new garage and got in the car, and Sachiko drove us out to the Wasteland.

The Wasteland was a broad stretch of barren, blighted land that ran for miles up to an old, abandoned monastery. The gray plains of the Wasteland appeared to be empty, but there was actually a vampire town known as Zamochit Village on its surface, and at its center was Rusalka Castle. The entire town was hidden from view by a charm, and you couldn't actually see the village until you entered it. There was also a barrier around Zamochit that prevented any non-vampire from entering. Somehow, I was immune to the barrier, and I could walk right through it without any difficulty—I still didn't know why I had this ability and other humans did not. I did know that Terrance had entered the village on at least one occasion—it was possible that the Order knew a way to get around the barrier.

But under ordinary circumstances, humans couldn't get past the barrier. And there was a further charm on the village that made people veer away from it and walk right around it—they were never aware that they were avoiding it, and anyone who was asked would have said that they'd walked straight across the Wasteland without obstruction. Zamochit Village was well hidden, despite the fact that it stood very close to human habitation.

Once we were far enough out into the Wasteland, Sachiko parked the car by the side of the road, and we both got out.

There was a definite chill in the air, and I shivered just a little as I looked out over the empty, gray field before us.

"Should we wait until morning?" I said. "I know night is when Zamochit is likely to be busiest."

"I think it's better to go in when everyone's up and about," Sachiko replied. "Especially since we're going to Rusalka—it's easier to get lost in a crowd. If we go in during the day, we'll really stand out. Especially these days—people are following a self-imposed curfew—no one wants to be caught out in the day when they're weakest."

I glanced over at Sachiko. "Last time we went to the castle, we went in disguise. Is this coat I'm wearing going to be enough?"

"You should be fine," Sachiko said. "The mood in Zamochit is tense these days. No one's going to be looking at us."

She set off across the blighted, barren plain in front of us, and I followed her.

Eventually, Sachiko came to a stop.

"This should be a good spot," she said. "Are you ready?"

"Yes," I said.

I watched as Sachiko stepped forward and disappeared.

Then I stepped in after her.

The air around me shimmered, and I felt a tingle, like a little electric buzz, as I stepped through the barrier. At the same time, the empty field that had been before me disappeared, and suddenly I was standing in a dark alley between two ramshackle houses. Sachiko was standing nearby, waiting for me.

"We'll go quickly, and we'll stay out of sight," she said. "Just follow me."

Sachiko walked swiftly to the end of the alley, and I followed close behind.

Zamochit was a haphazard collection of buildings and houses with a confusing tangle of streets. Streets stopped and started seemingly at random, and they often turned in unexpected directions—I had even seen a street that ran directly into a house. There were four tall towers that rose up over the village, and as Sachiko peered out of the alley, I could see one of the towers looming off in the distance. The towers housed guards who were charged with watching Zamochit's borders for trespassers. But thanks to the barrier, intruders were rare, and the guards were left with little to do. I knew from previous experience that they were seldom watching for anything.

After a moment, Sachiko stepped out into the street and motioned for me to follow her.

Although there were no streetlamps or other obvious sources of light, the entire village of Zamochit was lit with a soft, silvery light. The silver light was fairly dim, but it was enough for me to see by, and I had no trouble following Sachiko as she slipped silently through the streets.

Off in the distance, the vast outline of Rusalka Castle loomed over the village.

I had been to the castle and its Vaults before—I knew that getting in would not be easy.

As we hurried along, I saw a few shadowy figures that quickly slinked out of sight. As we rounded a corner, we came face to face with a tall, pale man dressed all in black. The man stared at us for a moment in alarm and then hurried off.

"See what I mean?" Sachiko said. "Everyone is tense these days. No one wants to deal with people they don't know."

Even as she spoke the words, however, Sachiko glanced over my shoulder at something.

I turned quickly. "What is it?"

"Nothing," Sachiko said. "Just a trick of the light."

She moved on, and I took one last glance over my shoulder before I followed her.

We hurried on through the zigzagging streets, and soon I had lost all sense of direction.

As we passed by a row of ramshackle houses, and Sachiko paused one more time to look behind us, I was struck by an unpleasant thought.

The houses we were standing near reminded me forcefully of a similar spot where I had first met a certain golden-haired vampire.

"Sachiko," I said, "what if we run into Veronika?"

"We won't," she said.

"She does live in Zamochit Village," I said. "This is the place where I'm most likely to run across her."

"It won't happen," Sachiko said.

"Why not?"

"Because she wants her price to be paid," Sachiko said. "And she knows she has to stay out of your way so you can do that."

"What if she decides it's not happening fast enough?" I said.

"Did she give you a time limit?"

"No," I replied.

"Then don't worry about her," Sachiko said. "Veronika is a skilled healer. And she's equally skilled at getting paid. She knows that she's set you an impossible task. And the only way she'll get what she wants is if she stays out of your way—clients don't deliver if they're being harassed. If Veronika hasn't given you a particular time limit, then you're not going to see her. She'll wait until you come to her."

"You're sure about that?" I said.

"Positive," Sachiko replied.

"Then who's following us?" I said.

"Who said anyone was following us?"

"Sachiko," I said.

"Okay, fine," she said. "I think someone's behind us, but I can't see who it is. I keep hearing little sounds, and I keep seeing someone slip out of sight, but I can't get a good look at them. I am sure it isn't Veronika, though."

I glanced back. "Should we go see who it is?"

Sachiko looked startled. "Do you mean, should we confront them?"

"Yes."

"No—absolutely not," Sachiko said. "In fact, what we should do is move a little faster—we should try to lose them."

She glanced up at the nearest building. "And the best way to do that is to go up. Are you ready?"

"Let's go," I said.

Sachiko grabbed my hand, and before I knew it, we were scrambling up the side of the house and onto the roof.

Soon we were jumping from rooftop to rooftop and getting steadily closer to the castle in the distance.

Sachiko moved swiftly, and I had no chance to look behind me to see if our pursuer was still following us.

I simply held on as the world blurred all around me.

Eventually, we came to a stop on the roof of a tall house with its own tower. The vast bulk of Rusalka Castle loomed close by, and we were near enough that I could see the guards patrolling the castle walls.

I glanced around at the rooftops nearby. "Did we lose them?"

"I don't know," Sachiko said. "Let's get under cover and then take a look."

She pulled me into the house through one of the windows, and then suddenly we were flying up a spiraling staircase to the top of the tower that I had spied from outside.

When we reached the chamber at the top, Sachiko released my hand and closed the door behind us. Then she looked out through the small sliver of a window that was set into the wall.

"I don't see anyone," she said.

I looked around the room. The soft, silver light that permeated the entire village shone in through the small window, and I could dimly see that the walls were hung with rich tapestries, and several large chests inlaid with jewels sat stoutly on the stone floor.

"What is this place?" I said.

Sachiko glanced around. "Probably the home of courtiers. As you get closer to the castle, the houses get nicer."

"Courtiers?" I said. "As in members of the court?"

"Exactly."

"You mean there are more of them aside from the king and queen and Innokenti?" I said.

"Yes," Sachiko replied. "There's a bunch of them—vampire lords and ladies with all kinds of titles."

"Vampire lords and ladies?" I said. "Are you sure this is a good place to stop?"

"We won't be here long," Sachiko said. "I just wanted to—"

She froze. "There's someone on the stairs."

I glanced toward the slender window, and Sachiko had the same thought.

"There's no other way out of this room," she said. "Look in the chests—look for anything we can use as a weapon."

I threw open the nearest chest, and all I found was a pile of diaphanous clothes.

Suddenly the door to the chamber flew open, and a tall figure stood silhouetted in the doorway.

It was William.

Chapter Thirteen

"William!" I said.

I ran toward him.

"Hey, I'm here too," said a voice.

Anton stepped into the room.

"Of course you are," Sachiko said.

Anton grinned. "Good to see you, ghost girl."

"I'm not the ghost girl," Sachiko said.

"I know," Anton said, "but it's a good nickname for you."

"What are you guys doing here?" I said. I should have been upset, but I was far too surprised for that.

"I came to find you," William said. "And Anton insisted on coming along."

"I'm the one who arranged the private plane," Anton said. "Without me *he* wouldn't be here."

"Why did you want to find me?" I said.

"Why?" William said in exasperation. "Katie, you disappeared—you went missing from your home. And it's been obvious for a while now that something's terribly wrong."

Sachiko walked over and took Anton by the arm.

"Come on," she said. "Let's leave these two alone."

"I don't want to leave now," Anton said. "It's just getting good."

"Come on," Sachiko said.

"What about the owners of the house?" Anton said.

Sachiko stopped. "What about them?"

"Well, they appear to be out at the moment," Anton said. "So we're in luck. But you didn't know that."

"Just get out," Sachiko said.

She pushed him out of the room and closed the door behind them.

"Katie," William said. "What are you doing?"

"You've got to go," I said. "It's not safe for you here."

"I've been hoping that you would come to me in your own time," William said. "But once you ran off, I had to come and find you. Katie, it's dangerous to keep everything to yourself. Just tell me what's going on."

"I can't tell you," I said. "And you really need to leave."

"It's about Veronika, isn't it?" William said.

I looked at him, startled. "How do you know that?"

"It wasn't hard to figure out. I've known for some time that Veronika was going to demand payment from you for saving my life. And then when I mentioned her, I noticed how you reacted. And then I saw Sachiko's name in your phone. It wasn't hard to put those things together—especially not when I consider how strangely you've been acting since your birthday party. Something happened that night."

"I've been acting strange?" I said.

"Something's been weighing on your mind since then," William said. "And if that something's me, I'm here to tell you that's not what I want. You don't owe me anything. You're not responsible for me—I am."

He paused.

"Won't you tell me what's wrong?" William said quietly.

"You're right," I said at last. "It is Veronika. She wants—"

I stopped.

"Yes?" William said.

"She wants your life back," I said.

I looked at William, but he simply nodded.

"She wants your life back," I said, "unless I can find the ghost girl for her."

William looked surprised. "There is no ghost girl. You proved that already."

"Veronika insists that there is," I said. "She said there's a real ghost girl who's behind all these disappearances—both the recent ones and the ones that happened several months ago. And you saw what happened to those vampires from the cave—they disappeared right in front of us."

"And why does Veronika care?" William said.

"She said the ghost girl has taken her Promised One," I said. "Veronika wants him back."

"I see," William said. "I get it now. So you find the ghost girl and rescue Veronika's Promised One, or else she will take my life away."

"Yes," I said. I glanced at him. "You don't seem too upset."

"I'm not," William said. "Katie, don't you get it? I love you. You matter more than anything to me—even more than my own life. And what you did when you saved me was a wonderful thing. You gave me my life back and gave me more time with you. But I didn't expect that safety to last forever. You've taken on way too much responsibility for me. And I'm sorry you felt like you had to tackle this on your own."

"William—"

"I am sorry, Katie," William said. "And you don't have to try to brush this off or try to make me feel better. I should have been honest with you from the very beginning. I should have told you things instead of keeping them from you. If I had, you might have trusted me. And then you wouldn't have felt so alone."

He took my hand. "Let me help you with this, Katie. Please."

I felt something slipping away from me then—a terrible weight was gone.

For a long moment, I couldn't say anything—the feeling was too great.

"Katie, say something," William said. "You're making me nervous."

"You can help me," I said at last.

William smiled, and I realized that I hadn't seen that in a long time.

In the next moment, he pulled me into his arms, and I hugged him back fiercely.

I felt, somehow, as if I had come home.

"So what's the plan?" William said.

"Well, Sachiko and I are here because vampires have been disappearing, and there seems to be a link between the disappearances and activity that the Order noticed at the Temple of the Moon."

"You told me about that," William said. "Why would that bring you to Zamochit?"

"Because I want to find out what's going on at the temple," I said. "But I don't know where it is. Sachiko and I thought we might be able to search the archives in the Vaults to find the location of the temple. If we can find the temple and figure out who or what is causing the disappearances, maybe we can find Veronika's mysterious ghost girl."

"Okay. So that makes sense now," William said. "I saw you go into Zamochit, and I assumed that you were heading to Veronika's house. When you turned away from it and headed toward the castle, I was puzzled."

"Why were you following us?" I said. "Why didn't you just let me know you were here?"

William looked sheepish. "I'm not sure. When I first realized you were gone, I was just frantic to find you. And after seeing Sachiko's name in your phone, I knew you had probably gone off with her. I waited out by the Wasteland, figuring you would come to Zamochit eventually to see Veronika. Then you and Sachiko did indeed show up, and then I didn't know what to do after that. I figured if I followed you, that the right opportunity would present itself. And it did—sort of."

He thought for a moment.

"How are you going to get into the Vaults?"

"Sachiko got me in once before," I said. "And she's going to help me get in this time too."

"I'd like to go with you," William said. "If I may. I can help you look through the archives. I assume that what you're looking for isn't just going to jump right out at you."

"I'd like that," I said.

William gave me a serious look. "I'd like you to help me with something too. The Vaults come first—absolutely. But afterward, I'd like you to come with me somewhere."

"Where?" I said.

"To the Black Tomb," William said. "I want to try one last time to look for the sword there."

"William," I said. My head was swimming—suddenly there were vampire tombs all over the place.

"I know," he said. "I mentioned this before, and you thought it was crazy. But just hear me out."

"William, you almost—"

"I know," he said. "I haven't forgotten. Please just listen."

"You have come a long way for me," I said. "I suppose the least I can do is hear what you have to say."

"Thanks," William said. He gave me his small, crooked smile. Then he paused as if gathering himself.

"I believe in the sword," William said at last. "I believe Ignis Sacer is a real thing, and I believe that with all my being. I know everyone says it's just a legend, but I know it's out there—and it's the one thing that can defeat the Werdulac."

"Even if the sword is real," I said, "it's only a rumor that it's in that tomb at all—and it was a false rumor specifically set up to trick you."

"But what if the rumor wasn't false?" William said. "What if it's really in there? I have a feeling about that place—that I saw something. I have to know what it is."

"But William, the tomb is the home of an ancient and powerful vampire," I said. "You know that—he attacked you. And presumably he's still in there. What if you don't survive this time?"

"But that's just it," William said. "This time you'll be with me—I won't be alone. We can watch out for each other."

"What makes you think the two of us can handle this vampire—even together?" I said. "I appreciate your confidence in me. But what good am I against an ancient vampire? I don't even have the clear fire anymore—and as far as I know, that was never any use against vampires."

William frowned. "I'm not sure that you need any special powers for this. I have a feeling that the vampire can be—reasoned with. All I need is someone smart and perceptive to help me keep an eye out—someone who can warn me if danger approaches."

"I don't know, William," I said. "It sounds like an awfully big risk for something we don't even know is there. And the risk itself is very real—we know for a fact that that vampire is real."

"Promise me you'll at least think about it," William said. "As crazy as it may sound, this means a lot to me. And I would really like to have you there with me."

"I don't know if I can even consider it," I said.

"Well, think about it this way," William said. "The Queen of the Moon is the Werdulac's sorceress, right? What if she's revived? What if she's working for the Werdulac, and this is all part of a bigger plan? How are we going to stop her?"

"I don't know," I said.

"With the sword we would have a chance against her," William said.

"Maybe," I said. "I'll think about it. And let's see what we find at the Vaults first."

"Yes, of course," William said. "Vaults first. Just think about it."

"I guess we should be going," I said.

I went to the door and opened it, and William followed me.

I had expected to find Anton standing outside, listening in on our conversation, but neither he nor Sachiko were anywhere in sight.

William and I went down the spiraling staircase to the level below, but no one was there either.

We continued down to the ground floor, and we found Sachiko and Anton in a very grand front parlor. Sachiko was looking out the window, and Anton was sitting at a piano plunking at a few keys.

"Sachiko made me come down here," Anton said, as we came into the room. "She said she didn't want me eavesdropping. She even told me to play this piano so I wouldn't overhear anything accidentally."

"Actually, I said that was annoying," Sachiko said, not taking her eyes off the window. "So are we ready to leave? Because the owners of this house could come back at any minute."

"Yes," I said. "And William's coming with us. He can help us search through the archives."

"What about me?" Anton said, getting up from the piano. "I want to go too."

"We're going to the Vaults," I said. "We're going to look through the archives to see if we can find where the Temple of the Moon is. I don't know if that's your kind of thing."

"Actually, I would like to have a look at the Vaults myself," Anton said. "Specifically, the inventory, which I believe is housed in the archives. I'd like to find out about the missing key that Innokenti wouldn't let me investigate."

Sachiko looked away from the window. "Missing key?"

"Oh, that's right," Anton said. "You weren't there for that conversation. After we had the earthquakes here and then the petty thefts started, I had the brilliant idea to check the Vaults to see if anything was missing—and something was—a key."

Sachiko frowned. "What kind of key?"

"I don't know," Anton said. "Innokenti stopped me from looking it up. But I would like to find out."

"That's actually very interesting," Sachiko said. "I wouldn't mind finding out about that myself."

"See?" Anton said. "I'm full of surprises. I'd say we're lucky to have me along."

"Okay," I said. "Let's get going."

"Follow me," Sachiko said. "I know the best way to get into the castle without being seen."

Sachiko stepped out of the house and slipped into the shadow cast by its tall tower in the silver light. I followed her, and William and Anton followed behind me.

Sachiko led us in a wide arc around the castle, and we stopped in the shadow of another towering mansion.

"So I've had a thought," Anton said as we paused for a moment.

"I suppose you think you know a better way into the castle?" Sachiko said.

"Well, yes," Anton replied. "But we'll get to that in just a moment. What I was thinking about were the petty thefts that coincided with the earthquakes here. I suggested that there was a connection, but that suggestion was rudely brushed aside."

"I never brushed that aside," Sachiko said. "I've never even heard you say it before."

"I know *you* didn't," Anton said. "But someone here did."

"Fine," William said. "Tell us your theory about the thefts. But do it quickly. We're a little busy at the moment."

"It's just like it was in Elspeth's Grove," Anton said. "With the earthquakes."

"There weren't any petty thefts in Elspeth's Grove," William said.

"I know," Anton replied. "That's because they weren't necessary. There was a full-scale mining operation there already."

"And your point is?" William said.

"My point is, the petty thefts involved rope, tools, and a wheelbarrow."

"I don't get it," William said.

"What happened every time there was an earthquake?" Anton said, turning to me.

"There was mist afterward," I said. "Mist only I could see."

"And where was that mist coming from?" Anton said.

"From the cave," I said. "Oh, I see what you mean. When we were down there, we saw—"

"*You* saw," Anton amended.

"I saw the mist rolling through the tunnels, and then the mist woke the vampires up."

William frowned. "And what does that mean?"

"It means there are tunnels here too," I said. "If there are earthquakes, that means there's mist. And if there's mist, it needs some place to flow through. The tools were taken to do the digging."

"Exactly," Anton said.

"So what were they digging out?" William said. "Just tunnels? Or is there another cave full of frozen vampires around here?

"Who knows?" Anton said. "But I suggest we keep an eye out. If we find any dusty vampires, we'll know what they've been up to."

"Okay," Sachiko said. "We'll be alert for dusty vampires. In the meantime, we've got to get into that castle. So I suggest we get moving again."

"About that," Anton said.

"Yes?" Sachiko said.

"I assume you're leading us around the back so that we can go in the way the trash comes out?"

"Why not?" Sachiko said. "It's worked for me before."

"It's a decent plan," Anton said. "But I have a better one."

"And what's that?" Sachiko said.

"I propose we go in through the library."

"The library?"

"You do know about the library, don't you?" Anton said. "I thought you knew all about the castle."

"I know about the library," Sachiko said.

"And you know the library is separate from the archives, right? I wouldn't want you to get confused."

"I know that," Sachiko said impatiently. "I also know there's no entrance to the library from outside. You have to be inside the castle already to get in. There's only one door."

"That may have been true once," Anton said. "But there's a way in now. The library crowd is clever. They've figured out a way to get in without going through security. Add to that the fact that many of them aren't allowed in at all because they aren't members of the court, and you've created a situation in which people are going to get creative."

"I don't see how that would work," Sachiko said. "Unless somebody actually carved a hole in a stone wall."

"That's actually kind of what it is," Anton said. "Trust me, I know it's there. I've used it myself when I wanted to get in without being seen."

He started forward. "Come on. It's this way."

Anton continued leading us around the back of the castle. We went out past the back entrance and then on beyond the carriage houses and storehouses.

Eventually, he led us all the way out to a short, round stone tower that was sitting all by itself at a fair distance from the others.

"This is just another storehouse," Sachiko said when we reached it.

"Correction," Anton said. "This is the storehouse for the library. You can see its importance relative to the other storehouses in its distance. And it's our way in—keeping us far away from guards and other suspicious onlookers."

"I don't see it," Sachiko said.

"Just wait," Anton said.

He walked around to the back of the storehouse, and we followed him.

"It's right here," he said.

Anton walked up to the storehouse, turned a little to the side, and then seemed to disappear into the wall.

"Is it another illusion?" I said.

"Yes," Anton's voice replied. "But it's not the magic kind—it's just an ordinary, physical optical illusion. Just come over—you'll see."

I stepped forward. The wall appeared to be solid at first, but as I got closer, I could see that there was an opening in the outer wall, and it actually wrapped around an inner wall, sort of like a snail shell. From a distance, the wall appeared to be all one piece—it was only up close that you could actually see the break.

Anton was standing in the alcove that was created by the outer wall.

"See?" he said. "The gray stone of the outer wall just looks like the gray stone of the inner wall. You can't tell the difference from far away. I don't know how long ago this was done, but whoever did it did a good job."

"How did you find it?" I said.

"I've told you before that I have sharp eyes," Anton replied.

William and Sachiko came up to stand beside me.

Sachiko ran a hand over the stone edges of the outer wall. "I have to admit this is actually pretty cool."

"Can we keep moving?" William said. "I don't think it's a good idea for us to be standing around like this."

"Relax," Anton said. "I didn't see any guards around, did you?"

"No," William said. "And that's a little worrying. Even if things are as lax as you've said."

"Don't worry," Anton said. "Like I said, I've been this way before. All we have to do is go through the library and then out into the castle. All those people reading in there probably won't even look up."

Anton led us along the outer wall to a break in the inner wall. Several columns of stones had been pulled out to form a space just wide enough for a person to slip through, and the new, false outer wall grew from the far side of the broken wall.

Anton walked up to the space in the wall and wriggled through it.

"This way," he said.

Inside the break was a small stone room, and as I stepped into it, I could see piles of books lying in heaps on the ground and a discarded library cart. The room was lit with a faint, silvery light, and I could see a stone staircase leading downward on the other side of the room.

Anton led us down the steps, and the floor before us slanted down into a tunnel that quickly leveled off. The tunnel was narrow, but it was lined with piles of books, broken shelves, and other odds and ends.

"Do all of these storehouses have tunnels that lead into the castle?" I said.

"Some do, some don't," Anton replied. "I'm not sure what the reasoning is behind which ones got one and which ones didn't. It's a little haphazard—like everything else in this village."

The tunnel soon slanted upward again, and before us was another set of steps, this time leading up to a door.

Anton hopped up the steps and pushed on the door, which opened inward.

"Wait just a second," he said. "I'll step in and make sure we're clear to go on."

Anton disappeared for a moment and then returned.

"Okay," he said. "It's clear. In fact, it's more than clear. You could even say it's wide open."

Puzzled, I followed Anton up the stairs and through the door.

William and Sachiko followed close behind me.

On the other side of the door was a small room piled with books that appeared to be another storage room. Anton led us through the room and out into the library.

We stepped into a large room with tables and chairs and shelves full of books. There was a large, ornate desk with an equally ornate chair that sat in a prominent space in the room and somehow gave the impression of being a librarian's desk. Beyond that were closed doors that might have led to private reading rooms.

"It looks just like a regular library," I said.

"It is just like a regular library," Anton replied. "It's just vampires happen to use it. I'll tell you what is strange, though."

"There's nobody here," Sachiko said.

"Exactly," Anton replied. "It's the middle of the night. Prime hours for this place."

"Maybe we just got lucky," William said. "We should keep moving."

"Like I said—relax," Anton said. "We'll just act like we've got business here and not like we're in a hurry. Besides, the archives aren't a priority for the guards. We should be able to get in and out with no trouble."

"I hope you're right," William said.

Anton led us out of the library and into the hall. The hall, like the library, was filled with the same silvery light that was found throughout Zamochit Village. The only difference was the light was just a little bit brighter in the castle—I knew that from previous experience.

As we stepped out into the hall, Sachiko stopped.

"What's that sound?" she said.

William and Anton both stopped and looked up as if listening.

"What? That sound like chimes?" Anton said. "Who cares?"

"What if it's an alarm?" Sachiko said. "What if somebody knows we're here?"

"It's not an alarm," Anton said. "I know this castle's security systems well enough, having defended it on more than one occasion. We don't have any alarms like that."

"I don't hear anything," I said.

"It's possible that it's pitched only for vampire hearing," William said. "But Anton is correct. It doesn't sound like any of the alarms this castle has."

"Well, we should stay alert," Sachiko said. "Whether it's an alarm or not, it's not normal."

"That's true enough," Anton said. "If they played these chimes all the time that would probably drive everyone crazy."

He started off down the hall.

"Where are you going?" Sachiko hissed. "The entrance to the archives is this way."

"I know," Anton said. "We're not going in that way. There's an entrance for the people who work there down this way. That's how I got in to look around last time."

"But didn't you get caught last time?" I said. "You said you were interrupted when you tried to look around."

"Yes," Anton said. "But last time I spent most of the time looking for the inventory. This time I know exactly where it is. Like I said, we'll get in and get out. And then we'll be gone."

Anton led us through the silver-lit halls to a small door at the end of a long corridor. We met no one on the way.

"Here we are," Anton said. "The staff entrance."

"Don't you think it's a little strange that we haven't seen anyone yet?" Sachiko said.

"Not worrying about it," Anton replied.

"And how are you going to get in?" William said. "I very much doubt that they leave the door open."

"I happen to have a key," Anton said, producing a card. "I took it with me when I left. With any luck, no one's thought to deactivate it."

He swiped the card over a little black panel next to the door.

A small click signified that the door was now unlocked, and Anton pushed it open.

"See?" he said. "I knew it would work."

"How long has the castle had a key card system?" I said.

"Not long," Anton replied. "It was an innovation of Innokenti's, actually. And it's only in a few places—it was something he wanted for the most secure areas first."

He ushered us all inside and then closed the door behind us.

I looked around. We were standing in a long, narrow room, lined with desks and tables. At the end of the room was a door.

"This way," Anton said.

He led us into a large, cavernous room that was noticeably dimmer than the other rooms we'd been through.

Fast footsteps approached us.

"You again!" hissed a voice.

Chapter Fourteen

I looked around. In the dim light, I could see a tall girl with glasses and glossy brown hair.

"This time you're really in trouble," the girl said. "This time you're going to the dungeons."

"Grace!" Anton said, smiling. "So good to see you again."

Footsteps came running into the room from behind us.

I turned to see a castle guard running up to us.

"Grace," the guard said, "the halls are clear now. We can—"

He stopped.

"Well, that was quick," Anton said. "How did you get here so fast?"

He looked around. "That sound really is an alarm, isn't it?"

I looked from the vampire girl to the guard and back again. I knew a thing or two about clandestine meetings.

"You're not here for us, are you?" I said to the guard.

"How do you figure that?" Anton said.

"For a start," I said, "he hasn't brought a weapon with him."

Anton glanced at the guard. "You're right."

I looked at the vampire girl. "Grace, was it? You two planned to meet up here, didn't you? And that alarm everyone's talking about— you set that on purpose."

Grace and the guard exchanged looks.

"I get it," Anton said, smirking. "Have we interrupted something?"

"I don't think that's quite what it is," I said. I turned to Grace. "We might have more in common than you think. We're not here to do anything wrong—we don't want to take anything. We just want to find out a few things. And I have a feeling you might want something similar."

Grace hesitated. "I did set off the alarm. It's the fire alarm. It was just recently installed."

"Maybe if we tell you why we're here," I said, "and you tell us why you're here, we'll see if we might have something in common. You guys both look like you're worried. Maybe we can help each other."

"Innokenti wouldn't like it," Grace said. She glanced at Anton. "He really wouldn't like it if he knew you were here. He ordered you not to return."

"Innokenti doesn't have to know," Anton said. "And I imagine he's out of the castle at the moment anyway. Besides he's not king of this place."

"He's not king yet," the guard said. "But everyone knows that's what he wants."

"See?" Anton said. "That's what I've been saying. The guy's not safe, and we have to look out for ourselves."

Grace glanced at William. "You—I know. You're William Sursur."

Then she glanced at me. "And you—you're human. What are you doing here?"

"Yes, I'm human," I said. "I'm risking my life in coming here to this castle. But I'm here for something that matters to me. Something that's more important even than my life."

Grace looked over at the guard. "I think we should at least hear what they have to say. What do you think, Dmitry?"

"I think anyone who is against Innokenti is a friend of mine," Dmitry said. "I'm happy to hear them out."

"All right," Grace said. "But we'd better move quickly. The rendezvous point for the fire alarm is just outside the front gate for the court. They won't be gone long."

Grace motioned us forward and led us through the vast, dark room that we'd found ourselves in.

"This way," she said. "We'll talk in here."

As we hurried through the room, I could vaguely see row after row of shelves stretching all the way up into the darkness. The shelves were filled with boxes.

"These are all the old files," Grace said. "And this is the old system. What we want is in the new system."

She led us quickly through the vast room to a door on the far side.

"Those are nice earrings, by the way," Anton said to Grace, as we paused by the door. "Are they antiques?"

I glanced over at Grace. She was wearing a pair of small, gold earrings in the shape of birds.

Grace looked uncomfortable. "Yes—they are."

Anton smirked. "Borrowed them from the collection, did you?"

"We don't have time to discuss that now," Grace said, producing a key ring that had a number of objects on it.

The door in front of us had an electronic lock just like the one on the outermost door, and Grace swiped us in with a card.

"This is why we had to come here during a fire alarm," Grace said. "Innokenti gets a notification in his office when this door is opened—and it also tells him who did it. We had to come in here while he was out of the castle."

She led us into a room filled with glass cases and closed the door behind us.

If anything, this room was even darker than the room we had just left.

"What is this place?" I said.

"This room houses the oldest part of our collection," Grace said. "Innokenti had this room constructed to protect it. The room and the cases are climate-controlled, and the light is low to help cut down on any further photo aging. The manuscripts in here are very, very old."

"Innokenti also set it up to restrict access," Dmitry said. "This way no one gets in or out without his knowledge."

Grace moved to one of the glass cases and opened it with a key from her key ring.

"You four can talk while we look," she said. "And make it quick."

"We want to know how to find the Temple of the Moon," William said.

Grace looked up at him sharply.

"We'd also like to get a look at the inventory for the Vaults," Anton said. "Something's missing, and I'd like to know more about it."

Grace glanced over at him. "Well, that second part's easy enough. I'm the chief archivist, and keeping the inventory of the Vaults is part of my duties. What's missing is a key."

"That part I know already," Anton said. "I was able to figure that out before I was rudely interrupted. A key was listed as missing, but its function was apparently kept in another document. I had to cross-reference some number to figure out what it was."

"As I was saying," Grace said, "I know what it is. The key leads to the Black Tomb."

"The Black Tomb?" William said.

"Yes," Grace replied. "It's been missing for months now."

"Hold on," Anton said. "Months? Didn't it go missing recently? Wasn't it one of the objects that was stolen during the earthquakes?"

"No," Grace said firmly. "I know what's in the collection and what isn't. The key to the Black Tomb went missing at the end of April."

I looked up sharply. "What does it look like?" I said.

Grace seemed puzzled. "The key?"

"Yes," I said. "I have a feeling it doesn't look like an ordinary key."

Grace put down the box she'd removed from the glass case and turned to a nearby shelf. She pulled down a large binder.

"I'll have that for you in just a moment," she said.

Grace flipped through the binder and ran her finger down the entries.

"Here it is," she said. "Lot 577351. Key to the Black Tomb."

She frowned. "It's described as a smooth, black rock shot through with bands of white."

I pulled the rock that William had given me out of my pocket.

"Do you think this fits the description?" I said.

Grace stared at the stone in my hand. "Yes, that's it. The Black Tomb isn't really my area of expertise, but it's made of onyx, and so is this stone from the looks of it. That would make sense—they would both have the same special properties."

"What properties are those?" William said.

"Black stones in general and onyx in particular are said to have powerful protective powers," Grace said. "They promote positive energy and block out negative energy."

"What do you mean by 'negative energy'?" Sachiko said.

"Well, I suppose you could call it 'evil,'" Grace said. "Onyx has the ability to ward off evil spirits—and also the ability to keep evil in. That's why it's so effective when used as a prison."

"A prison?" I said.

Grace nodded. "That's what the Black Tomb is. An ordinary tomb for an esteemed vampire is constructed after he dies his final death. But the vampire in that tomb was placed there while he was still alive to contain him. He was so powerful and so terrible that even other vampires feared him."

"Who is he?" William said.

"No one knows," Grace said. "His name has been lost over the centuries—as has the record of his crimes. But the memory that remains is a strong one."

"What is the memory?" William said.

"Fear," Grace said. "We all remember to be afraid of him. Anyone who lives here knows that."

"And yet somehow you had possession of this key," Anton said to William. "And you found your way inside. Do you remember who gave it to you?"

"No," William said.

"One guess as to who it was," Anton said. "It was the same person who wouldn't let me look through the inventory—it was Innokenti."

"You don't know that," William said.

"I don't know why you refuse to believe it," Anton said. "Someone at this castle set you up to go in there and get attacked—and he's the obvious person to have done it."

"You don't know that someone set me up," William said.

Anton turned to Grace.

"Does Innokenti have the authority to remove artifacts from the Vaults?" he said.

"Yes," she replied.

"Who else has the authority?" Anton asked. "Do you?"

"Well, no—not exactly," Grace said. "I can remove objects from their containers to study or restore them—all the archivists and historians can do that. But I can't actually remove anything from the Vaults or the archives. I have to do my work within these walls."

"But Innokenti can remove them?"

"Yes," Grace said.

"Who else?" Anton said. "The king? The queen?"

"Of course, in theory, the king and queen would have access to anything that they wished in the Vaults," Grace said. "But in actual practice, they would have to go to Innokenti to get permission. He's in charge of what goes in and out. Anyone who wants to remove anything has to apply to him."

"So if someone were to have an artifact in their possession," Anton said. "Say, this key for example, then they would have to have gone through Innokenti to get it."

"Yes—under ordinary circumstances," Grace said. "But the key is an aberration. Innokenti knew it was missing. The Vaults were attacked earlier this year by a member of the Order of the Hawthorne. He is known to have taken a sword—the Star of Morning—out of the collection. It is assumed that he took the key at the same time."

"An assumption that is incorrect," Anton said. "William got into the tomb before the Vaults were attacked. He went into the Black Tomb and got bitten before that Hawthorne guy ever got here."

He turned to William. "You may not remember that, but it's true."

Dmitry smirked at William. "What were you doing in the Black Tomb? Everyone knows it's dangerous to go there."

"William was looking for Ignis Sacer—the famous sword," Anton said. "Needless to say, he didn't find it."

"The Black Tomb is believed to hold a treasure horde of great significance," Grace said with dignity. "I would not be at all surprised to find artifacts of great value in there."

"It's believed," Anton said. "But do you know that?"

"No," Grace said. "No archeologist who has ever gone in has come out again."

"This is all very interesting," Sachiko said. "But we're here about the Temple of the Moon. Can you tell us where it is?"

"Grace can tell us," Dmitry said. "That's why I'm here too."

"Why do you need to know?" Anton asked.

"Because of what I've seen," Dmitry replied.

Grace closed the ledger and returned to the box she'd removed earlier.

"I know I can find it," she said. She opened the box and put on a pair of gloves. Then she picked up a pair of tweezers and began to sift through the papers contained within the box very carefully.

"So what have you seen?" Anton said to Dmitry.

"Shhh!" Grace hissed. "It took me a long time to narrow my search down to this box, and I need a few minutes of quiet. A lot of this stuff isn't in Russian or in any other modern language."

"I don't see why that should—" Anton began.

"Shhh!" Grace said. "We don't have a lot of time. And we've already wasted some of it talking about the key."

She returned to her work.

A moment later, she held out a hand.

"Dmitry," she said. "There's a magnifying glass on the table over there. Bring it to me."

Dmitry glanced around. "I don't see—"

"It has a metal stand with it," Grace said impatiently. "It's bigger than a regular magnifying glass."

"Oh, I see it," Dmitry said. He picked up a metal stand that had a square of glass in a metal frame attached to it.

He brought it to Grace, and she positioned it over the scrap of paper she was examining.

"I've found it!" she said. "It's faint, but I can read the writing. Come and see!"

William, Sachiko, and I each took a quick turn looking at the scrap of paper under the magnifying glass. In the dim light, I could see a map—the shape appeared to be the Black Sea. There were a number of tiny dots in the sea that I assumed were islands, and there was writing above and below the islands in a language that I didn't recognize.

"That's it!" Grace said excitedly. "That's the island her temple is on."

Anton had his turn at looking through the magnifying glass.

"I don't see how you can figure out anything on here."

"The island is quite clearly marked," Grace said. "It says, 'The Moon's Temple.' It's in the Black Sea close to the Russian coast."

Anton stepped back. "Well, that *is* the Black Sea. But I don't see anything like longitude or latitude on there. How are we going to find it? Just set out in a boat?"

"As I said—" Grace began.

"Yeah, I know," Anton said. "Close to the Russian coast. But this map isn't to scale, I'm assuming? And I'm also assuming that this map is at least a few centuries old—"

"It's a good deal older than that," Grace said.

"My point exactly," Anton said. "How are we going to find the island? And who knows if it's even still there?"

"That's not the only problem," Dmitry said. "The island itself is surrounded by protective spells—just like this village is. You can't see the island from the outside."

"Then what good is this going to do?" Anton said.

"I didn't come here to find an exact location," Grace said. "I came here to prove that the island exists."

"Was that in doubt?" Anton said.

"Yes," Grace replied. "Now we really should get out of here."

"Where are we going?" I said.

"To the Vaults," Grace said.

She led us out of the archives the same way we had come in. Then she led us through the silvery halls to a section that I recognized from my last trip—and at the end of it were the tall double doors that led into the Vaults.

There were no guards at the doors.

"Come on, quickly," Grace said. She hurried up to the doors and selected a big iron key from her key ring. Then she pushed it into the ornate lock and turned it.

She pulled one of the heavy doors open. "Come on."

"You guys go ahead," Sachiko said. "I'll stay here and watch for the guards. If they come back, I'll lead them away."

William stopped. "Are you sure you'll be okay?"

"I'll be fine," Sachiko said. "I'm very, very fast. They'll never catch me. Go on. I'll find you guys later if I need to."

"Trust me," I said to William. "Sachiko knows what she's doing."

The rest of us went into the Vaults along with Grace.

The Vaults were dimmer than the rest of the castle, just as the archives had been, and in front of us stretched a long, dark hall that was lined on one side by closed doors.

I knew from my last visit that behind the closed doors were "treasures"—or artifacts that were of great age and could be considered valuable—but also had the potential to be weapons. There were books, paintings, mirrors—and even quite a few actual weapons.

Grace led us to one of the doors and unlocked it.

"I believe we'll find what we need in here," she said. "Luckily, I'm one of the few people who can read it."

"Wait, so why doesn't it matter that we can't find the island?" Anton said.

"The king is trying to convince everyone that the Queen of the Moon is an imaginary threat," Dmitry said. "That the island is not real. No doubt under advice from Innokenti. But the rumors are everywhere. People are disappearing—even more than before. And the Queen of the Moon is behind it."

"How do you know the Queen of the Moon is behind it?" I said.

"Because her servant, the Acolyte, brags about it," Dmitry said. "She says the Queen is building an army, and she is looking for all of us to join."

He gave me a suspicious look. "How do you know about it?"

"Because of the Order of the Hawthorne," I said. "They said they've been watching the temple, and there's activity there."

"Aha!" Grace said, opening a wooden chest. "So someone does know where it is! In that case, it doesn't matter that the map didn't give us an exact location."

"Yes, but you didn't know that," Anton said.

"As I already stated," Grace said, "I was just trying to prove—to myself—that the island with the temple existed. And that fragment confirmed it—it's from an unimpeachable source. It's from an ancient book that is now lost to the ages."

"But—"

Grace began to pull tapestries out of the chest. "It didn't matter because I just had to prove it was there. Then finding it will be our next problem."

She rummaged through the tapestries, and, apparently not finding what she was looking for, she quickly rolled them up and put them back in the box.

"So is that what you're looking for here?" Anton said. "A map?"

"No," Grace said. "I'm looking for a way to stop her."

She opened another chest and began to pull out more rolled-up tapestries.

"Stop her?" I said.

"She's the one who's kidnapping people," Dmitry said. "She's doing it through her servant, the Acolyte."

"How do you know that?" William said.

"I've seen the disappearances myself," Dmitry said. "Vampires who disappeared right before my eyes."

"We've seen that too," Anton said. "That doesn't mean the Queen of the Moon is behind it."

"That one vampire did actually mention her," I said. "And the Acolyte."

"I'm trying to maintain a healthy skepticism here," Anton said. "I know what we know. I want to know what Dmitry knows."

Dmitry looked over at me. "The young human girl speaks the truth. One of the vampires who disappeared spoke her name. And there are whispers, rumors everywhere—"

Anton shook his head. "I'm not interested in whispers or rumors. What proof do you have?"

Dmitry drew himself up. "I have the word of Copper. He himself was taken prisoner and managed to escape. He told me what he saw."

"Copper?" Anton said. "What kind of a name is that?"

"Copper is one of the finest vampires I know," Dmitry said. "He's as good a warrior as you are, and I'll not hear a word against him."

"All right, all right," Anton said. "So this paragon Copper, what was his story?"

"He found himself on an island," Dmitry said. "He didn't know how he got there. But there were thousands and thousands of vampires there. And there was a woman—she called herself the Acolyte. She had control over a substance she called 'essence.'"

"And what's that exactly?" Anton said.

"It's a power she used," Dmitry said. "She could call it forth and use it on anybody she chose. She could bring people to her, and she could make them do what she wanted. And she could also revive long-deceased vampires."

"Technically, all vampires are deceased," Anton said.

"No," Dmitry said, "I mean the ones who are really gone—the ones who have turned to dust. Copper saw a box full of dust turned back into a vital, solid vampire."

"So that's how it's happening," I said. "We saw an entire cave full of vampires who were supposed to be just ashes wake up and then disappear."

Dmitry nodded. "That's exactly what Copper said. The Acolyte is working on orders from the Queen of the Moon, who is not yet free. She is using the essence, and with it, they can revive any vampire they want."

"Why would they want to do that?" William said grimly.

"To revive the army," Dmitry said. "To revive *his* army. It's all in the service of the Werdulac. They want to revive the entire army he originally went to war with."

"What about the Werdulac himself?" William said. "Can this essence be used to revive him too?"

"The way I hear it, he doesn't want that," Dmitry replied. "The essence takes over you completely. You have no will—you only do what the Acolyte tells you to do. The Werdulac would never want that—neither would the Queen of the Moon. They are both working on reviving and freeing themselves on their own. The Queen won't give up control to anyone, and neither will the Werdulac."

"So what are the kidnapped vampires for?" I said. "Are they part of the army too?"

"Could be," Dmitry said. "I think they'll be used that way in the future—probably they'll be the first ones sent in in any skirmish. But right now—they're doing all the work. They're excavating the Queen's temple—they're going to pull her up out of her tomb."

"Which is why we have to stop her," Grace said. "It's why we have to stop them all."

Grace had continued to look through the chests in the room. She stood now with her hands on her hips and surveyed the room.

"Does Copper know how to get to the island?" I said.

Dmitry shook his head. "Unfortunately, no. He was just summoned there by the essence, so he didn't see how he arrived. And he doesn't know how he left. He just woke up on a field with his friend lying on the ground beside him. His friend never woke up—and not long after he crumbled to dust. Copper figures the friend got him out."

"We'll worry about getting to the island once we find out how to stop her," Grace said. She looked around the room in frustration. "What we're looking for isn't in here. We need to move on."

"I thought you were the chief archivist," Anton said. "Don't you know where everything is?"

"I am the chief archivist," Grace replied. "But that doesn't mean that I know where every artifact is off the top of my head. And I'm not chief of the Vaults. Most of this stuff is available to me, but some of it is off limits to me—that's mostly the special section—the weapons and the most dangerous items."

She thought for a minute. "It's very possible that what we need is in there."

"So let's go break the door down," Anton said.

"I don't think we can," Grace said.

She looked down at her key ring, which also held the card she had swiped in the archives.

"I don't have the key that opens the room we need," she said. "But that room has also been upgraded to include an electronic lock. I wonder if I have access."

Grace hurried to the door. "Come on. Only one way to find out."

She ushered all of us out of the room and locked it behind us.

Then she took off down the hall.

William took my hand, and then he and I flew down the hall after her, with Anton and Dmitry following us.

We went down a flight of stairs and then stood before another large, imposing door.

Grace got out her key card and swiped it over the panel by the door.

I heard a click as the electronic lock opened.

"Well, that was easy," Anton said.

"This wasn't the door I was worried about," Grace replied.

She led us inside and down another hall.

Then she stopped before another door that was somehow more imposing than the others had been.

"This is the door I was worried about," Grace said. "This is the weapons vault."

I looked around. Even in the dim light, I could tell that the place looked familiar.

"This is the vault the Star of Morning was stolen from," I said.

Grace gave me a strange look. "Yes. How do you know that?"

"Everybody knows the Star of Morning was stolen," Anton said quickly. "It's no great stretch to figure out it was taken from the weapons vault."

"Yes—that's true," Grace said.

She gave me one last look and then turned to the panel by the door. After a moment's hesitation, she got out her key card and swiped it over the panel.

For a moment, nothing happened—there was no click from the electronic lock on the door.

Then a moment later, a small light over the panel lit up green.

The door in front of us opened silently of its own accord.

Anton examined the door as it swung open. "That is a pretty jazzy door. They spared no expense for that one."

We stepped inside, and I found myself standing in a room full of weapons—swords, spears, axes, daggers, and knives—and a number of implements that I didn't have a name for. I had been in this room once before, and the last time I had seen it, it had been in complete disarray—Terrance had taken the Star of Morning from the room and had left the place in shambles. Now, everything was stowed away in its proper place.

"After the break-in several months ago," Grace said, "and the theft of some very valuable artifacts, Innokenti had this new system installed for greater security. It's much harder for people to break into, and there is also a record now of everyone who goes in and out."

"Congratulations," Anton said. "You got us in."

"This still isn't what we're looking for," Grace said.

She led us to the center of the room and a wide circle that was set into the floor.

Oddly, there was a panel set next to the circle that was just like the panel next to the door.

"This is it," Grace said.

"You want to climb into the basement?" Anton said.

"We're already in the basement," Grace said. "This is a level below that. I really don't know if I have access to go down here. But I'm hoping if I got through the other layers of security, that I'll have permission here too."

She swiped her card over the panel, and after a moment, the light above the panel lit up in green just as it had for the outer door.

The circle in the floor slid away to reveal darkness underneath.

"There should be a staircase in here," Grace said.

She sat on the edge of the circle and dipped an experimental toe down into the darkness.

Grace seemed to find her footing, and then she began to descend what appeared to be a spiral staircase.

The rest of us followed her.

The staircase was pitch black to me, and the only light I had was what came from the circle above. As we continued down the staircase, even that light faded away, and I was left in darkness.

William took my hand and helped me as we continued on down the stairs.

Eventually, we reached what felt like solid ground.

"I can't see a thing," I whispered.

"Neither can we," Anton said. "Or at least, neither can I. I have to assume you guys are in the same boat as me."

"I'm not surprised it's so dark," Grace said. "Or that this is so far down. The objects in here are sensitive to light. It's best to keep them in the dark so they don't wake up."

"I have a flashlight," I said.

I reached into my pocket and pulled out my key ring with its tiny flashlight.

I switched it on.

A little pool of light appeared around me. I couldn't see anything beyond it except for William, who was standing beside me.

"Thank you," Grace said. "But we won't need it. There should be lights in here. People do have to come in occasionally."

I heard a soft sound as she moved away.

"Actually, maybe we do need it," Grace said after a moment. "There should be lights in here, but I can't seem to find them. May I borrow that?"

I held my little flashlight out, and moments later, it was lifted out of my hands.

I watched as the light danced around the room.

After a moment, the light stopped moving, and soon after, the room was suffused with a soft, silvery light.

It was very faint—just as it had been inside the archives.

Grace gave the flashlight back to me.

"I need to hurry," she said. "It's not safe to keep the lights on too long."

"So what are you looking for?" Anton said.

"A tapestry," Grace replied. "I think I see it."

She hurried to the other end of what I could now see was a small, round room.

The rest of us followed her.

Grace stopped in front of a thick, heavy piece of faded gold cloth that hung on the wall. A glass case was affixed around the cloth.

She leaned on the glass. "The writing is really faint. I wish I could remove the glass, but it's there to protect the artifact from contact with the air. It's possible it would also protect us from it."

"What is it?" I asked.

"It's a Sídh tapestry," Grace said. "It's very, very old. It was captured during the ancient wars centuries ago by the humans. They didn't know what they had and how important it was, so we appropriated it. It was made in commemoration of the Sídh victory over the vampires, and it includes a memorialization of all of the most powerful ancient vampires and how they were defeated."

"Does it say anything about the Werdulac?" William said quickly.

"I've never read it myself," Grace said, adjusting her glasses, "but from what I've heard, it only mentions him obliquely. It says

232

something like 'the Great Vampire was sent to his doom by the mighty Sídh.' This tapestry wasn't meant to be an actual, historical document. It was done to celebrate a victory. The references to the defeated vampires are more poetic than factual, but they do have some kernels of truth to them. The Hunter, for example, was defeated when the Sídh 'called down the stars upon him.'"

Grace frowned and took off her glasses.

"I don't really need to wear these," she said. "But the truth is that I never could get used to not wearing them. In this case, I think they're getting in the way."

She stepped close to the glass case again and peered inside.

I looked at the tapestry too. All I could see was faded gold cloth.

"I don't see any writing," I said.

"It's faint," Grace said. "Very faint. But it's there—words woven in gold thread. And it's in the ancient Sídh language. There aren't many who can read it."

Grace was silent for a moment.

"There!" she said suddenly. "There's the part about the Hunter. The text about the Queen of the Moon shouldn't be too far away. They were similar cases."

Grace studied the tapestry intently.

"I see it," she said softly. "There's not much here. It says, 'The Moon was defeated by the dark star.' Then there's an image here of a square with a bunch of light rays around it. I think that could be her tomb within the temple."

"So what does that mean?" William said.

"At the moment, I'm not really sure," Grace replied. "I'll need some time to puzzle it out."

"What did you mean?" I said. "When you said the Hunter and the Queen were similar cases?"

"The Hunter and the Queen both had Sídh connections," Grace said. "So their burial after their defeat was handled differently. They were both allowed to remain near the light."

"I know about the Hunter," I said. "His wife was preserved by the Sídh, and he fought on their side against his brother. They buried him in a cave."

"Which was open to the light," Grace said. "From what I understand, there was a big opening at the top. And it was also one of the tombs we knew about—because we could see it. It was exposed to the surface. And the Queen's temple was exposed to the surface also—because she herself was part Sídh. I don't think they could bear to bury her in darkness."

"She was part Sídh?" I said.

Grace glanced at William. "Yes, she was. She was full Sídh to begin with. Then she was converted by a vampire, and her conversion was successful. She became a full vampire and lived on blood and everything. I think her conversion was aided by her own magic—it was a transformation she wanted. She became a vampire with Sídh blood—and she had the full strength of each. Apparently she was quite a formidable creature."

"What kind of magic did she have?" William asked.

"All Sídh have magic of a kind," Grace said. "At least by human and vampire standards—even if it's just making themselves appear and disappear as they please. And then the Queen, who was apparently talented even by Sídh standards, became a vampire and studied the arcane art of vampire magic, which often, though not always, involves the use of objects as a conduit. She became quite a powerful vampire sorceress. She was the chief magic-worker of the Werdulac, and it was said she was so powerful that she could even draw a soul out of its body."

"So you say the Queen's temple is out in the open," I said. "And the members of the Order say they've been keeping an eye on it, but at the same time, the king is saying it's not real. How can he say that if it's out in the open?"

"From what I understand," Grace said, "we used to monitor the island until about fifty years ago—and then, as Dmitry said, it disappeared. No one can see it anymore. It seems to me that that must have been the time when the Queen herself woke up. She probably used her powers to put up a barrier around the island, making it invisible. I believe it's similar to the one that is placed around this village—it selects who can get in and who will be kept out."

"But why would the king say it wasn't real if it was once known?" William asked.

"I don't know," Grace said. "It's just another reason we can't trust the court."

"Hey, guys," Anton said. "Come over here and look at this."

Grace, William, and I turned.

Anton and Dmitry were standing in front of a painting that had originally been draped in black cloth, and Anton was holding it aside. The painting was immense, but despite its great size, it was difficult for me to see what was depicted in it in the dim light.

I went closer.

Up close, I could see a knight in a gold suit of armor. He held a sword, and its blade was turned downward with its tip resting on what looked like a book.

I could dimly see that there was writing on the blade.

"What does it say?" I said.

"Ignis Sacer," Grace replied.

Chapter Fifteen

I t says what?" William said.

"That's Ignis Sacer," Grace said. "The 'holy fire' sword."

"I thought it wasn't real," Anton said.

"Well, this is just a painting," Grace replied. "It's only a picture of the sword. It's not the sword itself."

"I know that," Anton said. "But I thought there were no pictures of it. I thought no one had ever seen it."

"There is this painting," Grace said. "But not too many have ever seen it. Very few people are allowed in the most secure areas of the Vaults. And I've only seen this painting once before—it was in a different section then. This area hadn't been built yet."

"Are you sure this is a painting of Ignis Sacer?" William said.

"That's what it says on the sword," Grace said. "You can see the letters running down in the direction of the book. And that's how the painting was introduced to me when I first saw it—as a painting of Ignis Sacer."

Dmitry glanced nervously toward the stairs. "We've found what we wanted, and I think we've been down here long enough. We should leave before the guards return to the Vaults."

"Does this prove that the sword exists?" William said to Grace.

"It proves that an artist chose it as a subject," Grace said doubtfully. "But an artist can choose any subject at all—they're only limited by their imagination. They can choose anything they can dream up. That doesn't mean it's real."

"That sounds like a 'no,'" Anton said. "I agree with Dmitry. We should get going."

"Who painted the picture?" William said.

"I don't believe anyone knows," Grace replied. "And there's no signature on the painting."

"Who's in the suit of armor?" I said.

"Who cares?" Anton said. "Let's go."

Grace glanced over at him. "I think they're right. We should go." She hurried toward a switch on the wall.

"If you would like to stand by the stairs with your flashlight," Grace said to me, "I'll turn out the lights."

I did as she asked, and moments later, we were plunged into darkness, except for my little light.

"I should go up first," Dmitry said. "If any guards are waiting for us, I'll take care of them."

I heard a soft sound as he rushed past me in the darkness.

I heard a rattling sound after that. I assumed Dmitry was ascending the stairs at great speed.

The rest of us moved up the staircase at a slower pace, and when we reached the top, we found Dmitry waiting for us.

"We are in luck," he said. "The guards have not returned to this section yet. But people are returning to the halls. We should hurry."

Grace led us quickly—but not too quickly—through the halls, and we exited the castle the same way we had come in—through the library and its storehouse.

Soon we were standing outside the stone structure with its hidden door.

"I suggest we all get away from here as soon as possible," Anton said. "It won't take them long to figure out someone was in the Vaults."

"What about Sachiko?" William said. "Shouldn't we wait for her?"

"She said she'll find us," I said. "She can do it. Don't worry."

"Grace and I need to go now," Dmitry said. "We have a lot of work to do."

"Wait," William said, "we can't just run off without a plan."

"We have one," Dmitry said.

"What is it?" William said.

Dmitry and Grace exchanged a glance.

"I think it's okay to tell them," Grace said after a moment.

Dmitry nodded.

"We came here to establish that the Queen's temple existed," Grace said. "And, if possible, find out how to stop her. Then we were going to head to the temple."

"How?" Anton said. "We still don't know where it is exactly, and as you said yourself, it's invisible."

"There are tunnels near Zamochit," Dmitry said. "Someone has been digging tunnels ever since the earthquakes. We planned all along to follow the tunnels to see if they could lead us to the temple."

Anton's eyebrows rose. "You think the tunnels go all the way to the Black Sea? It's nowhere near here, by the way."

"We had the plan before we knew where it was," Grace said. "Given all of the digging activity around here, we thought there was a possibility it could be close by. But I still think it's a good idea to search the tunnels."

"And why is that?"

"Because we believe that whoever is digging the tunnels has a connection to the Queen," Grace said. "And we think we can find someone or something in the tunnels that can give us valuable information. The tunnels don't have to go all the way to the temple to be useful. That was part of the plan too if it turned out to be far away."

"Fair enough," Anton said. "I'm in."

"You cannot come," Dmitry said firmly.

"What are you going to do?" William said to Grace. "Even if you do find clues, even if you do find the temple, how are you going to stop the Queen? You said you didn't know what that stuff on the tapestry meant."

"I don't," Grace said.

"Then what's the point of finding the island?" William said. "You can't stop the Queen and her army with just the two of you."

"What do you suggest we do?" Grace asked.

"I think we should go look for Ignis Sacer," William replied.

"Why?" Grace said.

"Because we need a powerful weapon to combat a vampire like the Queen," William said. "And I believe I know where it is."

"But the sword is just a legend," Grace said.

"No," William said, "we just saw it."

"That was only a painting," Grace replied. "You can paint a picture of anything you can imagine—it doesn't mean anything."

"But you also said that room was full of powerful objects, right?"

"Right," Grace said.

"And that room is the most secure one in the Vaults, isn't it?" William said.

"Yes," Grace replied.

"Then why would it be in there if the painting is just a fantasy?" William said. "What's the point of hiding it away if it isn't real? It seems to me that the only way there's power in that painting is if the sword it shows is real."

Grace paused. "That's actually a fair point. There's no reason to hide something away that has no value."

She thought for a moment. "So I'm assuming you believe the sword is in the Black Tomb? Especially since you went there and you have the key?"

"Yes," William said.

"We can't go there," Dmitry said. "It's far too dangerous."

"We have to try," William said.

"Did you actually see the sword while you were in there?" Dmitry asked.

"I—I don't know," William said. "I don't remember what's in there."

"Then the answer is no," Dmitry said. "There's no point in going to look for a weapon if we don't even know where the Queen is. Even if we found it, we'd have a weapon and no one to use it on."

"And there's no point in looking for the Queen if we don't know how to stop her," William said.

"I agree with Dmitry," Grace said. "We need to find the Queen first, and then we'll figure out what to do about her. I've heard the same rumor you have about the sword being hidden in the Black Tomb. But you've already been in there once, and you failed to find it. I don't think now is the time to try again. I'm sorry."

Grace and Dmitry turned to go.

"Wait," William said. "I have one last question for you."

Grace turned back.

"Can you tell me where the Black Tomb is?" William said.

Grace looked surprised. "But you've already been there."

"I know," William said. "But I don't remember anything about it. The only thing I remember is intending to go there. And I have a strong memory of finding something important. But I don't remember how I got there or even what the tomb looks like."

Dmitry gestured to Grace. "Come on. We have to go."

"The tomb isn't easy to get to," Grace said. "It's likely that someone had to show you. I've seen it once myself. I could take you there."

"No," Dmitry said. "Grace, we must go."

Grace turned to him. "Go on without me. Go to the main tunnel we talked about. I'll meet you there. The tomb isn't far, and I'll be with you soon."

"No," Dmitry said. "It's too dangerous for you."

"I'll be fine," Grace replied. "I'll just show him where it is—I won't go in myself. Then I'll return to you."

"Grace—"

"Dmitry, it'll be all right," she said. "Now go, please. I'll be with you soon."

Dmitry glowered, but he said nothing further. Instead, he disappeared into the night.

"Thank you," William said to Grace. "I really mean that. Thank you for doing this. It means everything."

He turned to me.

"I don't want to put you on the spot," he said. "And I know you've objected to this all along, so you don't have to—"

"I'll go with you," I said.

William looked startled. "Katie, you really don't have to—"

"I'll go with you," I said again. "I want to."

"But you've always said it's too dangerous," William said.

"You came here looking for me when I ran off to find the Queen of the Moon," I said. "And you never worried about how dangerous it was. And when you found out that Veronika had threatened to take your life back, you never worried about that danger either. You've been trying to share this with me the whole time, and I've been trying to shut you out. And even though there's great danger for you—and for me—I want to go with you. I want to help you. Like you said, we'll be together. And we can watch out for one another."

William took my hand. Then he turned to Grace.

"Will you allow Katie to come with me?" he said.

Grace shrugged. "If the human girl wishes to come with us, she certainly may. And who knows? Maybe she will see something our more powerful eyes cannot. The Black Tomb is a prison for a vampire built by vampires. Maybe a human will find a better way to slip through its defenses."

William turned to Anton.

"If you'll go with us too—"

"No," Anton said. "Absolutely not. This is crazy. There's a powerful, ancient vampire in that tomb that nearly killed you once. And now you want to drag Katie into that place too."

He turned to me. "Honestly, I'm astonished that you're agreeing—no, volunteering—for this."

"William has shown that he trusts me," I said. "And this is important to him. It's time for me to place my trust in him too."

"Like I said," Anton said, "this is crazy."

"What are you going to do?" William asked.

"You know, I'm just going to go off by myself for a little while."

"You can't follow Dmitry to the tunnels," Grace said. "He will never allow it."

"Yeah, I'd gathered that," Anton said. "You guys go off on your insane little mission."

With that, Anton disappeared.

"I can't believe he just left like that," I said.

"I can," William said. He turned to Grace. "Which way do we go?"

Grace glanced around at the spot where Anton had stood just a moment before. "Do you want to go after your friend?"

"No," William said. "We're better off without him."

"Then we should go quickly," Grace said. "We need to go to the other side of Zamochit. Just follow me."

She zipped off into the night, and William took my hand, and we followed her.

Since we were already outside the castle, we gave it a wide berth, and soon we were following the outer edges of the village, close to the barrier.

Grace continued to fly along, narrowly avoiding buildings and houses, and people on the street flashed by as little more than shadows.

Eventually, Grace stopped in the shadow of a tall tower, and William and I came to a halt beside her.

I glanced up. We were standing by one of the watchtowers that guarded the village's borders.

"Are you sure it's wise to stop here?" I said.

"We should be fine," Grace said. "I just need to stop inside for a moment."

She disappeared into the tower.

Moments later she was back.

"It's okay," Grace said. "I just wanted to make sure that no one was paying attention, since we have an intruder in our midst, and I wanted to scope out the way ahead. We're going the right way—it's sometimes hard to tell with the way this town is laid out."

"Where are we headed exactly?" William said.

"We're actually heading out near the Wasteland," Grace replied. "But we have to head out in exactly the right spot. Otherwise, we'll just wander around and never find it."

"And how do you know where the right spot is?" William said.

"We're going toward some of the only vegetation that occurs naturally in Zamochit," Grace said. "It's hard to miss it once you find it."

She rushed off again, and William and I took off after her.

We continued to fly along the outskirts of the town. Eventually, we came upon a section of the village that had a strongly unpleasant odor, and I figured we were passing by the heaps—the area of Zamochit where all the refuse was collected. I could just make out some dark mounds of mysterious origin against the streaking silver sky, and my suspicious were confirmed.

Luckily, we continued moving past the heaps, and soon the unpleasant aroma abated.

We continued on through the town, and eventually, Grace came to a stop.

William quickly stopped beside her, and I glanced around in the silvery air.

We were standing in the dusty backyard of a small house. Behind us was a fence, and beyond the fence was an equally dusty field. Standing out in the middle of the field was a small group of trees.

"That's where we're headed," Grace said, pointing to the trees.

She climbed over the fence, and William and I followed her. As we jumped down, we both kicked up a cloud of dust.

"As you can see, it's a bit dusty," Grace said. "The barrier is a little strange here—more of the characteristics of the Wasteland break through at this point. I don't know if the barrier is thinner or if it actually has some different properties here. But this part isn't quite like any other part."

Grace began to walk toward the trees.

"You're sure this is the way to the Black Tomb?" William said.

"You'll see," Grace said. "Just follow me."

William and I followed her across the field.

We reached the small group of trees, and Grace walked up to a large tree that had a branch hanging down.

"Can you see what's beyond that tree branch?" Grace asked.

William and I both looked.

"I don't see anything other than a few more trees," William said. "I certainly don't see anything that looks like a tomb around here."

"Just wait," Grace said.

She lifted the heavy branch and then let it drop back down.

"I still just see trees," William said.

Grace repeated the action two more times. Then something began to happen.

The area around the tree was largely dark, but there was still some silvery light filtering through. The area right under the tree branch began to darken, and I could see the landscape beyond it changing.

Where there had been trees, I could now see a swamp. And the swamp only seemed to exist in the area under the tree branch.

"What is that?" I said.

"I don't know how it works exactly," Grace replied. "But that's the path to the Black Tomb."

William stepped close and peered under the branch. "But that swamp wasn't there a minute ago."

"I know," Grace said. "I don't know what creates the path—whether it's using the properties of the barrier or some other magic entirely—but the only way to get to the swamp is by walking under this tree branch. You can't approach it from either side of the tree or even from the other direction."

"So there's definitely magic at work here in creating this path?" William said.

"Of some kind, yes," Grace said. "I couldn't say who'd set it up or why."

She paused. "Do you still want to go on?"

"Yes," William said quickly. "We have to."

"Then follow me."

Grace stepped under the branch and on into the swamp.

I went in after her, and William followed me.

I found myself standing on marshy, muddy earth that was very different from the dusty ground of the little copse of trees I had been standing in. There was a large body of water not far off, and out of the water grew tall, spindly trees. It was most definitely a swamp.

The swamp wasn't quite as dark as it had appeared to be from the outside, and a faint, bronze light, similar to the silver light of Zamochit, seemed to permeate everything.

I glanced back toward the tree branch we had walked under. I could still see the little copse of trees we had left behind and the silver light that shone through it.

I faced forward again. The swamp and its trees stretched ahead of me as far as I could see—there were so many trees, in fact, that it was much more like a forest. There were far more trees than there had been in the copse.

William glanced back at the tree branch—it looked to be the same tree on both the silver copse and bronze swamp sides.

"So how do we get back?" he asked.

"I've only been here once," Grace said. "But as far as I know, the entrance is always open on this side. The secret entrance with the trick door is only on the other side. All you have to do is come back to this particular tree."

"Well, let's hope that holds true for us," William said.

Grace moved forward into the swamp, and as William and I followed her, I made a point of looking for landmarks to help us find our way back. I mostly looked for oddly shaped trees or the occasional unusual small plant.

William seemed to have a similar idea in mind.

"There aren't too many landmarks around here," he said to Grace. "If you've only been here once, how do you know you're going the right way?"

"As I recall," Grace said, "you follow the water, keeping it on your right, and the tomb is all the way at the end. It's not a difficult path to follow."

I looked off along the water—I couldn't see the end of it.

But we walked along the edge of the water, with the bronze light shining off its surface, and eventually, we did reach the end of it.

Grace walked around the bank to the very tip of it and stood looking down at the water.

William glanced around. "I still don't see a tomb."

"It's right here," Grace said. "But we need to go down into the water."

I eyed the swamp warily. "It's underwater?"

"You have to go under the water to get to it," Grace replied. "But it's actually dry where the tomb is. You'll see once we get there."

William frowned. "That sounds dangerous, especially for Katie."

"We'll only be in the water for a moment," Grace said. "You'll see."

She stepped down into the water and kept going until her head was entirely submerged.

William turned to me.

"I doubt visibility is good under there," he said. "Let me go down and look for the tomb, and then I'll come up for you."

I nodded, and I watched as William plunged into the water.

The ripples from his plunge dissipated after a few moments, and I found myself staring into the water, trying to discern anything that looked like William or Grace—or even like a tomb. But I couldn't see anything under the surface of the water at all, and as I gazed into it, I noticed the strange, bronze light of the place reflecting off the water. The light was curiously attractive, and I found myself drawn to it. I reached out to touch the water, and as my fingers skimmed the cool surface, I was overcome by a desire to plunge in myself to see if I could catch some of that bronze light.

But as I began to pitch forward, I caught sight of my reflection in the water, and the sight of my own face was enough to pull me out of my trance. I grabbed frantically for the plants along the water's edge, and I was able to pull myself back in time to prevent myself from falling into the water.

I realized that I'd been kneeling on muddy ground near the water's edge, and I stood up quickly. I'd been warned once that the silver light in Zamochit could have a hypnotic effect on non-vampires, and I wondered if that was true of this bronze light also.

I stepped back from the water's edge and resolved not to let my attention wander again.

Moments later, William resurfaced, his dark hair clinging to his face and neck. He swam the short distance toward me and then climbed out of the water.

"Grace was right," William said, standing up and brushing the water from his face. "The tomb's not far, but you'd never find it if you didn't have someone to lead you to it."

He stopped and looked at the mud on my jeans. "Is everything okay?"

"Yes," I said. "I just got a little too close to the water."

"Well, if you're ready," William said, "I can lead you through."

He held out his hand.

I hesitated. "What's it like under there? Will I be able to breathe?"

"Yes, yes, of course," William said quickly. "There's air down there—and light. You'll be able to see and walk around quite comfortably."

I took William's hand, and I stepped down into the cold, murky water. The water wasn't very deep at first, and William and I had to wade in a little before the bottom dropped a bit, and the water came up above our waists.

William seemed to be looking for something with his feet. When he found it, he turned to me.

"Are you ready?" he asked.

"Yes," I replied.

He gave my hand a little squeeze. "Just follow me, and you'll be fine."

William moved forward, and he began to descend lower and lower as if walking down steps.

Soon his head was completely underwater, and I could feel him pulling gently on my hand.

I moved forward cautiously, and I could feel the ground beneath my feet change. The soft bottom of the swamp soon turned to something solid and flat like stone. I slid one foot along it and felt my foot drop off it into empty water. Carefully, I lowered my foot down, while still feeling the steady pressure of William's hand. After a moment, I found another stone surface below the first one, and I planted my foot firmly on it. Then I planted my other foot beside it. I repeated the process and found yet another stone below. There was indeed a set of steps below the water.

I walked down into the murky water until my head was submerged.

Though I wasn't really sure if it was a good idea or not, I opened my eyes underwater. The water was just as murky as it appeared to be above, and visibility was poor. I felt William tugging gently on my hand again, and I walked down the steps until I reached what felt like a broad, flat floor. William pulled me forward, and I felt my hand leave the water. A moment later, the rest of my body followed, and I stepped out of the water and into clear air.

I looked around.

I was standing in a long, narrow hallway, with a stone floor below and a dirt ceiling above. William was standing next to me, and behind us was a perfectly vertical wall of brown, muddy water.

I stretched out my hand and touched the water. The water sprayed a little where my fingers touched it, but other than that, the line of water was undisturbed, and the wall held firm.

"How is this possible?" I said.

"I don't know," William replied. "I suppose it's the same thing that makes the entrance at the tree branch work."

I looked around, suddenly startled. "And you're right—there's breathable air down here. I don't see how that could work either."

"For the moment, at least, it's enough that it is working," William said. "Maybe we should move a little more quickly—just in case. Grace is waiting for us."

William continued to hold my hand, and the two of us walked down the hall, with water dripping from our hair and clothes.

The hall was dimly lit, but it was no dimmer than the swamp above had been. And the light had the same strange, bronze cast that the light in the swamp had had.

I warned myself not to let the light get to me again.

We continued down the hall, and at the end of it, we found Grace standing beside a large, black wall. Set into the wall was an ornate door.

"This is as far as I go," Grace said. "Now that you're both here safely, it's time for me to leave. Just remember to go back to the tree branch to get out of this place—as far as I know, it's the only exit."

"You're sure you won't come with us?" I said.

Grace shook her head. "I have to get back to Dmitry. I've already wasted time by coming here."

"But aren't you curious as to what's inside?" I asked.

Grace glanced up at the big, black door behind her.

"I already know what's inside," she said. "This is a prison. It was designed to keep a very old and very powerful vampire inside. Besides, I don't think I can get in."

"What do you mean?" William said.

"This chamber is designed to keep a vampire in," Grace said. "And those same protections that keep that vampire in keep other vampires out. There are two reasons this tomb has remained unexplored. One, because most fear the vampire within. And, two, because getting in is very, very difficult even with the key—as I said, no archeologist who has come out here has ever returned."

"Then how did I get in?" William asked.

"You are different," Grace replied. "Everyone knows that you have Sídh blood. That may have given you the ability to slip past the protections."

She glanced at me. "Perhaps you were wise to bring a human companion. The protections should have no effect on her either."

"What about the sword?" I said. "Back at the castle, you seemed to think it was possible it was in there. Do you still think that?"

"I don't know," Grace said. "I hope you find it. I really do."

She glanced at us. "Do you have the key?"

"Yes," I said.

I drew the black rock out of my pocket.

"In that case, good luck," Grace said.

She disappeared down the hall.

"So I guess it's just us," William said. He looked at me in the bronze light. "Are you ready to go in?"

I looked up at the big, black door with its ornate carvings.

"Yes," I said. "Are you sure you want to do this?"

"I'm sure," William said. "Are you sure *you* want to do this? I feel like I've talked you into it, and I don't want you to go unless you're truly certain you want to."

"I'm sure," I said. "From now on, we do everything together."

"Then I'm glad you're here with me," William said. He glanced at the black door. "Would you like to do the honors?"

I looked at the rock in my hand. "I'm not entirely sure how this works."

"Neither am I," William said. He ran a hand over the door.

"There's an indentation just here," he said. "It's in the same spot where a lock would be on a normal door."

I ran my hand over the same spot and could feel the indentation too.

"I think you're right," I said. "It's the right shape."

I held up the rock. "Shall I?"

"Go ahead," William said. "I'll be ready for anything that happens."

William seemed to brace himself as if for an attack as I slotted the pointed end of the rock into the indentation.

For a moment, there was nothing—no sound, no movement. Then several long lines that had been cut into the rock lit up with a bright, white light. The lines extended in both directions on either end of the door, and soon the whole door was lit up. I heard sounds inside, as if bolts were being thrown back, and then the door swung open, revealing darkness within.

William and I stood silently for a long moment, but there was no movement from within the tomb.

"I'd like to go into the tomb first," William whispered. "I've been in here once before, so if I triggered any defenses then, I clearly figured them out and survived. It would make me feel a lot better if you just waited here for a moment."

I nodded, and William stepped across the threshold. As he did so, the interior of the tomb lit up with the same bronze light that was in the hall.

William quickly stopped where he was.

I could see that he was tense and listening. After a moment, he started forward again.

"Stay right there," William whispered.

I saw him move deeper into the tomb, and before long, he was lost to my sight.

After a few minutes, he returned.

"I don't see any sign of defenses," William said. "And so far, I don't see any sign of the vampire either."

He held out his hand. "Would you like to try stepping across the threshold?"

I took William's hand and took a step forward.

"Carefully now," he said.

I took another step forward, and now I was fully inside the tomb.

"Okay," William said. "Looks like you can cross with no trouble."

We both walked forward into the room.

Suddenly, the door slammed heavily shut behind us, and a voice rang out in the tomb.

The words were strange—they sounded a lot like Russian, but I couldn't understand them. After a moment, the words died away. Then the voice rang out again, and this time the words were in clear, modern Russian.

"Who disturbs my slumber?"

Chapter Sixteen

I could hear shuffling footsteps moving toward us, and at the end of the room, I could see a tall, white figure emerging from the darkness.

William quickly moved to stand in front of me.

The voice rang out again.

"Who dares—"

Then it stopped abruptly, and the figure shuffled closer.

"Oh, it's you, my boy," said the figure. "I'm glad you're no worse for wear."

I stepped forward, and I saw a tall, hairless man with very white skin and milky blue eyes.

He continued to shuffle toward us, but he wasn't looking at us—his eyes didn't seem to focus at all.

I wondered if he could see us.

"Yes, child, I can see you," the man said.

I looked at him, startled. "Do you read minds?"

The man appeared puzzled and replied without looking at me. "I don't know. I just receive impressions. Perhaps I read the question in your face. Perhaps not."

"Who are you?" William said.

"My name is Cyrs," the man said. "I suppose we weren't properly introduced last time, but then again, we didn't really have time to talk."

"Are you the one who attacked me?" William said.

Cyrs looked startled. "Oh, no. No, that wasn't me."

It was William's turn to look startled.

"You didn't attack me?" William said.

"No, no, my boy, it wasn't me."

"Then who was it?"

"The one who attacked you came in with you, though at the time I was under the impression that you didn't know he was there. I think he ambushed you."

"I was ambushed by someone who came in with me?" William said.

"Yes," Cyrs replied. "Though he didn't come in with you so much as behind you."

"So what happened?" William said. "Tell me what you remember."

Cyrs laid one long hand next to his forehead for a moment. "The door opened and you came through. You stood and looked around for a moment, and I came out to greet you. Then a man jumped on you—knocked you to the ground. He sank his teeth into your neck. Then you fought—I think a weapon of some kind was involved. The two of you rolled out into the hall. Then you both disappeared. I shut the door after that."

"Who was he?" William said. "Who attacked me?"

"I have seen him before," Cyrs said. "He is from the castle. I have seen him there—though whether I saw that with my own eyes or with my mind's eye, I am not sure."

"The castle?" William said. "Do you mean Rusalka Castle?"

Cyrs paused. "Yes, I think that is its name. I haven't been there in many, many years. Do you know, I remember when that castle was being built?"

"He was from the castle," William said. "Can you describe him?"

"I am not sure," Cyrs said. "He was a vampire in fancy clothes, and I have seen many like him in my time. If I saw him again, I might recognize him, but then again, perhaps not. But you, you are different, my boy. That is why I remembered you."

I eyed Cyrs uncertainly. He still wasn't looking at us.

"You're sure William was attacked by someone from the castle?" I said.

"Yes," Cyrs replied simply.

"But aren't you the vampire who's imprisoned in this tomb?" I said.

"Imprisoned?" Cyrs said. "Is that what they told you? This is not a prison. This is my home. And I am very happy here. I have not left in many, many long years."

"But isn't this the Black Tomb?"

Cyrs smiled. "I have heard that they call it that. Perhaps we can go sit down, and then I can explain a little. And then you can explain a little—for you are here for a purpose. No one ever comes here just to see old Cyrs. No one comes here just for the pleasure of his company."

Cyrs turned and began to shuffle back toward the dark end of the room.

As he walked away, I had a chance to look around for the first time.

The floor underneath our feet was black stone, but there was a thick, oriental rug a few feet from the door and a table with a vase on it next to one wall. Everything was clean, and there was no dust or mustiness in the air. The room, in fact, somehow gave the impression of being a foyer in a home.

"Please come this way, young ones," Cyrs said without turning to look at us. "The hall is far too drafty for proper conversation."

William and I both hesitated.

"Come," Cyrs said without stopping. "I mean you no harm, I can assure you. And I think I have something back here you would like to see."

William and I glanced at each other.

"Well," William said, "he hasn't attacked us so far. What do you think?"

"I think we should go with him," I said.

"I do too," William said. "But just be prepared to run in case something goes wrong."

I glanced behind us. "The door is shut."

"We'll worry about that when the time comes," William said.

Cyrs continued to shuffle off into the darkness, and William and I followed him.

As we walked along, the darkness was slowly suffused by the same bronze light that had lit up the area by the door.

Cyrs turned his head a little and smiled at us. "The light is for you."

As the light grew brighter, I could see that there were paintings on the black walls and more soft rugs beneath our feet. The place was surprisingly comfortable for a tomb.

Eventually, Cyrs stopped at a door and paused with his long, white hand on the handle.

"This is one of my favorite rooms," he said. "I would call it my 'grand parlor,' but I so seldom receive visitors that it really doesn't get to be used much in that way."

Cyrs opened the door and waved us in with one long hand. As he did so, the room within lit up with bronze light.

William and I stepped inside.

The room was large, and it was filled with paintings and sculpture. There were more soft rugs on the floor, and comfortable-looking sofas and chairs were arranged around the room. Something in a corner of the room glittered gold, and I was amazed at how opulent and immaculate the place was. Everything was clean and well cared for.

"I do apologize," Cyrs said. "I see now that you two are both damp."

He waved his hands, and a warm, gentle breeze wafted over us. Within moments, William and I were both dry.

"Please be seated," Cyrs said.

I selected a sofa with elaborately embroidered cushions and sat down. William sat down beside me.

Cyrs shuffled over and sat down on another sofa.

"William," he said to himself. "Yes, that seems right. I feel as if I would have known that was your name, even if the young woman had not said so."

Cyrs was silent for a moment.

"Ekaterina is your name," he said at last. "Though in English they call you Katie."

"Yes," I said.

"I see things, I hear things," Cyrs said musingly. "I'm not always sure what is in front of me and what is not. It's sometimes hard for me to determine what is solid reality and what is the world of the mind."

William and I exchanged a worried glance.

"You said this is your home?" I said.

"Yes, Katie, this is my home," Cyrs replied. "This is most definitely not a prison. I had this place built. Many long years ago, I took refuge in here from my fellow vampires. Few have set foot in here since then, though many, many want to. Do you know why they don't come in?"

"Why?" I said.

"Because they can't. It takes great strength to get through. You two must be very strong. The unworthy cannot get through even with the key."

William frowned. "Then why the stories?"

"The stories?" Cyrs said vaguely.

"Yes," William said. "The stories that there is an ancient and powerful vampire locked in a tomb who attacks anyone who tries to enter."

Cyrs laughed, and I was surprised by how loud the sound was.

"Is that what they say?" he said. "This is some kind of haunted place? No, I have not attacked anyone—I would not attack anyone. I am not strong—not in my body at least. The only strength I have lies in here."

Cyrs touched his forehead delicately with one long finger.

"If it came to a fight, I dare say I would lose. But this place is well protected."

"Why would people want to get in here?" I said.

Cyrs smiled. "They think I have treasure."

"Do you?" William said.

"That depends," Cyrs replied. "I believe the mind has great riches."

He paused. "I see you are disappointed. Is that why you came here? To find treasure?"

"We're looking for Ignis Sacer," William said. "The legendary sword."

"Ah, yes," Cyrs said. "A great treasure indeed."

"We're not looking for a treasure," William said. "We're looking for a weapon."

"A weapon, my boy?" Cyrs sounded amused. "And what would you use it for?"

"To defeat the Werdulac," William said.

A distant light appeared in Cyrs's eye. "Yes, now that would be something worth doing."

He raised a hand. "Can I offer you some refreshments? I understand humans often need food and drink."

A crystal decanter full of water and an ornate box lifted themselves off a table in the corner and floated across the room toward us.

Cyrs smiled as the decanter and box settled gently on the table in front of us. "I knew there was a reason why I asked for this to be brought in a few days ago."

"But—" William began.

"You aren't human?" Cyrs said. "Yes, I know. But the young lady is. And I sense that she could use some sustenance."

"That's not what I was going to say," William said.

Cyrs tilted his head. "Oh, I see. You are impatient to hear more about the sword."

"Is it here?" William said.

"In a moment," Cyrs said patiently. "I believe the young lady needs to rest a little. It seems to me that the journey here cannot have been an easy one."

I hesitated. Accepting hospitality from an ancient vampire in a legendary tomb seemed like a strange thing to do. And yet, Cyrs had not made any move to harm us—and if he did indeed know something about the sword, it might be wise to humor him.

I gave William what I hoped was a reassuring smile.

"Thank you," I said to Cyrs. "I would like that."

Cyrs frowned without actually looking at the table. "But how remiss of me. You will need dishes also."

He waved his hand, and a crystal glass and china plate floated over to us and settled down on the table.

"I hope you don't mind serving yourself," Cyrs said. "That way you can choose what you like."

"I don't mind," I said.

I poured out a glass of water from the decanter and opened up the box. Inside were rolls, pastries, and dried fruits.

"They are quite fresh, I can assure you," Cyrs said.

"Thank you," I said, as I started eating. "You said you just had this brought in?"

"Yes, I traded for it," Cyrs said.

"But you also said you haven't had visitors in a long time."

Cyrs smiled. "Yes, that is true. These visitors don't come in through the front door. In fact, they don't come in at all. They send things to me in their own way, and I send them things in mine."

"Do you mean you use magic?" I said.

Cyrs reflected. "I don't know. I suppose you could call it that."

"What do you trade?" William asked.

"What did I trade for the food and water?" Cyrs said.

"Yes," William replied.

"I traded the most valuable commodity of all," Cyrs said. "I traded knowledge."

"Is that how you get—sustenance?" I said.

Cyrs laughed his dry, rasping laugh. "No. I have become what might be considered a vegetarian—an extreme vegetarian—by vampire standards. I survive on the fish that populate this swamp. I have no desire to feed on the so-called higher animals any longer."

"And why do they call this place a tomb?" I asked.

I could sense William's impatience, but it seemed to me that it would be better for things to proceed a little more slowly—we had to let Cyrs get there in his own time.

"That is a good question," Cyrs said. "There's only me in here, and I am very much alive. I think it may have to do with the protections on this place. They are very dangerous for vampires— very dangerous. I understand that if the unworthy places the key in the lock, terrible consequences follow. I am not surprised they associate this place with an untimely demise."

Cyrs's eyes drifted vaguely in my direction. "But you two are different. Yes, you two are different."

He lapsed into silence, and I had a feeling he was thinking or dreaming—or whatever it was he did.

William moved as if he would speak, but I held up a hand.

In time, Cyrs stirred. His eyes seemed to focus for the very first time, and he looked at me—his eyes clear rather than milky. After a moment, he smiled a little, then he transferred his gaze to William.

"What a tangle you are," Cyrs said softly. "And not as young as you seem—at least not in terms of years. But your heart—your emotions—those are very young. Yes, I suppose this is not surprising."

Cyrs sat back in his chair, and his eyes clouded over once again.

"But you asked about my 'tomb,'" he said musingly. "However, it is nothing of the kind. I am safe in here. This is a sanctuary—in more ways than one. They used to call me Cyrs. And then it was the 'Old One,' and then they forgot that I was someone who had ever had a name. I became a ghost, an evil spirit, a boogieman. But I am none of those things. I am, in fact, a guardian. I am Cyrs the Guardian. That was what they used to call me."

"And what were you guarding?" William said quickly.

Cyrs smiled. "So impatient. But as I said, I am safe in here. I came here to get away from them all. I knew my duty would last for centuries, and I would be removed from society for the rest of my life. I won't last forever, but I will guard my secret for as long as I am able."

I could see that William was bursting to ask more questions, but this time he restrained himself.

"I knew them all, you know," Cyrs said. "The Werdulac and his family and his inner circle. I was young when they were building his castle. I knew this place had to be strong to keep vampires like them out. That's why it's made of onyx."

Cyrs tilted his head. "Do you know what's so special about onyx?"

"I've heard a little about it," I said. "Perhaps you could tell me more."

William made a sound that made it clear once again that he was trying to restrain his impatience.

"Onyx is black," Cyrs said. "And black is a protective color—the safest one there is. If you ever want something that's a protection against evil, find yourself a black stone. It's natural protection against supernatural creatures who mean you harm."

"I'll remember that," I said.

"Onyx has further powerful magic qualities in addition to its protective properties," Cyrs said. "It's formed in springs and caves by the most potent forces of the earth. And evil can be brought to a halt by its touch."

"Then that makes it ideal if you're protecting something from a vampire," I said. "Even a very powerful one."

"Yes, yes, it does," Cyrs said.

He paused for a moment. "Tell me again why you are here."

"We're here to find Ignis Sacer," William said.

"And you, child," Cyrs said to me. "Do you agree with this statement?"

"Yes," I said.

"And what do you want the sword for?" Cyrs asked. "I feel as if you've left something out."

"We want to use it against the Werdulac eventually," William said. "But first we want to use it to defeat the Queen of the Moon. And we need to do it quickly. There's activity at her temple, and we hear she's raising an army."

"The Queen of the Moon?" Cyrs looked startled, and his milky blue eyes darted back and forth as if he was searching for her in some place we couldn't see.

"Yes," William said. "Can't you see all this? Why do you need us to tell you?"

I quickly shushed William, but Cyrs seemed unperturbed.

"That's a fair question," he replied. "But as I have said, I don't know how I know things—I receive impressions, and I am not always sure what is in front of me and what isn't. And some impressions are very clear while others are fleeting. Besides, when you talk, I can read your voice too. I can see if it has the ring of truth in it."

"And?" William said.

"I think the two of you have been hiding," Cyrs replied. "You've both been hiding from who you are and what you are meant to do. You've always done just what you needed to do in the moment."

He paused. "But I sense that is changing."

Cyrs turned his head a little.

"Tell me, my boy, are you sure about this sword? Are you sure it exists?"

"Yes," William said without hesitation.

"Yet, it is said to be only a legend," Cyrs said. "And those around you doubt its existence. Is that not right?"

"That's right," William said.

"And as far as you know, no one has ever seen the sword, correct?"

"That's right also," William said.

"And yet you believe in it?" Cyrs said. "Why?"

"Because I know it exists," William said. "I'm sure of it."

"You have no doubts?"

"None," William replied.

I started to feel uncomfortable. It seemed to me like Cyrs was working up to telling William that he had made this trip for nothing.

"And what if I were to tell you that the sword isn't here?" Cyrs said. "What if I were to tell you further that it doesn't exist at all?"

"Then I would go somewhere else to look for it," William said.

"Nothing would shake you?" Cyrs said.

"Nothing," William replied.

Cyrs was silent for a moment. Then he nodded to himself.

"There's a reason you believe in it so strongly," Cyrs said. "I believe you have seen it. And what's more, you've probably held it in your hands."

William stood up suddenly. "Are you saying it's here?"

"I'm saying I have something to show you," Cyrs said.

He rose to his feet gracefully and extended one long hand in my direction.

"Would you care to come with us, my child? I think you will find this very interesting."

I rose also, and Cyrs shuffled to a corner of the room—it was the same spot where I had seen something gold glitter.

Cyrs stopped in front of a door that was set into the corner where two walls met.

"An awkward spot for a door," he said.

There was no knob on the door, but there was an ornament in the center—gold filigree surrounding an opal.

Cyrs waved a hand over the opal, and the door opened smoothly.

"This is a special room," he said.

Cyrs preceded us into the room, and as he did so, the interior lit up with bronze light.

He motioned for us to follow.

William and I stepped into the room, and I saw a number of striking objects, including a gilt chair and an enormous, highly decorated urn. But what really caught my eye was a pile of gold metal lying in a corner—it was clearly a suit of armor.

I rushed over to it.

"That's the suit of armor from the painting," I said.

William hurried over to join me.

"You're right," he said excitedly. "And that's the book from the painting."

I looked where he was pointing, and I could see a book with a brown cover and a red jewel in the center resting on a pillow. It was the same book the sword had been resting on in the painting.

William turned toward Cyrs. "Where's the sword?"

"That's it right there," Cyrs replied.

William turned back. "I don't see it. I see the suit of armor and the book, but I don't see the sword."

"It's the book," Cyrs said. "That's Ignis Sacer."

"Ignis Sacer is a sword," William said.

"And that book is a sword," Cyrs said. "It is no less than the sword of knowledge."

"But we saw it," William said. "There was a suit of armor, a book, and a sword."

"We saw a painting," I interjected, "in the Vaults at Rusalka Castle. The painting had those three objects in it."

"I see," Cyrs said.

"Have you seen the painting?" William asked.

"I don't know," Cyrs replied. "I don't remember. It has been many, many years since I was in the castle. I really don't recall."

"But you have the objects in it," William said. "All that's missing is the sword."

"And I tell you that the sword is not missing," Cyrs said. "The book is the sword."

"How can that be?" William said. "How can you defeat an ancient, powerful vampire with a book?"

"That is a very complex question, my boy."

"What's in it?" I said.

"What's that, my child?" Cyrs said.

"What's in the book?" I asked.

Cyrs smiled vaguely. "Finally, you have asked the proper question."

He shuffled over and waved a hand over the book.

"This book contains all of the magical knowledge of the Sídh," Cyrs said. "Spells, incantations, potions, descriptions of enchanted objects—all their weapons, so to speak."

I looked down at the book.

"Wow," I said. "That may actually be better than a magic sword."

"There are two problems with the book, however," Cyrs said. "The first is the language the book is written in. It was composed in the ancient language of the Sídh, and I, alas, have never been able to read it. But I sense Sídh blood in both of you, so it's possible one of you may know it or be able to learn."

Cyrs kneeled down by the book and placed one white hand gingerly on the cover.

"The other problem is more serious," he said.

He lifted the cover of the book carefully, and I could see that the page underneath was completely black.

"They're all like that, I'm afraid," Cyrs said.

Using one long, thin fingernail, he delicately lifted the top page to reveal the one beneath. Then he lifted two more. They were all black.

"I'd show you more," Cyrs said, "but if I lift any more pages, they will crumble. Unfortunately, I know that by experience."

"It's gone," I said. "The pages are so badly deteriorated that it can no longer be read."

"It's one of the perils of living in a swamp," Cyrs said, standing once again. "I am well hidden in here, but the place is very damp. When the book first began to deteriorate, I didn't know what to do. I certainly couldn't have turned the book over to the vampires—it was only safe in my hands. I suppose I hoped that some special property of the book would keep it from complete ruin, but unfortunately, that wasn't the case. Despite the magic in the book, there was no magic in the physical object itself. You should have seen it before the damp got to it. The letters were gold—truly lovely."

"So what you're saying is that Ignis Sacer isn't here," William said.

"It *was* here," Cyrs said. "But it has crumbled away."

"Can it be restored?" I asked.

"I don't know," Cyrs said. "I don't know much about books and their preservation. At any rate, I can't trust the vampires with the book, even in its decomposed form."

"It wouldn't have to be the vampires," I said. "Humans can do restoration work too."

Cyrs shook his head. "It's far too dangerous to give a book of this kind to humans. The book would swiftly be stolen from their hands and used for nefarious intent."

"Then we've come here for nothing," William said.

"Perhaps not," Cyrs said. "You may recall that I said you've probably held Ignis Sacer yourself—and by that I meant the original. This one is—was—only a copy."

"So where's the original?" I said.

"In the ageless realm of the Sídh," Cyrs replied. "They would never allow something as valuable as the original Ignis Sacer out of their sight."

"Okay," William said. "So how do we get to the realm of the Sídh?"

"You don't," Cyrs replied. "You of all people should know how difficult that is."

"But there must be a way," William protested.

"I'm sure there is," Cyrs said, "but I imagine that figuring it out would take a lot of time. And I was under the impression that time was of the essence—particularly in regard to the Queen of the Moon."

"Yes," William said.

"Then I suggest you find another way to go about defeating her without the sword," Cyrs replied. "You won't be finding Ignis Sacer today."

"That's wonderful," William said sarcastically. "I don't suppose you have any advice?"

Cyrs smiled. "So impatient, my boy. As it happens, I may know something that could help."

"What's that?" William said.

"I assume that if the Queen is causing trouble, she must be free of her temple?"

"Well, not exactly," I said. "From what we understand, she's 'freeing' herself, and most of her work is being channeled through a servant of hers known as the Acolyte."

"Then you have a little bit of luck there," Cyrs said. "I was going to suggest luring her back into her temple and then putting her back in her chamber of light. If she is already at the temple, then all that remains is to get her back into the chamber."

"When we went to the Vaults," I said, "we saw an ancient Sídh tapestry. It said, 'the Moon was defeated by the dark star.' Does this chamber have something to do with that?"

Cyrs reflected. "Yes—I can see that. I can understand why they would describe it that way. The Queen was one of the Sídh once—just as you were, my boy. But she wasn't banished—oh no. She chose to be transformed and leave the Sídh on her own. Her conversion was successful, and she became a truly powerful creature—a vampire with the power of the Sídh. And that's why, when she was defeated, they couldn't bear to bury her in the ground—and she wasn't burned to ash either. Instead, she was imprisoned in a chamber—which leads to a place known as the half-realm."

"The half-realm?" I said.

"Yes. It exists between our world and the Sídh realm—and it can only be entered into or exited from by magic. The chamber the Queen was locked in blocks out all light. And that takes away her power and puts her into a dormant state. The moon derives its light from the sun, so the way to defeat the moon is to block light from the sun. The Queen, as a member of the Sídh, derives her power from the sun. But as a vampire, her senses are too delicate to bear the sun's bright light. So as a vampire-Sídh, she derives her magic power from the milder reflected sunlight of the moon. Cut off her light, and you cut off her power."

"And they thought locking her in a dark box was better than burying her?" I said. "How's that any different from being buried in the ground?"

"The Sídh have a horror of the darkness that exists underground," Cyrs said. "They are creatures of the light after all. According to legend, they were banished underground when they were defeated by the humans, but I don't believe that was actually the case. They actually went to another realm—another plane of existence. It may be accessed at times from underground in this world, but that's not where they really are. Being buried in the earth is the ultimate horror for the Sídh. So they locked the Queen in a chamber above ground, separated from the great light above, so she wouldn't have magic, and she could no longer hurt anyone. The chamber the Queen was locked in—the chamber of light—is not dark. But it is also not lit by any natural source. Instead it is lit by the light of dreams. It's said that the Sídh left her a candle to sleep by."

"She didn't die?" I said. "Cut off from both light and vampire forms of sustenance?"

"No," Cyrs replied. "She went dormant. And it should have been enough to hold her forever—as it was, it worked for centuries. All the great vampires were defeated and burned by the Sídh, and there was no one left to help her. And the chamber is set at the heart of a labyrinth—one specifically designed to confound her. Should she get out of the chamber, the labyrinth is supposed to act as a secondary way to trap her. She must have had assistance to be revived—powerful assistance."

"So where is she?" William said. "Where is the island with the temple and the chamber?"

Cyrs was silent for a moment.

"I see water," he said at last. "As you said, she is on an island."

"Is that all?" William said. "Do you know which island? Where it is?"

Cyrs shook his head. "Alas, I am not a sailor. I cannot tell you where it is. But that is not all."

"What else do you see?" William said.

Cyrs shuffled close to William and placed his white hand on his arm.

"I saw it before," Cyrs said. "And I can see it again—glimpses of you—who you were. Would you like to know about your past? I can see that it is closed to you."

William looked startled. I could see that he was struggling within himself, and I held my breath.

It was everything he ever wanted—offered to him all at once.

William didn't look at either one of us, and for a moment, I think he forgot we were there.

Eventually, his face cleared, and he looked up at Cyrs.

"No," William said clearly. "I don't want to know. I've let my missing past haunt me for too long. It doesn't matter that I was banished. It doesn't matter that my own people cast me out and stole my memories. My future isn't dark any longer, and I don't have to believe I'm damaged or cursed. I can go on without my past and make my own life."

Cyrs smiled his vague smile.

"I think, my boy, that was the right answer."

Chapter Seventeen

He's just an old charlatan," William said.

Cyrs had let us out of his tomb and had given us the key to take with us. Then we had swum up to the surface of the swamp and climbed out of it—going back was definitely easier than going in had been.

Now, William and I were making our way to the tree that was the portal to this place, both of us damp and squelching as we walked.

"He doesn't know," William said. "He doesn't know anything."

I looked at William in the strange, bronze light that filled the swamp. His words were heated, but his face was hard to read. He didn't look angry exactly—he looked more forlorn than anything.

"Which part is it that's troubling you?" I said. "Is it the part about the sword? Or the part about your past?"

"Of course it's the sword," William burst out. "What else could it be? It's always the sword! Day and night it's the sword."

No sooner had the words left his lips than William looked at me, apologetic.

"I'm sorry," he said. "I didn't mean to shout at you. It's just—I really thought we were going to find Ignis Sacer this time. As far as my past goes—I meant what I said. I've finished grieving over what

271

I've lost. And if the Sídh don't need me, then I don't need them either. I don't need to know who I used to be. My future is what matters—my future with you."

"Do you really mean that?" I asked. Uncertainty nagged at me—somehow William's words about his past seemed so final.

"Yes, I do," William said. "No more pining over the past."

"But aren't you at least curious?" I said quietly. "It's not too late. I'm sure we can go back to Cyrs, and he'll tell you. I just don't want you to lose an opportunity to learn something that's important to you."

"You're important to me," William said. "I am curious, but that's all I am now—I don't have the horrible, all-encompassing desire to know that I once did. Maybe someday when you're safe, and I have time on my hands, I'll look into it again. But right now what's most important is securing your future. And that's why I'm so furious with myself. I thought we'd found the sword. But I let you down again."

"You didn't let me down," I said.

William did not respond.

"Do you believe what Cyrs said?" I asked. "Do you believe that the sword is actually a book?"

"I don't know," William said.

"Cyrs seemed pretty sure," I said.

"What about you?" William said. "Do you believe it?"

"I don't know," I said. "Cyrs did seem to know that you'd held Ignis Sacer in your own hands once. Somehow, I don't think that's a detail he'd just make up. Besides, he had a copy of it—albeit a damaged one. I don't have a hard time believing that a book of magic could be more powerful than a sword."

"Yes, he did have a copy of it," William said. "It's a shame it can't be read anymore. But Cyrs is right about one thing—we don't have time to go look for it right now. We have the Queen of the Moon to deal with, and she's not going to wait while we go looking for a book."

"So what about what Cyrs said about the Queen and the chamber she was locked in?" I said. "Do you believe that?"

"Yes, I do," William replied. "It seems consistent with the trap they set for the Hunter, and he had Sídh connections too, having fought on their side. What about you?"

"I believe it too," I said. "And it seems like the best plan we have at the moment."

"Yes, it does," William said.

"So we have to lead the Queen back into her chamber," I said. "And possibly through a labyrinth on the way, if I understood Cyrs correctly."

"I think that's right," William said. "It sounded like the chamber was at the center of the labyrinth—it was an extra layer of security meant to confuse her."

"Dmitry said that the Queen is 'freeing' herself," I said. "I wonder what that means? Is she trapped in the labyrinth right now? Is she still in the chamber right now, but it's open? Is she free of both the chamber and the labyrinth, but she's still trapped somehow?"

"Those are all good questions," William said. "I wonder about the chamber itself too. Is there a lock on it? Some kind of mechanism we have to get to work in order to keep her there? And how do we go about luring her anywhere in the first place?"

"I think I have an answer to that last one," I said.

William looked at me for a long moment.

"Katie, you can't," he said. "You can't use yourself as bait."

"Why not?" I said. "We know the Werdulac wants me, and the Queen wants to fulfill his plan. She's already building an army for him. I'm sure she knows about me by now."

"Katie," William said, "it's—"

"Dangerous?" I said. "Everything we do is dangerous now. I don't think there's any way to avoid it. Do you have a better plan?"

"No," William said resignedly.

"Then, I think we'll have to go with me as bait until we think of something else."

"I wish your friend Terrance was here," William said.

"Terrance?" I said, surprised. "Why?"

"He's your good friend in the Order, isn't he?" William said. "Maybe he would have a few ideas."

"Ideas about what to use instead of me to lure the Queen back in?"

"Yes—exactly."

I had to smile. "Well, I don't know about that. But I wouldn't mind talking to Terrance now too. I tried texting him before I left, but he didn't answer me."

"If he's working on the Queen of the Moon problem," William said, "he's probably busy."

"That's probably true," I said.

We'd reached the tree with the drooping branch through which William and I had entered the swamp, and now we stood looking at the scene on the other side. Under the branch, we could see the silvery light of Zamochit and the little copse of trees we'd left behind.

William paused. "Speaking of problems, I'm still wondering about that armor."

"In what way?" I said.

"Why have a suit of armor for a book?"

"I don't know," I said.

"I suppose we don't really have the time now to worry about it anyway," William said.

We both stepped underneath the branch and found ourselves back in the silvery light of Zamochit.

"It's about time you got back," said a voice.

I looked around. Anton was leaning against one of the nearby trees.

William whirled to face him.

"Surprised to see me?" Anton said.

"I'm not," I said.

"Thank you, Katie," Anton replied.

"I thought you'd gone," William said.

Anton sighed. "It's like you don't even know me."

"So what was that big production back there?" William demanded.

"That big production," Anton said, "was my distracting Grace and that guard guy, what's-his-name, so they would think I'd gone off in a huff. That way I could circle back and follow them. Or don't you want to know where those mysterious tunnels are?"

"You found the tunnels?" I said.

"I certainly did," Anton said. "I waited at a distance after you guys decided to go off with Grace to the tomb. I was just going to follow that guard guy—Dmitry—but then I figured I'd better keep an eye on the two of you. Once Grace left you in this interesting place under the tree branch here, I followed her to her rendezvous with her dashing guard. And thus I learned the location of the tunnels—or at least some of them."

"That's great, Anton," I said. "That's wonderful. Now we have a place to start."

William shook his head. "I don't know. I know Grace and Dmitry were very interested in those tunnels, but I don't think we'll find anything there. Anyone who was using them would have cleared out by now—just like they did in Elspeth's Grove. And I think it's highly unlikely that those tunnels lead all the way to the Black Sea and the Queen's island."

"You're just mad that I found them and you didn't," Anton said.

"No," William said. "I just think the tunnels are a dead end."

"At any rate," Anton said. "That's not all I found. On my travels back from the tunnels, I happened to find Sachiko. I showed her this place, and then she ran off to do some investigating. It seems that while she was distracting the castle guards, she happened to overhear something about a sighting of a member of the Order. She wanted to go see if she could find out a little more."

"A member of the Order?" I said. "I wonder if it was Terrance?"

"I couldn't say," Anton replied. "We'll have to see when she gets back."

He glanced at us. "By the way, what did you guys find in there?"

He gestured to the bronze-tinted swamp under the tree branch.

"We found out that Ignis Sacer is real," I said. "But it's actually a book—not a sword."

Anton's eyebrows rose. "That's interesting. How did you find that out?"

"Cyrs told us," I said. "He's the vampire who lives in the Black Tomb."

"The same one who attacked William?" Anton said. "And nearly killed him?"

"He didn't attack me," William said. "Someone else did."

"Did Cyrs tell you that?" Anton asked.

"Yes," William said. "And I believe him. He said it was someone from the castle—someone who followed me."

Anton whistled. "You know who the most obvious candidate is, right?"

"You think it was Innokenti?" William said.

"I'd bet very good money it was Innokenti," Anton replied. "So this book—did you see it? Do you have it?"

"We did see it," I said. "Or at least a copy of it."

"And?"

"It was unreadable," I said. "The pages are basically disintegrating."

"So Cyrs said Ignis Sacer is not a sword but a book," Anton said. "And then he shows you a book, but you can't read it."

"He did say it was a copy," I said. "The original is still out there. And in the painting we saw, the sword was resting on a book. Maybe it was just pointing to it."

"Maybe," Anton said. "There's definitely more to this story. But I don't think we have time to worry about that right now. The real takeaway is that you guys went into the tomb and did *not* come out with a special, magical weapon."

"That's right," I said.

"Well, on the plus side," Anton said, "at least no one got bitten by an ancient vampire. So what's our plan?"

"We may have a way to trap the Queen of the Moon," William said. "But first, we have to get to her island."

"What's that about a trap?" said a new voice.

Sachiko came zipping up to us, and she came to a stop gracefully beside me.

"Long story short," Anton said. "Katie and William met a vampire named Cyrs, but they didn't find the sword. But they may have found another way to stop the Queen of the Moon."

"Oh?" Sachiko said. "What's that?"

"Cyrs thinks we may be able to seal her back in her temple," William said. "The Sídh placed her in a chamber, and we need to lure her back into it."

"How?" Sachiko said.

"We're not quite sure about that yet," William said, with a glance at me. "We have to find the Queen of the Moon and see what the situation looks like when we get there."

"Works for me," Sachiko said.

"So did you find what you were looking for?" Anton asked.

"I think so, yes," Sachiko replied.

She turned to William and me.

"While I was at the castle," Sachiko said, "I overheard some of the guards talking. There are rumors about an American member of the Order being spotted in Russia. Ordinarily, that would mean Terrance—his skills and his knowledge make him a useful operative in difficult places. But it sounds like it wasn't him. From the description, I think it was that guy we saw back at your house—the one I left up on a roof."

"Dylan?" I said. "I wonder what he's doing here?"

"It sounds like he was headed in the general direction of the Black Sea," Sachiko said.

"So he's looking for the same thing we are," William said. "He's looking for the Queen of the Moon."

"Most likely," Sachiko said.

"Well, I just hope he doesn't get in our way," Anton said.

"He's far from getting in our way," William said. "In fact, we should be following him. He probably knows exactly where she is."

"Dylan probably does know where the Queen of the Moon is," I said. "Terrance knew, but he wouldn't tell me. And if he knows, I'm sure his backup does too."

"We should go after him right now," William said. He turned to Sachiko. "Do you think you could find Dylan?"

Sachiko frowned. "I'm sure I could—eventually. I just know his general direction—I don't have an exact location for him."

"What about the tunnels?" Anton said. "My news is important too."

"They'll take too long," William said dismissively. "And as I said, it's highly unlikely they lead all the way to the Black Sea."

"That's not the point," Anton said. "I never said they did. Besides, looking for this Dylan guy could take a long time."

"I still think we should try," William said. He turned to me and Sachiko. "What do you guys think?"

"I'd like to have a look at the tunnels," Sachiko said.

"But you're the one who found Dylan in the first place," William protested.

"Yes," Sachiko said. "I do think it's important to know what he's up to, and I would love to know where he's going, but I think we should look at the tunnels first. There could be something there that will lead us to the Queen faster."

"I agree with Anton and Sachiko," I said. "I think we should see the tunnels first."

"And I am being a saint and not gloating," Anton said.

"Fine," William said. "I can see that I'm in the minority here. I hope you're all right and we find something."

"I'll lead the way, shall I?" Anton said.

Without waiting for a response, he took off into the night.

Sachiko's figure blurred as she went after him, and William took my hand, and we zoomed after them.

We wound swiftly through Zamochit's twisting, tortuous streets until we reached the barrier. We sped through it, and I experienced a tiny tingle as I passed through—the tingle was usually a little more electric, but I figured our great speed had something to do with the diminished effect.

Within a heartbeat, we were out in the Wasteland, and I could dimly see a gray blur around me as we flew across it.

Before long, we had reached a nearby road, and we flew along it until we reached areas of human habitation.

Not long after that, we plunged into a forest, and Anton came to a stop in front of a grassy bank. The grass, like the leaves on the ground all around us, was brown and dry. I shivered just a little in the cold, and I glanced around when I heard the sound of water—a little stream was trickling nearby.

Cut into the bank was a doorway framed by wooden beams, and all around the doorway was a wall of cloth bags filled with what seemed to be dirt or sand.

"It's not the most high-tech arrangement," Anton said. "But it does the job."

"So this is why the shovels, ladders, and ropes have been disappearing from around Zamochit," I said. "Someone was constructing this?"

"Yep," Anton said. "The old-fashioned way still works even if you don't have fancy equipment. And this isn't the only tunnel—there are a few more around from what I understand. But I have a feeling that they all lead to the same place."

"Do you know that?" William said. "Or is it just a feeling?"

"No, I don't know that," Anton replied. "Just relax. We'll be able to go down and look for ourselves soon."

"Where are Dmitry and Grace?" I said. "Are they in there already?"

"Dmitry and Grace actually went into a different tunnel," Anton said. "Dmitry was waiting here at first, and then when Grace met up with him, the two of them left this entrance and went to another one."

William frowned. "Why did they leave?"

"I don't know," Anton said. "Grace arrived, Dmitry just nodded at her, and then the two of them went off."

"Why don't we use the entrance they used?" William asked.

"Because they used that entrance," Anton said. "This way we're less likely to run into them."

"Why don't we want to run into them?" William said. "We were all together not too long ago, and we were helping each other."

"I wouldn't say we were helping each other," Anton replied. "That was more of an uneasy alliance than a real partnership. I think we're better off without them—they have the potential to get in our way."

"But if all these tunnels lead to the same place," William said, "won't we run into them anyway?"

"Not necessarily," Anton said. "Now just get in the tunnel."

Anton walked in through the wooden doorway, and William, Sachiko, and I followed him.

I got out my little flashlight—we were walking quickly, and the little light that the night gave us soon disappeared. By the light of the flashlight, I could see earth walls and wooden beams like the ones in the doorway set up as supports.

"What are we looking for exactly?" Sachiko said. "Now that we're here, I realize that I don't know what we're hoping to find."

"Any sign that vampires have been down here," Anton said. "Basically, we're looking for a large chamber filled with empty coffins. And there may be artifacts—vampire artifacts—down here too."

"And what will the artifacts tell us if we find them?" Sachiko asked.

"What's with all the questions?" Anton said. "You wanted to come down here too."

"I still do want to be down here," Sachiko said. "I just want to know what's going on."

"It's not so much the artifacts themselves," Anton said, "but rather their presence—they'll tell us that the Queen would have used this place. And back in Elspeth's Grove there was an operation being run—with an office. If we find something similar, we may be able to find some paperwork—or something—that tells us where in the Black Sea this is all originating from."

"Well, that makes more sense now," William said. "Why didn't you say that before? That's a lot more reasonable than these tunnels stretching all the way to the Black Sea."

"I never said they did," Anton said. "And that's not all. I happen to be somewhat of an expert when it comes to ancient vampire artifacts. I think I may be able to find an object that creates a portal down here."

"And that makes less sense," William said.

"Just wait and see," Anton said.

We continued walking, and soon the tunnel we were following slanted downward sharply.

"Do you hear that?" Sachiko said. "It sounds like running water."

"You're just hearing the stream above us," Anton said. "It's nothing to worry about."

"No," Sachiko replied. "I don't think that's what it is."

She lifted her feet. "The ground beneath is growing damp and spongy. I think we should turn back."

"Don't be ridiculous," Anton said, but his words were drowned out by a shower of dirt.

Moments later, the dirt ceiling above us broke, releasing a torrent of water into the tunnel.

My feet were swept out from under me, and soon I was being sluiced down the tunnel by a strong stream of water.

I held on tightly to my little flashlight.

The light in my hand was the only thing I could see as I was swept along the tunnel, and eventually, I felt the floor beneath me give way completely.

I fell through the air and landed on a hard, cold surface. A torrent of water landed with me and sloshed over me before running across the floor and then dissipating.

I had managed to hold on to my flashlight, and I held it up.

In the little circle of light it cast, I could see that I was lying on a stone floor, and I could just make out William's form lying not too far away. He stirred and began to sit up.

"Well, now we know why Dmitry and Grace didn't want to take this tunnel," Sachiko said. "Apparently, it's not stable."

"Is everyone okay?" I said.

"Yes, we're fine," William said. He came over to help me up. "What about you? You're the most fragile one among us."

"I'm fine," I said. "What about this place we're in? Is it safe? Or is this whole place about to get flooded?"

"I think we're fine for the moment," William said. "But I don't think we should linger. The sooner we're out of here, the better. We'll have to look for one of the other tunnels to get out."

"Wait, wait," Anton said. "We're fine. The water is running off that way."

Anton pointed off in the dark in a direction I couldn't see, but I could see that there was a steady trickle of water running across the stone beneath my feet.

"So it's draining away," Anton said, "and while we're here, we really should have a look around. There's enough to see down here."

"Like what?" I said. I held my light up a little higher, but I still couldn't see much of anything.

"Well, there's this, for example," he said. He guided me over a few feet, and my flashlight picked out something on the floor that sparkled.

I bent down to examine it more closely. It was a dark blue stone set in a ring—a sapphire, possibly. Near it were more sparkling stones set into jewelry—red, green, yellow, and more blue—the floor was littered with them.

"And that's not all," Anton said.

He took me by the elbow and led me over to something on the floor that he nudged with his foot.

I held my light over it to examine it—it was a long, thin piece of wood that appeared to have been splintered. Stepping closer, I saw that there was more wood nearby.

"So there are jewels and coffins down here," I said. "Which means there were ancient vampires down here."

"Yep," Anton said. "Luckily for us, they're gone. Now, we're left with a big stone chamber full of vampire stuff. There are some chests down here too. Looks like this was another royal tomb."

"Royal tomb?" Sachiko said.

"That means it was one of the places where the Werdulac's followers were interred," Anton said. "It doesn't mean that any of the bigwigs were buried down here. It just means it belonged to the Werdulac. And I guess he saw himself as a king or something."

"Royal or not, we need to get out of here," William said. "I'm going to look for a tunnel out of here."

"What?" Anton said. "But we found what we were looking for. This is exactly what we were hoping was down here. We need to look through this stuff."

"There's no magic portal down here," William said. "And from the looks of this place, there isn't going to be an office with any paperwork or other clues around here. You do what you want. But once I find the tunnel, Katie, Sachiko, and I are getting out of here."

With that, William vanished into the dark.

"Now that he's gone," Anton said, "we can finally get some work done."

"Aren't you concerned about the possibility of flooding?" I said.

"Not at the moment," Anton replied. "I think we have some time."

He reached down and scooped up a handful of the gems on the floor.

"We keep finding these," he said. "I wonder why they don't travel?"

Anton placed them in his pocket. "I'll take a few of them, and maybe we can examine them later."

Sachiko suddenly appeared by my side. "I've had a quick look around. This chamber is definitely stable, and I imagine most of the tunnels are stable too, but I think William is right that we shouldn't linger. However, we should have enough time to take a quick look around."

Anton had disappeared from my circle of light, and I could hear signs of rummaging not too far away.

Sachiko looked toward the sound. "Although, for what it's worth, I don't think you're going to find a magical portal down here."

"There were 'transportation' artifacts," Anton replied from the darkness. "I think something like that would be quite handy."

"That doesn't mean there's one here," Sachiko said. "And the Queen seems to have her own method of transporting people—that mist that only Katie can see. So she doesn't need an artifact."

"But there has to be some way she's locating these places," Anton said. "Royal tombs were kept secret just like the other tombs—except for a few notable exceptions. It's not like the Sídh left a map for her."

"That's actually a good point," Sachiko said.

"Of course it is," Anton said. "Why don't you come over here and help me look?"

The two of them continued to talk, and I moved away from them—I couldn't help them look for artifacts anyway. And I had a strong feeling there was something else I should be looking for.

I stepped forward into the darkness.

It was disconcerting knowing I was walking through a vast, empty space, and my foot crunched occasionally on a precious gem or shard of wood that had been washed away from the area near Anton and the chests.

I walked until I could no longer hear the sounds of Anton and Sachiko's conversation.

Once they were out of earshot, I shut off my flashlight.

I had a feeling it would be better to sense rather than see what I was looking for.

I continued to walk in the dark. My eyes didn't really adjust to the light, because there wasn't any light down in the stone chamber, but somehow I grew accustomed to the darkness, and I was more comfortable moving in it.

I walked forward boldly, and a little wisp of something not far off caught my eye. I stepped closer to it and kneeled down.

A little shard of wood had a scrap of cloth clinging to it—it must have been torn off when one of the vampires broke out of his coffin. And clinging to the scrap of cloth was a tiny plume of white mist—it floated around the cloth, glowing softly in the darkness.

I didn't want to touch the cloth for fear of disturbing it, but here I had a piece of the mist.

As I was examining it, I saw another wisp of mist not far off.

I moved closer to it and bumped up against a wall.

I took out my flashlight, and I saw that the wisp was actually clinging to the opening of a round hole that was about a foot across.

Peering into the hole, I could see that it extended back as far as I could see—it was actually a tunnel. And lining the tunnel were even tinier wisps of mist—it was as if this was the last place they had dissipated from.

I leaned in a little closer. Beyond the light of my little flashlight, something glinted gold. Even the extra light from the wisps of mist was not enough to illuminate what it was—I could just make out a strange, hunched shape. And then just for a moment, I thought I saw a flash of red.

Without thinking about it, I began to sing the song my mother had taught me, and I reached out with my mind and heart for the clear fire—I had to have more light.

After a moment, sparks sprang to life all around me. I had summoned the clear fire—or at least as much of it as I was capable of summoning at the moment.

I had plenty of light now, but I was arrested momentarily by the sight of the sparks. The entire cave chamber was illuminated now, and the sparks filled the space like stars in the sky. It was a little like looking up at the constellations at night.

As I gazed up at the sparks, I suddenly realized that I wasn't alone.

Sachiko and Anton had come up to stand beside me and were now staring up at the sparks.

And then William appeared next, and seeing him in the light of the fragmented clear fire reminded me of the first time I had ever summoned it in the Pure Woods. He was staring at it in wonder, just as he had then.

"What happened?" William said.

"I needed a little more light," I replied.

"So this is the clear fire?" Anton said. "That thing you lost the ability to summon and use?"

"This is it," I said. "Sort of. It didn't used to look like this. It used to be all together in a sphere."

"Is it broken?" Anton said.

"I don't know," I said. "I don't know very much about it."

"Well, broken or not," William said, "it's beautiful."

"What did you need the light for?" Sachiko asked.

I turned back to the small, round tunnel. "There's something in here."

I peered into the tunnel—now I could see quite clearly a gold dome with a red jewel on one end.

"I think I can reach it," I said, leaning in and stretching my hand out as far as I could reach.

William moved toward me swiftly. "Are you sure that's a good idea?"

My hand touched something smooth and cold, and as it did so, the world in front of me disappeared, and I saw a flash of dark eyes. A moment later, I saw a statue turn its face toward me.

Chapter Eighteen

I stepped back from the tunnel quickly.

"What is it?" William said. "Are you hurt?"

He swiftly took my hands in his and turned them over.

"No, I'm all right," I said. "I just saw something—a vision. Eyes—and then a statue."

"What do you think it means?" Sachiko asked.

"I don't know," I said.

"Well, I'll tell you what I see," Anton said. He was leaning into the small, round tunnel. "I see a big, gold bug."

"A what?" I said.

Anton pulled his head out of the tunnel again, and in his hands he held the gold object I had glimpsed.

It was indeed a dome, as it had appeared to be, but it was flat on the bottom, with six slender appendages dangling down that appeared to be legs. There was a semicircle on one end with a red jewel set into it—it appeared to be a head. As Anton held it, the dome began to tremble and the legs began to move. The creature looked to be a giant, gold beetle.

"Shall I let it go?" Anton said.

Without waiting for a response, he set the beetle on the floor, and it began to scuttle around.

By the light of the clear fire, I saw it run over to a blue jewel that was lying a few feet off.

The beetle picked up the jewel with its forelegs and examined it excitedly, and then the wings on its back opened, revealing a hollow space. The beetle tossed the jewel into the space, and then its wings closed again. As the wings closed, the beetle began making a loud, buzzing sound.

The beetle then scurried off to pick up another jewel.

"What is that?" Sachiko said. "Is it a machine?"

"I think it's actually an old vampire artifact," Anton said. "I think we have some vampire magic at work here."

"What's it doing?" Sachiko asked.

"Aside from buzzing and picking up gems?" Anton said. "I don't really know."

"Well, whatever it is," William said, "I think we should get out of here."

"Now?" Anton said.

"Have you found anything?" William said. "Apart from that gem-collecting beetle?"

"No, but—"

"It's too risky," William said. "We can't stay down here and just hope that the tunnels don't collapse. I've found one that's stable, but there's no way of knowing how long that will last."

"I've found something," I said slowly.

William turned toward me. "What's that?"

"It doesn't require us to stay down here," I said. "It's just that I found some mist clinging to the tunnel where the beetle was."

"And what does that mean?" Sachiko asked.

"It's given me an idea," I said. "I think the mist I'm seeing is somehow related to the smoke trails I used to see with the kosts and the hybrids. I used that smoke to track them. If we can find more mist, maybe I can track it all the way back to the Queen."

"It seems to dissipate pretty quickly," William said.

"I know," I said. "But at least it's a chance."

"Well, let's discuss it above ground," William said.

I glanced around the cave and caught a glimpse of the gold beetle scuttling toward another jewel. Somehow, its determination made me feel uneasy.

"I agree that we should get going," I said.

"But I've hardly had time to look around," Anton protested.

"I can't make you go if you want to stay," William said.

"Fine," Anton said. "If you're all leaving, I'll leave too."

He glanced over his shoulder at the beetle. "But I'm strongly tempted to take that thing with us."

"Leave it," William said sharply. "We don't know what else it can do, and it's a complication we don't need. The safe tunnel's this way."

William hurried off across the big chamber, and Sachiko and I followed him.

Anton followed us after a moment.

William led us into another, smaller chamber, and I paused when I saw the tunnel opening he was leading us toward.

"Wait just a minute," I said. "I need to put out the lights."

I looked up at the sparks from the clear fire that dappled the ceiling and walls.

I closed my eyes and turned my attention inward. I focused on the clear fire.

I willed it to return to its hiding place.

When I felt the warmth of the clear fire leave me, I opened my eyes, and the chamber was black again.

William took my hand. "The tunnel's this way."

He led me along the tunnel, and I assumed that Anton and Sachiko were following—I couldn't see anything in the dark.

I managed to make it all the way up through the tunnel without stumbling, and eventually, we broke out into the open air.

It was still night, and we were now standing in a different part of the forest—there was no sign of the stream here.

"So where to now?" Anton said.

William looked up at the sky through the mostly bare branches of the trees that surrounded us.

"It's dark now, but dawn's not far off," he said. "Katie really needs to get some rest."

"I'm fine," I said quickly.

William gave my hand a gentle squeeze. "You may think you're fine, but the human body can only keep going for so long. You should sleep."

"We can go back to my house," Sachiko said. "It's safe there, and we can all recharge a little."

"That's great," Anton said. "But what do we do after that? I assume you're all going to veto the idea of coming back to this royal tomb."

"You assume correctly," William said. "There's nothing for us down there."

"Dmitry and Grace thought it was important," Anton said.

"And we didn't see them in that big chamber," William said, "which means that they didn't find anything and decided to move on."

"Or maybe they already found what they were looking for," Anton said. "Maybe we missed the important find."

"That's just speculation on your part," William said. "And Katie needs sleep. We'll figure out what to do in a few hours."

I was about to protest again that I was fine to go on, but then I felt myself swaying on my feet.

"I have to admit, sleep sounds good," I said.

"Then it's settled," William said.

He turned to Sachiko. "Lead the way."

Sachiko sped off into the night, and William and I followed her.

We soon came to a stop in front of Sachiko's door, and Anton arrived moments later.

Sachiko let us into the house.

"Would you like something to eat?" she said to me. "Something to drink? I do have a little bit of human food around here."

"A glass of water would be great," I said. "But then I think I'd just like to sleep."

"Works for me," Sachiko said.

She led me into the kitchen, and soon I had my glass of water. Then I went upstairs to my room.

I quickly fell asleep.

When I woke up, sunlight was streaming into the room. I glanced at the clock on my phone. I had only been asleep for a few hours, but I felt refreshed anyway and ready to keep going.

I went downstairs and found William, Sachiko, and Anton seated around the dining room table.

"I think we should go back," Anton was saying. "We didn't really spend any time there at all."

"And I think we should move on," Sachiko said. "There's nothing we can use in those tunnels."

The three of them looked up as I came in.

"Good morning, Katie," Anton said. "You're just in time to help us continue the argument we've been having for several hours."

Sachiko got up from the table. "You must be hungry by now. Can I get you some breakfast?"

"Just cereal would be great if you have it," I said.

"I do," Sachiko said. "I went on a breakfast food run this morning. Have a seat."

In a moment, I was seated at the table with a bowl of cereal and milk.

Sachiko sat down beside me.

"So the situation stands like this," she said. "Anton alternately argues that we should go back to the tunnels or go looking for Dmitry and Grace—he thinks the key to finding the Queen must be or has been in the tunnels. I think we might try tracking down Dylan—the guy from the Order. That could be time-consuming, but at least we know he's likely to know the location of the Queen. And William now thinks we should try your suggestion and see if you can track down some of that mist."

"Isn't that touching?" Anton said. "William has been arguing on your behalf. Of course, I have no idea how you're just going to be able to go outside and find a random piece of water vapor. Especially since—as William himself pointed out last night—the mist dissipates quickly. But that's just me."

"Why don't we just head out to the Black Sea?" I said. "We already know that's where the Queen is, and that's where Dylan was reportedly headed. If we go out that way, maybe I'll spot some more mist—and then I can track that to her island."

"Do you have any idea how big the Black Sea is?" Anton said. "We'll never find anything if we just randomly set sail on the water. We have to know where we're going."

"And how do we do that?" I said.

"We go back down into the tunnels," Anton replied.

"The tunnels that are in danger of flooding at any minute?" William said.

"Yes," Anton said. "Those tunnels. There's a clue down there somewhere. I know it."

"What about going back to the archives?" Sachiko said. "Grace had something like a map down there. Maybe that will give us an idea."

Anton shook his head. "That map wasn't even remotely to scale. I'm pretty sure they just stuck a dot anywhere they thought looked nice."

"I really think—" William began.

Anton cut him off. "How about this? Just humor me, and let's go back into the tunnels one more time. If we don't find anything, I'll go with you guys to the Black Sea where we can sail around and look for members of the Order or mist or whatever else you want to look for."

"No," William said. "We can't risk a collapse. You and I and Sachiko can probably make it out okay if the tunnels flood or cave in, but Katie can't survive something like that."

"The tunnels aren't that bad," Anton said. "We got in and out all right, didn't we? And it's not like it was a close call. We made it out in perfect safety."

"You really feel that strongly about the tunnels?" I said.

"I really do," Anton replied.

"Katie, you can't seriously consider this," William said.

"Maybe one last look is worth it," I said. "Anton isn't really the fanciful type."

"I'm really not," Anton said.

William turned to Sachiko. "What do you think?"

"Honestly, I don't think there's much in the tunnels besides a shiny gold bug," Sachiko said. "I think our earlier trip was enough to find anything worthwhile that was down there. But if taking one last look will silence Anton and get him to come along with us, I think it's worth it."

"You mean just humor him?" William said.

"That is what I suggested you all do," Anton said.

Sachiko put a hand on William's arm. "Don't worry. We'll get Katie in and out of there safely."

Anton stood up. "So let's get going, shall we?"

"I haven't actually finished breakfast yet," I said.

"Fine," Anton replied. "I'll go ahead and meet you guys there. I'll be at the unflooded tunnel we exited from. And I'll try not to make any big discoveries before you get there."

Anton's figure blurred and left the room.

I heard the front door open and close.

"I really think this is a mistake," William said.

"It'll be fine," Sachiko said. "We'll go down for a few minutes and look around. And it will keep him quiet."

I finished up breakfast quickly, and then we all went outside.

"Let's take the car," Sachiko said. "Anton's going to wear himself out expending so much energy during the day."

William, Sachiko, and I all got into her car, and she drove off quickly.

Before long, we had reached a familiar-looking wooded area, and Sachiko parked the car.

We all got out.

"It's this way," Sachiko said.

She led us through the trees and eventually, we reached the tunnel we had exited from last night.

Sachiko looked around. "There's no sign of water around here. We should be good."

She stepped into the tunnel, and William and I followed her.

Once we were fully surrounded by darkness, Sachiko took off down the tunnel. William took my hand, and we hurried after her.

Soon we were down in the vast stone chamber where we had been searching last night.

I held up my little flashlight, and I couldn't see anything beyond its small circle. I was surrounded by a sea of darkness.

"Anton?" William said. "Are you down here?"

"Yes," said a voice from a distance. "Just a minute."

A moment later, I felt a rush of air, and suddenly I could see Anton's face looming out of the darkness.

"Guess what I found?" Anton said.

"What's that?" William said.

"Vampire tracks," Anton said.

Even in the dark, I could see his smug smile.

"What are vampire tracks?" William said.

"You know, tracks left by vampires?" Anton replied.

"You mean footprints?" William said.

"You could call it that."

"That's not so remarkable," William said. "How do you know they weren't made by humans?"

"I just know," Anton said.

"Fine," William said. "Where are they?"

"They're up above us. They run right over this chamber."

"So you mean someone was walking on the ground above these tunnels?" William said. "That really could have been anybody."

"No," Anton said. "It wasn't just anybody. This place is pretty remote. It was Dmitry and Grace."

"And you know that?" William said. "Even without having seen them?"

"Yes."

"So what's the significance of that?"

"I don't know," Anton said. "But I bet there's a clue down here."

"That's great. That's very helpful," William said.

"That gold beetle," Anton said. "Do you know he's been busily working all night? He's right over there."

Anton stepped out of my little circle of light.

He returned a moment later with the big, gold beetle that we had seen last night. He held the beetle flipped over on its back, and its slender legs worked busily in the air.

Anton gave the beetle a little shake, and it rattled.

"Don't worry," Anton said. "He's just metal so that doesn't hurt him. But do you hear that? He's all full of jewels. He's been collecting them ever since we woke him up last night."

"Why is he doing that?" I said.

"Exactly," Anton said. "That's what I've been puzzling over since we found him. This little guy—he's just an artifact. He's not alive. Somebody wound him up and set him to work collecting all these jewels. The question is, who would do that?"

"The Queen of the Moon?" I hazarded.

"Again—exactly," Anton said. "Who else do we know who's interested in these underground burial chambers? No one I can think of—the Queen's really the only one who wants big, wooden boxes full of vampire dust. So why does she want this beetle to collect these jewels?"

"Maybe they're also vampire artifacts?" I said.

"Maybe," Anton said. "That's what I was thinking at first too. And then I got here, and I found the vampire tracks up above."

"You're not making any sense," William said.

"And every time you say that, you're wrong," Anton replied. "The vampire tracks don't run along a logical course. They run through the trees in a crazy way—they aren't following a clear path, and there appear to be two sets of them. It's like two people are following something small—something that winds around at times."

I glanced at the gold artifact in his hand. "You think they're following the beetle?"

"No," Anton said. "But you're on the right track. Much as Grace and Dmitry were."

"I don't see where you're headed with this," I said.

"He isn't headed anywhere with it," William said. "He doesn't know what he's talking about."

"No," Anton said. "I think I've figured it out."

He turned to me. "You can puzzle it out with me. You seem to be the only one here with an open mind."

"Okay," I said.

"So we've got this little guy here," Anton said, giving the gold beetle another rattle. "And as far as we know, he was sent by the Queen, and now he's picking up all these jewels."

"Right," I said.

"And we don't know why," Anton said, "but the jewels don't disappear when the vampires do."

"Right again," I said.

"So why is this little guy collecting jewels? The Queen already has what she wants—she has her reanimated vampires. What does she need the jewels for?"

"They're vampire artifacts like you said," I said.

"They could be," Anton said. "But I think their real significance is something else."

"What's that?"

"Well, I was wondering earlier about how the Queen was able to find these places," Anton said. "You remember how I mentioned that?"

"Yes," I said.

"Because it's not like the Sídh would have given her a map," Anton said. "They intended for her to be trapped forever. So then I thought about how this beetle has one of these jewels embedded in its head and how it goes around collecting them."

"Oh, I see," I said. An idea was forming slowly. "The beetle has been set to look for these jewels, and if he finds them, he finds one of these burial sites."

"As I said before—exactly," Anton said. "I bet he even drills."

Anton walked off, and I followed him with my flashlight.

He reached a wall and set the beetle up against it. The slender gold legs quickly latched onto the wall, and as I watched, the beetle's head began to spin. Within moments, it had drilled a small, round hole into the wall. As the hole grew, the beetle climbed inside and disappeared.

Moments later, the beetle reappeared. He clambered out of the hole and climbed down toward the floor. Then he scuttled off into the darkness.

"See?" Anton said. "He knows there are still jewels in here, so he turned right back around. There must be something special about these jewels—some unique quality they have. Otherwise, these beetles would be raiding all the local jewelry stores."

"You think there's more than one?" I said.

"I don't *know*," Anton said. "But I imagine so. That's the only way she could really do this."

"So the Queen of the Moon sends out these beetles," I said. "They find the jewels, and then that means that she's found one of these royal tombs. Then she sends the mist and brings back the vampires."

"That's what it looks like to me," Anton said.

"But how does she know when the beetles have found anything?" I said. "Do they have some way of signaling her?"

"I don't know," Anton said. "Maybe that's what the buzzing is—it happens every time the beetle picks up one of the jewels."

"So why do some vampires disappear and not others?" William said. "We were both surrounded by vampires down in the cave in Elspeth's Grove, and they disappeared, and we didn't."

"Maybe it has something to do with the jewels," Anton said.

"It can't be that," William said. "Vampires without jewels have disappeared—Veronika's Promised One, for example."

"That's true," Anton said. "I don't know everything yet. And I was working up to my big reveal."

Suddenly, Sachiko appeared by my side.

"Anton is right," she said. "The tracks up above are vampire tracks. I just went to see for myself."

"We already covered that," Anton said. "It was never in doubt."

"How do you know they're vampire tracks?" William said.

"Because of the speed," Sachiko said. "Vampires can travel much faster than humans can, so the footprints tend to blur and scuff together. There were two vampires, and they were traveling very fast."

"Grace and Dmitry?" William said.

"Seems most likely," Sachiko replied. "And they were taking an unusual path. It winds through the trees."

"So her you believe?" Anton said. "But not me?"

"Just think of it as confirmation," William said.

"Well, whatever it is," Anton said, "it leads into my next point."

"Which is?" William said.

"I know how to find the Queen."

"How?" William said.

"We just follow the tunnel the beetle made all the way back to her island," Anton said.

"That will never work," William said.

"Sure it will," Anton replied. "The tunnel's right over here."

Anton disappeared from my circle of light, and William took my hand and led me over to him. Sachiko followed us.

"See?" Anton said, indicating the small, round hole in the wall. "The beetle tunneled here after being sent by the Queen. All we have to do is follow it."

I peered closely at the tunnel. I could still see wisps of mist clinging to the inside.

"It could work," Sachiko said.

"There's no way," William said. "The tunnel's far too small. None of us could possibly fit in there."

"We're not going to go through the tunnel," Anton said. "We'll track it from above."

"There's no way to do that," William said.

"Of course there is," Anton said. "That's exactly what Grace and Dmitry are doing."

"It'll take too long," William said.

"Grace and Dmitry don't think so."

"Well, I do," William said. "We can't possibly get to the Black Sea in time. Even at our fastest speed it would take forever. And we don't know what type of geographical obstacles we could come across—there could be anything in the way—rivers, valleys, towns."

"I know what it is," Anton said. "I know how they're doing it."

"How?" I said.

"It's those earrings Grace had," Anton said. "I knew they were vampire artifacts. She sent one of the bird earrings into the tunnel. Then she's tracking the path using the other earring. It sends back a signal."

"So they'll follow the bird all the way back to the Queen?" I said.

"Yep," Anton replied. "The bird will fly all the way back to the source using the tunnel the beetle made."

"So what good will that do?" William said. "Even if we could track the bird or Grace and Dmitry? We still won't get there in time—we can't move fast enough."

"There may be another way," Anton said.

Once again, he disappeared into the darkness. When he reappeared, he was holding a long stick, which he held out horizontally. At the end of the stick was a pair of glasses.

"Have you ever seen one of these before?" Anton said.

"I can't say that I have," I said.

"It's called a pathfinder," Anton replied. "It's an ancient vampire artifact like the birds and the beetle. And like the birds, this artifact was used for tracking."

"Again, it's not so much the tracking as the speed that's the issue," William said. "Tracking anything won't help us if it takes us weeks to get there."

"Just wait," Anton said. "I hadn't quite finished yet. These glasses will help you pinpoint a spot on a map. While wearing them, you think of what you're looking for. Then you should be able to see the path appear in front of you on the map itself."

"There's no way that will work," William said.

"Well, these artifacts can be quite tricky," Anton replied. "Some of them are just junk, but some of them are the real deal, and this one happens to be the real deal. Of course, the real article does tend to be somewhat temperamental, and some work for everyone, while others only work for a select few that have a knack for it."

"And you happen to have the knack?" William said. "Is that what you're saying?"

"I don't know," Anton said. "I hope I do. And if not me, then I hope one of us does. Otherwise, as you keep saying, we are going to have a very long walk ahead of us."

"How do you know all of this?" Sachiko asked.

"I know a thing or two about vampire artifacts," Anton said. "It's sort of a hobby of mine."

"So how do we make this thing work?" Sachiko said.

"First we need a map," Anton said. "I don't suppose anyone happens to have a map of Russia on them?"

"You mean like a paper one?" Sachiko said.

"Yes."

"No," Sachiko replied.

"I thought not," Anton said.

"But I can get one," Sachiko said.

Sachiko vanished abruptly from my circle of light, and in less time than I would have thought possible, she was back with an armful of paper maps.

"I brought a few," she said. "Just in case we need some different views."

Anton selected one—a big map of Russia—and spread it out on the floor.

"Now let's see what we can see," he said.

Anton sat down and held the stick with the glasses out over the map. The glasses were about a foot from his face.

He looked the map over anxiously and changed position several times. Eventually, he lowered the glasses.

"It's no good," he said. "I don't see a thing."

"That's because you're holding the glasses too far away," Sachiko said. "Nobody could see anything through them that way."

"This is exactly how they're supposed to work," Anton said with dignity.

Sachiko held out her hand. "Let me try."

Anton held the glasses out to her, and she took his place on the floor by the map. At first she held the glasses up close to her eyes and peered over the map carefully. Then she held the glasses out by the stick, just as Anton had done.

"Do you see anything?" Anton asked.

"No," Sachiko said. "Maybe it's the wrong map."

She held out her hand again. "Give me the map of the Black Sea area. I made sure to bring one."

Anton sifted through the maps until he found the right one, and he handed it to her.

"Thanks," Sachiko said.

She spread the second map out on the floor and began to pore over it. Eventually, however, she sat back on her heels.

"Nothing," she said.

Anton looked up at William. "Looks like it's your turn."

William accepted the glasses and looked over the maps, just as Anton and Sachiko had done, but eventually, he too sat back and shook his head.

"So we're zero for three so far," Anton said. He looked up at me. "Would you like to try?"

"But I'm not a vampire," I said.

"It's true that these are vampire artifacts," Anton replied. "And vampire artifacts operate on vampire magic. But maybe magic is magic. And you're easily the most magical one of us here. Besides, it can't hurt anything—if they don't work, they don't work."

William held the glasses out to me, and I took them.

He moved aside, and I sat down next to him in front of the big map of Russia.

"What do I do exactly?" I said.

"Just hold the stick out in front of you," Anton said. "With the glasses at the end. I can take your flashlight for you."

I gave Anton my little flashlight, and he kneeled beside me, holding the light over my head.

"Now, just look through the glasses at the end of the stick. You don't need to bring them any closer. Just look through the glasses exactly where they are and look down at the map. And then think of what you need to find."

"This is a little awkward," I said.

"Yes, it is," Anton replied. "But that's how it works."

I looked through the glasses, as Anton had instructed, and I could see the map on the floor through them. The lenses of the glasses didn't change or magnify the map in any way—it was just like looking at the map through clear glass. I thought of the little bird earrings I had seen Grace wearing—I thought of one of them flying swiftly through the tunnel. But somehow that didn't seem quite right. My thoughts shifted then, and I thought of the wisps of mist clinging to the inside of the little, round tunnel. I could picture the wisps running all the way back down the tunnel—all the way back to their source.

"Anything?" Anton said.

"No," I replied.

"Keep looking," Anton said.

"I am," I replied. "It just looks like an ordinary map."

But as I stared down at the map, I thought I saw a flash of red.

"Wait," I said, "there's—"

"What?" Anton said.

"There's a line forming," I said.

As I watched, the flash of red settled onto the map and began to grow into a line. The red line started at our current location and began to snake across the map, winding slowly but surely across the countryside—across roads, cities, and rivers.

Eventually, the red line came to a stop.

It had come to a very decisive end in the Black Sea.

Chapter Nineteen

W hat do you see?" Anton said.

"There's a line," I said again. "A red line that runs across the map. It goes all the way to the Black Sea."

"That one may not be detailed enough," Sachiko said. She swept the map out of my way. "Try the other one—the Black Sea one."

I moved over to look at the Black Sea map, and I positioned my glasses over it once again.

At first I saw nothing, and then the red line appeared again. I watched it until it stopped.

"It stops right there," I said, pointing with my finger in the air since I couldn't reach that portion of the map. "Just off the coast of that town called Tayna."

Sachiko leaned over and placed her finger on the map.

"Here?" she said.

"That's the right town," I said. "Now down just a little down and to the left."

Sachiko kept moving her finger until she hit the right spot.

"There!" I said. "That's where the red line stops."

"I don't suppose anybody has a pen?" Anton said.

"Actually, I have one," Sachiko said, reaching into her pocket with her free hand.

"Why do you have a pen?" Anton said. "Do you always carry one around?"

"I bought one when I bought the maps," Sachiko replied. "I thought it might come in handy."

"You *bought* one?" Anton said.

"Of course I did," Sachiko replied. "I bought the maps too. That was actually the part that took the longest."

"It wasn't necessary to buy anything," Anton said. "That's all I'm saying."

"Yes, it was," Sachiko replied.

She looked up at me. "About here?"

Sachiko moved her finger from the map and replaced it with the point of the pen.

"Yes," I said. "That's right where the red line stops."

Sachiko made a mark with the pen and then quickly folded the map up.

"That won't give us an exact location," she said. "But it will get us closer than any other method."

As she gathered up the rest of the maps, she glanced up at me.

"How did you make the glasses work, by the way?"

"I don't know," I said. "I thought about Grace's gold bird first and nothing happened. And then I thought about the mist, and I pictured it traveling all the way through the tunnel. That's when the red line began to appear."

"Katie is magical," Anton said. "That's why it worked."

"We really should get moving," William said. "We don't want to spend a minute longer down here than we have to."

"What about these?" I said, indicating the glasses. "Should we take them along?"

"Just chuck them back in the pile," Anton said. "We already have what we need."

"Wait," William said. "They might be useful, and if we leave them here, we might not be able to come back to this place again if we need them later. Besides, we'll need to take a few bags anyway if we're going to take a plane."

"Are we going to take a plane?" Anton said.

"Of course we are," William said. "It's the quickest way to get to the Black Sea."

"We should go back to my house," Sachiko said. "We can get some stuff ready there."

Anton gave me back my flashlight, and we left the cave quickly.

We went back to Sachiko's car and drove to her house.

Once inside, William got to work on flight arrangements, while Sachiko and I went upstairs to pack a few bags.

I began to pack quickly, and as I worked, Sachiko came into my room.

"Do you mind if I go into your closet?" she asked. "I've got some guys' things tucked away in there too—you never know what you might need. I thought I would pack those up for Anton and William."

"Yes, of course," I said. "It's actually your room. And the stuff I'm packing to take with me is mostly your stuff anyway."

"Thanks," Sachiko said. "The things we do to not seem suspicious."

Sachiko bustled around swiftly between her room and mine. Soon she had three bags packed in the same time it took me to finish one.

Sachiko stood with her hands on her hips, looking at our four bags in a row.

"Are we good to go?" she asked.

"I think so," I replied.

After a brief stop in the kitchen so that I could pick up a few snacks for the trip, Sachiko, William, Anton, and I all went out to Sachiko's car, and then we were out on the road to the airport.

A few hours of driving brought us to the airport, and after another two hours of waiting, we were on our flight.

This time there were no first-class tickets, and we were all seated separately.

"Guess this will be time for me to get some rest," Sachiko murmured as we made our way into the body of the plane.

I found my seat by a window, and I pulled the shade down. As the plane took off, I decided to use the time to get some sleep too.

I woke up just as we were touching down again.

As the four of us left the plane, I could see that dusk was coming on.

Sachiko swept us into a rental car that she'd procured, and soon we were on our way to Tayna.

The sun had set fully by the time we made it into town, and Sachiko pulled into the parking lot of a small restaurant. The restaurant was on a cliff near the coast, and even in the dark, I could see waves crashing on the beach far below.

"You guys go in and make sure Katie eats something," Sachiko said, opening the car door. "I'll be right back."

"Wait," William said. "Where are you going?"

"I'm going to do a little reconnaissance," Sachiko said. "I'll see if the locals have noticed anything unusual. It may help us figure out where to go next."

Before William could reply, Sachiko had shut the door and vanished.

"I guess we're going inside," William muttered.

"I'm not," Anton said. "I'm going to have a look around too."

Anton got out of the car and disappeared.

"It's just you and me, then," I said.

"I think we're better off that way," William replied.

As the two of us got out of the car, I thought I saw the faintest wisp of mist float by me, and I turned toward it quickly.

William followed my gaze. "What is it? What's wrong?"

I looked all around in the night, but I couldn't see any hint of the wisp anymore.

"It's nothing," I said. "Just my eyes playing tricks on me."

William hesitated for a moment, scanning the night for any sign of danger.

Then the two of us went into the restaurant.

As we settled in at the table and gave our order, I noticed that William was staring at me.

"Is something wrong?" I said.

"No, nothing's wrong," William said. "I mean apart from our current predicament. It's just that we haven't really had a chance to talk since we left the Black Tomb."

"No, we haven't," I said.

"I'm glad you came with me," William said. "Really glad. I've realized that things are always better when you come along."

"Thanks," I said.

"I mean it," William said. "I may have said this before, but it's worth saying again. I was wrong to keep you out before—to run off and do things without telling you, without including you. I feel like a lot of things would've gone better if I'd only confided in you."

He paused as our order arrived—a sandwich for me, soup for him.

William pushed the soup aside and leaned his elbows on the table.

"The worst thing is that by keeping everything to myself, I taught you not to trust me. I taught you to keep things from me."

I looked up into William's eyes. He was clearly miserable.

"You didn't teach me not to trust you," I said quietly. "I trust you more than anyone else in the world. You don't have to punish yourself for this."

"Katie, when I think of—"

"William, it's all right," I said. "Everything's all right. You don't have anything to be forgiven for. And even if you did—I forgive you."

"I've put you in danger," William said. "By keeping you in the dark."

"I'm supposed to be in danger," I said. "I'm the Little Sun. And you've lost so much. I can't blame you for being secretive or for wanting to protect me. You don't want to lose everything again."

William nodded. "You're right that I'm afraid of losing everything again. And what I'm most afraid of losing is you. You're a bright, shining light in my life in more ways than you'll ever know."

He looked up at me. "But you have a destiny. You have an important job—a calling, really—that you have to fulfill. I realize that now. I can't stand in the way of that."

I reached for William's hand. "You're not standing in my way. In fact, I don't think I could do this—any of this—without you."

For the first time, my words seemed to get through to William, and I saw some of the tension leave his face.

"You think I help you?" he said slowly.

"I know you do," I said. "Like you said, things are better when we're together."

"So you really do forgive me?" William said.

"I really do. But as I said, there's nothing to forgive."

William was silent for a moment.

"Together," he said at last. "It's a hard word for me to believe in sometimes. I'm always so afraid to lose things—to lose you. But I think I'm finally starting to see that I don't have to be afraid that you'll disappear."

"I'm not going anywhere," I said. "I'm right where I want to be—I'm with you."

I finished my sandwich, and William prevailed on me to eat his soup, and then we went outside to see if either Sachiko or Anton was waiting for us at the car.

But the car was empty, and nobody was in sight on the little road that ran past the restaurant.

The night air was crisp and cold, but the countryside was beautiful even in the dark, and the sky above was a little cloudy and filled with stars.

William glanced around. "I suppose we should wait."

I turned toward William and wrapped my arms around him. William responded by wrapping his around me, and I leaned against him happily.

"It's so peaceful at this moment," I said.

William nestled his chin on the top of my head.

"It is," he said. "It's nice to enjoy just being with you. Maybe someday we can have nights like this all the time."

William held me a little tighter. "I can hear the water from here. The sound is very soothing."

I leaned against him and stared out into the night.

As I did so, I thought I saw another wisp of mist float by.

I pulled away from William and turned toward the wisp.

"What's wrong?" William said.

"Nothing's wrong," I said. "Would you mind if we just took a little walk down this road?"

William looked up at the road that ran past the restaurant.

"Sure," he said, but he gave me another questioning glance.

The road wasn't well lit, but the stars were out, and I knew William could see well enough in the dark.

We started off down the road.

William looked over at me. "It's clear that you're looking for something. Won't you please tell me what it is?"

I hesitated.

"I thought we were making progress," William said. "And if you'll recall, we both came here for the same reason."

"You're right," I said. "It's just that I'm used to having to hide when I notice something strange."

"You don't have to do that with me," William said. "I'll never doubt you."

"I can't be sure if I'm seeing what I think I'm seeing," I said.

"You don't have to be sure," William said. "Just tell me what you think."

"I think I'm seeing the mist again," I said. "The same mist I saw down in the tunnels in Krov. But it's very faint—it's like I'm just seeing little tendrils of mist. But I can't be sure I'm seeing anything at all. I could just be seeing what I want to see."

William took my hand. "If you think you see it, we'll go looking for it."

Our pace before had been a little hesitant—but now we walked with purpose. We continued on down the road, and soon the restaurant was lost to my view.

There weren't a lot of other buildings around, and the shoulder of the road we were walking on was fairly narrow.

I glanced over my shoulder.

William gave my hand a little squeeze. "You don't have to worry about cars. I can hear them coming, and I'll let you know. Just relax and focus on what you're looking for."

I turned back toward the road and told myself just to think of the mist.

William would watch out for me.

Our walk took us on into the starry night, and despite the fact that I didn't see anything, William continued to walk with me patiently.

Then a stiff breeze picked up, and as I turned my face away from the wind, I thought I saw a wisp of mist float past.

"There!" I said quickly.

I followed the mist with my eyes until it dissipated. It was gone quickly, but I was sure I'd seen it.

William turned to look. "You saw it again?"

"Yes," I said.

"Which direction did it come from?"

I turned my face back into the wind. "That way," I said, pointing.

William looked in the direction I indicated.

"That way leads down toward the coast," he said. "If we turn off on this road here, we'll be able to keep going in that direction."

William looked at me. "Don't worry—I can find the way back to the car."

We turned off onto the side road, and I felt the wind more sharply.

William put his arm around me.

"Anything?" he said.

I shook my head. "It's hard to see with the wind in my face."

"Let's try over here," William said.

He pulled me into the shelter of a nearby tree, and I was cut off from the sharp bite of the wind.

"Is that better?" William said.

"Yes," I replied.

"Let's just watch from here," William said. "We'll see if anything else goes by."

After a few minutes, our patience was rewarded—I saw another wisp of mist float by, borne on the wind.

"There's more mist," I said.

I stepped back to look around William, and I saw another scrap of mist float by his shoulder.

"There's another piece of it," I said. "It all seems to be headed the same way."

"That way?" William said, pointing the same direction I had earlier.

"Yes," I said.

"Well, that way definitely leads toward the coast. Let's just head for it and see what we can see once we get there."

"Works for me," I said.

William took my hand, and we headed off down the road again.

We had not gone far when a car pulled up beside us.

The window rolled down, and Sachiko looked out at us.

"Can I offer you a lift?" she said.

"Yes, thanks," I said. "I'd be happy to get out of this wind."

William and I both got in the car.

"So why did you guys ditch the car?" Sachiko asked.

"I thought I saw some mist," I said. "And we started to head toward it. I didn't know where it was coming from at first, and I wouldn't really have been able to spot it from a car."

"Understandable," Sachiko said. "Tracking is harder from a car. So where to now?"

"We were heading down to the coast," William said. "The mist seems to be coming from that direction."

"Makes sense," Sachiko said. "We know we're looking for an island. And it syncs up with what I heard in town."

"What did you find out?" I said.

"I looked up some connections I have in the area," Sachiko said. "That guy Dylan from the Order has been seen around here. In fact, I know exactly which part of the coast he's been hanging out on—the guy's not so good at being stealthy. With any luck, finding him should lead us right to the Queen of the Moon's island."

"That's great news," I said. "If the Order's here, then we're definitely on the right track."

"I learned a few other things too," Sachiko said. "There were powerful earthquakes that rocked this area not long ago—a whole series of them. And a vampire in antique clothes wandered into town a few days ago, and the local vampires didn't know what to make of him."

"That's good news but also deeply disturbing," William said. "That army of hers must be nearly ready by now—and who knows what the Werdulac means to use it for?"

He leaned forward in his seat. "How fast can we get to the coast?"

Sachiko shifted the car into gear. "It won't take us long at all."

As we sped along the quiet country road, I glanced into the back seat.

"Where's Anton?" I said.

"I don't know," Sachiko replied. "Last time I saw him, he was with you."

She continued to speed along the road, and after one more sloping turn, I could see the coastline and the sea up ahead of us.

"We're looking for a particular landmark," Sachiko said. "It's a rock formation with a flat top—that's where Dylan's been seen."

We drove along for a few minutes, and then William leaned forward.

"There!" he said.

Sachiko slowed the car, and sure enough, up ahead I could see an outcropping of rock with a flat top silhouetted against the night sky.

Sachiko pulled the car over. "It might be wiser to approach on foot. I doubt very much that Dylan will be happy to see us."

She parked the car in a wide, sandy spot by the side of the road, and we all got out.

"I think you're right," William said. "If we can find the location of the island without tipping off Dylan at all, I think that would be for the best."

"I'm the fastest one here," Sachiko said. "If you don't mind, I'll go on ahead to take a look around."

William and I both agreed, and Sachiko took off into the night, her figure blurring into a dark streak.

William and I followed at a slower pace.

As we walked, I saw more wisps of mist floating by me—they were definitely coming toward us from the water.

William glanced at me. "You see more mist, don't you?"

"Yes," I said.

He reached out to take my hand. "We're in this together—no matter what."

We had not walked much farther when we heard a cry.

"Sachiko?" I said.

"I think that was a man's cry," William said. "We'd better go have a look."

William and I sped off into the night, and soon we were near the base of the flat-topped rock.

William slowed down.

"We should be careful," he said.

The two of us walked silently toward the rock formation.

Suddenly, a large figure dropped down from a boulder right in front of us.

Even in the starlight, I could recognize who it was.

"Terrance!" I said.

The figure seemed startled. "Katie?"

He looked to William. "And it's William, right?"

"Right," William said.

"I'd ask you what you were doing here," I said. "But I pretty much already know."

Terrance sighed. "And I pretty much know what you're doing here too. I guess it was no use my not telling you where this place was."

He looked at William. "Sorry about jumping down on you guys, but I thought I sensed a vampire. I don't really feel it now—I must be off a little."

"So what was that scream?" I asked.

"That was Dylan," Terrance said. "He really is with a vampire. I thought you guys were bringing up the rear to attack. I'd better get over there."

Terrance started to run at a very impressive pace for a human, and William and I both ran after him.

William was careful not to outdistance him, and I glanced over at him. He seemed to feel the same way I did—I wondered how much Terrance knew about William, and how much it was safe for him to know.

We heard another cry, and the three of us came upon Dylan up at the top of one of the few trees that grew near the flat-topped rock. The tree was very tall, and Dylan had just broken one of the limbs that supported him.

Sachiko was standing at the base of the tree.

"Sachiko?" Terrance said. "You're the vampire who attacked Dylan?"

"I didn't attack Dylan," Sachiko said. "I just put him up out of harm's way."

Dylan snapped another branch and let out a small cry.

"I didn't know you were here," Sachiko said to Terrance. "I only heard about him."

She gestured up to Dylan.

"I'm a little better at disguising myself," Terrance said. "Dylan is still learning."

"Why didn't you answer my text?" I said. "You didn't have to tell me where you were—I just wanted to know that you were all right."

"I haven't read it yet," Terrance replied. "You can't always take your phone with you. You don't want it to buzz at the wrong time."

"So I can see that you have some unusual friends," Dylan shouted down from the top of the tree to Terrance. "If I promise not to hurt the vampire, can I climb down from here?"

"I can assure you that I am in no danger from you," Sachiko said. "Just as you are in no danger from me. But I do have to thank you—I found this place much quicker because of you."

Dylan threw Sachiko a baleful glance and began to climb gingerly down from the top of the tree. As he placed his foot on the next branch below him, the branch cracked.

Dylan froze.

"I can come up and help you down," Sachiko said.

"No, thank you," Dylan said stiffly. He maneuvered his way past the broken branch and climbed slowly and carefully down the tree. When he was close enough to the ground, he jumped the rest of the way.

Dylan walked up to Terrance. "This is highly irregular."

"I think you'll find," Terrance said mildly, "that when you're out in the field, a lot of highly irregular things happen."

Dylan stabbed a finger at Sachiko. "She's a vampire. I may not have your keen senses, but I've seen enough of what she can do to know that's true. Don't try to tell me she isn't."

"She is a vampire," Terrance said. "And a good person."

"And that one—Katie," Dylan said, pointing to me. "She's the one we're supposed to be protecting. She's not supposed to be here at all."

Terrance sighed. "Yes, she's the one we were supposed to protect. But you'll find with Katie that she's not so good at sitting on the sidelines."

Dylan turned to look at William. "And that guy—I don't even know who he is."

"That's William," Terrance said. He gave William a long, speculative look. "He's Katie's friend."

"The point is, he's not supposed to be here," Dylan said. "This mission is supposed to be secret. Civilians and vampires are not supposed to be involved."

"Things in the field are very different from the way they are in training," Terrance said. "You'll come to understand that soon enough."

"We have to send them away," Dylan said. "Now."

Terrance eyed the three of us. "Actually, I think we could use their help."

Dylan stared at Terrance. "You've got to be kidding. There's no way we can brief them. This mission is highly classified."

"I doubt they need any briefing—or at least not much," Terrance said. "The very fact that they're here tells me that."

He glanced at us. "Why are you guys here?"

"We're here to stop the Queen of the Moon," I said.

"See what I mean?" Terrance said. "So since we're all here for the same reason, I suggest we pool resources and work together." He turned to Dylan. "Sometimes in the field you get what I like to call 'accidental allies.' You'll find that out for yourself too."

"This is highly irregular," Dylan said again.

"Are you going to report me?"

Dylan stared at Terrance for a long moment.

"No," he said at last. "I'm not a snitch."

"Then let's get to work," Terrance said.

As we were talking, I had noticed more mist floating by, and now the mist was coming faster—I could see a steady swirl of white, luminous vapor.

I looked around, but I could no longer see the water—where we were standing, we were sunk in a little bit of a valley.

"What is it?" Terrance said. "What's wrong?"

"It's the mist," I said. "The mist I was seeing back in Elspeth's Grove—I can see it here too."

Terrance was instantly alert. "Let's get you up to our observation point," he said. "We'll see what you can see from there."

He jogged to the base of the flat-topped rock, and the rest of us hurried after him.

Terrance held out his hand to me. "I can help you up."

William stepped forward quickly. "I can help Katie. You go ahead."

Terrance glanced at William. "Do you know how to climb up a sheer rock face?"

"Yes," William said.

Terrance glanced at me.

"I'll be safe with William," I said.

Terrance gave a brief nod and then began to climb up the rock.

I stood at William's back and wrapped my arms around his neck, and soon we were scaling the rock wall after Terrance.

Before long, we had all made it to the top of the flat rock, and Terrance quickly crouched down.

"Get down!" he hissed. "We don't want to attract any unnecessary attention."

Dylan had already dropped down to the flat surface, and Sachiko, William, and I all followed.

As I did so, I looked out over the water below and saw an enormous, swirling mass of mist not far from the coast.

Chapter Twenty

Y ou can see it, can't you?" Terrance said.

"I can see a huge mass of mist," I said. "It's swirling around one particular point."

"That's it," Terrance said. "That's the island."

"The Queen of the Moon's island?"

"Yes," Terrance said. "None of us can see it but you."

I glanced around at the others. "You can't see anything out there at all?"

"I just see starlight sparkling on the water," Sachiko said.

"It just looks like open sea to me," William said. "I would never know there was an island out there."

"That's part of the Queen of the Moon's defenses," Terrance said. "When the Sídh first set the island up, it was visible to the naked eye—as was the Queen's temple. The Sídh's protections prevented anyone from entering the temple or setting foot on the island, but you could see it. And then one day, as the Queen began to free herself, she set up her own defenses—her own barrier like the one around Zamochit. This one, we believe, only allows vampires to get through."

"Then how do you know it's there?" I said. "How did you find this place?"

"I'll show you in just a moment," Terrance said. "But first, I think we should put our heads together."

"Not allowed," Dylan said.

Terrance ignored him.

"So the big news is that the Queen's building an army," Terrance said.

"Yes, I know," I replied.

Terrance blinked. "How do you know that? We only found out when I saw them all standing in rows down in the cave in Elspeth's Grove—that's why I had to leave so suddenly. So how did you—"

Terrance paused. "You know what? Never mind."

He sighed and continued. "So we figure she's raising an army to give to the Werdulac. And we've figured out how she's resurrecting these ancient armies."

"With essence," I said. "We heard about it in Zamochit."

"Yes," Terrance said. "With essence. From what we understand, the Queen distilled it from the bodies of the hybrids—they were part army, part experiment. And she can use it to reanimate vampires who have turned to dust."

"That's why all those bodies were dumped in the Wasteland," William said. "She used them all up."

"Exactly," Terrance said.

"What do you mean by 'distilled'?" Sachiko said. "How is this being done?"

"We don't know exactly," Terrance said. "We do know vampire magic is involved. The Queen of the Moon is the same one who created the emeralds for the Werdulac that mask a vampire's presence—and that can draw a soul out of its body. She must be using something similar to breathe life into a body that has long since disintegrated."

"The hybrids were part kost," I said. "And kosts are animated by evil spirits. Their whole purpose is to reanimate dead tissue. She must be using that somehow."

"Whatever it is," Terrance said, "it isn't good."

"That makes sense now," I said. "That's why I'm seeing the mist. I saw a smoke trail with the kost, and that's how I was able to track them. I saw one with the hybrids too, since they were part kost."

"And now you can see the essence," Terrance said. "Like I said, we didn't know what the Queen was up to until we saw all the vampires down in the caves. We knew the Queen's tomb was opening and she was being revived—and then we heard stories of ancient vampires appearing and then disappearing. And we knew there had to be some connection, but we didn't know what until I saw the revived army. And then when that army completely disappeared, we knew exactly where they had gone."

"So why does essence catch some vampires and not others?" William asked. "It took the ancient vampires that had been turned to ash, and it's taken some living ones too, but it certainly hasn't taken every vampire that's been touched by it."

"We've noticed that now too," Terrance said. "And you're right—it's not taking all of them. We're working off the theory that it's choosing the weakest individuals. I think essence has less effect on healthy flesh."

He walked across the flat-topped rock. "Come over here, and I'll show you where the Queen is right now."

"You can see her?" I said.

"Sort of," Terrance replied.

He led me over to two heavy-duty cases with monitors in them. Both of them showed a vague, fuzzy image of what looked like a Greek temple.

Terrance crouched down beside the monitors, and William, Sachiko, and I crowded around him. Dylan stayed right where he was.

Terrance pointed to one of the screens. "This one is from the stationary camera. And this other one is from our drone."

Sachiko peered closer. "I can see the temple. So cameras can see through the barrier the Queen set up?"

"These can," Terrance said. "Ordinary cameras, funnily enough, seem to be affected by the vampire barrier. If you train them on the island, you'll see nothing. The same is true if you turn an ordinary camera on Zamochit—you'll just see the empty Wasteland. But these are the very latest tech. And with them we can peer through a vampire barrier."

Terrance pointed again. "Do you see this large figure here? It's at one end of the temple and looks like a figure of a goddess?"

I leaned closer. "Yes."

"That's the Queen," Terrance said.

I looked again in surprise. "The Queen is a giant statue?"

"Well, actually, that's where she is right now," Terrance said. "The statue is the last of three traps that were designed by the Sídh to—well—trap the Queen. The first is the chamber of light—that was her original prison and some say an entrance to the half-realm. The second is the labyrinth. And the third is the statue—that's where she's currently trapped."

He pointed to the base of the statue. "Do you see this dark line here? That's a giant crack. Once the statue cracks completely, the Queen will be free."

William frowned at the screen. "How do you know she's in there?"

"For one thing, the statue has moved," Terrance said.

"Moved?" William said.

"Yes," Terrance replied. "We've been monitoring the temple for some time, and the statue's head moves. And every time the statue's head moves, an earthquake follows. And the earthquake comes from roughly the direction where the statue is looking."

"So the statue—the Queen—turns her head," I said. "And then she sends out the essence, causing an earthquake?"

"That's what we think, yes," Terrance said. "The royal tombs where the armies are are often thousands of miles away from here. It requires enormous amounts of energy to pump the essence that far through the earth. That energy is causing the earthquakes."

"So every head turn presages an earthquake?" I said.

"Every one but the last one," Terrance said. "The head turned about a day ago. There was no earthquake after that one. We don't know what it means."

I thought back to the beetle that had awakened and buzzed after we'd pulled it from its tunnel. I wondered if it was an active beetle that had drawn the Queen's interest.

"And you said you know about the labyrinth and the chamber of light already, right?" I said. "You know that we have to get the Queen back into the chamber?"

"Yes," Terrance said. "And I'm a little surprised that you already knew all about that too. But I guess I shouldn't be."

"Do you have any idea how we're supposed to get the Queen back in her chamber?" I said.

Terrance glanced at the image on the screen ruefully. "I think in order to get the Queen back in, we have to get her out first. That is, I think we have to get her out of the statue *before* we can get down into the labyrinth and then into the chamber. It's a closed system. So we'll have to break it open in order to get into it—and the statue is the only way."

"And then after she's free?" I said. "Any idea on how to lead her back in?"

"Not at the moment," Terrance said. "I was just going to improvise."

"I might have an idea," I said.

"Katie—" William said.

"It's the only plan we have at the moment," I said.

Terrance glanced from William to me. "I take it you're planning to offer yourself as bait?"

"Yes," I said.

325

Terrance rubbed his chin. "Well, it would probably work."

"We can't," William said. "It's far too dangerous."

"Until we have another plan," I said, "we'll have to go with it."

"We'll all be with her," Sachiko said.

Terrance glanced up at her sharply but didn't say anything.

"But the Queen is an ancient and powerful vampire sorceress," William said. "We're not talking about an ordinary vampire here—not to mention the fact that the Queen's army is in there too."

He turned to Terrance. "That's true, isn't it? That temple *is* where all the revived vampires have gone?"

Terrance glanced back at the screens. "Yes, that's true. The vampires are in there. You can't see any sign of them on the monitors because they're all dormant."

"What do you mean, 'dormant'?" Sachiko said.

"I mean they're all lying on the floor asleep," Terrance said. "I've been in there once. There are heaps and heaps of them everywhere. There must be thousands of them. But they didn't wake up when I came in."

"Why would they be asleep?" William said.

"It just makes sense," Terrance replied. "The Queen wouldn't want them milling around in there. She'd put them to sleep until she needed to use them."

"But we heard one wandered into town a few days ago," William said. "That one wasn't asleep."

"So a few of them might wake up on occasion," Terrance said. "We can handle one or two of them."

"It's still too dangerous," William said.

"William, I have to do this," I said. "I have to. I can't allow the Queen to break free. Especially not if there was something I could've done to stop her."

William was silent for a moment.

"I know you have to do it," he said at last, his face grim. "But I am absolutely coming with you—the whole way."

"Of course," I said. "We do this together."

Terrance shot a quick glance at William, but once again, he said nothing.

"So that's settled," Sachiko said. "What do we do now? Do we just head over to the island?"

"Pretty much, yes," Terrance said.

"Do we need any special preparation?" I asked.

"We're as prepared as we're ever going to be," Terrance said. "And now that you can see the mist surrounding the island, we can navigate by sight rather than using equipment—we'll be able to travel lighter."

Sachiko turned around. "Where's Dylan?"

I looked around also—the flat-topped rock was empty except for the four of us.

"I'm sure he's fine, wherever he is," Terrance said.

There was a splash then, from down below, and we all turned toward it.

Sachiko swiftly disappeared over the side of the rock, and Terrance, William, and I followed her.

We all reached the bottom and hurried toward the water.

Dylan was already standing on the beach, and by the light of the stars, I could see a boat out on the water. It was heading toward us from the opposite direction from the island, and it was moving toward us at a steady pace. The strange thing was—it appeared to be empty.

The boat was open on all sides—it appeared to be a simple rowboat—but no one was sitting in it, and it appeared to have no motor. How it was moving was a mystery.

"Do you think it's got something to do with the Queen?" Sachiko asked.

Dylan turned to look at her. "Hardly. I don't think she'd send a magic boat to collect us. Besides, it's not coming from the right direction. Even from here I can tell the island is the other way."

There was another splash then, just in front of the boat, and something small broke the surface of the water and then disappeared.

A moment later, there was another small splash.

The boat continued to move toward us, and as it reached the beach, a head popped up out of the water. It was Anton.

Soon he had reached the beach, and he was dragging the boat up onto the sand.

"I thought we might need a boat," he said. "Seeing as we're heading to an island."

Dylan launched himself toward Anton, and Anton put out a hand to stop him.

"Relax," he said. "I'm with them."

"How did you find us?" I said.

"You guys are so loud," Anton said, "that it was hard not to find you. I knew all I had to do was find a boat, and then eventually I'd find you guys."

"We already have a boat," Terrance said.

"Well, I didn't know that," Anton replied. "And I didn't know we'd definitely run into you guys from the Order. Anyway, I'm not sure we'll all fit in one—two is probably better."

"It doesn't matter," Dylan said. "We don't all need to go."

"Well, you can stay here, then," Anton said. He turned to Terrance. "I don't believe we've met. I'm Anton. And I'm a vampire."

Terrance held out a hand. "I'm Terrance—"

Anton interrupted. "I know who you are. I just don't want you and your friend here to get in our way."

"We're on the same side," Terrance said. "At least—at the moment."

"I can live with that," Anton said. He accepted Terrance's hand and shook it.

Anton glanced around. "So where is this island?"

"It's out there," I said. "I'm the only one who can see it."

"In that case, I want to be in your boat," Anton said.

"I'm the one traveling with Katie," William said.

"Calm down," Anton replied. "We can both go with Katie. It's not like this boat only holds two people."

"How about this?" Sachiko said. "Katie and I will take one boat—since we're both lighter, it will go faster. She can tell me which way to go, and I can row."

She turned to Terrance. "I'm guessing your boat is a rowboat also?"

"Yes," Terrance said. "Anything with a motor would be too noisy."

"Then you guys can go in the other boat," Sachiko said. "I imagine with the four of you it'll go pretty fast."

"I'm not going," Dylan said.

"Why not?" Anton said. "Are you scared of the Queen?"

"That's not it," Dylan said, smirking. "You'll see."

"Dylan is right," Terrance said. "Someone should stay behind in case we need backup. He can watch what's happening on the monitors."

He started up the beach. "Come on, Dylan. We'll get the other boat."

Dylan and Terrance soon returned, dragging a rowboat along the sand, and Sachiko and I pushed Anton's boat out into the water—his boat was the smaller one, so it made more sense for the two of us to take it.

Sachiko and I quickly set off—I sat in the bow to spy the way ahead, and Sachiko did the rowing. William, Terrance, and Anton got in the boat behind us and pushed off.

Steering the boat was not difficult. The island of mist loomed before us, a large, imposing mass. A white, luminous cloud wrapped around it, swirling as if stirred by an unseen hand, and I couldn't see anything of the land beyond it.

Sachiko continued rowing steadily, and soon were in amongst the mist. Moments later, the boat ran aground.

The boat hit the beach so suddenly that I was nearly thrown over the prow, and I heard a splash as Sachiko dropped one of her oars into the water.

She hurried to retrieve it. "Why didn't you tell me we were so close to the shore?"

"Sorry," I said. "All I could see was the mist—I couldn't actually see the land."

I could see the land now, however, and I stepped carefully out of the boat and onto the sand. As I did so, I felt a slight tingle run through me. I stood very still, and the feeling passed. Then I glanced around. The beach looked perfectly normal from what I could see, but much of the island was shrouded in mist, and I couldn't see any sign of the temple that we had seen on Terrance's monitors.

I heard a gasp from Sachiko, and I turned to see her standing up in the boat. She had one foot up in the air, and she appeared to be trying to step out of the boat.

"Katie?" Sachiko said. "Katie, where are you?"

"I'm right here," I said.

"Where?"

Sachiko lowered her foot back into the boat again and began to press on the air around her.

"All I can see is empty air and open water," Sachiko said. "Are you sure we're on a beach? Because I don't see anything like that."

I stepped back into the boat.

"Can you see me now?" I said.

Sachiko blinked in surprise. "Yes, I can see you. Where did you go?"

A moment later, the second boat came up onto the beach—this time more slowly. As the boat stopped, Terrance, William, and Anton all stood up.

Terrance looked over at us. "Any problems?"

"I seem to be able to walk up on the beach just fine," I said. "But Sachiko can't seem to get out of the boat."

"I was afraid that might happen," Terrance said.

"What?" William said.

"It's the barrier that the Queen set up," Terrance replied. "It seems to be very selective. Dylan, for example, can't get in."

"But I'm a vampire," Sachiko said. "I can get through the barrier at Zamochit with no trouble."

"This isn't the barrier at Zamochit," Terrance said. "The Queen has her own rules."

"But you got through at least once," Sachiko said.

"Yes, I did," Terrance replied.

"And Katie got through," Sachiko said. "I saw her disappear."

Terrance glanced at me. "Yes, I'm not surprised about that."

"So why could two humans get through when a vampire couldn't?"

"I have a special ability," Terrance said. "Magical barriers don't affect me. I think Katie may have it too—she's always gotten into Zamochit without any difficulty."

"But other vampires have gotten through," Sachiko said. "In fact, an entire army got through. So why not me?"

"I couldn't say for sure," Terrance said. "But it's very possible that it's connected to the essence—that is, that essence-infused vampires can get in—and out. But regular vampires might be blocked."

"In that case, I probably can't get through either," Anton said.

He attempted to get out of the boat and found—like Sachiko had—that his feet wouldn't go over the side.

He put up his hands, and they couldn't go past the edge of the boat either.

"How about that," he said. "I've never been stopped by a magical barrier before."

Anton glanced over at William. "I guess it's your turn."

William stepped out of the boat easily and then stepped back in.

"Okay, I just saw you disappear and then reappear," Anton said. "So I'm guessing that means you're allowed in."

He turned to Terrance. "How come he gets in?"

Terrance looked over at William. "I couldn't say—maybe there's something special about him."

Terrance's gaze lingered on William for a moment, and I was glad when Anton broke in again.

"So I guess this means Sachiko and I are staying here?" he said.

"I'm afraid so," Terrance replied.

"And Dylan up there on the rock isn't going to be much help as backup, is he?" Anton said. "Seeing as he can't get in either."

"You never know," Terrance said. "All he can do is stay alert right now—but that could change. You and Sachiko should stay alert too. With this type of stuff, anything can happen. At some point, we may need to make a quick getaway, and having you guys waiting here could be very important."

"Okay, guys," Sachiko said. "Be careful."

Terrance got out of the boat and began to walk up the beach. William and I got out of the boats too and followed him.

"So I'll just stay here, then," Anton called after us.

As we made our way up the beach, I could see very little. The mist pressed in on me on all sides, and all I could really see of the island was rocky soil and patches of scraggly grass. The mist, at least, did make the night much brighter for me, and I wasn't in danger of tripping over anything I couldn't see.

"So can you guys see the temple from here?" I said.

Terrance turned to look at me in surprise. "Yes. You can't see it?"

"No, all I can see is the mist."

"That's right," Terrance said. "I knew you could see it, but I didn't count on its being a factor on the island."

"We'll manage," William said. "You say you've been in the temple before?"

"Yes," Terrance replied.

"Do you know the best way in?" William said.

"Yes—basically right in through the front door. The temple is open on all sides, so there isn't really any hidden point to sneak in through. The front has the advantage of being the farthest away from the statue. We don't want to walk in right under the Queen's eyes."

The Queen's eyes. I thought back to the dark eyes I'd been seeing that had once turned to gold. I wondered now if those eyes belonged to the Queen.

"Terrance, there's something you should know," I said.

Terrance looked at me with concern. "What is it?"

"It's nothing dangerous," I said. "It's just that I need to tell you one last thing. We heard that the Queen was defeated by the dark star. Do you know what that is?"

Terrance shook his head. "No idea. But these tombs are all supposed to have a key—a fail-safe, if you will. Something that either resets the tomb, or will stop the vampire some other way in an emergency. With the Hunter the key was the sword—the Star of Morning."

"So the dark star could be something like that?" William said.

"Could be," Terrance replied.

"We'll have to keep an eye out, then," William said.

Terrance continued to lead the way, and the ground under our feet began to slope gently upward.

Soon Terrance stopped and held up a hand.

"I think we should proceed cautiously from here on out," he said quietly. "I don't see any sign of movement, but it is night—and any of these vampires could wake up at any time."

Terrance crouched down to the ground and continued up the hill slowly.

William and I did the same.

The mist still swirled around me and made it hard for me to see the way ahead. But as we continued up the hill, the mist began to thin, and as we reached the top, it cleared until all I could see of it was a white blanket that lay over the ground.

As the mist cleared, I could see the temple.

The temple of the Queen of the Moon looked very much like an ancient Greek temple, with columns along the front and sides and a frieze in a triangle over the front entrance. There were statues, too, that probably would have been gods and goddesses in a traditional temple, and by the light of the mist, I could see a large, imposing statue looming in the shadows at the back—the last part of the prison that held the Queen of the Moon.

Now that we could actually see the statue, Terrance held up a hand, and we all stopped, crouching down in the dry grass.

"So what's the plan?" William said.

"Well, that's the Queen right there at the back," Terrance said. "We'll go in and see if we can't make that crack at the base of the statue a little wider. I've been thinking that it may actually be possible for us to break in and get into the statue ourselves without letting her out. That would make things a little bit easier."

"And how do we break that crack in the statue open?" William said.

Terrance brought something out of a belt that was strapped around his back and chest—it was a silver rod that telescoped out into a stake with a very sharp point.

"I was going to use this," he said. "Other than that, we'll have to improvise."

I glanced at William. I knew he was perfectly capable of putting a good-sized crack in that statue with his bare hands. He still seemed to sense, as I did, that it might be wise to keep Terrance in the dark about his true nature. Terrance seemed to tolerate Sachiko and even Anton, but others might find out through him—and they might not be so forgiving.

We continued on toward the temple, and as we drew closer, I could see a wide set of steps leading up to a portico. I could also see more clearly the statues that stood in between the pillars that held up the frieze—they definitely did not look like gods and goddesses.

We reached the steps, and Terrance motioned for us to wait. Then he went silently up the steps and disappeared inside.

A moment later, he reappeared and motioned for us to follow him.

William and I went up the stone steps and walked in between the columns and the statues. I glanced up at a statue as we passed. The statue was on a pedestal, and it was a male figure of slightly larger-than-normal size. The face was classical in its lines, and the body was well proportioned. But its resemblance to classic Greek sculpture ended there. There was something menacing in the sightless eyes, and the well-muscled body seemed poised to spring into action—ready to attack at any moment. And in its hand was a sword made not of stone but of black metal.

William paused as we passed and glanced up at the sword. In a moment, he had climbed up onto the pedestal and had noiselessly relieved the statue of its sword. He climbed back down again, and we followed Terrance inside.

The temple itself was a wide space with a roof overhead, lined on either side with columns. The night air filtered in between the columns, and all the way at the back of the temple, set against a solid stone wall, was an enormous throne. And on the throne sat an equally enormous statue of a woman.

The arrangement of the woman's hair in ringlets and the way her clothes draped owed much to classical statuary. But even at a distance, there was an atmosphere of power and anger around the giant woman that was at odds with the graceful lines of her form. It felt at any moment as if the entire statue might stand and come toward us, and there was an ominous, black shadow lying on the steps that led up to the statue's throne.

And between us and the statue, there were thousands and thousands of vampires.

They were sleeping—lying on the vast stone floor, and their faces were beautiful and serene in the starlight. They were lying in heaps, their bodies jumbled everywhere, and every once in a while, there was one vampire who had managed to carve out a small space for his body alone. Most of them wore the antique, lace-trimmed clothes I had seen down in the cave in Elspeth's Grove, though their hands and necks were now bereft of jewelry. There were a few here and there in modern dress too, and I assumed they were more contemporary vampires that had been caught up by the essence along with their more ancient counterparts. But though they slept, they didn't breathe, and the entire temple was eerily quiet.

Off in the distance, I could hear the sea lapping against the shore.

"Follow me," Terrance whispered. "We'd better be very, very careful."

Terrance began to step cautiously around the sleeping forms, picking his way through feet and limbs and motionless bodies. William and I followed, and I strained my eyes in the dim light, watching to make sure that I didn't disturb so much as a lock of hair. The vampires didn't move or murmur in their heavy sleep, and as we made our way across the vast floor, the moon came out from behind a scudding cloud. The moonlight glinted off a sharp pair of teeth.

At long last, we reached the steps that led up to the statue's throne, and Terrance led us around to the side. There were vampires here too, though not so many, and it was almost as if they feared to get too close to their queen. I could still see the dark shadow on the steps in front of the statue, and even though I was much closer, I still couldn't tell what it was.

As we walked around the side of the statue, Terrance led us up the stairs to the base of the throne.

He pointed, and I could see a vast, dark crack that ran from the front of the throne all the way to the back.

"This is where we have to work," Terrance whispered.

He got out his stake and began to chip at the back of the throne where the crack was the widest. William joined him, using the sword.

But at the first sound of metal on stone, I saw the shadow on the steps at the front of the statue begin to stir.

As they continued to work, the shadow rose up as if getting to its feet, and I turned quickly to Terrance and William.

"Stop!" I hissed. "Stop!"

There was flash of light in the next moment, and I turned back to see dark eyes before me—the same eyes I'd glimpsed in visions when trying to summon the clear fire.

The figure standing in front of me had a staff in its hand, and it struck it once on the stone floor, causing it to glow with a strange, golden light.

By the light of the staff, I could see the figure was that of a young woman with very dark eyes and jet-black hair.

"The girl is here, my mistress!" the young woman cried. "She has come, just as you said she would!"

The young woman struck her staff on the floor again, and the eyes of the statue above us began to glow with the same strange, golden light. The crack in front of us also began to glow, and William, Terrance, and I all jumped back from it.

The head of the statue turned toward us, its sightless, golden eyes searching us out.

Then the statue itself began to rise.

Chapter Twenty-One

There was a small space behind the statue's throne, and Terrance, William, and I hurried to hide behind it.

The statue continued to rise, and as it did so, its eyes glowed even brighter. As the eyes glowed, so too did the staff in the hands of the dark-haired woman.

Terrance peeked around the corner of the throne. "So the dark-haired woman is the Acolyte. And the statue is the Queen of the Moon. I believe the Queen is transferring her power to the Acolyte through that staff."

"Is the Queen really that big?" I said.

"I don't think she fills that whole statue," Terrance said. "It's oversized on purpose—it is a trap, after all. But the fact that she can move it now tells me she's ready to break free. Then she won't need the Acolyte or her staff anymore."

As the statue stood upright fully, chunks of marble began to rain down on us from above. The eyes of the statue glowed again, and as they did so, the vampires around us began to stir.

"We'd better get that crack open," Terrance said. "We've got to get down in there."

We hurried out from behind the throne to see that the entire thing had actually split right down the middle. The broken throne began to fall in on itself, clogging up the fissure that had opened.

Terrance quickly turned back to the crack at the base of the throne and began to attack it with his stake. William joined in with his sword.

The statue made its laborious way down the steps and turned toward us. As the Queen reached the floor, the Acolyte raised her staff.

All the vampires around us began to get to their feet.

At the same moment, the statues at the front of the temple jumped down from their pedestals and turned toward us, brandishing their swords. They ran into the temple, slashing at the rising vampires.

One of the vampires in antique garb was struck by a sword—he collapsed into a pile of dust.

The statues began to cut their way through the crowd.

"Guys," I said, "we really need to hurry."

Terrance paused in his work. "Are those the statues from the front? Are they fighting the vampires for us?"

"They're fighting the vampires, yes," I said. "But I don't think it's for us. I think they're trying to get to the Queen—and to us. We are trying to break her tomb open at the moment."

The Acolyte and the Queen both turned toward the statues. As the Queen walked toward them, brushing her own vampires out of the way, the marble that encased her began to fall away. She was growing smaller by the minute.

William took one look at the melee and turned toward the base of the throne. He began to punch it, widening the crack until it collapsed completely. Then William put his shoulder against the throne and gave it a terrific shove.

I heard a loud clattering sound, and I turned to see the Queen sweeping her arm in a wide arc. Several of the statues went flying through the air, struck by an unseen force. They crashed against the columns, and I saw them fall into the crowd of vampires. The vampires quickly swarmed over them.

The Queen continued her forward progress, sweeping her arms and striking the statues with an invisible force, as more chunks of marble fell off her. Through a crack in the center of the statue, I saw a flash of pale, white skin.

William gave the throne one more terrific shove, and the throne crashed to the side, revealing a deep hole underneath.

Terrance was staring at William with something like awe, but he recovered himself quickly.

"Thanks," he said to William. "Let's go."

Terrance climbed over the rubble and jumped down into the hole.

William and I turned to follow, but something made me turn back.

I saw the towering stone figure of the Queen surge into the crowd once more. As she did so, the legs of the statue began to crumble, followed by the torso and the head. Soon, the figure of the Queen herself was revealed, and she fell to the ground, disappearing into the horde of vampires.

Before she vanished from my sight, I had a glimpse of a slender, pale figure dressed all in white, with long, silver hair. Even at a distance, the Queen was beautiful, and I had an impression of great power emanating from her.

William touched my shoulder. "We'd better go."

The two of us climbed over the rubble of the throne and jumped into the hole after Terrance.

The fall was quite far, but I managed to land safely, and it felt like the floor I landed on was stone. The area under the throne was cool and dark and silent—suddenly the noise from the battle above had disappeared completely.

I scrambled to my feet and got out my tiny flashlight. All I could see around me was darkness.

Terrance produced a flashlight and held it out in front of him.

"I have no idea which way to go," he said. "But we'd better move fast. I have no doubt that the Queen will be after us shortly."

"We should go this way," William said.

He moved off into the darkness.

Terrance and I followed him quickly.

I held my flashlight even higher, but I still couldn't see anything but darkness. I had a feeling that we were in a relatively close space, and I reached out my hand and touched a stone wall.

"What is this place?" I said.

"It's a tunnel," William said. "There are carvings in the wall—I think they might have been part of the protections that were meant to keep the Queen in. I would imagine there were carvings on the inside of the statue too."

"As a matter of fact, there were," Terrance said.

He held out a small chunk of stone to me.

"I grabbed this as it fell down," he said. "It's a piece of marble from the Queen's statue—I thought it might come in handy."

I examined the piece of stone in the light from my flashlight. It wasn't a big piece—it was actually not much bigger than a quarter—but there were tiny carvings on it—a bird, a sun, and a circle.

William glanced over my shoulder at the stone fragment.

"Those are the same markings that are on the wall," he said.

He led me over to the wall, and I leaned close to it. The carvings were there, but they were tiny—even in bright light, I might never have known they were there. And they were the same as on the stone fragment—a bird, a sun, and a circle, repeated in the same sequence. There were rows and rows of the same pattern repeated as far as I could see.

"This pattern must be repeated thousands of times," I said.

"More like millions," William said, looking down the hall.

Terrance leaned close to the wall and studied the markings thoughtfully—if he wondered about William's keen eyesight in the dark, he didn't say anything.

William turned swiftly to look over his shoulder.

"We should move," he said.

We had not gone far when there was a flash of light behind us.

I turned to see the Acolyte standing behind us. In her hands was the gold staff.

Terrance got out his silver stake.

"You guys go ahead," he said. "I've got some new stuff in this stake—puts vampires right to sleep. I'll catch up right after."

"Terrance—" I said.

"Don't worry," he replied. "It's not the Tears of the Firebird again."

"I know," I said. "I was just going to say, be careful."

"I got this," Terrance said. "Don't worry."

William grabbed my hand. "Come on. The labyrinth is this way."

William zoomed along at top speed for just a moment or two. Then he came to a stop.

In front of me was all darkness—I held up my flashlight, but it didn't illuminate anything.

I glanced behind me. We couldn't have been that far from Terrance and the Acolyte, and yet all behind me was darkness and silence too.

"Where's Terrance?" I said.

William glanced behind us also, and I saw a look of surprise spread over his face.

"What is it?" I said.

"I don't see him," he said.

"We should go back for him," I said.

"I'm sure he knows what he's doing," William replied. "Vampire hunting is his job, after all. We'd better keep moving."

I glanced back once more, and then I followed William.

The tunnel in front of us narrowed quite a bit, and we squeezed through into a large space. As we did so, the room in front of us lit up.

Once the initial flash faded away, I could see that the room was still largely dark. But projected on the walls and the ceiling of the room were tiny images—a bird, a sun, and a circle. They were little points of light that seemed to have been purposefully projected onto the room—but no source of light was visible. As I stood looking up at the images on the walls and ceiling, they began to move. The effect was disorienting.

William took my hand. "Our first choice in the labyrinth is up ahead."

So disorienting was the effect of the swirling images that I didn't realize that we were in the labyrinth already—we were actually in the first room, and at the end of it was a short hallway that led to two choices: we could turn right or left.

As we stepped into the hall, it lit up with the same three images, and the images quickly began to swirl around. The walls of both of our choices—right and left—did the same.

"We'll just keep going," William said. "Like a mouse in an experiment."

"Wait," I said. "Isn't the whole point of this to lure the Queen back into this trap? How do we know she's following us?"

"She's following us," William said grimly.

We hurried on through the labyrinth, and every time we reached a new corridor or room, the lights would reappear and begin their disorienting dance. I put away my flashlight—it wasn't doing me any good.

Once I glanced back and thought I saw something white behind us. But the flashing lights were so dizzying that I couldn't be sure what I saw.

We kept going, and then suddenly everything went black. The floor underneath grew sticky, and I found that my feet wouldn't move.

"Hold on," William said. "I'm coming to get you."

I heard a soft sound, and then there was silence.

"William?" I said. "William?"

In the next moment, I felt the floor give way, and I was falling through the air.

I landed hard on what felt like another stone floor.

"William?" I said.

It was just as dark below as it had been above, and I heard someone move toward me in the darkness.

"Katie, are you hurt?"

It was William's voice. I felt his arms go around me.

"I'm fine," I said. "What just happened?"

"I think we just moved down to the next level of the labyrinth," William said.

His words proved to be true, as he led me forward, and we found ourselves in yet another corridor. As soon as we entered it, the swirling lights started up again. But this time, William placed his hands over his ears and doubled over as if he were in pain.

I rushed to his side.

"William, what is it?"

"The sound!" he cried out. "That horrible sound!"

"I don't hear anything," I said.

William did not reply. He simply ground his hands against his ears.

"Come on," I said. "I'll lead you this time."

I urged William on gently, and he staggered forward.

We made our way slowly through the corridor and on into the next room where we had to make a choice of which way to go. Every time we entered a new room or corridor, the swirling lights began again. William didn't remove his hands from his ears or open his eyes, so we soldiered on with my leading the way, and every once in a while he cried out in pain.

I led William into quite a few dead ends, but we retraced our steps and kept going.

And then, all at once, the ground became slippery, as if it were covered with water, and I felt my feet get swept out from under me.

Once again, I was falling.

I landed on yet another stone surface in the darkness.

"William?" I said. "William, are you there?"

"I'm here," he said.

I got up and staggered toward the sound of his voice. Luckily, the floor underneath me seemed dry, and there was no sign of the slipperiness that had precipitated our latest fall.

"Are you all right?" I said.

"I'm okay now," William said.

"What happened back there?" I said. "I didn't seem to be affected at all."

"I heard some kind of high-pitched sound," William said. "It was almost too much to bear—probably too high a frequency for you to hear."

"But something that would work on those with vampire blood?" I said.

"It would certainly make getting through a maze a lot more difficult."

"So where are we now?" I said.

"I think we've reached the end," William said. "Or perhaps I should say the beginning."

He must have seen my questioning glance in the dark because he pulled me gently along with him.

"Over here," he said.

We walked a fair distance, and then William pulled me to a stop.

"Here," he said.

I got out my little flashlight and switched it on.

In front of me was a large, black, stone structure. It was oval in shape and rounded on the top, and down its surface ran a seam—it looked like the top opened up into two doors. The surface had a dull sheen to it, and carved across the two doors were large versions of the images we had seen in the labyrinth—a bird, a sun, and a circle.

"I think this is the chamber of light the Queen was locked in," William said.

I placed a hand on the surface—it was cool to the touch.

"Why is it closed?" I said.

"What's that?" William asked.

"Why is it closed?" I said. "If the Queen escaped, why isn't it lying open?"

"I don't know," William said. "The important thing is to get it open again. We can't lure her into it if it's shut."

William tried to prize the doors open with his fingers to no avail, and then he turned to look around in the darkness.

"There's nothing in here we can use as a crowbar."

I ran my fingers over the carvings.

"I feel like there's a significance in these," I said. "I doubt the Sídh had to pry it open."

William looked up sharply then, and I looked to see what had attracted his attention.

There was a gold glimmer off in the dark on the far side of the room. The glimmer was growing larger, and as it moved toward us, I could see the dark figure of the Acolyte.

"Stay here," William said.

He moved swiftly toward her.

The Acolyte quickly vanished into the darkness, and William disappeared after her.

I was aware at that moment of a soft glow behind me.

I turned to see a woman in white with silver hair walking toward me.

Her skin was very pale—even by vampire standards—and it seemed to shine with a soft, pearly glow. She looked as if she were lit from within by moonlight.

There was a soft, white light rising up in tendrils from the fingers of one of her hands.

"Hello, dear," the woman said.

A thrill of fear ran through me.

"You're the Queen of the Moon, aren't you?" I said.

The woman smiled. "Yes, and you must be Ekaterina. But I hear that you like to be called Katie."

The woman's Russian was antique, and there was something strange and a little hard to understand about it. All the same, her voice was lovely and soothing—like moonlight on the water.

"Would you like to see something pretty, Katie?" she said.

She moved her fingers gracefully, and I saw the tendrils of light separate from her hand and float just above it. The tendrils began to move as in a dance, and the effect was hypnotic.

Soon the tendrils formed a white, luminous flower—a rose.

At a gesture from the Queen of the Moon, the flower floated toward me.

"Isn't it lovely, Katie?" the Queen said. "I heard you like roses—there were roses growing at your childhood home in Krov. Wouldn't you like to smell this one? Breathe in its aroma? I'm sure it will remind you of home."

As I looked at the rose that floated just in front of me, I saw it change from white to a pale, blush color. Then I saw other roses around it—it looked just like the rosebush that grew in front of the house where I had lived as a child.

I leaned forward and caught up a flower in my hand. I drank in its heady scent.

I looked up to find a beautiful woman in white staring at me. I felt like I should know who she was, but I just couldn't remember.

"Hello, Katie," the woman said. "How are you?"

"I am happy," I said—and it was true.

"That's good, Katie, very good," the woman said.

She tilted her head to one side.

"I've heard that you can make a pretty light. Would you like to show me?"

"I can do that," I said—nothing would make me happier than showing off for my new friend.

I closed my eyes and began to sing. I thought of my mother and the Pure Woods. I thought of the clear fire and how it had shown itself in sparks—both in the plane and down in the tunnels.

After I felt the fire ignite within me, I opened my eyes.

Sparks appeared around me, lighting up the dark.

"Good, Katie, very good," the woman breathed.

The woman in white moved toward a big, black oval made of stone that was lying behind me—it seemed to be a container of some kind.

"Come this way, dear," the woman said. "And bring your pretty lights with you."

I turned toward the big stone and took a few steps.

"Good, Katie," the woman said. "Can you keep walking and place your hands on this stone?"

I nodded and kept going.

"It's funny," the woman murmured as I walked the short distance to the stone. "I didn't think the clear fire would look like this. But I suppose it will do."

I placed my hands on the stone just as the woman had asked, and I saw three carvings on it begin to glow—a bird, a sun, and a circle.

At the same time there was a screech from somewhere off in the darkness.

I looked up, and at first I saw nothing.

Then I saw two figures coming toward me.

"Concentrate, dear," said the woman in white beside me. "Think about how much you would like to get this box open. Then sing to your lights again."

I looked at the stone box again with its glowing carvings. I thought it would be nice to see what was inside.

I closed my eyes and began to sing.

I felt power surge within me, and I felt the stone move under my hands.

I opened my eyes and stepped back.

A seam of white light had appeared, running down the middle of the stone.

As I watched, the top of the stone opened out into two halves, and I saw white light pouring out of it.

"Katie!" cried a voice.

I looked up and saw someone running toward me—someone with a familiar face—a beloved face.

"William!" I cried.

Behind him was another familiar figure—this one black and gold.

I struggled for a moment to remember, and then the name came to me. It was the Acolyte.

I turned to the woman in white who was standing behind me.

"What is—"

But before I could finish my question, the woman raised her hand and threw it back in a sweeping gesture. It was the same motion I had seen a giant statue perform up above, and the effect was much the same as it had been then.

I saw William get lifted off the ground and get thrown into the darkness as if he had been struck a blow by a colossal hand.

"Foolish boy," the woman said. "You shouldn't have thrown that sword away."

"What have you done to William?" I cried.

I felt a great fire ignite within me, and the sparks that floated above me blazed with renewed intensity.

The woman in white—the Queen of the Moon—turned triumphant eyes on me.

"Thank you for opening the chamber for me, dear," she said. "You thought this was a trap for me. But it was really a trap for you. Did you really think it would be this easy to get to me? You got to me—you got down here—because I wanted you to."

"What have you done with William?" I demanded. The sparks above me began to move closer together, almost as if they were straining to reunite.

"I know this labyrinth inside and out," the Queen said. "Haven't I been traveling it for centuries? You and your boy never had a chance—you did exactly what I wanted you to do. Now you can stay in there nice and quiet until we have need of you."

The Queen raised her hand again and swept it toward me.

I felt myself get hit by a powerful force, and I was knocked off my feet. I fell toward the open doors of the chamber, and in the next moment I felt myself tumbling through them into nothingness.

I fell for a moment, and then I landed hard on the ground.

I looked up to see a white haze above me, and in the haze I could see the Queen of the Moon staring down at me.

She smiled. Then she stepped back, and I heard the sound of two heavy doors slamming shut.

The haze above me became solid.

I was trapped.

Chapter Twenty-Two

Everything was white.

Everywhere I turned, all I could see was a soft, featureless white—the clear fire had gone out.

I stood up, unsure of how much space I had, and I found that I seemed to have no ceiling above me and no walls around me. I stretched out my hands and touched nothing, and then I began to walk.

The space inside the chamber was far bigger than it appeared to be from the outside.

I frowned in thought. Cyrs had said the chamber might be an entrance to the half-realm, and as I looked around, I wondered if that was where I could be now.

He'd said the half-realm was a place in between two worlds—a border area between the human world and the domain of the Sídh. He'd also said it could only be entered or exited by magic. I didn't know anything about the Sídh realm, and I didn't particularly want to go there. So unless I found a way to cross back into the human world, I was going to be trapped here.

I remembered, then, a vision that had come to me while I was using the clear fire—I'd seen myself standing in a haze of white light.

The light wasn't as bright as it had been in the vision, but I realized now that it was the same place.

I'd seen myself standing in the half-realm. And something large had been standing beside me.

I looked around, and the vast, white expanse was just as featureless as it had been the moment before. I decided to see if I could summon the clear fire again—maybe it could help me find my way. At the very least, it would give me something to look at apart from endless white light.

I closed my eyes and began to sing. I concentrated and began the search within. Soon I felt the fire ignite within me, and I opened my eyes.

Floating in the white air in front of me were the red-and-gold sparks of the clear fire—it seemed to me that the summoning was getting a little easier each time.

The light of the clear fire was dimmed by the hazy whiteness all around me, but I found its presence comforting, and the fact that its sparks extended above me as well as in front of me at least gave me a way to measure a little distance.

The endless whiteness now had a little form.

I began to walk.

I thought back to the fact that the doors of the chamber had been closed—and the Queen had needed me to open them for her. So she had not opened those doors herself, and yet she had found a way to escape.

So how had she gotten out?

I kept walking, and soon I heard a sound.

"Katie!"

Someone was calling my name from a great distance—and the voice sounded familiar.

"William!" I cried.

I ran toward the sound, but it did not come again.

"William!" I cried again.

There was no response.

I slowed to a walk—but I kept going in the same direction.

Soon I heard other sounds—soft sounds—but they were far off, and I couldn't make out what they were. I saw vague shadows, too, far off in the whiteness, but I hesitated to turn toward them.

I didn't want to lose my sense of direction, and I was sure I'd heard William's voice.

The soft sounds continued, and eventually I saw something coming toward me out of the white haze.

I froze.

The shape continued to move toward me, and I saw that it was large and wide—with what looked like a long neck. I considered running, but curiosity got the better of me, and I stayed right where I was.

The shape came closer, and I could soon see that it was a horse.

The horse was all white, and it had large, dark, gentle eyes. It stepped closer to me.

"What are you doing here?" I said.

Moments later, more shapes loomed out of the whiteness. Soon, there were four more horses standing around me—all of them white with large, dark eyes.

I turned back to the first horse and held out my hand.

The horse nuzzled it gently.

I didn't hear a sound, but I felt something in my mind that felt vaguely like "hello."

I stepped back, startled, but the horse simply stared at me with its gentle eyes.

I remembered then that I had encountered a horse like this once before—back in Krov.

The horse had come to my rescue—had carried me to safety when my life was in danger. And just like with the other horse, I had a vague feeling that I could understand it—only this time the feeling was a little stronger.

I looked around at all the horses. They seemed curious, and I could feel kindness, patience. They seemed like they wanted to help.

The first horse I'd met whickered gently and then began to walk—its hooves made no sound. The other horses followed, and their steps were equally silent.

I decided to go with them—and we walked, the sparks of the clear fire creating some context in the empty whiteness.

We walked along for a short time, and then the first horse dropped back to walk beside me. He turned his head to look at me, and I reached out to pat his neck.

An image then formed in my mind of the vast, white space all around us. I could feel the word "distance." Then I felt the white space expanding somehow, and there was another word—"great."

"Great distance?" I said.

The horse kept walking, and I kept my hand on his neck.

Images continued to move through my mind. I felt "distance" again, and then I could see the white space shifting—it was almost as if there was a mist of the white space that moved and kept on moving.

I felt the word "change" float through my mind.

"Distances change here?" I said.

There were no more images in my mind, but I could feel a sense of approval coming from the horse.

I looked around at the vast, white expanse.

"Distances change...there are psychic, white horses," I murmured. "This really is the half-realm, isn't it?"

Again, I felt a sense of approval.

I looked at the horse. His head was down, and he was walking serenely forward—but I didn't know how he had come to be here.

"Are you a prisoner?" I said.

I felt laughter bubble up in my mind, and the word "happy" floated up to me.

"So not a prisoner, then," I said. "Why are you here?"

I had an image then of a white space that turned to blue above and green below, and I saw the same horse galloping across a grassy field.

354

I could feel the word "travel" in my mind.

"You're a traveler," I said. I looked at the other horses. "You're all travelers?"

I felt approval again from the lead horse.

"You travel from the half-realm into other worlds?" I said.

I felt approval again, followed by a little bubble of laughter—I took that as a yes.

"Why did you come to see me?" I asked.

I had an image in my mind then of the clear fire, and I felt laughter in my mind, followed by the word "happy."

So the horses had been attracted by the light—I could understand that in the featureless landscape.

My horse suddenly trotted off into the endless whiteness and then came back.

He did this a few times. Soon the other horses began to follow him.

I stared after them, puzzled.

The lead horse trotted up to me again. I placed my hand on his neck, and I saw an image of myself riding on his back.

"You want me to go with you?" I said.

The horse waited patiently.

"Okay," I said. I paused and looked up at the clear fire. I concentrated for a moment and sent it away. Then I turned back to my equine companion.

The horse was tall, and I wasn't an experienced rider, but somehow I managed to climb up onto his back with a minimum of difficulty—I had a feeling that the horse was aiding me in some way, but how I couldn't have said.

Once I was settled, the horse started off at a gentle trot. After a moment, he broke into a run, and the other horses went with us.

It was a strange sensation—riding across a featureless landscape with horses whose hooves made no sound.

It was hard to gauge time, but we rode at top speed for what felt like several minutes. Eventually, the horses began to slow, and I saw something large and dark looming up ahead.

My horse soon came to a stop, and the others stopped beside him.

In front of us was a large, dark rift in the sky. It was jagged and black, and it appeared to have perforated the air—it seemed like there was a crack in the world.

The other horses danced nervously near it, and I could feel my own horse shifting underneath me uncomfortably.

I leaned close to the horse's ear. "What is it?" I said.

An image formed in my mind then of the Queen of the Moon. I saw her rise up into the sky and then disappear.

"That's how she got out?" I said.

I felt approval coming from the horse along with a feeling of unhappiness.

So that was how the Queen had escaped—through the rift in the sky.

I felt my horse shifting his weight again, and then he trotted in a circle around the other horses before returning to his original spot.

A moment later, another image formed in my mind—this time I saw myself rising up into the air and disappearing into the rift.

I understood well enough what that meant—I could escape the same way the Queen had. But as I stared up at the rift, I realized that wouldn't solve anything—I could get out, and possibly trick the Queen into getting back into the chamber, but she'd simply get out again through the rift.

It seemed to me that the Queen hadn't just been wandering around in this white expanse. Even though this was the half-realm and she apparently couldn't leave it on her own, there must have been a more secure area she'd been banished to.

I reached down to pat my horse on the neck. I wanted to ask where the Queen had been confined, but that seemed to be a complex question to ask. I would have to make it simpler.

"Nervous?" I said to the horse.

He danced a little in response.

"Is there another place that makes you nervous?" I asked.

The horse suddenly stood very still. I could feel tension in his body.

"There is, isn't there?" I said. "Can you take me there?"

The horse hesitated for a moment and then began to walk. The other horses followed at first, but as we continued on, I sensed uneasiness in the other four. They began to fall behind us, and then one by one, they dropped off. Soon we were walking alone.

Distances were hard to judge in this place, and so was time. But it seemed to me that it wasn't long before we were approaching something shadowy off in the distance.

As we drew closer, my horse went slower. Soon, he came to a complete stop.

In front of me, I could see a large stone block—it appeared to be made of onyx, and it was shaped like a funeral bier. Around the base of it were fresh flowers, and floating above it was something very strange.

It was very long and very thin at the top and bottom—it was an elongated diamond shape, and it was deeply, deeply dark—it was so dark that it somehow went beyond black. And without any means of support, it was hanging above the bier in the hazy whiteness of the half-realm—it was a large, dark diamond hanging in the air.

I had a feeling I was looking at the dark star.

I patted the horse on his neck and assured him that it was all right to go closer, but he didn't move.

I slid off his back and gave him a reassuring pat on the neck. Then I began to walk toward the stone bier.

I glanced back once, and my horse was standing still, watching me. Even at a distance, I could read anxiety in his gentle eyes.

I went on and soon reached the stone and star. Up close, I could see a slight shimmer in the area around the bier—almost like a barrier. I put my fingers up to it and felt a slight tingle. Then I stepped through to the other side.

I was instantly struck with a crushing heaviness, and I sank to the ground. I found myself kneeling by the flowers at the base of the stone bier, and even in my discomfort, I noticed how fresh they were. The flowers appeared to have been placed there that very day—but I had a feeling that they'd actually been there for centuries. Whatever else was happening in the strange spot with the dark star, anything that was placed here would be well preserved—including me. I knew I had to move.

But moving was growing increasingly difficult.

Once I'd stepped inside the barrier, the light had grown much dimmer, and I could see the dark star above through a haze that somehow looked like the sun setting at dusk.

I looked down and couldn't really see a floor beneath me—all I could see was the white haze of the half-realm, much dimmed. But I could still feel the floor, and I crawled along it, trying to get back to the barrier.

My whole body felt heavy, and movement was getting more and more difficult.

I reached what I thought was the edge of the barrier, only to find that it had moved—I could see it shimmering just out of reach of my fingers. I crawled closer and reached out with my hand again, only to encounter empty air and no tingling sensation. The barrier had moved once again.

My body was getting heavier and heavier, and my eyelids began to close involuntarily.

I began to think about how nice it would be to go to sleep.

But I pushed myself to keep going, and I dragged my heavy body to the end of the bier—I thought I would try to reach the barrier from a different side.

I reached out my hand once again, but as before, the barrier had moved. There wasn't any way for me to reach it.

I closed my eyes and rested my head down on the ground.

I would just rest for a moment.

I felt myself sinking into sleep.

But something was nagging at the back of my mind—something I had to do—and I forced my eyes open.

I saw a tiny, white point of light shining through the gloom at me. And somewhere distantly, I heard a voice calling my name.

"Katie!"

I forced myself to sit up.

I had to get out of here.

I made an effort to clear my head and focus on what I had to do—the Queen had gotten out of here, and I could escape too.

I focused on the point of light that I could see on the other side of the bier, and I began to drag myself toward it.

Sure enough, as I drew closer, I could see that the point of light was actually a long, thin line of white light running all along the floor. Just as in the outer chamber, there was a crack here too. That had to be the way the Queen had gotten out.

I pulled myself toward it, fighting the heaviness of my body the whole way. But soon I was within reach of the white border, and when I stretched my fingers out toward its edge, it didn't move away.

I slipped my fingers through the barrier, and I felt a slight tingle run through me. Using that one hand as an anchor, I pulled my arm and my head through the barrier. Once my head was free, I began to feel much better, and soon I had pulled the rest of my body through.

I lay on the strange, white ground for just a moment, feeling energy flowing back into my body. I heard a soft sound, and I rolled over to see my horse standing not far away, watching me with anxious eyes. He was much closer than he had been when I'd first approached the dark star. When he saw me sit up, he walked over to me silently and nuzzled my ear—I could feel concern radiating off him.

I stood up and looked at the stone bier with the dark star floating over it. It seemed to be a good trap, but I had the same problem with this trap that I'd had with the rift in the sky—even if I could lure the Queen back in, she would just get out again.

There had to be something else I could do.

I thought back. Terrance had said something about a key—some kind of fail-safe that could lock the whole trap down again or stop the Queen some other way. With the Hunter that key had been a sword—the Star of Morning. Placing it in the proper place had reset the entire trap.

What if there was something like that here?

And then I remembered—there was a sword here too—or actually quite a few of them—in the hands of the statues. And the Queen had been careful not to touch the statues when she'd attacked them—she'd sent out some kind of energy instead.

"You shouldn't have thrown that sword away," the Queen had said.

If anyone knew how this trap worked, it was certainly the Queen. I had to find one of those swords.

I stood up, and the horse moved to stand beside me protectively.

I reached up to pat him on the neck.

"It's time for me to leave," I said.

The horse seemed to understand, and soon I was up on his back again.

"Katie!"

I heard William's voice again, and I turned sharply toward the sound.

My horse started to move at a gentle trot and then broke out into a gallop.

"Katie!"

As we rode along, my horse's hooves pounding the ground silently, I heard William's voice again and again—sound seemed to travel far in this strange, silent place.

Before long, we were in sight of the rift in the sky again. It stretched in the quiet, white air, dark and unnatural. My horse drew to a stop and stood still, though I could feel tension in his body. The sight of the crack in the sky was somehow profoundly wrong.

I heard William's voice again.

"Katie!"

The sound was much louder here, and I wasn't surprised—it only made sense that William's voice was entering the half-realm through the rift.

"William!" I called up to him.

"Katie?" William was startled, and his voice was full of hope.

"William, I'm coming!" I shouted.

I leaned over my horse's neck, and I pointed up at the rift.

"How do we get up there?"

An image formed in my mind of the horse running at full gallop across the vast whiteness that surrounded us. Then a word floated up in my mind.

"Fast."

"Fast it is," I said.

My horse turned back and began to trot away from the rift in the sky. We kept going until the rift had disappeared from my sight completely.

Then he turned back and began to gallop.

The horse went fast—faster than he had gone before with me on his back. As we approached the rift, the horse began to rise in the air, his hooves treading the white air as easily as they had the white ground. His hooves moved silently, and the only noises I could hear were the motion of his limbs and the sound of his breathing.

We rose ever higher into the air, and soon we were hurtling toward the rift in the sky. We passed through it, and suddenly the white light all around us disappeared.

We were back in the darkness.

My horse trotted to a stop, and I slid down off his back.

As soon as my feet touched the floor, the horse took off at a gallop again. I watched his white form for just a moment, and then he began to fade—soon, he had disappeared completely.

I looked around in the darkness. I could see neither the gold staff of the Acolyte nor the pale glow of the Queen.

"William?" I whispered.

I heard a soft rush of air, and then I felt warm arms wrapping around me.

"Katie, are you all right?"

I couldn't see his face in the darkness, but that was undeniably William's voice.

"I'm all right," I said.

"How did you get out?" he said.

"You didn't see the horse?"

"The horse?"

"Yes—the white horse," I said. "He carried me up into the sky and then out here."

"I didn't see anything," William said. "I've been calling your name, and I thought I heard you answer me. And then all of a sudden I saw you standing out here again."

"Well, it doesn't matter now," I said. "What does matter is that there's a crack in this chamber of light—like the crack at the base of the statue. Even if we could lure the Queen back into the chamber, she'd just get out again."

"So what do we do?" William said.

"We have to get one of those swords," I said. "One of the ones that those guardian statues have. Terrance said that there's always a key to a trap like this. I think the swords are the key."

"Okay," William said. "Let's go get one."

"Wait," I said. "What happened to the Queen?"

"The Queen disappeared as soon as she locked you in the chamber."

"Which way did she go?"

"I don't know," William said. "I was so busy trying to get you out of the chamber that I didn't notice. I think she must have gone back up to the surface. And I assume the Acolyte went with her."

"So we have to go back through all of the traps?" I said.

"We did it once," William said. "The second time should be no problem."

William took my hand, and we began to speed back toward the temple. The very first hurdle was the fall that had dropped us down to the level of the chamber of light. William somehow negotiated that—"It's not as far down as you think," he murmured—and we managed to make our way through the sound barrier that was so painful to William and back up through the other big fall. We made our way through the rest of the labyrinth, and William helped me to climb back up to the base of the statue.

We paused to look out through the rubble.

A fight was still raging out in the temple, but it was pretty clear that the Queen and her army were going to win.

Three statues were still fighting the vampire army that filled the temple, but the others seemed to have been overwhelmed by sheer force of numbers—I couldn't see any sign of the vanquished statues or their swords—they were probably hidden by the crush of bodies.

As for the Queen, she was standing not far away from us on a tall pile of crumbled stone, watching with satisfaction as her vampires pressed in on the statues.

A flutter of motion at the side of the temple caught my attention. Between two of the columns, I could see a growing crowd of vampires assembling on the grass outside the temple. The Acolyte was standing at the head of the crowd, holding her gold staff high, and more and more vampires were joining the crowd every moment.

It was dark, but I could see the moon and stars, and by their light, I thought I could see something large and metallic waiting beyond the crowd of vampires—it looked like an airplane.

William moved restlessly beside me, and I turned back toward him.

"What do we do with the sword once we have one?" he said.

"I think we should touch her with it," I said. "She seemed to be avoiding contact with them before."

"Do you know that will work?"

"No."

"Well, it's worth a try," William said.

We watched for another few moments, and then he stirred again.

"I'll be right back," he said. "I'm going to get a closer look."

William waded into the melee, and I soon lost sight of him in all the commotion.

I briefly considered following him—I wasn't doing much good where I was—when I saw something gleaming dully on the far side of the room. It was one of the black swords. Both it and the statue that had wielded it were lying underneath a piece of the giant stone arm that had once encased the Queen.

There was a lot of open space between me and the sword, and there wasn't much cover.

I began to creep toward it.

I had not gone far when I felt someone tap me on the shoulder.

I turned to see William.

"I just did a quick circuit of the battle out there," he said. "I didn't find anything."

"Well, I see something," I said. "Right over there."

William followed my gaze.

"I see it," he said softly. "It's going to be hard to get to that sword without being seen by the Queen."

As he said the words, the Queen's head turned toward us. We were hiding behind a large chunk of stone, and we both ducked down even lower.

I peered around a jagged corner of the stone—I could see the Queen coming toward us.

"I'm going to go," I said. "The Queen will follow me. Get that sword."

William started to protest, but I had already jumped up.

"Over here!" I said. "I bet you didn't think you'd see me again so soon!"

I had just a moment to see the Queen scowl, and then I ran for the side of the temple.

I reached the open air between the columns and jumped down to the grass below. I could see the Acolyte assembling more vampires, and I could see more clearly the outline of a large jet that appeared to be waiting to take them somewhere.

I ran away from the Acolyte, and I glanced back to see where the Queen was.

She was still following me.

I continued to run over bare rock and grass, and I began to run down the hill away from the temple.

As I ran, someone suddenly stepped out in front of me. It was the Queen.

"Hello, dear," she said.

I quickly skidded to a stop. I glanced back to see if I could catch a glimpse of William—there was no sign of him.

"Clever girl," the Queen said. "You're right—I didn't expect to see you again so soon."

She moved one of her hands in a graceful gesture.

"Would you like to see something, dear?"

Glowing white tendrils began to form over her fingers as they had once before—this time they were even brighter.

I began to back up. Then I turned and ran back the way I had come.

Suddenly, the Queen was in front of me once again.

"I draw my power from the moon," she said. "When its beams touch me, I am capable of great magic. Would you like to see?"

The Queen's fingers moved gracefully, and soon I could see a small figure made of white light floating just above her palm—it was William. I knew to be careful of her magic, but I was startled.

"Who is he, dear?" the Queen said. "Do you really know?"

"I don't need to know who he used to be," I said.

The Queen smiled softly. "I see—so you love him, and he loves you. You are sure of him?"

She paused and tilted her head. "But you are unsure of yourself. You don't know if you are worthy of the great power that has been entrusted to you—is that it?"

"I—don't know," I said.

The Queen stepped toward me. "Yes, I see it. You don't know if you can do this. You don't know if you can protect people the way you are supposed to. I can see it, Katie. You struggle with your power. And you have no one to guide you."

I felt her words drill into me and bury themselves deep within me. She was right—I didn't know what I was doing, and I didn't have anyone to show me the way.

"Let me guide you," the Queen said. "I know what you should do. You should forget about your powers and just go home where you will be safe. Would you like to go home again?"

I nodded. I would like to go home.

"Katie!" A voice cut through the thick fog that seemed to surround me.

I turned to see William rushing toward us—he was carrying one of the black swords in his hand.

The Queen made a small gesture with her hand, and the tendrils of white light in her hand coalesced into a solid sphere. She hurled the glowing white sphere at William, and it struck him squarely in the chest.

William went soaring in the air, and so did the sword. William fell heavily to the ground, and the sword landed harmlessly in the grass.

The Queen lifted her hand again, and the sword went flying through the air. Moments later, I heard a splash.

I ran toward William, but he was already getting to his feet.

He reached out a hand to me. "Let's get out of here."

But before William had even taken a step, the Queen appeared in front of us.

In her hand were more swirling tendrils of white light.

"Hello, lovely boy," the Queen said. "Can I ask you a question?"

"Don't listen to her, William," I said. "It's a trap."

William, however, was already transfixed, and his gaze was locked on the white light in the Queen's hand.

I tugged on William's arm. "William, we have to go."

As I watched, the white light in the Queen's hand formed itself into a figure—it looked like me.

"Yes, you love her," the Queen said softly. "But there's still something bothering you, isn't there? You fear loss."

The figure in the Queen's hand shifted—it grew taller and broader. Soon it looked like Cyrs.

"Yes," the Queen said. "You long for knowledge—knowledge of the past. If you had your past back, maybe you would not fear the future so much. And you're right—he can tell you what you want to know. Though you turned him down, you still want to know."

The Queen drifted close to William.

"What if I told you that I can tell you what you want to know too?"

"Don't listen, William!" I said, pulling on his arm. "We've got to run!"

But William simply stared at the white light.

The Queen turned a satisfied expression on me. A moment later, tendrils of white light appeared in her other hand.

"Where were we?" the Queen said softly. "I believe you wanted to go home. I believe you wanted to leave your powers behind and never worry about them again."

I looked into the white light. I saw my house in Elspeth's Grove forming out of the white tendrils that swirled and danced.

I could go home—I could leave everything behind—I could lead a normal life.

That was what I wanted, wasn't it? Just to be normal?

But doubt tugged at the back of my mind. I *had* wanted that once. I'd wanted to be free of my powers—free of the clear fire. But now that it had gone—now that I struggled to find it—I realized how important it was to me. I realized I needed it—I needed to be who I was meant to be. And I had seen so much trouble, so much darkness—so much danger out in the world. I wanted to help, and I knew now that I could, and I didn't have to be afraid.

I wanted the clear fire back. I wanted to be the Little Sun.

It was who I truly was.

"What's that, dear?" the Queen said softly. "I haven't heard your answer yet. Don't you want to go home?"

I forced my gaze away from the white light, and I looked up at the Queen.

"No," I said.

The Queen blinked in surprise. "What did you say, dear?"

"No," I said more loudly. "No, I don't want to go home. I want to stay right here and fight you."

The Queen gave me a startled look. Then a smile curved her mouth.

"Aren't you the clever one?" she said. "But it doesn't matter. You're still trapped—I've still got your boy. And you'll never leave while I have him, will you? So come along, now, both of you."

I looked over at William. His eyes were still locked on the white image in the Queen's hand. She began to move away, and William began to follow.

The Queen smiled. "See? You're powerless. Come along, dear, and we'll find a better place to lock you up. You're both my prisoners."

"No!" I shouted. "No! I am not your prisoner! I'm free! William and I are both free!"

The Queen laughed—a high, mocking sound. "And how will you stop me? A girl with half her powers, afraid of her own abilities? What will you do?"

I didn't know what I would do—I just felt anger welling up within me. I reached inside myself for any power I had to throw at her—anything at all, and then I concentrated hard and flung it all at the Queen.

There was something like an explosion then. The Queen was knocked off her feet, and I saw what looked like a riot of stars above me.

The clear fire had appeared—still in its broken form—but this time all the sparks looked like bright, blazing stars. It looked like I had constellations dancing over my head, and their brilliance was dazzling.

William was still on his feet, and he looked around dazed, as if coming out of a stupor.

He blinked in confusion. "What's going on?"

"The Queen," I said. "We've got to get out of here."

William's eyes oriented quickly on a white form that was struggling to get to its feet.

"Back to the temple," he said, grabbing my hand.

As he did so, the clear fire abruptly went out, and the two of us hurtled back toward the temple.

We reached it to find that the battle was nearly over—there was only one lone statue fighting on, and most of the vampires had gone to join the crowd around the Acolyte and the plane.

The Queen was a white streak just behind us, and I searched frantically for a way to stop her.

And then William and I both saw it. We looked at each other, and William nodded.

Then he took my hand, and we plunged into what was left of the battle.

I caught a glimpse of the Queen following us. I saw with alarm that she was growing larger and larger by the moment.

Soon, she was as large as her statue had been.

"You're mine!" the Queen thundered. "This prison was built for me, but soon it will hold you! You are my prisoners!"

The Queen swept her arm in an arc, and the vampires in her path were brushed out of her way by an unseen force. The last statue teetered on his marble legs and fell to the ground.

The Queen laughed—a great, booming sound—but William and I kept running. Soon we were close to what we were looking for.

One of the fallen statues was missing an arm and both of his legs, and he lay on his side, hacking futilely at the air now that most of the vampires had gone to join the Acolyte.

But his good hand still held his sword, and he continued to swing it though no enemies were nearby.

William and I ran right at the statue, and the Queen followed us.

We ran right underneath the chopping arm.

Realizing too late just where we were headed, the Queen tried to stop, but her great mass kept her going. Her giant foot just grazed the statue, and the statue brought its sword down on her toe with little force.

But it was enough.

The dark star I had seen down in the chamber of light suddenly appeared over the giant Queen's head.

The star was indeed dark—far darker than the night sky, and the Queen stared at it in horror.

The spot on her toe where the sword had touched it turned gray, and the dark color quickly swept up her foot to her leg. The Queen took a step back, but the darkness continued to cover her—it was dull, gray, and looked like marble.

The Queen was being turned to stone.

Within moments, the gray stone swept over the Queen's entire body and up her neck. The last part of her to be turned was her face.

There was a great cracking sound as the transformation was complete.

I looked up. Standing in front of us once again was an immense statue of the Queen of the Moon.

Chapter Twenty-Three

I looked around. The dark star had vanished, and all around me I could hear soft sounds.

I turned to see the vampire army crumbling to dust. Some of the recruits, however, were modern vampires—these looked confused and dazed for a moment. Then they began to run off into the night.

There was another sound then of an engine, and William and I ran to the other side of the temple. We were just in time to see an airplane taxiing down a dirt runway. After a few moments it took off into the night sky.

"I think the Acolyte was on that," William said.

"I think you're right," I said. I glanced around. "At least she won't be taking an army with her."

As I watched the last of the vampires scurry off, I saw someone coming toward us through the darkness.

Whoever it was, he was moving fast, and I could feel William tense by my side.

But as the figure drew closer, I could make out a familiar form—it was Terrance.

He hurried into the temple and stood staring at all the rubble and the heaps of dust. Then he looked up at the towering statue of the Queen.

William and I hurried over to him.

"I see you two have been busy," he said.

"Just a little," William said.

Terrance glanced around. "So where's the Queen? Did you get her back inside the statue?"

"Actually," I said, "I think she is the statue—she's turned to stone."

Terrance nodded. "You must have found the fail-safe, then."

"I think we did," I said. "It was the swords the smaller statues had. One touch and she began to transform."

"Makes sense," Terrance replied. "It was a last-ditch effort. If the Queen escaped her prison, the Sídh had to have a way to stop her quickly."

He looked up at the statue. "They didn't want to destroy her—she had been one of them after all—but they knew they had to do something if she got out."

I looked over at Terrance. "Are you okay?"

"Yeah," he said sheepishly. He ran a hand over the back of his neck. "The last thing I remember is heading back to face the Acolyte—she must have taken me out. I woke up underground in the darkness, and I had to find my way out. When I got back up here, you guys were gone. So I went to look for you."

He glanced over his shoulder. "I did get back in time to see the Acolyte boarding that plane—and to see the other vampires that were with her crumble into dust."

"So what do you think the plan was?" William said. "Was she going to make a whole bunch of trips to ferry all these vampires off the island?"

"I think so," Terrance replied. "And it would have taken quite a few trips. There were thousands of them here."

"Any idea where they were going?" William asked.

Terrance shook his head. "Unfortunately, no. Maybe Dylan will have spotted something from the coast—at least a general direction." He glanced around. "Speaking of Dylan, maybe we should get back to the boats."

"Shouldn't we take one of the swords with us or something?" I said.

"No," Terrance replied. "We should leave this one for the Order. There's a lot here for them to clean up and explain to the locals."

The three of us left the temple and began to walk back down the hill toward the coastline. The night was wearing away, and the dark sky was turning to gray—dawn wasn't far off. As we approached the coast, I could see that all the mist was gone—the essence had vanished along with the Queen.

We hurried down to the boats, and I could see Anton and Sachiko waiting for us—Anton's hair and clothes were wet.

"What happened to you?" I said as William, Terrance, and I all made it down to the water's edge.

"I fell in," Anton said shortly.

"He was leaning against the barrier," Sachiko said. "When it disappeared, he toppled over into the water."

"You were being cavalier," William said.

"No," Anton replied. "I was being vigilant. I wanted to know if anything changed with the barrier—and I found out."

"So I'm assuming you guys were successful?" Sachiko said.

"It was these two," Terrance said. "They turned the Queen to stone."

"You mean she's back in her statue?" Sachiko asked.

"Nope," Terrance said. "She is the statue this time. They sprang the final trap, and she's not coming back."

Sachiko's eyebrows rose. "Wow. You'll have to tell me about that once we get somewhere safe."

Terrance glanced over at William and me. "Shall we head back to the mainland and the stakeout point? Maybe Dylan saw something useful."

"That's an excellent idea," William said.

We all got back in the rowboats, and soon we had reached the opposite shore. Dylan was already standing on the beach waiting for us.

Dylan walked up to Terrance as he got out of the boat.

"What happened?" he said. "I saw the island suddenly pop into view."

Dylan pointed, and we all turned to look—the island was indeed visible from the shore.

"What happened?" he said again.

Terrance grinned. "Ask them—they did it."

Dylan turned to William and me.

"She's gone," I said simply.

"Turned to stone," William added.

Dylan stared at us for a long moment. He seemed to be struggling with something, and several warring emotions played out over his face.

Eventually, he seemed to find peace within himself.

"Good job," he said at last.

"Did you see the plane?" Terrance asked.

"Yes," Dylan replied.

"The Acolyte was on that plane," Terrance said. "Any idea where it might be going?"

"Not beyond a general direction," Dylan said. "We don't have the right kind of equipment here to track a plane. I'll see if I can get some eyes on it."

Terrance turned to us.

"Dylan and I should probably wrap things up here," he said. "Why don't you guys go get some rest?"

"Is there anything else you need from us?" William said.

"We'll find you if we need you," Terrance said.

We said our goodbyes, and then William, Anton, Sachiko, and I went to find Sachiko's car.

We found it without much trouble, and William looked for hotels while Sachiko drove.

William located a likely looking one, and Sachiko drove us up to a cheerful, brightly lit hotel. We went into the lobby, and even though it was the early hours of the morning, there were people up and about—they appeared to be on vacation.

Sachiko got rooms for us, and we had a quick conference in the hall.

"I know things seem to be safe," William said. "But I think we should have a look around just to be sure. I think I should check out the immediate area around the hotel, Sachiko should check out the wider neighborhood, and Anton should check out the beach and the coastline."

"Where should I check?" I said.

"I think you should go up and get some sleep," William said. "I'm not trying to sideline you. It's just that there may be stray vampires wandering around here, and I think it's a good idea to make sure that the area is clear. Besides, you've already vanquished one vampire tonight. You've certainly done more than your share."

"I agree with William," Sachiko said. "You should get some rest—let us take this one. We're just going to look around. And you need sleep more than we do."

"Okay," I said. "I'll get some rest." I didn't feel particularly tired, but the others did have better eyesight and much faster reflexes. Things would probably go much quicker without me.

"Why do I have to check out the coastline?" Anton said.

"I just thought you'd be good at it," William said.

"I get it," Anton said. "You don't want to leave your girlfriend alone with a handsome devil like me."

"Just get going," William said. He turned to me. "I'm going to do a quick circuit around the hotel and then work outward from there. I'll be back soon."

William, Sachiko, and Anton all left, and I went upstairs to my room.

As I walked down the hall to my room, I had the feeling that I was forgetting something. But nothing came to me, and I shook the feeling off.

As I opened the door, I felt a cool breeze brush past me.

I hurried to the window to close it, but it was already shut. Puzzled, I went back to close the door and then sat on the bed.

I felt a sense of fatigue settle over me, and I closed my eyes. When I opened them, someone was standing in front of me.

The figure was very pale, and she was dressed in white—for one horrifying moment, I thought the Queen had returned.

Then I took in the blond curls and the sweet, angelic face.

It was Veronika.

"Hello, kitten," she said.

I felt a stab of fear for William as I realized what I'd been forgetting.

"Veronika," I said quickly. "What are you doing here?"

She smiled. "I came to check on you."

Veronika's smile was sweet, but I knew she was anything but.

"How did you find me?" I said.

Veronika's smile deepened, showing her dimples. "I have my ways."

I wondered, then, how far away William was. I hoped he wasn't close enough for Veronika to sense him—if he was, he could be in great danger.

"I need more time," I said.

"Do you?" Veronika said. "Now isn't that interesting?"

"I know why you're here," I said. "You want payment—and I've almost got it for you. We've done the hardest part—we've found the ghost girl—the real ghost girl—and we've defeated her. All the ancient vampires crumbled into dust—but the modern ones ran off. If your Promised One was here, he was probably part of that group that scattered. If you give me more time, I'm sure I can find him."

Veronika gave me a long look. "Where is William now?"

"He's far away," I said. "Very far away. You won't be able to find him tonight."

Veronika continued to stare at me, and after a moment, her lips curved into a slow smile.

"That's good," she said. "Then we'll have plenty of time to talk."

She sat on the bed next to me, and she drew up her tiny, delicate feet and tucked them up beside her. Her feet, as usual, were bare.

"So tell me, child," Veronika said. "How are you?"

"How am I?" I said.

"Yes."

"I'm fine," I said. Veronika was close enough that I could feel the coldness of her skin, and I found myself moving away involuntarily.

Veronika noticed the gesture and smiled once again.

"Come, Katie," she said. "Tell me about your grand adventure. How do you feel now that you've defeated the real ghost girl?"

"It was the Queen of the Moon," I said. "She was the ghost girl—she was the one who was taking all the vampires. She brought them to her island—she was raising an army for the Werdulac. The Queen used to be his personal sorceress."

"I've heard of her," Veronika said.

"Your Promised One must have been fairly sick at the time the Queen took him," I said. "We figured out that the essence—that was the spell she used—only works on the most vulnerable vampires. That's why it worked on the Werdulac's old army—she was resurrecting the most vulnerable vampires of all—the ones who had been reduced to ash."

"Yes, my Promised One was very ill," Veronika said.

"Then we should go find him," I said. "If he's sick, he probably hasn't gone far."

Veronika tilted her head. "Do you really want to go with me to find my ailing Promised One?"

"Yes," I said. I stood up. "I said I would find him, and I will."

Veronika remained seated. "How brave you sound. But how do you feel?"

"How do I feel?" I said.

Veronika suddenly came to stand beside me in one swift, graceful movement.

"Your William isn't here, and neither is my Promised One," she said. "We can talk freely."

"I don't understand," I said.

"What if I told you William doesn't matter?"

"Of course William matters," I said. "He means everything to me."

"In this case something else matters more," Veronika said.

"What could matter more than William's life?" I said.

"In this case we're talking about a different matter. Isn't there something you want to tell me?"

"Are you trying to trick me?" I said.

"What were you looking for?" Veronika said.

"I was looking for the ghost girl so I could find your Promised One and return him to you."

"And did you find her?" Veronika said.

"I told you yes," I said. "We found her."

"And what did you do?" Veronika said.

"We stopped the ghost girl," I said. "We turned her to stone."

"I wasn't asking about 'we,'" Veronika said. "I was asking about you, and you alone. What did you do?"

"Me?" I said.

"Yes—you. What did you do that no one else could have done?"

"I see what you're doing," I said. "This is a trick. You're trying to get out of this on a technicality. You're going to say that the bargain was between me and you, and if anyone else helped, our deal is invalid. You're trying to say that you're going to take William's life back because I had help, and I didn't find your Promised One. But I won't let you take William's life away. I blocked the Queen with the clear fire, and I can block you."

"You summoned the clear fire?" Veronika said.

"Yes," I said.

"You have your power back now?"

"Yes," I said. "It's a little different than before, but I have it back."

"Then you have indeed defeated the ghost girl," Veronika said. She smiled. "And that is what you did yourself."

"What does that mean?"

"It means there is more than one way to be a ghost." Veronika moved toward the door. "You are free now, kitten. Your debt is discharged. William's life is now his own."

"But I didn't find your Promised One," I said.

"I never asked you to find him," Veronika said. "I only asked you to find her—and you've done that."

"But you said—"

"No, I didn't," Veronika said. "I said I wanted to find the ghost girl because she had taken my Promised One. Your own overdeveloped sense of responsibility led you to believe I was asking you to find him too. But I didn't ask for both things—I only asked for one. I will find my Promised One myself."

"Then what was that interrogation about?" I said. "Why did you try to make me think you were here to collect William's life?"

"I never said that," Veronika said. "I merely hoped that along the way you had found something else of value. I was only trying to help."

"You were trying to help?" I said.

"Yes, of course. I never wanted William's life. I only wanted the ghost girl to be stopped—and without me, you wouldn't even have known she existed."

"You're unbelievable," I said. "Are you really trying to pretend that you did all of this out of the goodness of your heart?"

"Yes, I am unbelievable," Veronika said, dimpling. "I often amaze myself. Enjoy your lovely boy—be grateful I gave him back to you. Goodbye, kitten."

With that, she vanished.

I sat down on the bed again.

A moment later, the door flew open, and William came into the room.

"Katie!" he said. "Are you all right?"

He crossed the few steps that separated us and gathered me into his arms.

"I thought I saw—" he began.

He stopped.

"You did see her," I said. "Veronika was here."

"I should never have left you alone," William said. He took my face into his hands. "You're sure you're all right?"

"I'm fine," I said. "All we did was talk. It was you I was worried about."

William brushed a hand over my hair. "You never needed to worry about me. I know you went to Veronika to save my life. Any debt that is incurred because of that I'm happy to pay."

He gave me a searching look—as if he wasn't quite sure that I was really okay.

"What did she want?"

"She said that we were both free," I said. "She said we don't owe her anything any longer."

William relaxed. "She really said that?"

"She really did."

"You never had to worry about her," William said. "You never had to go through this alone."

"I know that now," I said.

William pulled me into another embrace, and I relaxed against him for just a moment. Then I looked up at him.

"Can I tell you if I'm worrying about something else?" I said.

William was suddenly alert. "Of course."

"Do you mind if we go somewhere else?" I said. "I feel like I need some air."

"Sure," William said. "Wherever you want to go."

Our hotel was by the water, and we walked out onto a balcony that overlooked the sea. The air was chilly but not unpleasant, and as we looked out over the water, we could see the first rosy rays of dawn lighting up the sky.

"It's a beautiful morning," I said.

"Yes, it is," William said. He was staring at me steadily, and I could tell he was worried about what I was going to say.

"You don't have to be worried," I said. "I'm the one who's worrying here. I'm concerned that I'm holding you back."

William looked puzzled. "Holding me back?"

"It's just that both Cyrs and the Queen mentioned how much you want to know about your past," I said. "How much you want your memories back. And you told Cyrs that you didn't need them—that you were happy enough as you are. But the Queen was able to hold you with that idea—transfix you."

I looked up at William. "I was just wondering if you really are happy here with me. If your past is more important to you—if you need to find out who you are—I want you to do that. I want you to do what is most important to you."

William quickly took my hand. "You're what matters most to me."

"You don't have to say that," I said. "You don't have to look out for me. If there's something you want more, you should search for it. I can't imagine how horrible it must be not knowing who you truly are."

"I want to be here," William said. "I want to be with you. I do want to know who I am—but I want to be with you more. You need me right now. And I need you."

"You won't regret not going to find your past?" I said.

"No," William replied firmly. "What I told Cyrs is true. I do want to know, but if I never find out who I am, that's okay. And that's okay because I've found you. You've given me a new life—one where my past doesn't matter. I want to be with you right here at this very moment. You're all I need, and nothing in my past can change that. I want to be with you—more than anything."

I leaned against William then, and he wrapped his arms around me.

"I'm glad you're here," I said.

"I'm glad I'm here too," William murmured. "There's nowhere else I want to be more."

He ran a hand over my hair. "I love you, Katie."

We kissed, and I felt everything fading away. We kissed again and again, and I felt as if I had fallen into a beautiful dream.

William wrapped me in another tight embrace then, and I hugged him back fiercely. I never wanted this moment to end.

"We can't stay here forever," I said.

"No, we can't," William said. "But you're safe for now."

"The Queen was building an army," I murmured. "I have to go find the Werdulac. I have to stop him before he's free. But where do we start? Where do we begin our search?"

"I don't know," William replied. "But you shouldn't worry about that right now. You should go and get some sleep. I can tell you're tired."

"I am tired," I said. "But I feel like we should get going. I think we should head to the nearest airport."

"There's time," William said. "Just give yourself one more day."

"One more day?" I said. "How about one more kiss?"

William smiled. "Now that sounds like a plan."

We kissed again, and this time I let myself drift away.

Thank you for reading!

Thanks for reading *Ghost Girl*! If you enjoyed it, please leave a review at your retailer of choice:

Amazon
Barnes & Noble
Kobo
Apple (iBooks)
or
Goodreads

Thank you very much!

Sign Up!

Sign up for Catherine's newsletter to get news about new releases, giveaways, and other fun stuff!

You can find the form at //eepurl.com/cXS5_z.

Other Books by Catherine Mesick

Pure, Book 1 of the *Pure* series

Firebird, Book 2 of the *Pure* series

Dangerous Creatures, Book 3 of the *Pure* series

Coming Soon!

Little Sun, Book 5 of the *Pure* series

About the Author

Catherine Mesick is the author of *Pure, Firebird, Dangerous Creatures*, and *Ghost Girl*. She is a graduate of Pace University and Susquehanna University. She lives in Maryland.

Visit the author's website at catherinemesick.com and her Facebook page at facebook.com/PureBookSeries. You can also connect with her on Twitter at twitter.com/CatherineMesick.